DARK

LACEY LEHOTZKY

First paperback edition June 2024

ISBN 979-8-9883620-5-0 (paperback)

ISBN 979-8-9883620-4-3 (e-book)

Book cover and interior art by Beholden Book Covers

Edited by Kaitlin Ugolik Phillips

Published by The Lehotzky Group LLC

www.laceylehotzky.com

MORE BY LACEY LEHOTZKY

A Choice of Light and Dark
Chained
Light
Dark

PRONUNCIATION GUIDE

Agrenak - AG-ren-ak
Aress - AH-ress
Béke - BE-k
Blire - B-lire
Cazius - KAZ-ius
Drazen - Dray-zen
Domi - do-mi
Endre - EN-dre
Északi - EE-sah-kee
Este - esh-te
Félvér - fell-ver
Izidora - iz-i-dawr-uh
Kazimir - kaz-imir
Kaztar - kaz-tar
Kirigin - ki-ri-gin
Kriztof - KRIS-tof
Liliana - lil-i-ana
Radence - RAY-dense
Ruslan - ROO-slahn
Ryza - RYE-zah

Telivér - tell-i-ver
Vaenor - VAE-nor
Vadim - vaa-deem
Valynor - VAL-noor
Vasvain - vas-vain
Vaszoly - vaas-o-ly
Vlisa - vlis-a
Viktor - vik-tor
Zalan - ZA-lan
Zekari - zek-AR-i
Zheka - zeh-kah
Zuriel - ZUR-iel

CONTENT WARNING

Dark is suitable for audiences of 18+. It contains scenes that sensitive readers might find disturbing. Your mental health matters, and you should make the choice with which you feel most comfortable.

This is by no means an exhaustive list of trigger warnings, and you can check the author's website for the most up to date list.

Trigger warnings: Flashback of rape and sexual assault, gruesome torture with gore, kidnapping, stalking, nightmares, flashbacks, panic attacks, suicidal ideation, graphic violence, and mentions of physical, verbal, mental, emotional, and child abuse. The explicit sexual content in this book contains group sex scenes, orgies, anal play, impact play, breath play, and more.

Eszaki
Iron Realm
Day Realm

Night Realm
Crystal Realm

A CHOICE OF LIGHT AND DARK PLAYLIST

Hunting Season - Ice Nine Kills
Watch The World Burn - Falling in Reverse
There's Fear In Letting Go - I Prevail
Werewolf - Motionless in White
Masterpiece - Motionless in White
No Masters - Bad Wolves
I Will Not Bow - Breaking Benjamin
Fallen Angel - Three Days Grace
Infinite - Silverstein, Aaron Gillespie
Riot - Three Days Grace
TRIALS - STARSET
Don't Stay - Linkin Park
Face Everything And Rise - Papa Roach
Say You'll Haunt Me - Stone Sour
Last to Know - Three Days Grace
Without You - Breaking Benjamin
Pain - Three Days Grace
Whispers in the Dark - Skillet
Take Me Back To Eden - Sleep Token
Whatever It Takes - Stephen Stanley

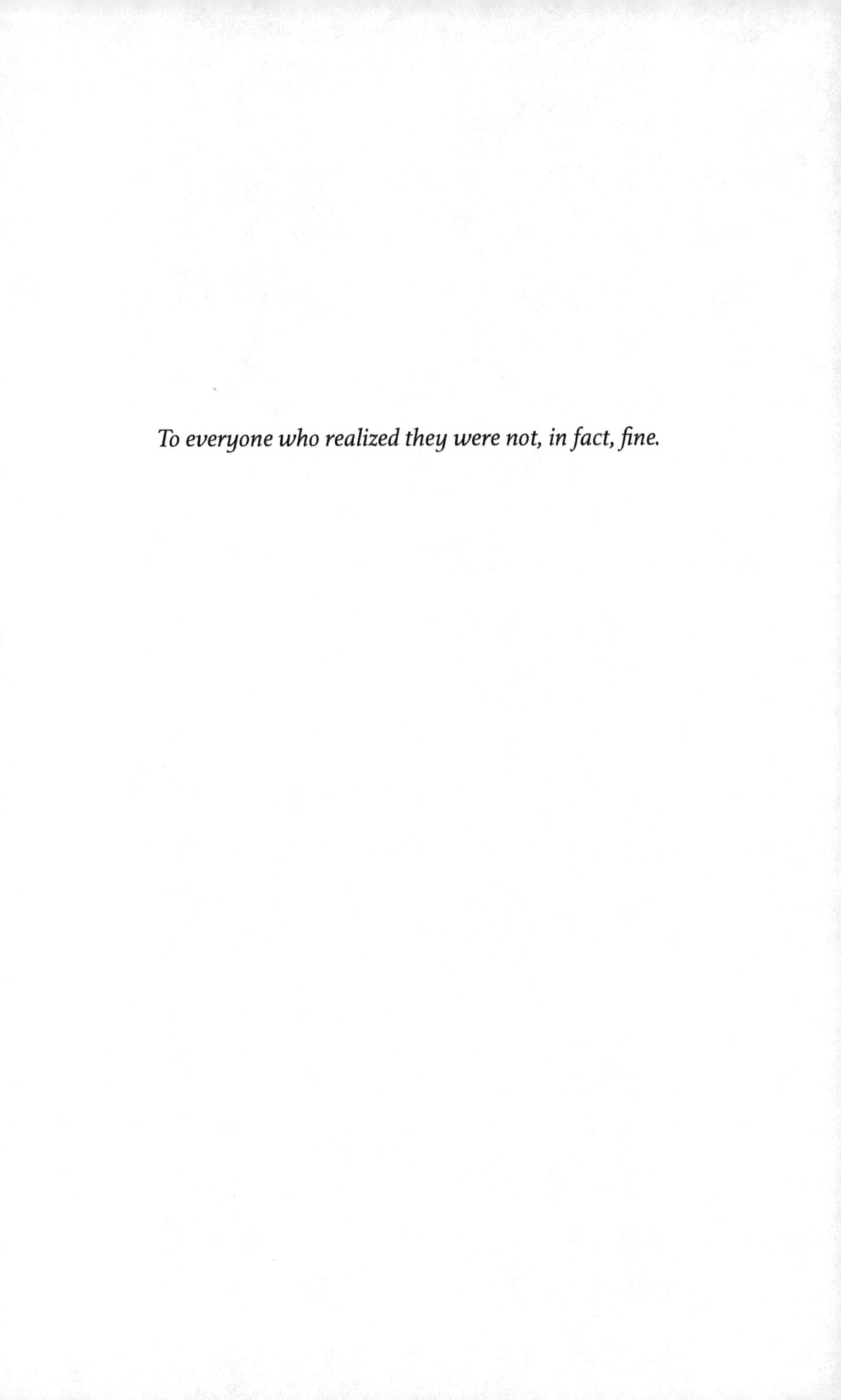

To everyone who realized they were not, in fact, fine.

YOU ARE CORDIALLY
INVITED TO

BÉKE

HOSTED BY

THE IRON REALM

Schedule Of Events

DAY 1	OPENING BALL
DAY 2	ARCHERY COMPETITION
DAY 3	TRADITIONAL HUNT
DAY 4	SWORDS COMPETITION
DAY 5	STRENGTH COMPETITION
DAY 6	HORSEBACK COMPETITION
DAY 7	FREE DAY
DAY 8	GODDESS OFFERING
DAY 9	MASQUERADE BALL
DAY 10	ARTISANAL FAIR
DAY 11	LANTERN RELEASE
DAY 12	TALENT SHOWCASE
DAY 13	CITY-WIDE PARADE
DAY 14	WEDDING + CORONATION

PROLOGUE

Silence greeted the group of Iron Fae as they entered the hewn cave. The air was still, like the mountain was holding its breath, waiting for the scene it knew would unfold. The tallest and broadest of the group stalked forward, nostrils flaring as his keen senses caught the metallic scent of blood.

"Spread out and search," he growled, drawing black flame into his palms.

The heavy footfalls of his soldiers broke the silence as they fanned out around him, hugging the walls of the living area that looked like it had been used only hours before, though its former occupants were nowhere to be found. He waited, heart racing, jaw clenching, until one of his soldiers shouted, "They're dead!"

"What do you mean 'They're dead'?" Banishing the dark fire, he stomped deeper into the cave, the smell of metal becoming almost unbearable in the stagnant air. Pools of ruby greeted him along his path until he stood before an ocean of blood and piles of bodies shoved against the cave's carved walls.

Deep blue eyes met his from across the red pools, dark

brows pinched slightly together, giving a warning look. "Ruslan..."

"Don't, Drazen," Ruslan snapped, scanning the dark floor for signs of what had happened. "Can we get some more fucking light in here?" His neck was growing tight and hot, and he cracked it, vertebra by vertebra, to relieve some tension.

The space was illuminated moments later with the fire his soldiers cast into the air, heating the chamber around them and cooking the cold bodies lining it. Crouching down, Ruslan studied the footprints leading to and from the red ocean. The oldest markings led forward, a set of seven large boots whose outlines were nearly dried on the stone. The newest led backward and down another hall, though there was an eighth set of smaller footprints, bare of any shoes.

The way he rose off the ground was predatory, sucking the air from the lungs of his regiment as they waited with bated breath to see what their volatile commander would do. Without a word, he stalked forward, and they hurried behind, holding the firelight high for him. Sweat dripped down his forehead as Ruslan followed the twists and turns until he reached a cavern so dark and so deep, that the light of dozens of males barely broke through.

Another body slumped there, lines of blood indicating he had been dragged by two of the intruders.

Ruslan stepped into the middle of the space, a war playing out in his mind as he tried to wrap it around what he was seeing. Iron chains wound haphazardly against the stone floor, the shackles on the ends broken open and gaping like a snake's mouth prepared to strike. Further away, a thin, worn mattress disregarded him, and even further, a stone tub turned its back on him.

There was no sign of the mate he'd waited for twenty-one years to claim. Red and black coated his vision as he lost control, horns protruding from his skull and hands morphing into talons. He released a roar so violent it shook pebbles loose above them, creating a rainshower of rock. The firelight faltered as his soldiers covered their bare heads.

Stomping down the hall, he followed the tiny footprints until he reached the lip of the cave, staring down as the brilliant sun rose over the Agrenak Mountains. His second roar was violence incarnate, vocalizing twenty-one years of anguish, and even the mountains dared not interrupt his rage, allowing the sound to echo among their peaks until his throat was raw and bloody, and he felt more lost and broken than he ever had before.

I

THE COMPETITION

1

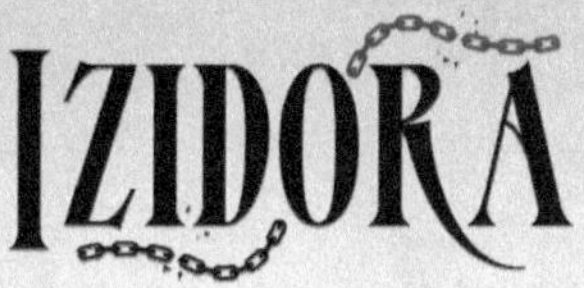

IZIDORA

Béke Day One

Light blinded me momentarily before pain speared through my middle, tearing me apart from the inside. I took a staggering step forward, plunging my foot into the ankle-deep snow in the courtyard of Ryza Citadel in the Iron Realm, as I laid eyes upon the male I had loved first.

Kazimir was haggard, with a thick beard and grown-out black hair that made him look like he'd been living in the woods since we'd parted. His deep emerald green eyes held none of their prior sparkle, even when our eyes collided across the snow-dusted ground and the rest of the world dropped away. The bruises that marred the spaces beneath his eyes were not the most alarming change in him; it was the oily aura that surrounded him, as if he'd fallen into a pit of tar and not quite managed to free himself of the sticky substance when he'd escaped.

The Goddess's Prophecy came screaming back to the forefront of my mind, and doubt threatened to drown me as the words played like a haunting tune.

"The ones that are part of all will be born under a full moon
Her white light will fill the land
But her mates darkness will rise
Kings will fall
Rivers will run with blood
There is a choice
Follow the light
Descend into the dark
The harrowing pass decides it all"

Darkness bled through every pore in Kazimir, and as I reached my empath magic out to brush against his mind, I beheld thickly coiled black ropes caging it in. With horror, I recoiled in on myself, shifting toward Ruslan instinctively, and returned to the present moment.

The guests arriving for Béke, a two-week celebration of peace between realms, had dismounted, handing their reins to waiting stablehands, while a handful of footmen trotted toward a carriage, opening the door and assisting four females down the steep steps.

"Liliana!" I cried out when the long chocolate-brown locks of my best friend peeked out of the carriage. Her seafoam green eyes popped up in recognition of my voice, a wide grin spilling across her face as she dropped the hand of the Iron Fae male helping her onto the snow-packed ground and sprinted toward me. Forgetting the two males whose eyes were locked in a staredown, I threw my arms wide and embraced my friend.

"Izidora! I've missed you so much," she breathed in my ear, her bubbly voice hitching.

Ruslan hummed his amusement beside me, causing me to hold my friend at arm's length and look at the second male I loved. Her eyes shone like a mirror of my own, and I quickly introduced them. "Liliana, this is King Ruslan of the Iron Realm."

Her greedy eyes drank in his frame before she dipped into a polite curtsey. "Pleased to meet you, Your Highness."

Ruslan's signature smirk returned, his smoky eyes dancing as he looked at the Night Fae female. "The pleasure is all mine, Lady Liliana. I hope to get to know you better in the coming weeks." Then, he turned his attention to our other guests, and my cheeks flamed as I realized Liliana and I had forgone all protocol in our excitement.

"Welcome to the Iron Realm. I am King Ruslan, and this is my mate and future queen, Princess Izidora of the Night Realm. We are glad you could join us, not only to celebrate Béke but also our upcoming wedding and coronation, taking place the day after the end of the feast. We hope you'll extend your stay to celebrate with us."

If the news shocked any of the attending nobles, none let it show on their bland expressions. Even the Night Fae kept their expressions neural, if not a touch hostile, especially from Kazimir as his attention flitted between Ruslan and me. King Azim had died only the day before, so there was no way any of them knew of Ruslan's elevated status prior to this very moment. But court politics was a game well played by all in attendance, and I had no doubt that they'd whisper about the changes once they were out of earshot.

Liliana jabbed me in the side with her elbow, and I shot her a look that said, 'we'll talk later.' My attention was pulled by an elegant female with platinum hair flowing loosely over her shoulders who was clapping her hands together. "I do love weddings!"

A lithe male with white hair proffered his hand to Ruslan. "King Ruslan, it is a pleasure to make your acquaintance. I am King Airre of the Crystal Realm, and this is my mate, Queen

Immonen." He trained his blue eyes on me, and I offered my hand to him. He grasped it, planting a formal kiss on the back. "Princess Izidora, you are even more beautiful than High Lord Kazimir described. I do hope to learn more about you both in the coming weeks."

My cheeks flamed, though I offered King Airre a polite smile after a cursory glance to the male beside me. Ruslan seemed unfazed by King Airre's flattery, his attention pointedly fixed on Kazimir during our exchange. The corner of Ruslan's lip twitched up as if he was goading Kazimir into saying something about me or his newfound status as king of the Iron Realm.

"As do I." A dark-skinned female stepped forward, and I curtsied to her as Ruslan lifted her hand. Queen Viktoria's beauty was striking, her colorful ensemble a bright and cheery distraction from the tension that floated around us like falling snow.

Kazimir's eyes bored into me, but I kept my gaze firmly on the monarchs of the Day Realm. The tug around my middle became insistent enough that I spared a glance behind them, my gaze colliding with two emerald orbs that held a touch of something foreign, something that made me want to glance away as quickly as I could.

"Queen Viktoria, King Consort Geza, I look forward to making your acquaintance as well," Ruslan acknowledged with an air of formality. "Drazen will show you to your rooms. After such a long journey, I'm sure you'd like to freshen up before the opening ball tonight."

"That is most kind of you, King Ruslan," Queen Viktoria remarked. "I am quite tired from our travels."

Drazen, Ruslan's cousin and closest confidante, stepped forward, beckoning the travel-weary monarchs into the halls of Ryza Citadel. I dipped my head politely to the passing Crystal and Day Fae in their respective entourages, until another forceful tug on my middle yanked my gaze to the approaching Night Fae.

Viktor and Vadim, Liliana's brother, led the party, followed by a familiar pair of Night Fae, with Endre and Kazimir bringing up the rear. The way Endre repeatedly glanced at Kazimir sent my stomach plummeting to the cold ground. Kazimir's eyes never left me, sending shivers down my spine as they approached.

The males swept into deep bows before Ruslan and myself, though by the set of each of the Nighthounds' jaws, I understood they were displeased in their display. Ruslan made no move to return the gesture, and tension rolled off of him in thick waves that clawed at my shoulders. Tapping into the clear crystal in my chest wrapped in white flames and moonlight, I released a tendril of my empath magic, siphoning his fear.

"King Ruslan, thank you for having us at this year's Béke," Viktor began, though his voice was tight. "We are representing the Night Realm at this year's feast. I am afraid we are also road-weary, so we'll have to do introductions later."

"Of course," Ruslan replied haughtily, glancing briefly at Viktor before ghosting his hard gaze across the rest of them. "Drazen will show you the way."

"I'll see you later, promise," I whispered to my friend, who nodded and strode toward her brother as he passed. Kazimir's mouth opened for a fraction of a second before closing again, Endre yanking on his arm to lead him along behind the rest of the Night Fae. My body felt that acute ache once he rounded the corner and disappeared into Ryza Citadel.

I blew out a long breath, looking at the male who still stood beside me as our entourage dispersed. His smoky eyes were filled with anxiety, the emotion resonating through our connection even more deeply. "We're okay," I reassured him, knowing that his worst fear of being abandoned was screaming at him to do something to save himself.

"Promise?" His raspy voice was no more than a whisper, and for a moment he reminded me of one of our first times together, when he allowed me to see the vulnerable child that still lived inside him.

Standing on my tiptoes, I brushed my hand across his cheek. "Promise."

But as we entered Ryza Citadel, hand in hand, I began to worry that Béke was going to be more taxing than I anticipated, especially with the oiliness that exuded from the male who saved me from the cold, dark cave.

2

KAZIMIR

Béke Day One

I felt as if I'd been run through the middle with one of the decorative swords that hung along the walls of the main hall. A tug I hadn't felt in months screamed at me to break free of Endre's bruising grip and race back to the courtyard, snatch up my mate, and carry her off with me.

Izidora looked *happy*. She'd stared up at Ruslan like he was the air she needed to breathe until her attention fell over me, and then, just as fast as she'd looked at me, she turned away to embrace Liliana.

I was nothing to her.

After I'd spent most of my life searching for her, after I'd saved her, after I'd gathered a fucking army for her, she couldn't care less about me.

Izidora. Was. Mine.

And I would simply have to remind her of that fact. The binding magic that had begun eating away at the light parts of my soul reared its beastly head, thrumming with the promise of blood and vengeance. But if I wanted to win her back, the monster winding its way around my magic had to remain locked away. Swallowing the surge of rage at her rejection, I refocused on the halls before me, memorizing the way to our apartment in the citadel and any other interesting-looking doors we might need to explore later.

The Iron Realm had been breeding races from across the continents to create a more powerful race of Fae, and we needed to know everything we could about the program if we had any chance against them in battle. Our army was tucked safely in the Day Realm, and we had two weeks to gain as much information as we could before they marched on the Iron Realm.

The deeply tanned male had already directed the Crystal and Day Fae to their rooms, and he seemed unbothered as we traipsed the halls of his home, like his enemy wasn't lying in wait to tear him and his people apart at a moment's notice. "Here's your suite. The opening ball starts in four hours."

If Kaztar or Viktor acknowledged him, I did not hear, because all my focus was on reining in the black beast in my chest that screamed at me to return to Izidora. We stumbled into the ornate living area complete with a blazing wall-sized fireplace and six doors leading into lavish bedrooms. The wealth and power of the Iron Realm were on full display, egg-sized gemstones embedded in sconces along the wall, fur rugs lining the floor, and massive bedrooms and en-suite bathrooms with deep soaking tubs asking to chase away the bone-deep chill that clung to each of us.

Vadim whistled as he wandered around, running a hand over his beard as he surveyed the space. "This is nice as fuck."

None of us could argue with him.

"And there are more than enough rooms for everyone," he added, giving Liliana a sidelong glare as she snatched Endre from me and dragged him to a room at the back of the suite.

"Exactly, so there's no need for us to share a wall, brother," she cooed, batting her lashes at him before shutting the door in his face.

"Fucking Fates, she's going to be the death of me," Vadim groaned, earning a snigger from Viktor and myself. The laughter eased some of the tension in my chest, though it wasn't enough to completely dull the edge of the knife stabbing into me.

"Domi and I will take this room here," Kaztar teased, indicating a half-open door closest to the exit. "Don't want to share a wall with Liliana and Endre, either." The male snatched his wife's hand, tugging her to him and whispering in her ear, causing red to cascade across her cheeks. "We'll see you guys in a few hours."

I ground my teeth as they disappeared into their room, wishing that Izidora had paid me enough attention, had given me something to know that dragging myself around the continent again was worth it.

What if she wasn't my mate?

That niggling worry that had plagued me since our ride between the Crystal and Day Realms voiced its opinion, sending another surge of rage up my spine.

What we shared was real.

As if he sensed the direction of my thoughts, Vadim bumped my shoulder, tearing me from the spiral that was dragging me down. "I'm going to take a bath because my balls have retreated inside my body. And since I got a good look at the females roaming the halls, I'm going to need them later."

Mine and Viktor's eye rolls were simultaneous. "You can't stick your dick in an Iron Fae female on our first night, Vadim," Vitkor griped.

"Why not? Who said we can't enjoy the spoils of war, prior to the war? Plus, we've been working so hard lately. I need to relax before things get bloody. It wouldn't hurt to use that time to gather information, seeing as we've gotten a lot of *valuable* information over the years using that tactic." Vadim's evergreen eyes sparkled as he recalled other Békes where we'd used our charm to search for leads on Izidora's location.

"Shh, not so loud," Viktor snapped, glancing around us. "They could have spies in the walls for all we know."

"All the more reason for me to soak in the bath." Vadim waggled his eyebrows, then disappeared into a room across from Liliana and Endre's. "See you assholes later."

And then it was only Viktor and me standing amid opulence and luxury.

"Kazimir, are you okay?" My friend's sage green eyes were pinched at the corners, and I knew he worried about the unstable binding magic slithering in my chest.

"Fine," I lied through my gritted teeth.

I was not fine – not when I'd saved Izidora, only for her to reject me when I came to her rescue again.

"I don't believe you," he said, smoothing a hand over his already perfectly styled black hair and rubbing the back of his neck. "I'm not Endre, and I don't know the right words to reassure you, but you are not fine. Judging by the way Izidora looked at Ruslan, she does not appear to be here against her will any longer, and that has to sting."

More like a punch to the gut that knocked all of the air from my lungs.

I ran a palm over my face and blew out a breath. "I need to get her back."

A slow smile spread across Viktor's lips. "Now that I can help you with. Why don't we wash up and start strategizing on how to make it happen?"

I nodded. "Thanks, Viktor. Meet in an hour?"

"Done."

———

STEAM ROLLED off the surface of the water in a soaking tub large enough for two people, and the earthy scent of lavender filled the air. My toes stung as I stepped into the waiting water, life returning to them after our long ride through the snow. The tingle that spread through my body as I sank was a welcome reprieve from the chill that felt bone deep. Dunking my head underwater, I washed away the grime gathered from long days and dusty roads, surfacing when my lungs screamed for air. After the fifth time, I settled back against a rolled towel on the lip of the tub and pulled my father's journal from the dark wood table adjacent to me.

I prayed there was something between these pages that would help me, because I felt like I was drowning in despair as everything I'd worked for, everything I was so certain of, came into question. Nothing of note was on the first few pages, so I continued flipping through them, the scent of ink and parchment joining the earthy scents of my bath salts.

My father did not keep an accurate account of each day, but rather random thoughts and ideas as they came to him. I was about halfway through when I stumbled across the words 'Izidora is an empath' written and underlined. My heart skipped a beat, body trembling as I searched the surrounding pages for any context or date to indicate when it was written, but nothing stood out. Empaths were extremely rare, and I only knew of one in history – a Crystal Fae who was killed for her gifts after she used them to influence the outcome of a war.

Fucking Fates, that was it, that was why Ruslan wanted her.

She was an empath, and a powerful one at that if she had imbued me with strength while Viktor and I had sparred. She not only possessed the ability to influence emotions – she could manipulate others' actions. Her empathy was why her emotions were so tied to her magic and how she gained strength from embracing them.

Could her Angel blood enhance these abilities too?

I spent so many years searching for Izidora that I had only heard stories about the races who lived across the continents, and the only one I had met was a Wolf Shifter female whom we rescued all those years ago.

I flipped through the journal again, hoping to uncover other insights that might aid our efforts. My heart stopped at the last entry, and I read and re-read those words – the last ones my father ever wrote.

Kazimir, if you are reading this, then I am most likely dead. After your mother passed, my grief led me on a dark road, one that resulted in consulting a medium at the Crystal Realm, if only to hear Klariza's voice one last time. Instead, I received a reading that foretold the date of my death. I never told you because I wanted you to live your life without constantly thinking about how many grains of sand remained in the hourglass. My heart is full knowing that you found your mate, even if neither of you has realized it yet. I am so proud of you, my son, for the strong, principled male you have become. The Goddess truly blessed me with you, and I want you to know how much I love you. I am eternally thankful for the years we spent together on the road, for not many fathers get the opportunity to spend so much time with their sons.

Remember who you are in your darkest moments, and you will always triumph.

My throat thickened and I swallowed hard as I wrangled for control with the sorrow that speared its way into my heart. The memory of our last night together surfaced, reminding me how sad he had looked and how guilty I had felt for leaving him alone. He had been grieving the last moments of his life while I had assumed he had been missing my mother. I wished he had told me, but I understood why he kept it from me. He thought to give me this one last gift, knowing I would need to hear his words from beyond this life. A shudder wracked my body, and I closed the journal, placing it on the stool, only a breath away from succumbing to the anguish that wreaked havoc on my soul.

The heat surrounding me did nothing to warm the chill that settled deep in my bones.

Water splashed over the sides of the tub as I reached for my leather bags, digging through them until I found those scraps of lace I'd stolen from Izidora's room at Este Castle before we departed. Bringing them to my nose, I inhaled deeply, her rosy scent so faint after all the times I'd buried myself in her.

No, no, no. I couldn't lose this too.

I threw the scraps to the side, gripping the edges of the tub so hard the marble cracked beneath my fingers. Darkness surged in my chest, knocking the air from my lungs as my vision flashed between red and black and white. I plunged beneath the water in an attempt to regain control, waiting well beyond the point of my lungs burning before freeing myself from my watery prison and sucking down steamy air.

The shift in my body's priorities cleared my mind, allowing me to calm down and think logically about what actions came next. I needed to remember myself, the male who wanted nothing more than to save his lost princess, who led his friends on countless raids, who battled and fought for those he loved.

My reflection caught my attention, water dripping off the ends of my long, unkempt hair and the beard that had started to mimic Vadim's. I looked haggard and a touch crazed, and nothing about the male staring back at me was familiar.

It was time to stop pitying myself and return to the strong male I was.

Pushing out of the warm bath, I pounded a path to the mirror, dripping along the tiled floor, and found a razor sitting alongside the basin. Scraping it across my face, I trimmed the hairs until they barely dusted my skin, showing off the cut of my jaw. The motions were soothing, methodical, and allowed me to put my mind to a singular task.

My attention turned to my hair once I finished my beard. The mess that had grown out over the past few months needed a serious cut. Strip after strip of black hair fell away, some landing over my broad shoulders, others tickling my feet as they piled on the cool tile. The sides were shaved down until they mirrored the length of my beard, though I left it longer on the top, tousling it with my fingers until I was satisfied with how it settled across my head.

I healed the bruises beneath my eyes, the dark purple bags lightening and smoothing, until the emerald of my eyes shone beneath the dark brows set firmly over them. By the time I finished, I recognized the male in the mirror. Bracing my hands on the countertop, I turned my head this way and that, giving myself a final once over. Izidora would remember this male as the one who saved her, who brought her into the world and showed her all that she could be.

All doubt fell away like a shedded skin, and I straightened to my full height, ready to take on Ruslan and the rest of the Iron Realm.

It was time to win back Izidora, and with Viktor's aid, I was certain I could do it.

3

RUSLAN

Béke Day One

Izidora's reassurance was a balm, but it did not heal the fear seared into my soul. The way she stumbled forward, the way their eyes locked, the way he looked at her, had my heart reforming its cage of ice, preparing for the worst. Even still, the side of me that held that cocky confidence screamed within me for doubting myself. But on this matter, this choice of light and dark, I wasn't sure who Izidora would choose. I'd changed so much since I'd snatched her from Este Castle, and that was because of her. I wanted to be a better male for her, but the fear of her leaving me was making it hard.

As we trekked through the bejeweled halls of Ryza Citadel toward the spire that held our apartment, I tried and failed to clear my head, and it wasn't until Izidora placed her hand in mine that my chest finally eased. She siphoned my fear, and not for the first time, I welcomed it. "Clear your emotions when we get back to our room, sprite," I murmured, not wanting her to suffer with the depths of my acute pain.

"Let's do it together." She bumped her shoulder into me, but with her petite size, she only managed to bump my elbow.

"Sure," I replied, opening the heavy metal door to the spire. I scooped Izidora into my arms without warning, needing to feel her closer. She did not protest; instead, she sighed and burrowed into my chest, melting the ice I'd already built up. Her unrestrained affection was everything.

"You seemed excited to see Liliana," I commented as I climbed stair after stair.

If we were to stay here long term, I really needed to install a lift.

Her laugh vibrated against my chest. "Sorry about the lack of decorum."

I nuzzled my nose into her hair. "Nothing to apologize for. I like seeing you happy."

"I'd like for you to get to know her, and for her to get to know you," she replied, tipping her head up to look at me. Her dark lashes brushed against her high cheekbones as she blinked. "We were instant friends, and I've never had a female friend besides her." She paused, and I sensed a darkening shift in her emotions as she slumped against me, hiding her face. "I hope she still wants to be my friend."

My heart panged with her whispered words, and I squeezed her tighter as if I could fend off her fears. "With the way she greeted you, I have no doubt."

We'd reached the door to our apartment, and a sentry – one of the Félvér, the half-bloods who resulted from Rares's experiments – opened it for us, allowing me to keep Izidora in my arms until we were safely inside our bubble of peace.

Rares.

I ground my teeth at the thought of the old Mage, who'd barely managed to appear in the courtyard alongside us to greet our guests. I needed to speak with him and ensure he *never* made a piece of jewelry like the enchanted one I'd almost given

Izidora that afternoon. The thought that I had requested he craft something that ensured my mate would not choose another made me sick, and I'd never been so disappointed in myself.

I meant what I had said to Izidora, and that I would spend the rest of my life redeeming my mistakes, that being the second biggest one. The first had been not checking on her like I had so desperately wanted to do before she came of age.

The fire roared in its hearth, and with the thin, black fabric Izidora wore, I knew she was cold. I placed her on the sofa in front of the fire before fetching a fur blanket from the basket beside it and tucking it around her.

"You take such good care of me, Ruslan." She beamed up at me, her expression reaching into my chest and forcing my heart wide open. Then, she stretched her tiny hand to stroke the soft hairs coating my jaw.

I caught her wrist, turning my face and kissing her palm. "You deserve to be taken care of. Would you like to read to pass the time before the feast? I am so proud of you for finishing a book all by yourself."

"Only if you lay behind me so I can point out the words I am struggling with."

"Deal. Let me see what we have here." I left her on the sofa while I browsed the stack of books Drazen sent over, landing on a fantasy that was more challenging than the romance she'd finished before we greeted our guests.

I kicked off my boots and tossed my suit jacket across the back of a nearby chair, then returned to the couch. Izidora scooted forward, leaning away so I had room to settle behind her. I wrapped her up in me so her head lay against my thumping heart. "Give this one a try," I said, handing her the leather-bound book.

"Age of Dragons." She read the title perfectly, and I gave her a tight squeeze of affirmation. The smell of old parchment wafted up to my sensitive nostrils as she opened to the first page, her bright voice slowly enunciating every word. She was over five pages in before she stumbled across a word she did not know.

"Anonymous," I breathed in her ear, eliciting a shiver that had my cock standing to attention.

"Anonymous," she continued, her voice hoarser than before. I grinned behind her back, pleased with the impact that small act had on her.

Our bond heated, that thirst to be closer to her driving me to snake my arm around her waist and flex my hardened muscles against her ribs. "I can never be close enough to you," I murmured, burying myself in her rosy scent and hoping to die right then and there with my mate in my arms. Fuck the rest of the world. If I could have my mate whisper those sweet words of acceptance, I'd give it all up just to spend my days like this.

Her breath hitched, but she continued to read. I wasn't a male who leaned heavily on the support of the Goddess or the Fates, but in that moment, I prayed to anyone who would listen to let her choose me.

4

KAZIMIR

Liliana wore the same dress she'd worn the night Izidora was kidnapped from Este Castle, the nude glitter catching the light of the giant fireplace in the living area of the suite. Between the reminder of that night and the way Endre looked at her with pure adoration, waves of irritation and jealousy shot down my arms, curling my fingers into my palms until the nails bit into the skin. Domi dripped jewels, and if I didn't know any better, I would have said she belonged in the Iron Realm.

Vadim sprawled across a couch, drink in hand, and he whistled when Viktor and I emerged. "Looking sharp, Kazimir."

"Thank the Goddess you finally shaved that awful beard," Liliana laughed.

"I appreciate you all letting me know I looked like shit before," I deadpanned.

Vadim and Viktor snorted, the former tipping the last of his drink into his mouth before rising from his seat. "Anytime, brother," he teased.

Kaztar cleared his throat, swirling ice around his glass. "Shall we convene with the Crystal Realm before we go to the feast?"

"Lead the way, Kaztar," Viktor said. "There are a few items of business I'd like to discuss."

Tucking his wife's hand into the crook of his arm, Kaztar led us through the maze of halls until we stopped in front of a large set of double doors. He knocked four times, with a long pause between the third and fourth – the signal we'd agreed upon before arriving in the Iron Realm.

High Lord Tukka answered the door, his hungry expression sweeping up and down Liliana appreciatively before acknowledging us and allowing us to pass. Endre's fists curled and uncurled as he passed through the door, and I bit my lip to hide the snicker that threatened to escape as he became possessive of Liliana. She soaked up every second of the males silently promising war over her, much to Vadim's dismay and Domi's amusement.

King Airre settled a dainty tiara over his wife's head, and Aake and Mikko, the other High Lords of the Crystal Realm who joined us, lounged in the middle of the large, open apartment with tall windows and high ceilings. When Queen Immonen rose, she spun to face us immediately, clapping her hands as she beamed over our appearances. "You all look lovely! Please, have a seat anywhere you'd like, there is more than enough room."

We spread out among the array of couches, chairs, and poufs, the High Lords of the Crystal Realm passing around glasses and drinks while we chatted. Once the monarchs had been served, Viktor cleared his throat. "What do you think happened to King Azim?"

King Airre blanched, his lips forming a thin line as he shook his head. "I can only assume that he is dead, though by natural or unnatural cause is certainly up for debate. If I had to guess, I would say that Ruslan is king by force. I knew King Azim long enough to know his tells and how to approach him – I guess not well enough to know about the experiments done in secret within these very walls – but we will have to dance delicately with King Ruslan until we have more information. I do not think this will change our other plans," he finished with a low whisper.

"I don't like the male. There is something almost manic about him, almost like he could be welcoming one moment and have you pinned beneath his sword the next," High Lord Tukka declared, betraying the true depth of his emotion with the way his knuckles tightened over the arms of the chair.

"That we can definitely agree upon, Tukka," Viktor said grimly.

The queen tapped her finger on her chin for a moment, and we fell silent, waiting for her to speak. "We should have a day for just us females. I'd like to get to know Izidora better, and perhaps Liliana and Domi can coax some truth from her. The Iron Realm has natural hot springs that run from the mountains, and the water is incredible for your skin. I will suggest a day at the spa for us."

Liliana beamed, excitement bursting from her at the idea of pampering and relaxation. "That is a brilliant idea, thank you, Queen Immonen."

"King Ruslan better not deny me this. I went on my own when we were here four years ago, and my skin was soft for months afterward." The queen swooned, a dreamy expression crossing her face, rendering it serene.

Her husband lifted her bejeweled hand and planted a light kiss on the back of it. "I'll ensure you get to go before we leave, my love." Liliana and Domi's sighs were audible as they watched the tender moment between the mated pair.

King Airre glanced at the large clock pinned to the wall. I

followed, noting that the time for the ball drew near. Nervous anticipation settled in my gut, the sick feeling hollowing me out and setting me on edge. I glanced at Endre, whose half-smile bolstered my confidence.

I would show Izidora that I was the better male, and she would come running back to me before the night was over.

"Who is ready to make an entrance?" I grinned roguishly as the High Lords jumped to their feet, mischief and plotting in each of their expressions. King Airre and Queen Immonen followed shortly after, the latter gliding in front of us to the double doors, head held high and shoulders back in a display of regal confidence.

"We will show the usurper what real monarchs look like," she announced as her husband captured her arm to lead her out of the room. I always liked the queen, but statements in support of my claim and against Ruslan made me a lifelong fan. High Lords Aake and Mikko opened the doors for them, then fell into place as we marched to the ballroom.

Kaztar and I led the Night Realm's entourage a few paces behind, just enough distance to appear loosely united rather than plotting an attack on the Iron Realm. The halls passed in a blur as I held my focus on the task at hand, until finally we rounded the corner to the richly decorated entrance of the ball-room. Soft silks draped the door, pinned in place by obsidian spikes, and on either side rows of perfectly polished guards stood, backs ramrod straight, against the walls. They didn't even blink as we passed them, and a wave of hatred washed over me at Ruslan's clear display of mistrust and arrogance.

The reception line spilled out the door, and Queen Viktoria and King Consort Geza were already in it.

Perfect timing.

I strained my ears to hear the words she spoke to a few of the nobles of the Iron Realm, but her voice was lost amid the dim roar that echoed in the cavernous room beyond the metal doors. She disappeared beyond my view, moving deeper into the space where I assumed Ruslan and Izidora waited.

Endre grasped my shoulder and leaned forward to speak in my ear. "Get through this ball without pissing off Ruslan and getting us all killed. Or getting pissed off and killing Ruslan."

Before I could respond, Viktor added, "You want Izidora to remember who you are, and acting... *Irrationally* will not help. Either way, let's get out of this alive, yeah?"

He wanted me to contain the binding magic that slumbered within my chest, ready to fight at the slightest provocation. "I am planning on controlling myself."

We entered the ballroom, and a line of noble Iron Fae waited to greet us.

Fucking bastards.

They got to chain Izidora in a cave for twenty-one years and then show their faces like nothing had happened? I still couldn't comprehend how Izidora was so willingly hanging on Ruslan's arm after what the Iron Fae did to her. None of this made any sense, and I needed answers. Ruslan clearly had some sort of power over her that was making her act this way. It was the only explanation.

The first of the lords of the Iron Realm dipped his head, and I gritted out my pleasantries, not listening to his response as I concentrated on the sweet sound of Izidora's voice as she greeted Queen Viktoria. Her words were indistinguishable, but I would recognize her tone across lifetimes, the sound of home always calling me to her.

Behind me, Kaztar and Domi redeemed my coolness with polite flattery.

I reached the High Lords, two young males whom I had not met before. They regarded me with vicious intent. One licked his lips as if he anticipated a delicious fight breaking out later.

Something between a grin and a baring of teeth held my lips wide as I stepped up to them. I refused to bow my head, and they did the same as we locked eyes. "I don't think I have met either of you before. I am High Lord Kazimir Vaszoly."

"You haven't. I am High Lord Slavian and this is High Lord Anton," the blond male said, gesturing to the deeply tanned male to his right.

"Which houses do you belong to?" I asked politely, though I couldn't care less who they represented. My focus was on reclaiming my mate, standing mere feet from me.

"I am House Vitali," Anton replied.

"Ah yes, I remember your father from my last visit to the Iron Realm. How long ago did he pass?" I feigned a hint of sadness.

Anton's eyes flashed as he snarled, "Don't pretend like you care. You only want to know how long I've warmed his seat."

I raised a brow but said nothing as I turned to Slavian. "And your house?"

"House Romanuk. I remember your father from his last visit to the Iron Realm. Why are you here in his stead?" His words were barbed and aimed to wound. Grief that gave way to rage surged through my veins, awakening the binding magic in my chest, but I held my expression firm, shoving my desire to strangle him down for a later time.

"He died during the attack on Este Castle. I am the Head of House Vaszoly now."

Anton's face went wolfish, and I swore his eyes flashed yellow momentarily. "Welcome to the club of young High Lords. We'd love to take you out during your time here and show you the best spots to find willing females who would do anything to bed a bachelor Lord."

I assessed the two standing before me, and it was clear they were used to getting their way, their cocky arrogance on full display to the world. "I'll let you know if I grow bored in Ryza

Citadel. If you'll excuse me." I quickly extracted myself from the conversation, avoiding the temptation to punch them in their smug faces as they suggested I forget about Izidora for a more willing encounter.

As I greeted the remaining High Lords, Queen Immonen's airy voice drifted down the line from where she and King Airre spoke with Ruslan and Izidora. "...your circlet is gorgeous! King Ruslan, you must allow us females to have a spa day while the males get together. Your future wife needs to look her best on your wedding day!"

Bile rose in my throat at her false praise, but she was certainly adept at getting what she wanted, because Ruslan acquiesced. "While my mate is already stunning, I cannot deny the request of such a kind queen. Princess Izidora and yourself will find much common ground in that regard."

"You are such a gem! I cannot wait to get to know you better, Princess Izidora," Queen Immonen finished with a kiss on either cheek.

"Likewise, Queen Immonen," Izidora responded in kind, her warmth toward everyone but me like a punch to the gut.

Only a few Fae remained between my mate and me. Hearing Ruslan voicing his claim to her over and over cut deep into my soul, for I knew she was mine and not his. My binding magic agreed. But I gritted my teeth and steeled my spine against it as High Lord Tukka finished with them, then I took the final step toward her.

I ignored Ruslan, instead taking Izidora's hand in mine and caressing it with a featherlight, sensual kiss. Her pulse fluttered in her wrist as I pulled my lips away. "Izidora, I am so happy you are safe and sound. We unanimously proclaimed you queen despite your absence. We eagerly await your return, as do your people, who love you dearly."

Tears welled in her big, beautiful eyes, but she held the same serene smile as she spoke to me at last. "I am glad to see you are well, Kazimir. And to hear that all my people are well. I look forward to celebrating this time of peace with you and the rest of the Night Fae."

Her formality stung like the lashing of whips, and the coolness she showed me despite this insistent tug between us had me wanting to hurt her like she continued to hurt me. "Unfortunately, not all of your people are well. We lost many the night Ruslan attacked Este Castle, including my father." A low growl came from the male beside my mate, but I did not heed his warning. "Kriztof, Kirigin, and Zekari gave their lives for you, My Queen. I hope it was not in vain."

A tear rolled down either cheek, taking with them a line of black. Her expression dropped, and she took a nearly imperceptible step closer to Ruslan, whose hand immediately found her lower back. I wanted to remove them from his body immediately. She looked to the ceiling, blinking rapidly, while her fingers swiped at her eyes.

"I think you should move along now," he snarled, his glare hot enough to burn.

I scrutinized him as we stood only a breath from each other. The hint of madness Tukka had noted was carefully masked, but there. Ruslan's shoulders were tense beneath the well-cut suit as if he were prepared to strike at any moment. A flash of teeth showed pointed canines, and I sensed he would be an equal foe under the onslaught of the binding magic I hid in my chest.

"Kazimir, would you mind grabbing a drink for Domi? She is parched," Kaztar butted in, shooting me a look that told me I needed to relax.

"Certainly," I gritted out, then stalked away from the receiving line. I did not go far, choosing instead to wait out of sight for the pair to finish speaking with Ruslan and Izidora.

"High Lord Kazimir and myself are representing the Night

Realm at this year's Béke at the behest of the council, since our monarch has not yet been formally crowned," said Kaztar. "In our entourage, we have the sons of High Lords Erik Adimik and Tibor Zadik, and the son and daughter of Lord Nikolai Arzeni. They send their apologies for not being able to attend this year's festivities, as we must keep our realm running smoothly in the queen's absence." Kaztar was a brilliant courtier and one I was grateful to have on my side.

"Thank you, High Lord Kaztar. Enjoy the opening ball." Ruslan's insincerity dripped through every word. I fixated for as long as I could on Izidora, watching her greet Liliana and Endre before Kaztar blocked my vision.

"Do you want to win her back or not?" he hissed. "Because you're not off to a very good start. Pull it together, Kazimir."

Kaztar gripped my upper arm and steered me toward one of the long bars lining the room, where he ordered whisky for us while Domi ordered wine. The glass was finely crafted and inlaid with gems, and I gritted my teeth momentarily before loosening my jaw and sipping. The burn seared my throat before settling in my belly, though it didn't satiate the fervent need to follow that string that led me to Izidora.

The wood bar held me up as I surveyed the room buzzing with activity. The mingling crowd was thick with females bedecked in jewels of every color, their male companions joining them in slim-fitting suits. Off to the side, a group stuck out of the normal crowd, their clothing simple yet elegant, and by the looks of them they were clearly not Iron Fae. One in their number had hair whiter than Queen Immonen, and I would have mistaken him for Crystal Fae if it weren't for an ethereal aura that surrounded him. Around him, five others with various shades of dark hair and red eyes shifted to look at me as if they sensed my attention on them. The tall Angel turned, his piercing blues pinning me in place from across the room. He said something to his companions, after one last glance over his shoulder.

"Are those Angels and Demons?" Domi gasped as she noticed the group.

"I think so, but I never spent enough time around the port in Vaenor to meet one before. Have you?" I questioned.

Kaztar stepped forward, narrowing his eyes to get a closer look. "I met an Angel once – he was an explorer. I bought him a drink and he told me that the Angels and Demons like to keep to themselves," he recalled. "They live for millennia and hate involving themselves in the petty affairs of the mortals, as he called us." He shrugged, then downed the last of his drink and set the glass on the bar. I did the same. The rest of the Night Fae had finished moving through the receiving line and were gathering across the room.

"What do you think they are doing here?" Domi whispered as we pushed through the crowd.

"Shh, not here, Domi," Kaztar replied. "There are too many open ears."

Indeed there were. Every Iron Fae assessed us as we passed them, regarding us with suspicion. Their stares did not affect me, for they were against me, and I did not care to win their approval – my sole focus was rescuing my mate from the Iron Fae again.

Would the Angel help us do that?

Izidora was part Angel, and from what Queen Liessa's former maid had told us before we departed for Béke, the non-Fae were in the Iron Realm against their will. Perhaps we could convince the Angel and the Demons to side with us, and in exchange for their help, we'd free them from the clutches of the Iron Realm.

About halfway across the room, Kaztar and Domi interrupted my plotting with an excuse that they wanted to sit, tired after riding for weeks on end. Bidding them goodbye, I continued to my friends, arriving just in time to witness Endre loop his arm around Liliana's waist. But she stared off into the distance at the young High Lords in the receiving line, curiosity cocking her head ever so slightly to the side.

"Can you get me a drink? I need one." She turned her attention to Endre, batting her long lashes and offering him a soft smile.

"A glass of bubbly wine coming up." Endre dropped his arm from her hip after giving it a gentle squeeze. I clenched my fists.

"I need a glass of something strong. Anyone else?" Vadim offered, stepping forward to join Endre.

"I do," Viktor and I said in unison.

Vadim and Endre chuckled, then pushed through the crowd, retrieving the liquid we needed to make it through the evening. I scanned the room, finding no sign of Ruslan and Izidora.

Where had they disappeared to?

My gaze landed on High Lords Slavian and Anton, sauntering up like they owned the citadel and boxing Liliana in. Both looked her up and down, Anton licking his lips appreciatively and rubbing his hands together. She shot them both a sideways glance, then flicked her hair over her shoulder.

"Can I help you?" She crossed her arms and popped out a hip, her attention raking over Slavian, and then drifting onto Anton.

By the way Viktor crushed his lips together, I knew he and I felt the same about the two males. I eagerly waited for Liliana to tear them to pieces. If wars could be won with sharp words in place of swords, she would be queen of the world.

"The real question is, can we help you?" Anton said smoothly. "I'm High Lord Anton. Pleased to meet you..." he paused, waiting for her to fill in her name.

She turned her back on the male, faced Slavian, and cocked

a brow, waiting for him to speak. His eyes flashed with delight at her defiant attitude. "I am High Lord Slavian, and I would love to get you a drink."

"Get me a drink, or get me drunk?" she quipped.

"Get you a drink, get you drunk, get you off, probably in that order," Slavian purred, teeth raking in his lower lip suggestively.

Viktor barely held in a snort while I lifted my hand to cover the smile threatening to break free. Endre and Vadim were fast approaching, both fixated on the two males standing on either side of Liliana. Between High Lord Tukka and these two, Endre was going to fight someone before this trip was over.

They circled around, listening intently. Vadim slipped a drink in my hand, then one in Viktor's as he stepped between us. Endre sidled between Anton and me, clearing his throat as he passed Liliana her bubbly wine. "I believe she already has a drink."

"Are you going to get in on this?" I whispered to Vadim.

"Not a chance. Let's see if Endre is worthy of my sister," he chuckled darkly. "Though I hope he does not scare them off completely. I hear they spend copious amounts of time with willing females, and I can take them up on their offer if I grow bored here. There's a reason I pushed Liliana along to Izidora in the receiving line."

I returned my attention to the growing tension before me. "I think the Lady can speak for herself," Slavian purred. "Anton and I can show you *such* a good time while your companions are off playing politics. You look like a female who likes to have fun."

She sipped her drink, sighing after the cool liquid hit her tongue. "What gave it away? The wine or the cut of this dress?"

"While that dress looks damn good on you, it would look so much better on my bedroom floor. But I'm offering other fun as well. I can take you places you've never been before, beautiful," Slavian promised, his tone dripping with lasciviousness.

Endre snarled low at Slavian's provocative undertones, and Liliana scowled at him before turning her attention to Anton. "And what are you offering?"

"The same as my friend here. Tell me, have you ever been worshiped like the Goddess? Because we know just a place to make that happen. In fact," he glanced around at all of us surreptitiously before continuing, "we should all go tonight for the after-party. This event is too stuffy for a bunch of young blood like us."

Endre growled a warning, but Liliana pointedly ignored him. "Sounds fun. How do we get there?"

The liquor caught in my throat, and I coughed, trying to clear my airway. Liliana was wild like the creatures of the forest, and not even Vadim could control her. She was open to anything, and dragging us along with her? That was simply an extra flair of fun for her. Endre clenched and unclenched his fists as she flirted with the two males, making arrangements for us to meet them once the ball concluded. For a moment, I thought he might break his jaw from the way the muscles in his cheek feathered.

"I'll need your name so that our security knows to let you in," Slavian pointed out, thumbing his lower lip.

She batted her dark lashes at him before offering it up. "Liliana."

Slavian lifted her hand, kissing the back of it lightly before bowing and backing away, melting into the crowd with Anton. "I look forward to seeing you there, Lady Liliana."

"Why did you agree to go?" Endre snapped the second the pair were out of earshot, pushing his messy hair out of his face as he towered over her.

Liliana tipped the last of her drink into her mouth and then shrugged. "You didn't stop me." He bent his head close to her, furious whispers passing from his lips to her ears, and then reversing direction.

Vadim snickered beside me. "She did that on purpose to test him."

I whispered back, "I gathered that much."

"We're still going, right?" he clarified, hissing like the alcohol burned his tongue.

Before I had a chance to respond, a gong reverberated throughout the room, signaling the time to find our places. Toward the back of the space, hundreds of tables were neatly arranged, all holding place cards and elegant dining ware. I checked table after table, searching for my name, but each came up empty. Only a handful of people still waded through the sea of tables looking for their seats, and when I reached the last table and still found none, I dropped into an open chair, flicking the name card away without looking.

Feeling eyes on me, I glanced to the high table to find Ruslan's sardonic smirk.

Petty bastard.

If he was secure in his relationship with Izidora, he would not feel the need to slight me and control her. I bared my teeth in his direction, and he merely sipped his drink and turned away, ignoring me and adding to my ire.

Each Night Fae was seated at a different table around the room, no doubt another strategic move on Ruslan's part. Liliana was at the table beside mine, positioned – unsurprisingly – between High Lords Slavian and Anton. Endre was farther away, staring daggers in their direction; if looks could kill, the two would be bleeding out onto the iron gray tablecloths draped over the circular tables.

At least High Lords Soma and Domon sat at my table. I engaged the High Lords of the Day Realm in conversation as we waited for our meal to be delivered. The metal goblets at the top corner of our place settings were already filled with dark red wine, and I gulped down the dry liquid until only a drop remained at the bottom. Not a moment later, a young servant appeared, pitcher in hand, and refilled my drink.

High Lord Soma lifted his goblet in my direction, and High Lord Domon and a few others surrounding us mimicked him. "Let us drink to our friendship, but remember that Béke's competitions start tomorrow, and after that," he grinned deliberately, "we will see if we are all still friends."

I lifted my goblet in turn, saluting my table companions, then drained the second glass. My nerves started to settle as the alcohol relaxed me, forcing me to focus on the present moment rather than the unknowns that lay before me. The Day Realm's High Lords played the role of jokesters and entertainers, keeping the entire table engaged and laughing, even through the serving of a dozen ostentatious courses. For the most part I ignored the high table, save for a few glances at Izidora, who spoke jovially with Queen Viktoria and Queen Immonen.

Memories of our meals together, both on the road and at my family's estate, Zirok, flooded my mind. The sound of her laughter as the Nighthounds entertained her with stories of misadventures, the way she unabashedly ate every crumb of the sweet treats that were piled on her plate. The memory of her burning her mouth on a slice of fresh-baked pie came too, a grin tugging at my lips before a stone settled in my gut, wishing that Kriztof, Zekari, and Kirigin were with us in the Iron Realm. Together, we were an unstoppable force, and without them I felt unmoored, like an essential part of me was missing.

She'd laughed with them, with us, with me.

And now, she did it with *him.*

A slow, classic tune filled the air, and one by one Fae stood from their tables, laughing and throwing their fine silk napkins over their plates. They wove their way to the dance floor, picking up mid-song and twirling around.

From the opposite end of the room, I had a *fantastic* view of Ruslan and Izidora, hand in hand, joining the couples already dancing. He pulled her flush against him, hand splaying over the bare skin of her lower back, a finger dipping beneath the black fabric that barely covered it.

Her smile was devastating.

I rose without thinking from my seat.

Her expression was exalted as he spun her and then yanked her back to him.

I pushed forward through groups of Fae taking far too long to move.

She laughed, breathless and happy.

The glass I had been holding shattered, my magic and my mind screaming for me to act, *to save.*

She was happy without me.

And I would not stand for it.

I stalked toward Ruslan and Izidora, intent on snatching her away from him the moment I reached them. As the final note lingered in the air, I parted the crowd roughly, earning scandalized looks from the finely dressed couples standing at the edges.

Izidora found me immediately, her head jerking in my direction as that tug between us became insistent. Ruslan whipped around after her lips parted, and I bowed my head to her before holding out my hand. "May I have this dance, My Queen?"

Ruslan smacked my hand away with a snarl. "She will not dance with you. Not after you upset her earlier."

I stepped closer to him so we were nearly nose to nose. My blood burned hot in my veins, dark magic simmering just below the surface of my skin. "What are you afraid of, Ruslan?" I crooned. "I am simply a High Lord asking his queen for a dance. She has chosen you to wed, after all."

His eyes flashed with black fire, his mouth forming a hard line as he stared me down. Endre and Viktor watched the interaction cautiously, ready to jump in should I lose control.

Should I have goaded Ruslan? Probably not.

But did I care? No.

I was better than Ruslan, and I needed to remind Izidora of our love so she would willingly leave his side and rejoin me in our bed. Ruslan needed to be embarrassed in front of his people, his new reign tarnished by his inability to keep a female.

Neither of us yielded to the other, two males resolved to win this power struggle, even as people started to stare and whispers overtook the music in volume.

"I'll be okay, Ruslan." Izidora placed her small hand on his chest, a gesture of reassurance that made my nails cut into my palms. Ruslan scowled at me a moment longer but eventually caved. Whether it was because he tried to appear like he was not fazed by my request, or because he wanted the approval of his people, I did not care, because I had won the first battle.

"Fine," he spat out through clenched teeth. He barely stepped away from Izidora, and I bowed to her reverently before tucking her hand into the crook of my elbow and leading her onto the dance floor. Ruslan vibrated with barely restrained rage as he watched us together, his eyes never leaving us as I circled deeper into the crowd of dancers.

Izidora was guarded as we began to spin among the couples, her aquamarine eyes hard in a way they'd never been before as she pointedly looked everywhere but my face. She didn't melt into me like she did Ruslan, so I pulled her closer, needing to touch her in every way possible after so long apart. But she pulled back as much as she could, like she did not want to touch me, so similar to the first time we rode Fek together. Much like then, my heart sank, and my fingers dug into her back as I forced her closer again.

"Kazimir, you're hurting me," she frowned, finally looking me in the eyes.

"Izidora," I croaked, unable to say more as my every sense was overcome with her closeness once again. Her rosy scent filled my nostrils, smooth skin brushed my palm, petite frame pressed firmly against my body, big eyes drinking me in. All of it was intoxicating and all-consuming.

"Kazimir, loosen your grip."

"Izidora, I've worked so hard to get to you. You have no idea what I've done over the past months." I tried and failed to keep the desperation from my tone.

"And you don't know what I have either." Her voice was flat and her face lacked all semblance of joy.

"What did he do to you? What is he threatening you with?" My voice was a little too loud, and the couples around us regarded us for a moment before moving along.

Izidora's iciness deepened with the unwanted attention our conversation was bringing. "He's done nothing wrong, Kazimir. But I've changed – a lot."

"Then let me get to know the new you. I have a surprise for you. Please, let me show you how much I love you." I was begging, but I didn't care – not when losing our bond was the price of failure.

Her aquamarine eyes wavered, bouncing between mine as she chewed her lip. "Fine. We can spend some time together tomorrow."

I released a breath, a weight lifting from my chest with her words. "Thank you, Izidora."

Her lips pressed into a firm line as we continued the steps of the dance, but I couldn't waste a single moment I had with her. "I still love you, Izidora. Don't you still love me?" My voice broke over the question, along with my heart.

A tear spilled down her cheek, and guilt flashed in her eyes. "Kazimir, I–"

Before she could finish, Ruslan yanked me back, separating me from Izidora.

"What the fuck," I snarled, shaking his hand off of me.

"Song is over," he hissed, wrapping Izidora possessively under his arm. She made no move to fight him.

I clenched my fists, still hearing the same tune playing. "You can't handle another male threatening what you think is yours, can you? You're just an insecure child playing king."

He dropped his arm from Izidora, and then he took a menacing step toward me.

"Ruslan!" Izidora reached for his sleeve and missed.

"She chose me, and you can't handle that," he seethed, popping one knuckle after another as he puffed himself up.

I straightened to my full height and bared my teeth, not backing down, not when I'd been preparing for this fight for months.

I took a step forward. "It seems to me like she was not actually given a choice. What do they call that? Oh yeah, rape. As if she did not experience enough abuse at the hands of your people, you had to continue it."

Horns sprung from Ruslan's head as he shoved me with all his strength, forcing me to take a stumbling step back. "She came to my bed willingly. She even asked nicely. And she had no thought of you."

The only color I saw was death as I dove for his midsection, pulling us both to the floor. The crowd parted as their king and I each grappled for control of the other. Ruslan swept my legs out from under me so that I landed hard on my back, air whooshing from my lungs as he rained heavy blows on my face. I trapped his arm before he could land another punch and rolled him off, retaliating with a hard elbow to the ribs followed by a sharp hit on his jaw.

Ruslan spat blood into my face, and I jerked back, giving him the opening he needed to stand up and throw a knee to my face. I dodged at the last second, catching the back of his leg and standing, off-balancing him as I kicked his other leg out from beneath him. He landed with a heavy thud, and I dove to follow him, fist poised to strike again, when a set of hands dragged me backward. I struggled against them, my vision tunneled on a grinning Ruslan who pushed himself off the floor.

"Kazimir, calm the fuck down. We can't do this here," Viktor warned, giving my arm a harsh yank, trying to ground me. But I was too far gone.

Ruslan flashed his bloody teeth and spat ruby on the ground. "That's right, run away like the weak male you are. No wonder Izidora chose me. A real male would fight to the death."

"Let's fucking go." I yanked out of Viktor's grip, raging to finish what I'd started.

I stomped toward Ruslan, who used the opportunity to lunge and yank me to the ground with him. He wrapped his legs around my shoulders as I fell on top of him, locking them together so I was gasping for breath and blood in my brain. My vision clouded, stars dancing in my eyes as I struggled to free the knife hidden at my ankle.

But the darkness embedded in me sang and filled my veins with power, giving me strength. Knife in hand, I stood with him still wrapped around me and stabbed into his side. He grunted, legs releasing my neck, but dropped them to my hips instead, launching me back with a powerful kick. The crowd caught me as Ruslan popped to his feet, his roar shaking the chandeliers hanging from the ceiling as he clutched his side.

Drazen burst through the crowd and grabbed Ruslan from behind before he could move forward and continue our fight.

He shouted past me, "Get him out of here!" as Ruslan's eyes flashed with dark fury. Izidora's hands were pressed against Ruslan's side a moment later, white light flashing beneath her fingers as she healed him.

The sight of her so quickly coming to his aid boiled my blood.

Viktor's hands were on me again, with Vadim assisting him as they fought to return me to myself.

"Come on, Kazimir," Viktor ordered as they hauled me through the crowd of people, and once Ruslan was out of sight, rage's hold fell away as if it were never there at all. I slumped into the chair they threw me in once we left the ballroom, head in hands as I processed my massive mistake.

Vadim snorted, "At least he hit you first."

"I can't believe you called him a rapist," Viktor groused.

"You heard that?" I questioned with a defeated sigh.

"Oh, yeah, we heard the whole thing. As did half the room. It was not a good look for you, especially if you want to win Izidora back. We talked about this." Viktor pinched his brow, then ran a hand over his dark hair to smooth it. He opened his mouth to admonish me again but was interrupted by Endre and Liliana bursting from the ballroom.

A breath of relief left Endre's lips as he saw me slouched in the chair, guarded from repeating my earlier actions. "I told you not to piss him off."

"Yeah, well, he pissed me off." I defended my actions, even though I was fully aware that I had acted like an ass.

"I also told you not to get pissed off and kill him." Endre glared at me from above like he was scolding a petulant child.

"Well, he is alive isn't he?" I gestured toward the ballroom, where the revelry continued as if the King of the Iron Realm and a High Lord of the Night Realm hadn't brawled in the midst of it.

Vadim snorted again. "Only because Viktor pulled you off him, so don't make that excuse. You did in fact stab him."

And I didn't feel one ounce of remorse.

Silence stretched between us. I ran a hand over my face, wincing as I brushed over a bruise.

"You look like shit, Kazimir." Liliana reached her fingers to my face, touching my aching cheek. When I jerked under her touch, she ordered me to hold still. Silver light caressed my face, and I let her heal me, though I probably didn't deserve it. She was not a gifted healer like Endre, so the fact that she had offered to heal me at all spoke volumes.

The doors banged open behind us, and High Lords Slavian and Anton spilled into the hallway, both obviously drunk.

"There you are! Come on, Kazimir, let's go find some willing females." Anton stumbled over to me, grabbing my arm in an attempt to take me with him. I shrugged him off immediately, and Slavian took that to mean that they needed to try harder.

"Anton, you idiot, he does not want another female right now. What he needs is a strong drink and some herbs from Steel," Slavian chided, hiccuping over his words.

Anton wagged a finger at his friend as he clung to his shoulder. "You're right, Slavian. Some herbs will do him good."

"Liliana! Make your friends come with us," Anton exclaimed when he noticed her kneeling before me.

"I think we've had enough excite–" Endre started before I interrupted him.

"Lead the way, Anton." Endre glared and I merely shrugged. Ruslan's words still echoed in my head, and I wanted to drown all my thoughts in whisky. If Izidora went to his bed willingly – no, I didn't even want to consider it.

The drunk High Lords sang an off-key tune as they led us to the courtyard, a fresh layer of snow covering the ground. Anton whistled at a male leaning against a closed carriage. "Take us to Steel!"

The driver pushed off the frame, opening the door for us and waiting until we were all inside before closing us in. It was a tight fit, and Liliana sat on Endre's lap, twirling her fingers in his dark locks while shamelessly flirting with the two High Lords. His hands twitched over her thighs, subtly bunching up the glittering fabric in his tense fingers. Beside me, Vadim and Viktor spoke in hushed tones, leaving me alone to witness the antics across from us.

Instead, I watched the capital of the Iron Realm pass us by, trying not to think about the noises Izidora made as Ruslan gave her all the pleasure she wanted.

5

RUSLAN

Béke Day One

Izidora fussed over my wound as we pushed our way through the throng of Fae and Félvér to a quieter location in a room adjacent to the massive ballroom. The sweet taste of victory masked any pain I might have felt, knowing that Kazimir had made a fool of himself in front of the monarchs of the Crystal and Day Realms by fighting with and then stabbing me.

Convincing Queen Viktoria of the Day Realm and King Airre of the Crystal Realm to ally with me, to create a unified continent where all were welcome, pure-blooded or not, would fly along if Kazimir continued to act like an asshole at every turn.

There was no doubt in my mind when the group had arrived simultaneously that they'd already thrown their lot in with Kazimir and the Night Fae, yet his actions were the first slice I'd needed to tear their alliance apart. A small smile tugged at my lips until Drazen and Izidora's raised voices caught my attention.

"...what did you expect would happen with the two of them

in a room together?" Drazen hissed, looking down at Izidora, whose hands were balled into fists and planted on her hips as she glared upward, not backing down despite the half-Dragon towering over her. Pride swelled in my heart as she faced him head-on, and even though I was beyond pissed that Kazimir had hurt her, I was proud of her for standing up for herself then, too.

"I expected both of them to behave!"

"Kazimir was the one who started it," Drazen pointed out.

Izidora's pink pout dipped into a frown. "Ruslan didn't have to goad him."

I stepped forward and took one of her slender arms from her hip, pulling her to me. I had to crane my neck to look down at her, and her aquamarine eyes were teeming with emotion. "Yes, I did. No male will *ever* lay an unwanted hand on you and go unpunished for it. It is only because you have requested time to make your decision that he is alive at all right now."

She raised a brow at me. "You seem fairly confident that I'll choose you in the end."

The smirk that rose to my face was a well-practiced one, aimed to hide the hurt that twisted my heart into a thousand knots. "You will."

And maybe if I said it enough times, I'd actually believe it.

That deep-rooted fear of abandonment, of being utterly unloveable because of how fucked up I was, challenged my words, clawing them back down my throat and replacing them with the ones I actually wanted to say.

Please don't leave me.

I swallowed them down. After almost succumbing to the fear prior to the arrival of our guests, I'd vowed to allow Izidora time to make her choice, and I would *never* break a vow to her. Never.

Unlike Kazimir, who, if I had to guess, was rolling toward Steel with Anton and Slavian at this very moment. The two young Félvér High Lords were guaranteed to indulge in their desires, dragging the Night Fae into the haze of lust that covered every inch of the place. Sex ruled the Iron Realm just as much as the gems we mined in the mountains and the metal we crafted into unbreakable armor and weapons.

In Északi, power ruled above all, and the Iron Realm, long thought to be the weakest realm, had been harboring secrets for more than a century. The power we'd amassed would soon be flashed before the other monarchs, and I'd show them why they should leave the blood-purity mindset behind. Before Béke was over, they'd be begging to unite with us.

So, let Kazimir fuck some Félvér females at the club and forget about the fiery female still standing before me, eyes glittering as she tipped her head up, sending her soft, chestnut hair spilling down her back.

"Does it still hurt?" she asked, referring to my already-healed wound.

"Sprite, this is not even close to my worst injury. I will be fine." Her long lashes fluttered as I stroked her cheek, then tucked her hair behind her pointed ear. She chewed her lip for a moment before nodding and stepping away. Before she got far, I grasped her wrist and tugged her to me, wrapping my arms around her waist as I inhaled her rosy scent. "Thank you for healing me. Be sure to keep your magic well full, just in case you need it."

She huffed a laugh. "I will."

Izidora may grow tired of my constant reminders to take care of herself, but I didn't give a fuck. She was *everything* to me, and I would die if something happened to her. That was why I'd pushed her so hard during our time together, and I'd watched her inner flame grow from a burning log into a wildfire. She was a true force of nature who knew just how powerful she could be. I savored the feeling of her small body pressed against mine like one might savor a decadent dessert, my shoulders dropping a little as she stroked a soothing pattern against my chest.

Drazen cleared his throat as Zuriel, the only Angel remaining in the Iron Realm, glided into the room. His icy eyes ghosted over the three of us before settling on me. We'd formed a tenuous relationship as he'd spent countless hours training with Izidora, teaching her how to use her empath magic and pull from her ever-deepening well.

"Glad to see you're okay, Ruslan." His deep, melodic voice floated through the small space, and Izidora pulled out of my embrace, turning to face her cousin.

"It means a lot that you came to check on me, Zuriel," I replied, actually meaning my words.

The Angel only shrugged, his expression betraying nothing, per usual. "The guests are restless, wondering what will happen next after the exodus of their host and the representatives of an entire realm."

"They can wait," I declared, attention bouncing between Drazen and Zuriel as an idea began to form in my head. "Actually, I need to speak with both of you. I believe we have an opening to carry out my plan for the Félvér."

Drazen's dark brows rose over his deep blue eyes. The male was intimately familiar with my longtime wish for the Félvér to be free to roam the continent. After all, he was one of the only people I trusted, and he headed my personal guard – the whole Iron Realm army, too, now that I was king. But Zuriel's face remained as cool as ever, not even a twitch of his eyes or mouth to betray his thoughts. The Angel always knew more than he let on, and I wondered if he had already guessed my plans or knew of them some other way.

"The Night, Crystal, and Day Realms arrived as a united front. But with Kazimir's behavior tonight, I wonder if that alliance might have cracked, even a little." My gaze fell over

Izidora, who had spun to face me when I spoke the name of her other potential mate. "I know you share my feelings about wanting our people to be free, so I hope if you do... choose him, you will still help me carve out freedom for the Félvér."

She nodded, waiting for me to get to my point.

"If we can continue to break their alliance, then we might have a chance of opening the minds, and doors, of the other realms to uniting for the good of our continent and all those who inhabit it. Zuriel, coordinate with the other Telivér to be more visible throughout Béke. I don't want you to hide as you have in the past. If we're going to push for this new way of life, we need to lead by example."

Zuriel's facade cracked for a moment as a softness bled into his eyes. "It would be my honor."

"And Drazen," I continued, "let's show off the Félvér superiority as much as possible in the competitions. I want to impress the fuck out of the other monarchs and show them why the 'pure blood is the only way to maintain power' mindset is bullshit."

A wicked grin crossed his face, and he straightened the pile of black hair atop his head. "Oh, I can guarantee that. I'll get our strongest, fastest, and best fighters to compete for the Iron Realm."

My heart soared on the wings of this new plan, and a feeling of rightness settled over me. It was time to shed the skin of the sadistic prince and become the wise, ruthless king that I needed to be. For I could be both, exacting the pain and pleasure from those who served me at just the right moments to ensure compliance and cooperation. It would be a mistake for anyone to see this softening as anything other than preparation for an unyielding, relentless pursuit of what I wanted.

There could be no dark without light; there could be no pain without pleasure. The highs and lows of life were there to make me feel fucking alive. Those dark parts of me would never leave, but allowing fragments of light to pierce the dark would guide me down the path of victory.

"But what happens if we fail to convince them?" Izidora asked. As a Félvér, Izidora had just as much reason to want acceptance for those with mixed blood as Drazen or myself.

"Then there will be war, and a bloody one at that. It will be the Fae against the Félvér, mirroring the war between the Angels and the Demons millennia ago. I'd like to avoid the near-genocide that happened during that war at all costs." I was more than serious, too. Félvér blood was precious, and losing our brethren would eat away at the tendrils of light lifting the darkness from my heart. A flash of my siblings' faces crossed my mind, but I shoved them away, unwilling to allow my father's fucked up games to derail me.

Zuriel's facade cracked again at the mention of the war, a heaviness settling over his usually light posture. "It is also something I would like to avoid," he announced, his voice carrying a grimness that made me wonder if he had fought in it.

"Then we will not fail," Drazen promised, the confidence and surety in his voice dispelling the shadow of doubt that had begun to creep in around our small group.

After all, I *always* got what I wanted, a fact that I'd made clear to Izidora from one of our very first conversations.

I wanted to be king of Északi.

I wanted the Félvér to be free.

I wanted Izidora to choose me.

And nothing would stop any of those wants from coming to pass.

"Perfect. It's settled then. I will work on the other monarchs," I announced.

"What can I do to help?" Izidora asked, her bright voice drawing my immediate attention.

I closed the distance between us, using the tip of my finger to tilt her head up to look at me. "You focus on your choice. After that, I'll let you know."

Please choose me.

The words were unspoken, but she heard them all the same. She saw to the depths of my soul, the parts of me I hid from those who would scrape at the already raw wound.

And at the same time, I saw to the depths of her own, and there was a heaviness there that no one should have to bear. The gravity of her decision weighed upon her, and with only a slight pinch in her eyes, she hid it better than I realized. I bent down to plant a featherlight kiss on her lips, if only to steal her attention away from the choice that ate at her mental capacity.

She was my Angel, my light in the dark, and for her, I could do anything.

A soft noise caught in her throat as I pulled away. "Thank you," she whispered, only for me to hear. A quick glance up showed Zuriel and Drazen with their heads together, plainly busying themselves with other matters while I had a moment alone with my mate.

"I will always take care of you, sprite. Even when it hurts me to do so."

"I know," she breathed, her fingers stroking the stubble dusting on my strong jaw, and I let go of the tension I'd been holding there. Her touch soothed the fear that held my teeth in a constant ache. "I love you, Ruslan. My dark king."

Trapping her palm against my face, I turned into it, leaving my lips lingering there as I stared deep into her soul and watched it come alight at our contact. The thread that tied us together hummed contentedly, finally satisfied with our proximity. Izidora was like a drug I could not get enough of, and the constant need to touch her was becoming overwhelming.

How was I supposed to run a kingdom and host a two-week-long celebration when all I wanted to do was hide away with my mate?

"We should return to the party. I did not get to finish dancing with you, sprite."

The smile that she offered me was like glittering diamonds, making my inner Dragon purr contentedly. "Let's go."

I slipped my hand around hers, leading her toward the half-open door, Zuriel and Drazen continuing their low conversation behind me as we made the short walk to the ballroom. I didn't bother listening to their plans, trusting they would carry out their respective tasks. But the second we returned to the ballroom, all eyes fell over us, and my high was replaced with cold fury.

Blood still stained the floor where I had fought with Kazimir, and the memory of Izidora's pained face as she danced with him flooded my eyes.

I would erase every memory of him from her mind, body, and soul.

Leading her straight to the dance floor, I ignored the whispers and stares, guiding her into the middle of a number she did not know. And yet, she trusted me to lead her, following along with my steps. Contentment settled my racing heart, knowing that I held something precious with her that Kazimir no longer did – trust.

6

Béke Day One

Kazimir made Ruslan who had spirited me away from the Night Realm look as angelic as Zuriel.

The male who once made every effort to ensure I felt safe and cared for now slashed me with harsh words, intentionally, in our first conversation since the terrifying moment that I was ripped away from him in the ballroom of Este Castle.

How could he drop the deaths of those we both cared about so casually within moments of speaking?

His obsessive glances throughout dinner had my stomach in knots. It took every ounce of willpower I possessed to focus on my conversation with Queen Viktoria. My body screamed at me to both run to him and flee from him every time I felt him look my way. My mother's words from the enchanted necklace Zuriel had given me echoed through my mind – a warning from beyond this life.

Then, he insisted we dance.

He did not care when I told him he hurt me; his fingers only tightened on my back and in my hair, ignoring the steps of the dance to keep me crushed against him.

Was what I had thought of as intensity and passion purely obsession on his part?

After all, he had spent a large portion of his life with me as his only and every thought. As much as I hated it, I understood where his mind could have gone twisted, exacerbated by our potential mating bond.

A potential bond that nearly tore me in two as I stood in the bathroom of mine and Ruslan's apartment in Ryza Citadel. I felt as if I were being ripped apart from the inside as one half of me was pulled to the adjacent bedroom, where the male who protected me lay, while the other called for me to run through the halls to find the male who hurt me.

I checked my back in the mirror as I undressed. A darkening mark lay across my lower spine, and I healed it before Ruslan could see. He was still so angry, it ate at my skin through the walls. He'd remained true to his word and given me space to work out my choice until it became painfully obvious that Kazimir was hurting me. I hated that my petite frame made me physically powerless against these large males. The ever-deepening well of power that came from my magic – that was the key to my survival.

Still, Ruslan intervened to protect me, not possess me, like Kazimir was so plainly trying to do. Their fight had been brutal, though not as brutal as it could have been. Ruslan absorbed a knife in his side like it was nothing, then stood, still ready to fight if only to see no harm come to me. If it hadn't been for Viktor and Vadim corralling Kazimir, one of them would have ended up dead.

Stabbing Ruslan with a knife hidden on his person during a feast to celebrate peace was not the way to win me back, and it was totally out of character for the male who'd rescued me from the cave in Vasvain, the highest peak in Északi.

Had he gone so mad from loss that it warped his mind?

Grief and anger were intimately intertwined, dancing together as they skewed all sense of reason, space, and time. While my grief had turned into a thirst for vengeance, Kazimir's had morphed into something oily and sinister.

How would he have reacted if I'd finished my words and told him that I loved Ruslan?

I was too exhausted to think any longer. I turned my head to plait my hair, then winced as soreness from Kazimir's rough grip bloomed. I healed that too. The past two days had been a whirlwind of emotion, and more tension only awaited over the coming days.

Would the discord between them suck all the oxygen from any room where they were together?

And then there was the matter of uniting the realms. Ruslan didn't need my help – didn't want my help – until after I'd made my choice. The reality stung like a whip across my back, and it didn't occur to me until that moment how much I *didn't* know what I truly wanted out of life. I'd spent so long only thinking of the next moment, the next problem, that I hadn't considered what lay beyond solving them, especially what came after choosing between Kazimir and Ruslan.

Did Ruslan fear that I would oppose his goals if I did not choose him?

I was a Félvér, half Angel and half Night Fae with a hint of Crystal and Day, and I wanted to be accepted as I was.

Would my friends look at me the same once they knew?

My head throbbed as a barrage of questions pounded against the inside of my skull, and I shook it in an attempt to silence my inner thoughts. The white-knuckle grip I held over my emotions was all I could do for the moment because I needed to survive the next two weeks, figure out who the fuck my mate was, and then possibly destroy the world in the process.

No big deal.

Except, it was, and the thought itself nearly sent me into a panic attack. The room swam before me, and my breath caught in my chest. I gripped the counter beneath me with that same intensity, trying to force stillness where there was only chaos.

Too much too much too much.

I was suffocating; there wasn't enough air.

I can't I can't I can't.

My body was simultaneously freezing and sweating, and I wasn't sure if it was tears or perspiration that dripped down my cheeks.

No no no no no no...

I squeezed my eyes shut, trying to force the tidal wave of overwhelm back into its typically tightly locked box.

But my inner voice screamed one phrase over and over again until I felt like it would deafen me.

I was not okay.

A truth I'd been hiding from myself, only accentuated when both males stood before me. The pressure of it all crashed over me, forcing my head underwater and drowning me.

I was shaking uncontrollably, and an anguished cry left my lips of its own accord.

"Sprite?" Ruslan was by my side in an instant, filling my nostrils with his cedarwood scent. I opened my eyes to see the panic in his own, and without thought, I reached for him, needing his warmth and comfort.

"What's wrong?" he asked gently against my hair, smoothing it down my back in soothing strokes.

"I-I-I'm not okay," I stuttered out through sobs that felt like they would never end.

How could I have thought I had a handle on this?

His arms tightened around me, providing pressure, warmth, and stability to my unmoored state.

Sobbing, hiccuping, gasping, the waves of emotion crashed through me, and I panted out everything I was feeling, needing to free myself from the burden of my thoughts. "I can't do this. I'm so scared. Why is this happening to me? I don't want - I don't want this. I can't, I can't... It's all so much. The choice. The feelings. I don't want to feel anymore. I've hurt so much for so long, why is this my life? Why can't it be easy? Haven't I suffered enough?"

Ruslan said nothing, allowing me the space I needed to feel.

But I didn't want to feel, not when every emotion was like a stab to my soul, more painful than any whipping I'd ever received.

"*Please*, make it stop... I hurt so badly." My voice cracked and shuddered as I begged someone, anyone, to hear me and *do something* about it. Because I was not okay, and I was powerless to it.

Grief burst from the depths of my pain, so acute that it was as if someone stuck their finger in the raw wounds that had once flayed open my back, and twisted it.

I grieved for the loss of my friends – Kriztof's jokes, Zekari's kindness, Kirigin's silliness.

I grieved for the loss of Cazius, who treated me with nothing but the utmost respect.

I grieved for my mother and her suffering at the hands of King Zalan.

I grieved for Ithuriel, my father who lost his wings for wanting to be with his mate.

I grieved for Ruslan, forced to fight and kill for his place at the Iron Realm.

But most of all, I grieved for myself.

For growing up without love and safety. For doing what I had to do to survive the cave. For my identity and power being stripped from me. For not knowing my name or what I looked like until I left. For believing everything I was told because Kazimir showed me kindness for the first time in my life. For a life filled with one impossible decision after another.

I was not okay.

My empath magic had opened up a rawness in me I hadn't begun to process, or comprehend, and I knew, deep down, that this pain wouldn't go away until I felt every last drop of it, and let it go.

Kazimir's cruel comments had been the key that unlocked the floodgate and left me shattered on the bathroom counter, breaking so violently in Ruslan's arms I wasn't sure I could ever piece myself back together. I hated Kazimir for it, just a little.

Would I ever be okay again?

The pain felt infinite, as if the time I sat there had no beginning and no end, and this would be my existence forevermore.

"It hurts... it's too much. It's too big, I can't handle it on my own. I can't do this, Ruslan, I can't do this." My nails dug into his back and I pulled him as close as I possibly could, the sobs wracking my entire body, despite his firm embrace. My cries echoed off the walls around us with the force with which they left my body, barely muffled by Ruslan's chest.

"I'm so sorry, my sprite," Ruslan murmured, puncturing my thoughts and grounding me into his arms again. "You don't deserve this pain, to hurt like you are. I would gladly take all of it on, for you."

If only it were possible to transfer the wounds on my soul to another; but I would never give them to Ruslan, whose soul was just as scarred as my own.

"Please," I begged, though I wasn't sure what for. I only wanted the pain to stop.

"You are safe, here and now, with me, Izidora. I've got you," Ruslan replied, beginning to gently rock us back and forth.

Tears carved paths down my cheeks as he hummed a tune I didn't know, and my mind latched onto it, *anything* to slow the tide of emotion still washing through me. His heart beat strongly against my ear, and I listened to that too, trying to anchor myself amid the storm that raged within.

"You are safe," Ruslan repeated, then returned to his song, creating deep rumbles in his chest to soothe me.

Exhaustion from fighting and gripping my emotions finally washed over me. My breaths slowed, and I was able to suck down one ragged breath after another. "Ruslan?" I whispered, needing to hear his voice.

"Yes, sprite?" he murmured, still not releasing me.

A light sigh released the last of the air in my body, and my eyelids drooped as I relaxed into his embrace. "Why are you always so warm?"

"Because I am a Dragon. Fire runs through my veins. And it's a good thing too, since you are always cold," he huffed a laugh into my hair. "Do you want to go to bed?"

"Tell me a story until I fall asleep?" I murmured.

Ruslan chuckled; this had become our nightly routine when I couldn't sleep, and he was always willing to oblige my requests. I wrapped my legs around his waist, still tucked into his chest, and he walked us into the bedroom, laying me gently down and then crawling in next to me, pulling me beside him once he settled. I curled into him, needing every inch of my skin to touch his. A deep exhale slipped out, and my heavy, swollen eyes began to close.

Ruslan cleared his throat, then launched into a story for me. "Once upon a time, a Dragon fell in love with an Angel…"

A small smile settled on my face as I listened to his highly embellished tale, losing myself among his words, until finally, I began to fade in and out of the story, drifting away to the land of sleep. I barely woke when he shuttered the lights in our room and turned us to the side so his entire body could sleep flush with mine.

7

KAZIMIR

Béke Day One

The door to the carriage opened with a blast of frigid night air, and we stepped into the snow before a slate stone building decorated with metallic climbing ivy. The craftsmanship was impeccable, and if it weren't for the silvery color, I'd think that the Iron Fae had enchanted vines to withstand the harsh winters. Vadim whistled as he examined the filigree etched into the doors, the whorls and dainty details drawing out a story I did not know.

We pushed through them when Liliana complained of the cold, and a bulky male waited just inside the entrance, his face serious until he saw Anton and Slavian.

"They're with us." Slavian jerked a thumb over his shoulder, swaying slightly.

"Your usual table is available, My Lords," the male replied, moving out of our way so we could enter the dimly lit area. Anton and Slavian descended a set of stairs to a sunken level below, the beat of drums building with each step into the earth.

The air smelled of herbs, metal, and sex, and I soon learned why, when we cleared a fog of smoke and landed on the floor where scantily clad males and females served drinks and sacks of herbs to groups of people lounging in the middle. Off to the sides, curtained rooms both hid and revealed half-naked bodies writhing together while others smoked the herbs in front of them. The High Lords sauntered to a larger space at the back of the room, pulling aside the curtain for us to pass. The beat of the drums quieted as we took seats on the deep couch lining the walls.

A female appeared a moment later with a bottle of amber liquor and glasses for all of us. "My Lords, so glad you are here tonight. It was getting boring without you." She batted her lashes as she placed everything on the table in front of her.

"Zoya, I hope you'll join us later." Anton pulled her into his lap, and she giggled, placing her hands on his chest.

"Do you want me to bring you something stronger?" She trailed a finger down his abdomen until it disappeared from view.

"Nothing too strong, Zoya, as this is our guests' first time experimenting." Anton gestured to us where we sat toward the back of the room.

She hopped up from his lap with a sly grin, spinning to face us. "Welcome to Steel, My Lords and Lady. You will certainly enjoy your time with us." She bit her lip as her eyes trailed over me, stopping at my groin. "I'll be back in a few moments with your herbs." She swayed her barely covered hips as she walked away from us.

Vadim whispered next to me, "I think this is the best decision we've made in months."

Viktor and I snorted simultaneously, though I got the sense he was ready to let loose himself. Endre sat protectively next to

Liliana, who was unfazed by the whole experience, as if she had frequented it many times. Slavian started pouring drinks for us, sliding them down the long, narrow table in each of our directions before pouring the last one for Liliana and handing it to her with a grin.

"To our health." He raised his glass, then threw back the liquid. We replied in kind, and the alcohol burned on the way down, not in an unpleasant way. He immediately poured another round for us all, and I embraced the second shot, needing the buzz to drive away the image of Izidora spread before Ruslan that kept appearing behind my eyes, triggered over and over again by the sensual space we found ourselves in.

I rolled my shoulders, feeling the effects already, my body loosening along with my tongue. "What is this place?" I asked Anton, who was already pouring his third glass.

"It's a place where you can lose control and experiment. Every desire you've dreamed of can be fulfilled here. Steel is very exclusive, and only the best Félvér work and play here."

"Félvér? What is that?" Viktor leaned forward, resting his forearms on his thighs to hear him better over the thrumming music.

"Those of us who have mixed blood, we call ourselves Félvér. I am half Wolf," Anton explained, his drink sloshing. Viktor and I shared a look that said 'we'll play dumb' since we already knew about Izidora's half Angel heritage, but any additional information about these Félvér would only serve to help us in the coming fight. Anton's lips were loose now, and if he was willing to share, who were we to deny him the opportunity?

Viktor didn't hesitate to continue with his questioning. "Interesting, I've never met a Wolf before. What abilities does that give you?"

"Well, not to brag, but my mother is an alpha. I can fully shift into a Wolf," Anton boasted unabashedly, then he jerked his thumb in Slavian's direction, spilling alcohol in the process. "Slavian here is part Demon, part Centaur, but he only got horns and wings from his mother."

Zoya pushed aside the gauzy curtain a moment later, then laid sacks of herbs on the table. Anton pulled her into his lap once again. "Zoya is a Wolf also, and she likes to play." He nuzzled her neck, and she sighed and leaned back into him. He trailed a hand down the bare skin on her front, slipping a hand under the fabric that covered her hips. She moaned as he touched her.

"Come back later and bring more friends," he purred in her ear, before removing his hand. She straightened her skirt, flashing him with a seductive smile, then disappeared into the dimly lit room beyond.

"So everyone here is Félvér?" Viktor clarified.

"Yup. Let's see, we've got more Wolves out there, a few with Demon blood – you're going to love them, most of them are incubi like Slavian – a couple of Dragons, I think she's a Mage..." Anton trailed on as I blinked rapidly, processing everything he said.

If so many Félvér hung out here tonight, how many more were out there? And if they had other magic outside of Iron Faes' elemental magic, how would we take them on in battle?

"We're pretty progressive here you know, not like the other realms who are all 'pure blood is the only way to maintain power' bullshit. Plus the Félvér have way more fun than you Fae," Anton finished, his finger wagging as his words slurred even more.

I bristled at his insinuation that the other realms were so rigid in their beliefs. Before I could open my mouth to protest, Viktor's elbow dug into my side, and he topped off everyone's glasses in rapid succession.

"I'll drink to that." Slavian chuckled, lifting his glass before downing it. "Let's break out the herbs now, Anton." He reached for a bag and pulled an apparatus from beneath the table. Taking a pinch of herbs in one hand, he stuffed it into a small opening before lighting it and bringing it to his mouth. He sucked in a deep breath, then exhaled a plume of smoke into the space. It smelled sweet and earthy, like rain on a spring day.

"My turn." Liliana eagerly held out her hand for the apparatus.

"Not so fast, beautiful. You'll hurt yourself if you don't know what you're doing. I'll help you." He placed the apparatus to her lips, then flicked a mote of fire to his fingers. "When I put my finger here, you breathe deep into your belly. Hold it for a moment, then exhale slowly."

Endre's eyes were hard as he watched Slavian and Liliana flirt, a muscle feathering in his jaw. Liliana's green eyes locked on Slavian's gray ones as he placed his flaming finger on the herbs. She inhaled slowly, then stopped as he took the apparatus from her. She held for a beat, then released a tendril at a time before forming an O with her mouth and blowing rings in Slavian's face.

I leaned over to Vadim. "You know she's done this before, right?"

"I do now," he huffed and I followed with a low laugh. She clearly kept a lot from us.

"How long until Endre snaps?" Viktor joined our hushed discussion.

"Why is Endre allowed to snap but I am not?" I quipped.

"Because when we found Izidora, you found a temper. Endre is too nice. My bet is he won't break in public," Viktor snickered.

Vadim grinned wolfishly. "If he wants Liliana, he has to earn her. It's not his fault that she wants to test him. Deep down, she wants him to succeed, and I think he knows that. I bet he loses it in the next hour, especially if Slavian keeps touching her."

"If Endre hadn't had his heart set on her for the past six or so years, I think he would have dropped her rather than keep fighting. He is a stubborn male. I give him until the end of the night," I chimed in.

"Six years?" Vadim exclaimed in a hushed whisper.

"To be fair, he never said anything, but Kazimir and I always knew," Viktor shrugged.

Endre declined the herbs, so he passed them along to Vadim. "This shit better make me forget that last statement," he grumbled.

Slavian leaned forward with his fiery finger to light Vadim's pull. He repeated Liliana's motion, but instead of holding, he came up coughing and wheezing.

"Happens to everyone their first time," Slavian laughed and then passed the apparatus to me. I debated for a moment before deciding that if I truly wanted to let go, I needed to act like it. So I put the herbs to my mouth, inhaled deeply as Slavian lit them, held my breath as he pulled away, then exhaled slowly through a wide mouth, only coughing slightly at the end. Viktor ended up joining as well, leaving Endre the only one without a hit.

Anton refreshed the now-burned herbs, then puffed a few times. Slavian refilled all our glasses, offering another cheer before we all chased the herbs with more liquor. My whole body tingled, and I felt like I floated rather than sat on the couch as the drink and smoke sank into my bones. Thoughts of Ruslan and Izidora disappeared from my mind, and all I could focus on was what was right in front of me, which a moment later included three females and a male pushing through the fabric that separated us from the main area. Zoya followed them in, her bronze skin shimmering as if every speck of light in this place reflected off of her. I blinked a few times, noticing that every newcomer's skin shimmered in some way. I shed my suit jacket, then rolled up my sleeves, turning my arms over and examining a similar sheen on my own skin.

The three other females pushed past Anton and seated themselves between him and Viktor, lashes fluttering in our direction. Out of the corner of my eye, I saw Endre eye a redhead appreciatively, scooting toward Vadim slightly and away from Liliana. I guessed he was intent on playing games if she was.

"I'm Taya," the redhead introduced herself, then gestured to the females beside her. "This is Aliana and Natasha. And he is Atros." She jerked her head to the male who sat beside Anton, taking hits of the herbs.

"Lovely to meet you ladies." Vadim leaned forward, rubbing his palms together and licking his lips. Endre and Viktor shrugged out of their jackets and lounged casually against the couch. "Can we get you anything to drink?"

"Oh, no, we're perfectly fine. We've already had a lot of herbs," the black-haired female, who I assumed was Natasha, trilled.

"Natasha, switch places with me, I want to sit next to that one," the blonde said, her hazel eyes glued to Viktor's torso.

"Ugh, you always go for the tall ones, Aliana," she replied, but instead of switching places, she settled herself between Vadim and me. His eyes went feral as he looked her up and down, stopping on the low cut of her skin-tight dress before returning to her face. "And what are you?" he asked.

"Demon," she flashed her teeth with a low laugh. Vadim only grinned as he yanked her to his lap. She straddled him, and I decided I'd had enough of watching them.

Anton passed the herbs to me, and I took two long drags, this time easing the smoke out of my mouth without a cough. Zoya sat on his lap, and he lazily stroked her bare skin, his fingers like a blur as I watched. The male sucked on his neck on the opposite side, and Anton tipped his head back to rest on the wall behind him. "The Félvér are looser than you rigid Fae, Kazimir. Relax and enjoy the ride," he moaned as Atros stroked his groin.

My skin heated and tightened. I needed relief, so I unbuttoned the top of the shirt I still wore, but none came as I caught sight of Viktor and Aliana wrapped around each other beside me. My eyes trailed to my left. Endre held the herbs in his hand, finally giving in as the smoky air filled with breathless moans and wanton pleasure. He blew smoke into Liliana's open mouth, who sucked it in before blowing it back to him. She climbed into his lap, clasping her hands on his face and kissing him deeply as he dug his hands into the flesh of her ass. Slavian kissed her bare back, trailing his fingers lightly down her sides.

I swallowed thickly as my groin heated, and in a blur I could not quite follow, Taya sat on my lap, wrapping her arms around my neck. She walked her fingers up my chest to my open shirt, pulling the fabric aside to reveal my tattoos.

"I do love males with ink." She batted her lashes and leaned in to kiss me. I turned my head, wanting to avoid kissing her, but I was not sure why. Didn't I want another? A flash of something like hurt washed through me as a pair of aquamarine eyes filled my vision. The thought and the feeling left as quickly as they came when she licked from the top of my chest to my ear, sucking it between her teeth. Her hand found my hardness and palmed it over my pants. I would have jerked away, but my body was so loose and relaxed that I only leaned back and allowed it to happen again and again. She unbuttoned my shirt and ran her tongue down, down, down my abs until she reached the waistband of my pants.

I looked up to find my friends in similar states of undress, Viktor kneeling on the ground, spreading the legs of his female companion, Vadim outright thrusting into his. Atros knelt between Anton's legs, his head bobbing up and down while a fully naked Zoya kissed Anton, and his fingers found the apex of her thighs.

A moment later, Taya freed my cock, then sucked it into her mouth, hollowing out her cheeks as she swallowed me.

"Fuck, I should not be doing this," I moaned, but I did not stop her for I barely remembered my own name. Her head was a blur, and I only watched for a moment before glancing at Endre, who had Liliana's dress hiked up to her waist. She moved above him, but her mouth was locked on Slavian's hardness, and Endre looked both pissed and pleased as he ground into her from below. Both of them were too preoccupied to glance in my direction and see what was unfolding between me and the female on her knees.

Taya's teeth grazed the sensitive underside of my head, and I groaned, fisting my hand into her hair and pushing deeper into her mouth. My world devolved into madness as she took all of me, soaking my shaft up and down. She glanced to her left, eyes heating when she saw Viktor and Aliana switching up positions. She rose and grabbed my hands to move me so I stood above her as she laid on the couch.

Viktor had positioned himself behind Aliana, who was on knees and elbows, her face slightly above Taya's hips. The blonde female grinned, then lifted the thin dress covering Taya to reveal her core. It was wet and glistening in the dim light, and Aliana purred at the sight before licking from bottom to top. She sucked her clit into her mouth at the same time Viktor thrust into her from behind and the three released a collective groan.

Taya's hand found my shaft and stroked as Aliana continued to lick and suck her core. I stepped closer, and she took me in her mouth, humming over me as her pleasure built. I grasped the back of her head, holding her steady as I pumped in and out. She began to whimper, and Aliana slipped two fingers inside her, curling and stroking in time with the thrusts that pounded into her.

Viktor and I locked eyes, a small smile splaying across both our lips. The carnal pleasure we participated in was wild and freeing. Taya's moans became more frantic, the vibration around my cock sending tingles up my spine. My balls tightened, and I breathed through my nose, trying not to lose control so quickly.

I released her head as she came with a cry, her body arching off the couch as Aliana thrust her fingers in deep, tongue firing rapidly until her body came down. When her orgasm subsided, Taya returned to my cock, sucking it into her throat while her fingers found my balls, cupping them and stroking them lightly. With a curse, I found my release, filling her mouth as she swallowed down every last drop. I braced myself on the wall in front of me as the room started to spin.

Taya guided me down beside her, and as my back hit the couch, she slurred, "Watch." I followed her gaze to Anton, Atros, and Zoya who were all completely naked and writhing together. Taya's hand found her dripping center and dipped a finger inside as she watched them.

Atros spread Anton's cheeks and entered him from behind as he pulled Zoya onto his cock. Anton thrust into her over and over, groaning as Atros moved behind him. Natasha appeared in a blur at the edge of my vision, sidling up to Taya and stroking her breasts as she watched the three move together.

I turned my attention to them as Vadim slid behind her, positioning himself before thrusting into her from behind. The females kissed and stroked one another until Natasha slipped off of Vadim and pushed Taya to the couch, spreading her legs and joining them with her own. "Watch us," the redhead purred to Vadim and me, and my eyes locked on the two beautiful females writhing together below us. I found my cock in my hand

and pumped slowly as breathy moans and wet sounds rose between them.

The dim, smoky room smelled of pleasure and sweat as partners switched, new combinations formed, and we came over and over and over again. I lost myself in the erotic dance, my body humming, floating, as time blurred together. I barely remembered stumbling to my bed at Ryza, let alone how I got to Steel, as my mind completely blanked of anything but gratification.

8

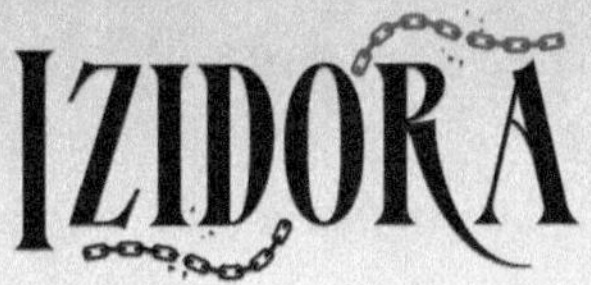

IZIDORA

BÉKE DAY TWO

A white void surrounded me; no matter which way I turned, it was endless. "Hello?" I called out, but the only response was the echo of my own voice. I picked a direction and ran. My lungs burned as I sprinted, trying to find a way out.

There!

A black speck in the distance caught my attention. I changed course, racing straight for it. That speck turned into a square, then into a rectangle, and I skidded to a stop in front of three black doors, stark against the limitless white. The one on the left was embossed with an iron sign that read 'Ruslan.' 'Kazimir' was painted on the one on the right. In the middle, a blank one waited, blacker than the cave where I'd spent most of my life in chains. I hesitated in front of the doors, my heart pounding as indecision swept through me.

"My child, you have been given such a tough choice."

I spun around. "Mother?"

A female with chestnut hair and jeweled green eyes gazed at me with so much love it physically hurt. The color of her hair perfectly matched my own, and I saw so much of myself in her. Beside her, another female floated, nearly impossible to see with her ethereal, translucent form. Both her hair and eyes were so white that they blended into the space around us. With a gasp, recognition washed over me – the Goddess.

My mother tore my attention from the Goddess when she spoke. "You have been given this mountain because you alone can move it. You are so strong. So brave. I am so proud of you, Izidora." The warmth in her tone caressed my very soul.

I leaped to embrace her, but my feet would not move. My arms flailed as I grasped for her motherly love, stymied at every chance of closeness with her.

When the Goddess spoke, her voice was haunting, ethereal, and sent a cold shiver down my spine. "The Fates are fighting me, trying to end this world. One of these doors will save us all; the others will damn us all. You must choose quickly, for we rest on a knife's edge."

"But which is the right one?" I tried to keep the desperation from my voice, but my question slipped from my lips with a breathy, unsure air.

The Goddess only shook her head, her white hair floating around her as if she were underwater. "The future becomes darker the longer you wait to make your choice, no matter which choice that is. You must make haste, do not delay, for you will plunge the world into chaos if you wait."

"Chaos? How?" I pleaded, desperate for some sign, some information that would help me.

"The Fates only allow me glimpses into the outcomes they weave, and if I share too much, they will change it out of spite. Choose quickly, as the fate of our world rests on your shoulders," the Goddess warned.

"But I can't, not when I don't know who is light and who is dark!" I protested, turning to my mother and scrutinizing her features as if she could hint my way to the right answer.

A male appeared beside my mother, his arm encircling her waist.

White wings sprouted from his back, mirror images to my own, and the structure of his jaw reminded me so much of Zuriel.

"My daughter, with the gift passed down from your grandmother, you know what lies within each male's heart. You are not one to be led by your head, but by your heart. Use it to guide your decision." My father passed along his advice, and hearing his voice directed at me for the first time nearly brought me to my knees. I could only stare at the three floating figures before me, urging me onward without realizing the weight of making such a huge decision on my own.

White deepened into gray as darkness closed in around us, and my parents and the Goddess faded from view.

"Wait!" I tried to move once again but remained trapped. "Please, I only want to touch them," I begged the Goddess.

"I will allow it if you promise to choose within the next week, Izidora," she murmured, her voice haunted. "My magic is weakening and my time is running out."

"I promise, I'll do whatever you want, please just let me hold them." This was my only opportunity to do this, and there was no way I was letting it slip through my fingers.

With a wave of her hand, she lifted me from the ground and floated me between my parents. Tears streamed down my face like a rainstorm as they enveloped me in their arms. Their touch was like coming home, and I savored every precious second offered to me.

"You are so loved, Izidora." My mother's final words were swallowed by black as all light disappeared around me.

My face was wet when I awoke, and the world around me was dark.

That wasn't a dream.

Though I had been asleep, I knew in my gut that the white void had been somewhere beyond this world. The Goddess had appeared to me alongside my parents, and I'd made a bargain with her to make my decision in the next week.

How was I supposed to make a decision when making the

wrong one would plunge our world into chaos? Whatever the fuck chaos meant? Would choosing the wrong mate cause the sun to explode and end life in our world? Or would it spark a war that sent rivers around the continent running with blood? Between Ruslan and me, we'd already killed two kings. Who was next? Was Ruslan one of them?

Panic clawed up my throat, and a fresh wave of hot tears spilled down my cheeks. I was so fucking tired of crying. It seemed like that was all I had done the last few days, from having my heart nearly broken by Ruslan's request that Rares enchant a ring so I would not leave him to my breakdown the previous night after realizing how much my trauma still clung to me.

Ruslan's arm twitched around my stomach, startling me from my spiraling thoughts.

I needed to calm down.

I was still drained, still so raw, and I didn't have the energy for a repeat episode. A grounding exercise Zuriel had taught me sprang to mind, and I rotated through it, trying to regain control of my mind and my racing, aching heart.

My fingers clutched the warm blanket covering my shoulders, ghosting over the soft material, and I inhaled deeply, savoring Ruslan's woodsy scent. His heat on my back eventually relaxed my shoulders, and I exhaled, long and slow, causing him to stir.

"Are you ready for breakfast?" Ruslan's sleepy voice rumbled against my back.

Releasing a yawn and stretching out the stiffness that had worked its way into my muscles with the panic, I nodded. "So many responsibilities as hosts."

And as the person who could potentially turn the world over to chaos.

Ruslan grunted in response, pressing up on an elbow to

plant a kiss on my collarbone. "I need an assistant so I can spend all day in bed with you."

My belly heated at his words, thighs dampening as he trailed the rough pads of his fingers down my chest and circled my nipple. "Ruslan..." I moaned when he pinched and rolled it. His morning arousal pressed into my back, and I ground shamelessly against it. The way Ruslan touched me always got me out of my own head, and I fucking needed that.

"Sprite," he croaked, "as much as I would like to fuck you senseless right now, I am afraid we're already late. If we want to unite the realms, we need to show the other monarchs why we're worth supporting."

A heavy sigh deflated my chest and my desire. "I know. Do you think they've noticed the Félvér and Telivér hanging about? Zuriel and the Demons were at the feast last night, along with most of your guards."

"Our guards." He dusted his lips across my neck. "Anton and Slavian made themselves very known to the Night Fae. Hopefully, they didn't scare them off with their drunkenness."

"Is that why I didn't meet them before yesterday?" I grinned, teasing Ruslan over his protectiveness.

"That... among other reasons." Ruslan threw back the blankets, exposing my bare skin to the cold air.

"Must you do that every morning?" I griped, reaching for the warm fur.

Ruslan pushed off the bed, yanking my ankles until my center was lined with his hardness at the edge of the bed. He towered over me, wearing nothing but his devastating smirk, then planted his hands on either side of my head, caging me into his warmth. My breath hitched as he dipped his head close to mine. "I can think of other ways to get you up."

I chewed my lip as a flush crept up my chest. "I think I'd like that better."

Ruslan tsked. "Who knew you were such a dirty little Angel for me?" A hand crept down the sides of my ribs, eliciting a shiver as he trailed his fingers over my hip bones, finding my clit with a finger and pressing. "Is that how you want to be woken up, sprite?"

"Maybe you should experiment with it for a few days. See if that gets me out of bed any faster." I gasped as he traced my center, wetting his finger before returning it to my clit.

"Then that is how I shall wake you tomorrow." His finger slipped inside me, curling against the spongy inner wall. "And the day after that." My legs snapped shut of their own accord before dropping wide. "So wet for me already, sprite. Be a good girl and come quickly so we can greet our guests."

Another finger joined the first, and I ground against his hand, needing more fullness. Two wasn't enough, not when I'd been split apart on his thick cock more times than I could remember. "I need more to come," I begged.

Ruslan removed his fingers, only to bring them hard against my center, drawing a gasping breath from my lungs as I arched off the bed. "I'm going to fill your greedy cunt, and you'll feel me dripping between your thighs all day. Understood?"

"Understood," I breathed as he gripped himself and lined up with my entrance. In one powerful thrust, he speared into me, and I was so deliciously filled with him. His hands gripped my hips as he pounded into me from the edge of the bed, and I fisted the sheets to hold myself in place.

"Your breasts look so good bouncing up and down as I fuck you," he growled, quickening his pace. He hiked one of my legs up toward his shoulder, deepening the angle and sending tingles across my body as my walls began fluttering around him.

"Ruslan," I moaned his name as he ground his hips against mine, filling every inch of me. His free hand dropped to my swollen clit, rubbing it in a circle to match his hips, and I was so close to coming already. The thread that tied us together hummed excitedly as the tension building in my core ratcheted up to the point of snapping.

He growled his approval when I ground against him. "Come all over my cock, mate. I want to hear you scream my name as you fall apart."

Mate.

At that word, my body exploded, and stars filled my vision. Ruslan's strong hands caught my back as I arched off the bed, and he drove his hips up and into me, mercilessly pounding through my orgasm. The world went black around me, and there was nothing but the feel of him inside and around me.

"Fuck, Izidora, I love you," he ground out, his hips jerking as he released inside me.

My chest heaved, and my eyes fluttered into focus, colliding with his smoky gray ones. I loved Ruslan with every part of me, and yet I couldn't give him everything he wanted. Not yet. I needed to be certain, especially after my dream, that I was making the right choice.

But was I selfless enough to save the world if that meant choosing the male I loved less?

I had promised Kazimir time alone, and I hoped that would light the path I was supposed to take.

Reaching up a hand to stroke Ruslan's face, I said, "I love you, Ruslan. You make me feel alive."

He pinned my hand beneath his, leaning into it. "Let's get you some food before you start getting grumpy."

"Hey! I do not get grumpy," I protested, a grin spreading across my face, even as he pulled out of me.

"Yes, you do, especially with how hard you train." Ruslan strode to the bathroom, returning with a wet cloth and running it over my body to clean me. Then he tossed it aside and held out his hand to me. "Come," he said, and I took it, allowing him to pull me off the bed and lead me to the wardrobe, where he pulled out clothes and began dressing me.

I playfully swatted at his hands but allowed him to continue because his careful attention caused my body to hum in the most delicious way.

It was so nice to be taken care of.

———

SURPRISINGLY, Ruslan and I were not the last to arrive in the dining room with a view that overlooked all of Radence. When the Night Fae spilled into it, nearly half an hour after we did, all but High Lord Kaztar and his wife, Domi, looked like they'd rather be dead than attending breakfast. Liliana's makeup was smudged and smeared under her eyes, giving her the appearance of a raccoon, while Endre pressed a cool glass of water to his forehead. Kazimir, Viktor, and Vadim were equally as disheveled, though Vadim wore a smug grin as he shoveled greasy food into his mouth.

Anton and Slavian sauntered toward them, offering Vadim a high-five before sticking around to chat. Slavian couldn't tear his eyes away from Liliana, who gave him more attention than I thought she would. I elbowed Ruslan in the ribs, jerking my head in their direction. "I'm guessing Anton and Slavian had something to do with why they look like drowned rats?"

He snorted, popping a pastry into his mouth and chewing. "I'd wager they are the cause of it."

I caught Liliana's attention, and she excused herself before dragging over to our table and plopping in the chair across from me. "I feel like I could die," she moaned from where her head was buried in her arms. "Can you please put out the lights?"

I shoved my glass of water in her direction. "Drink this, it will help."

She picked her head up enough to pull the water in her direction and tilted the glass to her lips. Little rivers spilled over the sides and onto the table, coating her chin along the way. Once she finished it, some color returned to her cheeks. "Why do you look so chipper?" She dried her face, then tucked her chocolate brown hair behind her pointed ear as she regarded me, a slight upturn of her lips betraying her suspicions.

"I got a good night's sleep," I lied, a grin tugging at my mouth.

"Did Anton and Slavian drag you to Steel?" Ruslan asked, bracing his elbows on the table as he leaned into our conversation.

"That they did," she groaned, but there wasn't an ounce of regret in her tone.

"Steel?" I stopped my contraceptive tea just before my lips, looking to Ruslan for an explanation.

"It is an establishment that I own. A Félvér club, if you will. Anton and Slavian are my best customers," he shrugged noncommittally.

"What Ruslan is not telling you is that it is one of the most incredible experiences of your life. You should join us next time." Liliana's eyes glittered with mischief, and my heart leaped at the thought of all the mayhem I'd been promised she and I could cause.

Before either Ruslan or myself could respond, a tug around my middle jerked my eyes up to meet a pair of deep emerald ones. Kazimir stood just behind Liliana, hands clasped behind his back and waiting to be invited to speak. Ruslan tensed beside me, and I automatically grabbed his hand, stroking the back of it with my thumb in an attempt to calm us both. Kazimir still exuded that oily presence, though it was tempered compared to the previous day.

"Izidora, I believe last night we agreed upon an outing today. I'd love for you to accompany me on a ride through the city."

Liliana whipped her head around, apparently just noticing Kazimir had joined us. He kept his gaze trained on me with a ferocity that was remarkable considering the rage that rolled off Ruslan. He squeezed my hand beneath the table, and I pushed soothing emotions in his direction, turning his anxiety and anger into calm.

"I'll send for my mount to be saddled," I replied.

"No need, our horses are already prepared to go. I will be waiting for you to finish breakfast." He sketched a quick bow and retreated to the safety of the Night Fae before Ruslan could object.

The male beside me cracked his neck and huffed a breath before his lips found my ear. "Leaving you alone with him will be hard for me, and I will suffer through it because you deserve the space you need to make your decision. I will spend the rest of my life making up for my mistakes, but please, please protect yourself, sprite. You are so much stronger than you used to be. Don't forget that."

I turned to face him, letting him see the adoration I had for him. "You've taught me well. I will keep my talents hidden until absolutely necessary." After all, Kazimir had been the first to call me an insidious bloom, and that was a motto I'd imprinted on my soul. I'd told Kazimir that I had changed, but he did not need to know the details of my newfound power. That power was what would protect me against these much larger males, and I planned on hoarding the knowledge of it like it was my greatest treasure.

Liliana wisely kept her attention on her nails as we spoke, only looking up once Ruslan cleared his throat. "Will you be participating in the archery competition this afternoon, Lady Liliana?"

"Absolutely. And you can call me Liliana, no need for fancy titles between friends, right?" She flashed him a disarming smile.

"Liliana, it is. Now," Ruslan pushed back from the table, looking down at me, "I must attend to my kingly duties. I'll see you before the archery competition, sprite." He planted a light kiss on the top of my head and darted from the room. My body sank with his absence, but as I reached my magic out to feel his emotions, I grasped that he needed to put some distance between himself and me as I prepared to go off on my own with Kazimir.

"Izidora, we've got so much to catch up on, but I know you need to get this conversation with Kazimir out of the way. We can gossip later, maybe even with Domi and Immonen. You're going to love them," she grinned.

"I seriously cannot wait. I need to hear more about this life-changing experience you had at Steel," I teased.

"But before you go, tell me... do you love him?" I knew she meant Ruslan.

"Yes," I breathed, closing my eyes for a moment before confessing the secret that had plagued me since I heard it. "But both Kazimir and Ruslan are my mates."

"Shut the fuck up," she gasped. "You get *two* mates?"

I shook my head, my dreamlike encounter returning in full force. "I have to choose, and soon."

Her mouth popped open into an O. "Shit, Izidora. We definitely have to talk more about this later, with fewer ears around." She glanced around the room at all the Fae and Félvér in attendance.

"Please. I need advice," I begged, reaching my hand across the table and placing it on hers. Maybe with Liliana's help, I could reason out which male was the right choice.

She covered my hand with her other, holding a soft smile on

her face. "I promise. Now, go to Kazimir. I think I know what he has planned for you."

I drained the last of my tea, the taste not entirely pleasant, especially as I was reminded that only Ruslan ever offered it to me. The chair scraped against the ground as I pushed back, leaving Liliana to pick at the food left on my plate. Kazimir rose to meet me in the middle of the space, and I left a healthy distance between us, turning for the open doors and striding into the main hall of Ryza Citadel.

"You look lovely this morning, Izidora," Kazimir said from beside me.

I wore the fur-lined boots Ruslan had gifted me, and I was grateful I'd also grabbed the matching cloak before we left our apartment in the spire. The diamond at my throat caught the light of the mid-morning sun as we entered the courtyard, and despite a brisk breeze blowing through it, I remained warm wrapped in the white fur. "Thank you, Kazimir. You've looked better." My tone was light and teasing, like we'd used to play with one another, but his emerald eyes flashed with a darkness I'd never seen before.

"I've felt better." His tone was flatter than I'd ever heard it, and I began to wonder why he bothered asking me to join him if he wasn't going to show me the same warmth he had after rescuing me from the cave.

Did he even care about me then?

We walked in tense silence toward the stables. I was unsure what to say to the male who had rescued me, showed me the first bits of this big beautiful world we lived in, but who I now held so much doubt about. Flinging my unanswered questions at him so soon would not do either of us any favors, especially as his attention sent shivers of two kinds down my spine.

"I have a surprise for you," Kazimir said before we rounded the corner, breaking our silence.

"Oh?" was all I managed as my stomach turned over.

"Look forward," he commanded.

I straightened my gaze to find Fek saddled and ready to go, his long black mane falling over his eyes, front foot stamping and breath fogging in the morning air. Beside him was Mistik, her dapple gray coat gleaming in the morning sun.

"Mistik!" I bounded forward, the mare's eyes lighting up as I approached. She released an excited neigh and surged forward, catching her groom off guard as she trotted toward me. He stretched for the rope attached to her bridle and missed as Mistik raced straight toward me, all else forgotten. Through blurred vision, I stroked the mare's silky nose, blowing in her nostrils as we reacquainted.

"Liliana rode her here just for you," Kazimir murmured from behind me, and I was too filled with joy for his presence to startle me. Swiping at my eyes, I planted a kiss on her nose, then faced the male I loved first.

"Thank you for bringing her to me," I whispered, voice thick with unshed tears. Learning to ride her, in addition to the mare's freely-given affection when I needed it most, had been exactly what I needed in the weeks following my exit from the cave and entrance into a world I'd never known.

"Shall we ride?" Kazimir offered, striding toward Fek and holding out an apple slice for him.

I wanted nothing more than to be back in Mistik's saddle. "Yes. I can show you around the city, and maybe we can stop at one of my favorite markets," I suggested, hauling myself up and over the mare I loved so dearly.

"Lead the way," Kazimir said, mounting Fek and spurring him alongside Mistik.

As we exited the stables, we passed Savich, a Bear Shifter Félvér, and his mounted regiment returning from their patrol. I nodded to him, and he shot me a lazy grin before it fell away when he noticed my company. Then, he offered me a look that said 'be careful' and continued riding.

Kazimir and I would not truly be alone on our trip through Radence.

"You know him?" Kazimir asked when we were out of earshot, a hint of disdain in his voice.

"Yes, he is one of my friends here in the Iron Realm," I stated. "He's Félvér – those of us with mixed blood. There are a lot of Félvér about, if you haven't noticed."

Our horses' hooves clopped against the stone path as we descended the hill away from Ryza. "I learned a thing or two about Félvér yesterday," Kazimir gritted out.

His tone bothered me, but I said nothing as I fell into the sway of Mistik's stride. The sun caressed my face, bathing me in what little warmth it had to offer on the bitterly cold day, melting the remnants of the past few days' snows from the cobbled streets of Radence. "The market we're going to has a sweet shop that I adore," I offered by way of conversation when we reached the bottom of the hill and turned onto the main thoroughfare.

"Are cinnamon rolls still your favorite treat?" Kazimir asked wryly.

"They are." I allowed my lips to lift in a smile.

How could a few months apart put so much distance between us?

The doubts in my mind lay between us like an ocean trench, and I knew if I didn't voice my questions soon, I'd never move forward with Kazimir.

"So, Izidora, tell me what you've been doing during your time in the Iron Realm," Kazimir said politely, and I welcomed his attempt at conversation.

As we navigated the capital's bustling streets, I told him of my physical training, magic training – leaving out the most important details of my empath powers – and how I'd grown to love the Félvér, as each of them was unique and they all had backgrounds that fascinated me. He remained silent, and when minutes passed without a response from him, I wondered if he'd listened at all.

The colorful market appeared after our next turn, and my shoulders slackened in relief. A hitching post stood just outside it, with a few other horses already tethered and waiting for their masters. I dismounted and tied Mistik at the end, leaving room for Fek.

The market was crowded, and we had to weave through Fae laden with goods as we traveled the path to the sweet shop. A bell rang as we pushed through the door, and the baker looked up from his work. "Princess Izidora, how lovely to see you again." His golden eyes narrowed over my shoulder for a fraction of a moment before returning to me. "What can I get for you today?"

I approached the glass container blocking the treats from being snatched without payment. "What would you like, Kazimir?" I called over my shoulder. He pressed forward, joining me at the display, and my body simultaneously heated and chilled at his proximity.

"We'll take some fresh cinnamon buns," he hummed, his hand skimming up my arm.

"Coming right up. Feel free to sit, and I'll bring them to you." The baker motioned us away with a sweep of his hand.

My breath hitched as Kazimir flattened his palm on my lower back and led me to a table in the corner of the small shop, adjacent to the large window overlooking the market square. My skin was alight beneath my cloak where he had touched me, and I drew a slow breath as I settled in the seat with my back to the wall. Kazimir sat across from me, that oiliness gone from his aura, and I saw the male I fell in love with staring back at me, his lips stretched in a smile. "Remember when we stopped in a baker's shop much like this one on the road to Vaenor?"

The memory leaped to the front of my mind, the smell of baking cinnamon triggering a vivid recollection. Kazimir and I had sat on a bench in a very similar square and eaten them together. He had swiped a bit of icing from my face, and I had sucked it off his finger. My cheeks now flamed because that moment had held the promise of more as tension built between us. "I do."

"You looked so beautiful that day. The sun was starting to put color on your cheeks, and you had started opening up to us more. We'd answered a nearly endless stream of questions about the world around us, and yet you always wanted more. You bested me in a stick fight that day, and if I had to guess, it was because of those cinnamon rolls," he laughed.

"Who needs magic when you have the power of cinnamon rolls?" I joked, feeling a bit of tension melt from my chest as we shared memories.

"Your magic is nothing short of incredible. How is your flying?" he asked.

The baker appeared with a tray of steaming buns dripping white frosting over the sides, and my mouth watered as he placed them between Kazimir and me. "Thank you," I grinned at him, and the baker flashed me a wink before disappearing behind the counter.

"Flying is much better. The strength training I've been doing with Ruslan has helped tremendously." I plucked a sticky bun from the tray, my fingers immediately coated in gooey frosting, and took a large bite, moaning as the flavors melted over my tongue.

Kazimir's eyes darkened, sending a shiver down my spine, as he watched me pull the treat away from my lips. "Good," he mumbled, reaching a finger to stop a line of frosting tumbling down my chin. I froze as he swiped at it, leaving his finger dangling between us with an unasked request. I swallowed down my food, breath catching as I debated my next move.

Do I lick it off and keep this peace between us, or do I show my suspicion of him and risk that sinister aura returning?

I must have hesitated a moment too long because Kazimir brought the finger to his lips, nostrils flaring as he inhaled and sucked the icing from his finger, emerald orbs trained on me. "I still remember how you taste." His voice grew husky, and I nearly dropped my cinnamon roll as he ensnared me with his words. "The most divine wine I'd ever tasted. I could drink from you for hours."

My core heated under his unrelenting gaze. "Kazimir, I–"

He shook his head, interrupting me. "Eat. I have things to say."

Warily, I brought the treat to my lips, taking a smaller bite as I waited for his next words.

He braced his forearms on the table, flexing his fingers before exhaling and shaking his head as if to clear it. "When Ruslan tore you from my arms, I felt like an absolute failure. I'd broken my promise to you, to always keep you safe. My father told me with his dying breath to go to you, my mate. I went out of my mind that night, pushing Fek to his absolute limit as we raced through the woods surrounding Vaenor seeking you. I'd have given my life to see that you were never chained again, and I worried for you every day, because I knew being bound again would end in your death. I vowed to myself, *to my father*, that I'd save you again. I was too thick-headed to see that we were mates before that night, and I'd give anything to travel back in time and accept our bond before you were kidnapped again." His throat worked, and he looked at his folded hands before returning his intense gaze to me.

The roll turned to ash in my mouth, and I barely managed to

swallow it down around the guilt lodged there. "Kazimir, there's something you need to know."

His dark brows pinched together. "What is it?"

"Have you heard the Goddess's Prophecy?" I reached for a napkin to wipe my fingers, freeing them of frosting.

"I have. The Goddess spoke to us on the day of the funerals at Este Castle." Kazimir leaned forward, his attention wholly focused on me, and the air dropped a dozen degrees around us.

"The original language of the prophecy called for two mates."

The words were like a fallen glass between us, shattering the tentative peace we'd formed.

Kazimir growled, a sound so low it was barely audible, but it sent goosebumps across my skin all the same. His fingers dug into the table so hard the wood splintered, and onyx flashed across his eyes. "I will not share you with that motherfucker."

I shook my head, leaning back to free myself of Kazimir's space and throwing up an invisible mental shield to block out the rage he emanated. "I must choose one."

If my first words were like shattered glass, those four were like an explosion. Kazimir shoved to his feet, knocking his chair and the table behind him over with the force of his fury. His fists landed on the table in front of me with a thud that made the tray jump, and he towered over me, mere inches from my face. "Then you will choose me."

My body tensed as I prepared to fight for my life. I was a survivor, and more than that, I was an insidious bloom, and my thorns were well hidden. I reached out a tentative hand, placing it atop Kazimir's and siphoning away his anger, so subtly he did not notice. The natural progression of his breathing indicated it was working, until he shook his head then backed away and straightened the mess he'd made. "I'm so sorry, Izidora. I don't know what came over me. You know I would never hurt you."

But he had, in fact, hurt me the previous night.

Was it intentional? Or was he so crazed from our separation that he no longer had a grip over his actions? Or was it something else, something connected to this new, sinister oiliness that had arrived with him?

It was time for my questions to be answered.

"I have some things to say of my own," I pronounced, sitting taller in my seat and puffing out my chest. Kazimir resettled in his chair, lifting a cinnamon roll to his mouth and taking a bite.

"I think you manipulated me to get what you wanted. You planted the idea of taking the throne in my head, telling me that King Zalan would marry me off the second we arrived at Este Castle. You used my feelings for you to get what you wanted, and that is not okay."

Kazimir only chewed, not denying my accusation. I ground my teeth and continued. "I told you I did not want children, and yet you did not provide me with contraception, or even tell me that was a possibility. Why?"

His eyes widened a fraction before he schooled his face again. I reached a tendril of my magic toward his mind, sneaking through the ropey cage, and was met with a flash of his desire to impregnate me. I recoiled, bile rising in my throat, and fisted my cloak in my hands.

"Are you going to say anything?" I snapped.

He placed his roll on a plate, then wiped his hands before speaking. "My love for you is why I encouraged you to take the throne. Why is that such a bad thing?"

"Because you made me think it was my idea! I couldn't read, and my only contact with Fae outside of my guards and keepers was you and the Nighthounds. I trusted what you told me, but as it turns out, I shouldn't have trusted a word you said. Now answer my other question." How could he not understand what a massive betrayal all of that was? I was ignorant, naive, and relied on everyone to tell me about the world. In fact, my entire world had been them once they rescued me. How was I supposed to know what I didn't know?

Kazimir ran a hand over his face, releasing a heavy breath. "This is not how I wanted our date to go."

"Well, this is how it is going. I can't move forward with my choice until I get some answers," I hissed.

"You are mine, Izidora. You always have been, and you always will be. From the time you were born, you've been mine. I scoured this continent for you. I fought for you. I lost friends for you. You are my mate." His voice broke on the last word, and he captured my arm, dragging out my hand from beneath the table and holding it. "I love you, Izidora. Is that not enough for you?"

The plea in his words softened the wall I'd thrown up between us. "It's not enough when the fate of the world rests upon my choice," I whispered, the weight of that decision settling across my shoulders like the heaviest of fur cloaks.

"What can I do to show you that I'm the right choice?" Kazimir was nearly begging, his desperation evident through our physical connection, and that tug that pulled me to him vibrated with anxiety.

"I don't know," I breathed, my eyes pricking. It was the truth, for something had changed within him, throwing everything I thought I knew about which male was the dark and which male was the light into question. It was apparent that something dark had risen in Kazimir, too, during our separation, just as the Goddess's Prophecy had described my mate doing. Both Ruslan and Kazimir now held threads of dark as much as they held threads of light. In truth, both of them were shades of gray, which only made interpreting the prophecy that much more difficult.

"I want to follow the light, whatever that means. But there is something sinister swirling around you, Kazimir, and I do not like it," I finally said.

That darkness flashed across his eyes again, and a muscle feathered in his jaw as if he was clamping down on something trying to crawl up his throat. A moment later, it vanished, and the male who'd rescued me from the cave returned. He blew out a long breath. "I will show you, Izidora. Give me time to show you, please."

I closed my eyes, blocking out the pain written across his face. "I will make my choice in the next few days," I announced. "So far, I don't see how I can choose you. Do whatever you think you must to prove to me that you are the light."

He leaped to his feet and crossed the table, embracing me without warning. I stiffened under his touch and did not relax until he'd stepped away. "I have no doubt that I will."

I skirted around him and walked to the front door. "We should get back for the archery competition."

He did not protest, following me like a wraith as we pushed through the crowded streets and returned to Mistik and Fek. As we retraced our path through the city, the clopping of the horses' hooves did nothing to drown out the screaming thoughts in my head.

Was there a chance that Kazimir could change for the better? Or was he already so far down this oily path that it would be impossible to climb back up? His words and his actions were antithetical to one another, something that, as I had learned during my time in the cave, screamed untrustworthiness. It set my teeth on edge, and my shoulders climbed higher toward my ears at the perceived threat.

The realization that his actions reminded me of the males who had abused me stole the breath from my lungs.

But what if I doomed us all by choosing Ruslan? The course of history rested upon this choice of light and dark, and who was

I to affect the outcome of millions of lives? Lives I'd barely considered up until this point, and only because Ruslan had become king of the Iron Realm and the weight of his responsibility had been thrown in my face. Never before had I seen what that responsibility entailed, and in only a few days it had become abundantly clear that there was more to it than greeting his people and the nobles of the other realms.

The few moments of exposure I'd had to leadership in the Night Realm had been choreographed by Kazimir and the Nighthounds, and with the secrets and lies I'd uncovered since arriving in the Iron Realm, how could I trust them to assist me in governing, let alone in making a decision with such tremendous consequences?

Which male was the right choice?

9

RUSLAN

"Ruslan!" Drazen called through the haze of my thoughts. Sweat poured off of me as I continued to pound into the bag of sand hanging in the barracks outside Roc Palace, the home I'd built for Izidora and myself into the side of my favorite mountain in the Iron Realm. My knuckles screamed in protest as I landed another heavy blow, the already raw skin cracking and sending ruby rivulets running down my arm.

"What do you want, Drazen?" I snarled at my half-Dragon cousin, not paying him any more attention than that as I continued to pound away the pain that cut deeper than any knife. Before I could land my next blow, the male caught my arm and swung me to face him. My chest heaved with the relentless effort I threw into beating the bag while my brain flashed images of Izidora falling back into Kazimir's arms.

"She's not going to leave you." Drazen's deep blue eyes were filled with conviction, but I shrugged off his grip.

"You don't know that," I growled, reaching for my discarded

shirt to wipe the sweat from my face and neck. My hair dripped a steady stream down my back as I stared Drazen down.

"Savich saw them leaving and sent Kriath to follow them." Kriath was one of the Félvér in my personal guard, and he was one of the few who could execute a full shift into his inherited form. His Eagle was beautiful and large, and because his eyesight was keen, he could fly lazy circles far above Radence, out of sight from below.

"And?"

"And Kriath said that their interaction didn't go very well. He said Izidora seemed tense on their way back to the castle." Drazen blew out a breath, reaching up and tugging on the messy knot of hair tied at the crown of his head.

It wasn't until my chest loosened that I realized how tight it had been. My breath flowed easier, and I sank onto the padded ground, waves of relief washing over me. "They're already back?"

"Yes. And the archery competition starts in an hour. You need to wash up, because you are, in fact, hosting this year's Béke." Drazen pinched his brow. "I see you trying to do better, Ruslan, I really do. I know this isn't easy for you, but even if Izidora chooses him, you know I will always be here. We might not have grown up together, but I will always be loyal to you. I can't love you like she can, but I promise I'll never leave."

His words were like a punch to the gut and comforting hug wrapped into one, and my throat thickened, rendering me unable to speak. Finally, I managed, "Thank you, Drazen."

He proffered a hand to help me to my feet, and I accepted it, pulling him into a quick embrace before heading out of the barracks. "Besides, who else is going to call you out on your shit?" His grin was impish, and he elbowed me in the ribs as we entered the wintry sun.

"No one, unless they want to end up dead." I huffed a laugh, the darkness that called to me lifting for a moment. "Are we flying back?" I asked when no horses greeted us at the adjacent stables.

"We are. The courtyard at Ryza was too packed for me to ride out," he shrugged. "At least it's a nice day."

Without bothering to pull my shirt on, I loosed my black, taloned wings from my back, letting them flare wide before settling behind me. Drazen's lapis lazuli Dragon wings flared through his enchanted armor, and we shot into the cloudless blue sky, soaring on the bitter winter wind toward Ryza. The citadel watched over Radence like a hawk, missing nothing from its seat on a hill in the center of the city. Its black spires beckoned me forward, and I aimed for the largest tower at the edge of a rough cliff, not wanting anyone to see my bruised and bloody knuckles before I had a chance to heal them.

Strength, wealth, and power. Those were the attributes I wanted on display during Béke, and showing up with a wildness that spoke to how close I was to losing my shit would not do, especially not after my fight with Kazimir the previous night. Blood dripped from my palms as I dug my nails in, remembering his insult. *Rapist.*

The male was disgusting, stooping so low when he knew what Izidora had experienced. If only I could get Drazen to chain him up with the others, I could torture him until he begged for mercy I would not give.

A wicked grin spread across my lips as we approached the wall-sized windows of my apartment, my blood heating at the thought of the surprise Drazen was helping me concoct for Izidora. Soon, I'd be ready to show her the lengths I would go for her. But until then...

I knocked against the glass that opened from the inside, startling Izidora from where she lay on our bed. Her eyes were red and puffy, and I nearly broke the glass to get to her when I saw the pain written across her face. She rushed to the window, unlatching it and pushing it open. In a carefully calculated move, I banished my wings and rolled over my shoulder onto the dark wood floor, landing safely in our bedchamber. Drazen mimicked me and then Izidora shoved the window shut, blocking out the cold air.

"I didn't know you could do that," she murmured, awe in her voice.

Pushing off the ground, I caught her in my arms and pulled her close. "I would have shown you sooner if you'd made the flight from the roof of Roc to the ground, sprite. Master that, and I'll teach you this."

She didn't argue, burying her face into the dried sweat on my chest. Drazen cleared his throat, raising a dark brow and shooting me a look that said, 'I told you so.' I rolled my eyes and jerked my head, indicating that he could go.

"I'll be back in half an hour to go over the rules for the archery competition," Drazen threw over his shoulder, shutting the door behind him. I waited until his footsteps retreated out the main door before extracting Izidora from my embrace.

"What's wrong, sprite?" I crouched down so we were at eye level, and the redness was more apparent with our faces a breath apart.

She closed her eyes and shook her head. "It's just so much pressure. The fate of the world rests on my shoulders. Who am I to choose what happens next? I don't even know what will happen! Only that if I choose wrong, I'll plunge the world into chaos or something, whatever that means. Why can't there just be a clear answer!" The frustration eating at her was evident in her tone and the way her fingers twisted in her tunic.

I brushed my knuckles across her cheek, leaving a smear of my blood in their wake. "There is no stronger Fae, Félvér, or Telivér in all of Északi. Each of us is given a battle we must wage, and while some get off easy with the extent of their battle, others, like us, must carry longer and heavier campaigns to reach our highest potential."

She blew out a breath, nodding. When I pulled my hand away, she murmured, "You're injured." Her eyes widened, and she snatched my hand in midair and turned it over to assess my knuckles. In a flash, her white magic appeared, settling over them like a warm blanket, knitting the skin together and removing the swelling. With pride blooming in my chest, I lifted my other hand, allowing her to repeat the process before her aquamarine eyes narrowed on me. "What did you do?"

"The battle I must face is fear of you abandoning me, mate. We cope in different ways." I spoke through gritted teeth, not wanting to delve further into the fact that the only way for me to feel better was pain. Fastening my hand around her wrist, I jerked her to me. "Come shower with me and wash away all the blood."

Her lips parted slightly, and her heavenly arousal filled my nostrils. With the silence filling the space around us, the fluttering beat of her heart was like a drum, and I swore the hum of our bond was just underneath it.

"I wanted to enter the competition," she breathed. "Shouldn't I head to the arena so I am ready when it starts?"

"If I remember correctly, I am the king of the Iron Realm, and I get to decide when the competition starts, as well as who is allowed to participate. If you want to participate, then you shall." My healed hand found Izidora's chestnut hair, yanking it back so her throat was bared to me. I grazed my teeth along her exposed lifeline, eliciting a shudder and spreading goosebumps across her exposed skin.

"A quick shower," she conceded, her words breathy and soft. Approval rumbled in my chest as she broke my grips and tugged me behind her to the bathroom, turning the knobs until the space filled with steam.

My cock rose to attention as she stripped off her leggings and tunic, and I wasted no time removing my pants and showing her how much I wanted her. Her gaze snagged on my hardness before I walked her backward into the waiting water. Before I could say anything, she grabbed a bar of soap and rubbed it across the hard planes of my torso, soaping away the layers of sweat that clung to my skin. They washed down the drain along with my fear as she continued to shower me with her touch, and when she dropped to her knees before me, I nearly came undone.

She glanced up at me through her thick lashes, then flicked her tongue under the head of my cock. I groaned, "You look so fucking pretty kneeling before me. Now suck my cock into that pretty mouth of yours like a good girl."

Her eyes were molten, and she popped her mouth into an O before taking me down her throat with a single bob of her head. My abs tightened as I watched my shaft disappear completely, the suction created by her throat causing me to moan. She repeated the motion until her gags were too violent and she came up coughing for air. The water sprayed all around us, and she blinked droplets from her lashes, chest heaving, looking up at me like I was all she needed in this world.

Threading my fingers in her wet hair, I guided her head back to my erection. "Open wide because I'm not going to be gentle," I growled, and she sucked in a breath before obediently dropping her jaw. I buried myself in her mouth, not stopping until I hit the back of her throat, and then I began my relentless pace, her teeth grazing the underside of my cock and driving me wild.

Spit dripped down her chin as I fucked her face, and her nails dug into my thighs, but she did not tap them or ask for a reprieve. The sight of my mate taking everything I could give her had my balls tightening, and I knew I was close.

"Get ready to swallow me down," I grunted, my thrusts becoming erratic as waves of pleasure started at the base of my spine. With a groan, I emptied hot cum into her mouth, my cock throbbing and jerking with each subsequent release. I watched her throat bob as she swallowed it and then she stuck out her tongue, showing me what she had done. Releasing her hair, I pulled her to her feet and kissed her deeply, my tongue sweeping across hers and tasting the saltiness leftover from my release. "You're so fucking good, sprite."

"Does this mean I win the archery competition?" she grinned against my mouth, and I released her so I could gaze at the sparkle in her eyes.

"If there was a competition for sucking dick, you'd definitely get first prize," I told her.

She grabbed soap for herself, washing quickly while I did the same. Drazen would return any moment, and if he found us fucking, I'd never hear the end of it. But as the high of coming wore off, that fear crawled its way up my spine, constricting my lungs and robbing me of air. Izidora seemed almost as out of sorts as I did, her eyes glazed over as if she were deep in thought while she rinsed her hair. I exited the shower, grabbing towels for both of us, and we dried and dressed quickly, entering the living space at the same time as Drazen.

"Ready?" the half-Dragon asked, a thick, black brow raised in our direction. With his heightened senses, there was no doubt he knew what we'd been doing in his absence.

"Let's go," I confirmed, striding toward the door with kingly, purposeful steps. I snatched the Iron Crown from where I'd carelessly tossed it earlier and placed it on my head as we exited into the hallway.

"Who do we have representing the Iron Realm?" I asked Drazen.

"Kriath, Artur, Savich, and myself from your guard, and I believe Anton and Slavian have also thrown their names in. There are some of the lesser nobles and a few members of the Iron Realm's archery unit participating as well. All in all, maybe forty?" he responded.

"Wait, who am I representing?" Izidora jumped in, and my heart sang. She didn't default to representing the Night Realm, and that gave me hope.

Drazen responded before I could open my mouth. "Well, since the Night Realm nobles have made it clear they still see you as their leader, I would say the Night Realm." I sucked in a breath as we entered the stairwell leading us to the main floor. "But if you'd rather represent the Iron Realm, I don't think we'd oppose it," Drazen added.

Our footsteps echoed around the stone staircase as Izidora considered her options. "Why does the representation matter anyway?"

"The games we'll play over the coming weeks determine an overall winner of the friendly competition. There will be group and individual prizes for each event as well. It's mostly about bragging rights and an opportunity for the host realm to flaunt their wealth and wares," I said, stepping onto the landing and holding the door open for my cousin and my mate to pass through.

"Prizes?" Izidora beamed with a twinkle in her eyes. "What sort of prizes?"

With an amused huff, I captured her waist and pulled her into me, planting a kiss on her wet hair. "Not the kind of prize I'd give you, sprite."

Drazen rolled his eyes and shouldered past. "The Iron Realm most often awards gems and metalwork as prizes."

"I do like gems," Izidora sighed, and my stomach dropped because the one precious ring I had given her had been ruined by my selfishness and impulsiveness.

"Then I'll have to get you some more, mate," I whispered in her ear. "I want you to be dripping in more ways than one." Her cheeks flamed as I pulled away from her, and a smirk played across my face as I received the reaction I wanted. Then, I dropped my hands and followed Drazen down the hall, leaving Izidora to jog to catch up with us as she recovered.

"So, what's the rest of the schedule going to be?" she asked, slipping her hand in mine, and the ache in my chest that was always there eased immediately.

"Well, the first few days are competitions, like archery, swordsmanship, strength, horsemanship," I elbowed Izidora, knowing that would be her favorite, "and tomorrow we'll have a hunt for the males, and the females can go to the spa. Then there are a few days of celebration of the Goddess and her lasting peace, including a ritual offering, masquerade ball, artisanal fair, and lantern release. After that, we'll have an entertainment show, and the last two days are spent celebrating from dawn until dusk," I explained.

"And whoever wins the most of these competitions gets awarded a grand prize?" Izidora asked.

"Exactly," Drazen replied. "So, who do you want to represent, the Night or the Iron Realm?"

Izidora chewed her lip, and my heart galloped in my chest as I waited for her answer. If she chose the Iron Realm, that meant I was one step closer to sealing our mate bond. But if she chose the Night Realm...

"Can I remain neutral?"

Fuck, if those four words didn't both wound me and reassure me.

Drazen shrugged. "I don't see why not."

"Then that is what I will do," she declared as we joined the throng of people bustling down the main hall and out into the afternoon sun.

Horses were tacked and ready to ride, and those staying in the citadel departed in droves down the long, sloped path into Radence. As we mounted and joined the fray, I observed just how many residents trekked to the arena set on the outskirts of the city, with rows and rows and rows of seating climbing toward the sky to give all in attendance a view of the competitors. The hum of excitement was palpable, given that these next two weeks were filled with drink, food, and fucking, a much-needed reprieve from the long, harsh winters and the back-breaking work in the mountains.

Izidora waved to people she knew as we passed them, and many Fae and Félvér stopped their progress to bow to their king. The lightheartedness and joy of my people managed to lift a little of that tightness from my shoulders, and by the time we reached the arena, I'd relaxed into my role.

A stage had been erected to one side, the wood planks creating a shelter from the wind that blew down from the nearby glacial peaks. The Demon Dragon sigil hung from a beam at the back, showing everyone in attendance exactly who was in fucking charge of the Iron Realm. The maw of the black dragon dripped blood, matching its fiendish ruby eyes and bright red horns. It was intimidating and powerful, which was exactly why I'd abandoned the sigil of my father, the late King Azim, in favor of it.

"Good luck, sprite." I bid Izidora goodbye after we secured our horses, squeezing her hand before ascending the steps to the platform. I braced my arms along the back of the throne in the center of the stage, Queen Viktoria already seated off to my left. I nodded to the pregnant monarch, her hands resting across the furs piled over her belly to ward off the chill.

Then I turned my attention to the crowd of competitors and onlookers.

Five stations had been set up, each fully stocked with quivers filled with arrows, though each competitor brought their own bow. The throng of people filled me with joy as I saw Fae of every race, Félvér who lived in the Iron Realm, and the Telivér who had remained behind after I released them from their magical chains to the Iron Realm, mixing and laughing with one another.

This was how the continent should be.

Swallowing down my smile in favor of a smirk, I stepped forward, shooting a blast of black fire into the air to garner the attention of the crowd. A hush fell over it, and all eyes were on me.

"Béke is a time of peace, where all the races of Fae gather to celebrate our benevolent Goddess and her infinite wisdom. However," I paused, allowing my expression to shift into a devilish one, "that doesn't mean our *friendly* competition has to be boring. The Iron Realm plans on winning this year, so don't hold back, because the competition will be fierce."

Cheers erupted from the gathered Iron Fae and Félvér, while teasing boos resounded from everyone else.

With a casual, indifferent air, I leaped from the platform, landing lightly in the space below, and strode toward the closest station. Drazen had already laid out a ceremonial bow and iron arrow for me, and I notched and drew it, taking aim at the target. Black flame erupted along the bolt as it flew straight and true to the center, flaring briefly before extinguishing completely.

"Let the games begin!" I shouted.

10

IZIDORA

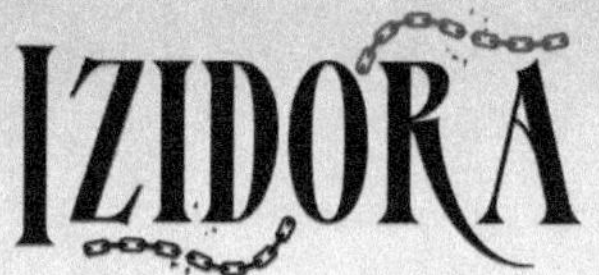

BÉKE DAY TWO

Ruslan fired four more iron arrows into the target, his aim near-perfect. Cheers erupted from the Iron Fae and Félvér watching as our king set a high bar for his subjects to follow. When he finished, he returned to the stage at the far end of the range, joining Queen Viktoria to survey the competition below. The high-backed chair where he lounged glittered with precious gems, and he looked every bit the ruler he was. I bit my lip and blushed as he caught my eye and winked.

Drazen nudged me forward, and I realized I was being herded toward a quickly forming line where contestants queued to give their names and realms in exchange for a number. Liliana was ten paces ahead of me, and as if she could sense my attention on her, she turned, waving.

The line moved quickly until suddenly we stood before the booth.

"Izidora Valynor," I said to the male who marked names.

"What realm?" he asked, not looking up from his paper.

"None," I said, though my voice did not hold much conviction. I couldn't choose – not yet, not when the pressure of my bigger choice loomed over me like an executioner's blade.

He handed me a number – ninety-four. "Strap that around your arm," he instructed.

Drazen fastened it for me, then secured his own place in the competition. He fetched a bow for me, this one much smaller in size than the ones wielded by the large males in front of me. Zuriel joined us in line, along with a few of the Demons I had begun to recognize as they emerged from their cocoon of safety.

"What realm are you representing?" Drazen asked them.

The taller male Demon, whose black hair seemed to suck in all the light around it, replied first. "We decided to represent our continent, Keleti, rather than any realm."

Drazen nodded, not seeming surprised by their choice.

"Each Telivér has chosen to represent their respective continent as a way to show worldwide unity," Zuriel explained, and I knew my cousin well enough now to know that pride filled his voice.

Before, it had struck me as odd that Zuriel had not hated or rebelled against the Iron Realm that kept him chained to this continent with magical binds, but there was something about the way he spoke of the continent of Angels and Demons, Keleti, that made me think he was happy to leave it behind.

Around us, conversations were loud and filled with laughter, and I opened my empath magic to absorb the positive energy buzzing in the air, replenishing my stores for whatever may lie ahead. Ruslan constantly reminded me to keep up my strength, and I loved that he chose to empower me so often. It helped me remember just how powerful I was when moments of self-doubt crept in.

Absentmindedly, I played with the string on my bow, letting my thoughts drift, but when we were about halfway through the line for the archery stations, it broke, stinging my finger as it whipped to the side. I cursed, and Drazen looked it over. "There are more bows around the corner there." He pointed in the direction of a small building overflowing with various goods and leftover building materials. "Test out a few until you find one that you can pull. I don't think there are any smaller ones left."

"Hold my spot!" I tossed over my shoulder as I jogged away. Dozens of bows lay against the wall, and I picked up the smallest one I could find, pulling back on the string and testing its flexion. I tried two more before the hairs on the back of my neck rose, causing me to pause and scan my surroundings. All I heard were the shouts and cheers of the archery competition in the distance. Otherwise I was alone.

But Kazimir had to be nearby, otherwise this tug low in my belly would not be so insistent.

The last bow I tested was sufficient, and I hurried back to the safety of where Drazen, Zuriel, and the Demons waited in line, that sense of being watched never leaving me, even as the line grew shorter. I craned my neck, searching the crowd for any sign of Kazimir, but he never appeared.

"Who are you looking for?" Drazen asked.

"Kazimir," I whispered under my breath, knowing his keen senses would pick up on my words while the Fae around us would not.

Drazen whipped his head around, searching for the male. "I don't see him. Why are you looking for Kazimir?" His voice dropped into a serious tone, a hint of concern peeking through. Zuriel took a step closer after making his own scan of our surroundings.

Blowing out a breath, I decided to admit the truth to them. "Because I can *feel* him like I can feel Ruslan. When I went to get a new bow, I felt like someone was watching me, and I felt that tug like he was around. But there was no one over there, except for me."

Drazen's dark brows pinched above his lapis lazuli eyes. "What's his Night Fae magic?"

I chewed my lip, debating about revealing Kazimir's magic to someone who could be a possible foe, depending on which mate I chose. I decided on vagueness. "Other than offensive blasts and such? He uses shadows."

"And you searched the shadows too?" Zuriel questioned, giving me a light nudge to step forward in line and close the gap I'd left in my absentmindedness.

I nodded.

"Well, Ruslan, Zuriel, and I have trained you well. I do not doubt that you can hold your own these days. But we'll watch out for you, Izidora." Drazen's mouth was pressed into a firm line, and reaching out with my empath magic, I read his worry.

"Thanks, Drazen."

Liliana stepped up to the free slot on the range, and I turned my attention to my friend, watching the smooth way she notched her arrow and drew the string back, blowing out a breath as she loosed it. She sank five arrows into the center of her target, better than the two males on either side of her. With a wry grin, she winked at the Crystal Fae who gaped at her – High Lord Tukka, if I remembered correctly – and strutted away from the slot.

My eyes were still on my friend when Drazen nudged me forward again. Gripping the new bow, I trotted to the slot on the end, feeling a prickle on the back of my neck again. My eyes darted around the space, but most onlookers were focused on the contestants readying their bows. Ruslan caught my eye from across the range, giving me an encouraging nod. Drawing a deep breath, I snatched an arrow from the quiver and notched it, trying to ignore the anxiety skittering across my skin.

The arrow left a twang in its wake as it sailed across the range toward the waiting target, burying itself in the highest ring. I cursed the feeling that had me on edge and tried again. Again the arrow flew toward the target, landing just below the first. The third attempt resulted in a similar placement, and I paused my firing to center myself. I allowed the world to drop away as I focused on my breath, shutting out the sight, sound, and smell of everyone around me until I was only aware of the smooth wood of the bow in my left hand, the firm feathers brushing against my right fingers, and the string in between them.

Insidious bloom.

Lifting the bow and arrow, I drew back with all my strength, looking down the tip of the bolt to the black circle in the very center of my target. The dark dot morphed into the tangled mess of feelings I had about my choice and the burden I'd never asked for. When the surge of anger and grief rose in me, I let it fly along with my arrow, both burying themselves in the center of the target. Before I could be shaken out of my focused state, I grasped and notched the next arrow, firing it straight and true, reuniting it with its brethren in the center.

The Iron Fae manning the targets unclipped mine and wrote my number down, signaling the end of my turn. Ruslan caught my eye again as I slipped through the crowd to the waiting contestants, finding Liliana amongst a trio of males.

"Your last two shots were incredible, Izidora!" she grinned, pulling me in for an embrace.

"All five of yours hit the center," I shrugged as I squeezed between her and the Crystal Fae. "High Lord Tukka, so nice to see you again."

"Likewise, Princess Izidora. I've heard so much about you these past few months," the male responded, smoothing his long blond hair away from his face. My stomach dropped because I knew all of his information had come from Kazimir, and the female he saw before him was so different from the one I had been the day I had left the Night Realm with Ruslan.

"Where are the others?" I asked Liliana. *Where was Kazimir?*

"Endre, Viktor, and Vadim went off with Kaztar and Domi to check out the leaderboard. I haven't seen Kazimir since you both returned from your date." Her voice dropped low and she tilted toward me. "How was it?"

I blew out a breath, fingers fidgeting over the bow in my hand. "Honestly, I don't know. He's... different. I can't quite figure out what it is, though. The prophecy does call for 'her mates darkness to rise' which only makes this more confusing." I paused for a moment, then relayed my current situation like I had to Drazen. "I feel him here, but I can't see him. Yesterday, this morning, this afternoon... whenever I see him, I get that tug that pulls me toward him, but I also get this sick feeling in my stomach, and my skin feels like someone is driving pins and needles into it."

"Shit," she hissed. "That's not good, Izidora. But you're right, something has changed within him since Ruslan showed up. I think the males know, because when Kazimir gets the slightest bit upset, they all walk on eggshells around him until he calms down. Want me to see what I can pry from Endre?"

"Please," I sighed. "How is that going, by the way?"

A gong sounded from somewhere nearby, breaking our conversation and drawing our attention to the stage where Ruslan rose from his seat and unrolled a scrap of paper. A hush fell over the crowd as he opened his mouth to speak. "The finalists from each realm are as follows: Lady Liliana Arzeni from the Night Realm. High Lord Tukka Raita from the Crystal Realm. King Consort Geza from the Day Realm. Artur Lovav from the Iron Realm. And this year, we have a fifth category: the world at large. Their representative is Gozzak, of Keleti."

I whooped for my best friend, who wore the confident smile of a female who held not an ounce of self-doubt. "You will win!" I pushed her forward toward the waiting targets, and she winked at me before striding off, High Lord Tukka on her heels. His interest in her was obvious, and I covered my mouth with my hand to hide a snicker as he took his place beside her. Artur I knew from Ruslan's personal guard, and Gozzak was the male Demon who had stood in line with us. I'd had a brief interaction with King Consort Geza at the ball the previous night.

But my allegiance lay firmly with Liliana, and as I dug my nails into my free palm to ground against that creeping feeling across my skin, I hoped she'd choose me if I accepted the mating bond with Ruslan.

"Zuriel?" I reached out to him through the mental connection shared by all Angels.

"Yes, cousin?"

"Can you come stand with me?"

"I'll be there momentarily."

Ruslan had just finished explaining the rules of the shootout when the Angel pushed his way past the Iron Fae surrounding me. His white hair was pulled up and away from his face, showing off the sharp lines of his brows and jaw, and his ice-blue eyes skimmed over me before facing the range where the finalists had lined up to take their first shot.

"Want to tell me why you're so tense, cousin?" Zuriel asked in my mind.

"Kazimir, still. I don't like that I can't lay eyes on him."

"No harm will come to you while I am here. Or while Ruslan is here. Or Drazen. You have so many people in your corner, Izidora. Not like you need them. You've grown so strong since the first day we met. Do you doubt your abilities?"

His words were like a punch to the gut because they were

true. Self-doubt nearly crippled me, compounded by the impossible choice that lay before me. *"Yes."*

A cheer went up from the crowd as all five fired their arrows at once. Liliana, High Lord Tukka, and Artur's arrows sank into the center of their targets, and King Consort Geza and Gozzak each gave a friendly wave to the crowd before stepping away from the range, having been knocked out of the shootout.

The three drew arrows and lined up their next shots, waiting for Ruslan's command to fire. A hush fell over the crowd in eager anticipation of who would be eliminated that round. The twang of the bowstrings releasing filled the air a moment before three arrows thudded into the bales of hay, all three in the dark center. Not a drop of sweat graced Liliana's brow as she notched another arrow, her seafoam green eyes trained down the range and chest proud as she held her bow steady. Ruslan's command fell again, and High Lord Tukka's arrow went a little too wide, knocking him out of the competition. He bowed to the other contestants, then joined King Consort Geza and Gozzak a few paces behind the others.

Liliana and Artur locked eyes before returning their attention to the targets down range. Drawing a deep breath, Liliana returned to her starting position, seeming to block out the world around her as she waited for the next call.

Come on, Liliana.

They shot five perfect shots in a row, and the tension in the crowd was as taught as their bowstrings as they lined up for their sixth, both black centers nearly blotted out from fletching. I held my breath as they drew, then closed my eyes as they released, too anxious to watch the arrows fly. The roar of the crowd snapped them open, and Liliana leaped into the air with a squeal. Darting my gaze down range, I saw Artur's arrow in the white space alongside his other arrows, making Liliana the winner of the archery competition.

"Let's go, Zuriel!" I exclaimed, tugging on his arm as I pushed through the crowd toward my friend, who was on her way to the stage where she would receive her prize. Endre, Viktor, and Vadim emerged from the crowd, joining Liliana in her celebration, and I jogged to catch up with them.

"I knew you would win!" I grinned, embracing my friend when she broke apart from Endre.

"Me too," she laughed, dropping my arms before arching an eyebrow as she noticed the male behind me.

"Oh my Goddess, you're just as bad as Vadim," I teased, low enough that Zuriel couldn't hear me.

"You must introduce me later," she whispered, before Endre tugged on her arm, snatching her attention.

My blood heated, and I whipped my head around to find Ruslan a few paces away on the platform, holding a shiny black box tied off with a silky gray bow. His smoky eyes glittered when he saw me, and my body relaxed as he neared. "Hold the box for me while I present the prize?"

"Absolutely." I had to tip my head all the way back to look up at him, and for a moment it was only us among the mountains, with the wind pulling at the loose strands of my braid and ghosting across the fur that peeked out from our jackets.

Zuriel cleared his throat, breaking the trance, and Ruslan grabbed my hand, leading me toward the front of the wooden platform. Ruslan handed me the box before turning to face his people.

"Lady Liliana Arzeni has won this year's archery contest! It is my honor to present her with a prize," he lifted the lid from the box with a flourish, "a hand-crafted bow made from the lightest metal in the Iron Realm."

My jaw dropped at the beautiful metalwork that lay among sheets of soft velvet in the box. When Liliana lifted it, the sun caught the tiny gemstones encrusted on the sides, inlaid in an intricate filigree that was nearly transparent. With how light the box was, I would have never guessed that inside lay a beautiful bow. Liliana tugged on the string, watching the bow flex as easily as any wooden one. "It is an honor, King Ruslan." Liliana sketched a quick bow, and the crowd cheered at her victory.

"This concludes the day's events, and I wish you all a nice evening of celebration," Ruslan boomed over the crowd, dismissing everyone with a wave of his hand. We remained on the stage while people began reclaiming their horses and trekking back to Radence.

The Nighthounds, minus Kazimir, joined us on the platform. Vadim took the bow from Liliana, assessing it thoroughly, turning it over in his hands, and testing its movement and lightness. "This craftsmanship is like nothing I've ever seen."

"And it's all mine, brother," she teased, snatching it from his probing fingers.

"You won't even let me fire it once? I am the one who taught you how to shoot after all," he grumbled, smoothing his beard with his hand.

"The student has become the master," she shrugged, and I bit my lip to hide a snicker.

Ruslan's hand found the small of my back and I leaned into his touch, feeling both of us relax with the physical connection. Endre and Viktor's eyes darted to Ruslan's disappearing hand, and something flashed in both their eyes that I couldn't quite read. Tuning into that flame-wrapped crystal in my chest, I pushed my magic toward them, trying to discern their emotions. Mine were so frayed that I needed to know what they were feeling, and yet I was still afraid of what I would find.

A swirling mix of anger, guilt, and anxiety bled from both of them, though what drove each emotion, I could not decipher. I had hardly spoken to my friends since they arrived in the Iron Realm, and this chasm between the Night Realm and myself was growing deeper with each passing moment of awkwardness that went unacknowledged. It was clear they had not found what they were expecting when they rode upon Ryza Citadel, and now none of us knew how to proceed.

Where was Kazimir?

As if he heard his name in my head, he appeared at the bottom of the platform, looking up at those of us gathered above him. His emerald eyes collided with mine for only a moment before moving on to Liliana. "Congrats, Liliana," he said. "Your shots were excellent. You make the Night Realm proud."

She flicked her braid over her shoulder. "I know. You are all lucky to have me." That earned a chuckle from the males on the stage, including Ruslan, Drazen, and Zuriel. It struck me then that every person I cared about was gathered in the small space, and yet I felt so lonely, unmoored and adrift in my anxiety.

The scattering of my friends reflected my feelings, too. The Nighthounds gathered on the opposite side of the wooden planks, while Liliana stood proudly on her own in the middle, though a hair closer to where Ruslan, Drazen, Zuriel, and myself stood. It was a perfect metaphor for the feelings rising from the people around me, and I choked on my breath as I opened myself up to the collective tension of the group.

Was there any way to repair the rift and bring peace?

Or would choosing one side over the other only end in war?

11

KAZIMIR

Why did I go to Steel again last night?

My head pounded with each strike of Fek's hooves against the packed earth beneath us as we trekked along the winding path deep into the Agrenak Mountains, where the traditional hunt would begin. The noble males from all the realms bundled in our thickest furs, bracing against the cold that swept from the sheer mountain faces overhead. Snow still blanketed them, despite much of it disappearing around Radence. The sun glittered off the snow, forcing me to squint against the glare as it pierced into my skull.

Since the very first Béke, the *friendly* hunt had been a competition to prove the prowess of the hosting realm's hunters, with only bows and arrows to take down the large game. In the Iron Realm's case, that was a rare white stag that had been spotted late yesterday afternoon by one of the mountain patrols. Ruslan led our pack, followed closely by King Airre and King Consort Geza, the three creeping along the narrow, icy trail, bows half-cocked as we searched for any sign of the stag. Endre kept his bow slung across his chest as he crouched down to read the prints in the snow. He was only here because we planned on serving our kills tonight for dinner. For him, killing animals for sport was distasteful, and I was inclined to agree with him, especially when the meat could feed a hungry village for at least a day.

I hung back, wanting as much distance between Ruslan and myself as possible. The bastard had completely ignored my existence since we'd departed early this morning to ride toward the breaking dawn. Still, I did not trust that his evasion was born of indifference.

The cold air burned my lungs as we climbed deeper and higher into the Agrenak Mountains that surrounded the Iron Realm like an impenetrable shield. The day was cloudless and clear, the snow glittering and reflecting in our eyes until we crossed into the shadow of one of the many peaks.

"Here!" Endre shout-whispered as he spotted tracks in the deep snow.

"Well done, High Lord Endre," Ruslan commended. He glanced around like he was searching for something, and upon spotting it he motioned, "This way."

A steep incline and boulders funneled us higher up the mountain, and I had to sling my bow across my back to free my hands to use among the slippery rocks.

"Why we can't just fly up is beyond me," Vadim cursed under his breath from behind me. I snickered and kept pushing, my muscles straining and breathing uneven until I reached a small overlook that housed the rest of the hunting party.

Endre crouched once again, reading the indentations in the snow that scattered in all directions. Ruslan knelt beside them and I took the opportunity to peer over the ledge, soaking in the sweeping view below while I caught my breath. A blanketed valley opened up before us, and in the distance, a slender stream of smoke indicated a small mining village nestled among the white powder. The visibility at this altitude was incredible, and and through the peaks, I thought I glimpsed the ocean.

"Beautiful, isn't it?" Ruslan's raking voice sounded over my ear, breaking the trance that the mountains held over me. Backstepping, I spun to face him, calling my magic just below my skin should I need to fly or fight. But he seemed unfazed and merely stepped to my side, joining me in appreciating the view.

"This is one of my favorite spots in all the Agrenak Mountains. I planned on bringing Izidora here one day, but we had too many pressing matters to attend to and could not find the time to sneak away for a hike."

I said nothing, watching him out of the corner of my eye. The leash I held around my dark magic was taught, and if I so much as breathed, it might snap. Ruslan may have had Izidora these past few months, but she was mine first, and I needed to keep my cool if I wanted her to return with me to the Night Realm.

"Just down there, I killed my brother Damir to secure my place as heir apparent." He paused, letting his words sink in. "Nothing in my life has been handed to me. I had to fight for every scrap since I was a small child, and that has made me stronger than I ever thought possible. Don't underestimate me, Kazimir, and don't think for a second that I will not fight to the death for Izidora."

I clenched my jaw and fists, trying to hold back the biting words that wanted to escape my lips. Instead, I exhaled through my nose and replied coolly, "I look forward to your death."

He looked me up and down, a wicked grin playing on his lips as his eyes glinted with black flame. "I think I may have finally found a worthy opponent. You too have a darkness inside you. I look forward to seeing the full extent of it."

Cocky bastard.

Movement caught my attention on the mountainside below us, just over Ruslan's shoulder. A large rack of brown antlers surged upward, and I quietly unslung my bow, drawing an arrow from the quiver. He followed my line of sight, then stepped quietly to the side, pulling the string back and aiming at the same time I did.

The stag bounded closer, and the tip of my arrow followed him until he turned sideways once more. Then I released the arrow in the direction of the majestic white creature's heart. Ruslan's arrow followed a moment later, mine landing first with a solid thud while his flew just off the mark. The stag stumbled and collapsed to the ground.

"I am more than a worthy opponent, Ruslan. I am better than you," I smirked, then turned on my heel and walked away from the ledge. A snarl sounded behind me as King Airre whooped at the size of the rare white stag's antlers.

"Beautiful shot, High Lord Kazimir! Look at the size of this beast. We will certainly feast tonight," he enthused.

"Does this mean we can go now? I am freezing my balls off. Give me the heat of the beach any day over the cold in the mountains," King Consort Geza laughed, clapping me on the shoulder in congratulations.

The sound of snapping wings turned me around. Black leathery wings sprung from Ruslan's shoulder blades and he shot into the air, backflipping and then diving to the dead stag. The hunting party hurried to the cliff and peered down as the king of the Iron Realm grasped the brown antlers in his hands and lifted both the large carcass and himself with one strong flap of his wings.

"I thought Iron Fae did not have wings," High Lord Soma of the Day Realm whispered off to my left. Murmurs of agreement floated through the group, and Ruslan smirked as he lowered himself and the stag behind us. I hadn't thought Ruslan was a pure-blooded Iron Fae, but his leathery wings and horns were a confirmation of my suspicions.

"I'll fly the carcass to Drazen and then return to escort you down the mountain," he announced, then winked at me and took off into the sky.

How dare he steal the spotlight away from me? The stag was my *kill.*

Suffocating the urge to leap into the sky and race after the bat-winged mongrel, I turned to Viktor, whose brain worked overtime analyzing the situation. The abilities Ruslan displayed today would certainly need to be accounted for, but it wasn't my biggest concern about him. If he wanted to continue stealing *everything* from me, he was going to have to pay.

Slavian and Anton sauntered over to where the Night Fae stood in a semi-circle, trying to keep warm as a strong wind blew through the mountains. Slavian's mischievous expression told me exactly what he intended to discuss, and it had nothing to do with Ruslan or the stag.

"So will you be joining us again tonight?" Slavian addressed us once they were within whispering range.

"Where exactly is that? My suitemates have been coming in at odd hours the past two nights. Must have been quite the party," Kaztar chuckled.

Licking his lips, Anton looked him up and down. "The place is called Steel. You are welcome to come and bring your wife. We will show you a good time."

"That they will, Kaztar," Vadim crooned, rubbing his hands together. "I think I'll join you again tonight."

Snorting at Vadim's enthusiasm, I glanced at Endre who did not seem pleased with the suggestion of another venture to the wild establishment. Not that I could blame him – I needed to stay far away from that place and any temptation. "Does Ruslan ever go with you?" I asked the young High Lords.

Slavian laughed darkly. "It's his club, so yeah, he used to. He hasn't been in years though. Such a shame, he was always a good time."

"That's why I'm never getting married," Anton chimed in. "Why tie myself to a single person when I can have all the males and females? At the same time, too."

I understood why Vadim was so eager to return – he and Anton shared a similar outlook on life.

I glanced around, watching for any sign of danger. If Ruslan planned on having me killed, doing it while he was not around gave him an airtight alibi. And yet, after his revelation and display, I sensed that he truly wanted a fair fight with me. If what he said about his brother was true, he was no stranger to fighting for his life, which made him a dangerous opponent. When someone's back was against a wall and they were trying to survive, they would do anything to take one more breath. Ruthlessness ran through his iron blood, and if we went head to head, only one of us would walk away with our lives, of that I was certain.

Cold bit at my fingertips and toes the longer we stood stationary, and I shifted from foot to foot, trying to bring heat and blood flow back to my body. Too much time had passed. I looked up to the sun, trying to gauge the hour, when I noticed movement high above us. Squinting, I realized it was not an animal traversing the snow-covered rocks above. It was other rocks tumbling down, and as their momentum increased, they brought more with them.

Adrenaline flooded my veins as the ground beneath my feet began to vibrate. "Avalanche!" I yelled to the group, the sounds of cracking ice and falling rock finally reaching our sensitive ears.

A tidal wave of white tumbled closer and closer to us, and without thought I shouted out orders to save us all, knowing there was no time to escape down the steep, rocky path we'd ascended. "Vadim, Viktor, Kaztar, take the Day Fae into the air and out of danger. Return for the rest of us when they are out of harm's way. Airre, Tukka, use your air magic to assist them, then help Aake and Mikko freeze the snow to the side of the mountain. Slavian, Anton, deal with the rocks so they don't smash us to pieces."

Each male sprung into action, unquestioningly falling into line as we worked together against the mighty forces of nature. I snapped out my wings, shooting into the air and scanning for any sign of Ruslan as my friends scooped the Day Fae into their arms, and with the strength that comes from mortal peril, launched themselves into the air and flew with all their might away from the tumbling earth.

Endre joined me in the sky, ready to swoop in to grab the six males waiting below. They braced themselves, digging their heels into the packed earth as they wielded their magic. Slavian and Anton gritted their teeth as they slowed the descent of the ice and rock mix, buying time for my friends to get King Consort Geza, Soma, and Domon to safety. Carrying Izidora's light frame through the mountain tops had been much easier than carrying full-grown warriors, and I prayed to the Goddess to give the males the strength to return to help with the Crystal Fae.

King Airre and High Lord Tukka turned back to the fray, joining High Lords Mikko and Aake in freezing as many rocks as they could. But the avalanche tumbled closer despite the sweat pouring from each of them.

"Kazimir! We aren't going to be able to hold it off much longer. I can carry Anton straight up if you can carry the other four," Slavian yelled, his legs beginning to tremble. I searched the horizon for any sign of my friends or Ruslan, but we were alone.

"Take King Airre and Mikko! Tukka and I will remain," Aake offered himself in sacrifice, calculating the number of wings versus those remaining to be saved.

"Hang on a moment longer!" I ordered, hoping, praying for someone else to return. They obeyed, digging in with determination as the massive icy wave inched closer and closer. A shadow passed over my head and I glanced up to see a set of massive black wings soaring above me, the wind knocking me off balance momentarily.

Ruslan circled above the avalanche, then roared so loudly I was certain he would cause further damage. But instead of continuing descent, the ice and snow evaporated as if it were nothing, black flames licking it, consuming it until nothing remained but a fine mist that floated off on the breeze. Anton and Slavian dropped the stones into the remaining snow with a huff, then collapsed to their hands and knees, chests heaving.

Endre rushed to their sides, immediately dropping to his knees and assessing the two High Lords for injury. The Crystal Fae sat in similar states of exhaustion, and I could only stand and flex my fingers, running a hand over my face as I watched over the fallen Fae before me.

Ruslan saved the fucking day.

"You are a true general, Kazimir. You remained calm and clear despite looming death above us. I will gladly follow you into battle again." King Airre's words were sincere, but they tasted like ash.

I felt Ruslan's presence behind me, and I spun just in time to watch him land, talons in place of hands, horns protruding from his slick hair, and his leathery wings splayed wide.

"You saved us all," I uttered, a bitter mixture of shock and anger swirling in my gut.

He shrugged. "I passed your friends on my way back, and they told me there was an avalanche. It would not be a good start to my reign to have your blood on my hands."

King Airre heaved himself to his feet beside me. "I am grateful for your help, King Ruslan. But if I may ask, what did you do? And why do you have this?" He gestured to Ruslan's changed anatomy.

"This is my shifted form. I am part Demon and part Dragon, coming from my mother's side. I breathe black fire in this form, which I used to vaporize the avalanche." He sheathed his talons and then looked at me. "I can carry two back to the horses, if you and Endre can get the others."

I nodded through clenched teeth, and Slavian shifted to reveal black wings, differently shaped than mine and Ruslan's, and horns. He grasped Anton from behind, then launched into the air. King Airre stood in front of me and Aake stood in front of Endre. We secured them, then followed Slavian into the sky. Ruslan followed with Tukka and Mikko on either arm a moment later. The Crystal Fae used their last remaining magic to create a wind at our backs, propelling us forward until the horses and others came into view. I breathed a sigh of relief, sweat soaking through my clothes as we descended and landed a little too roughly.

Viktor tossed me a waterskin, and I gulped down the cold liquid, then used the back of my hand to wipe sweat from my brow.

"You were brilliant back there, Kazimir," he said. "Glad to see some of the old you resurfacing. Cazius would be so proud of you right now."

But the glory wasn't all mine.

Shaking off the intrusive thought, I pulled my friend in for an embrace, grateful he was alive and well. "I am glad for it too," I said. Then, in a much lower voice, "We have much to discuss about Ruslan's powers upon our return." One dip of his chin was all I needed to know he understood.

"Well, after that shake-up, I am pleased that I brought wineskins. Who wants some?" Drazen grinned, holding up one in each hand. Vadim snatched one immediately, followed by a chuckling Tukka. We passed around the skins, and once I had my drink, I strolled toward Ruslan. He stood off to the side with his horse, away from the rest of the group.

I held the skin out to him, saying nothing.

We regarded each other for a moment before he took it from me, then drank down a hefty measure. I would be lying if I didn't admit that I respected him a bit more for his heroic actions, though I wished I'd been the ultimate savior. Not that the binding magic in my chest agreed, its desire to strangle our opponent fighting against my own desire to appear calm and collected in front of the other male nobles.

Without another word, I left the wineskin with Ruslan, then found Fek and pulled an apple from my saddlebags. My dependable mount bit into it greedily, then stamped his foot when he was finished as if to say, 'it's cold, let's get the fuck out of here.' I chuckled and rubbed his nose in agreement. Once the stag was secured to the litter behind two horses, Drazen called for us to mount up and we began the long journey back to Ryza Citadel, shaken but alive.

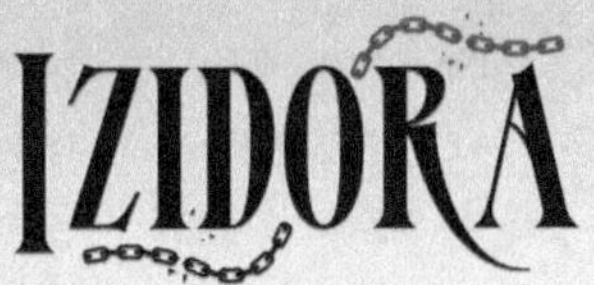IZIDORA

Béke Day Three

The morning was blisteringly cold, but I welcomed the refreshing sting against my face as Zuriel and I rode out of the city. A thick blanket of snow covered everything in the valley that nestled Radence, and even the peaks surrounding us were nothing more than white spears in the sky. Mistik's back swayed beneath me as we walked at a slow pace in the direction of Roc Palace, and beside me, Zuriel rode Twilight, her black coat shining beneath the winter sun.

"So, cousin, want to tell me why you wanted to go for a ride so early?" Zuriel said finally once we'd left the city behind. Only snow-dusted fences and curling chimney smoke accompanied us now, save for the occasional bleat of a sheep penned in a field.

Fog graced the air in front of me as I blew out a long breath. "I had a breakdown two nights ago."

"What triggered it?" my cousin asked gently.

My throat thickened, and tears pricked my eyes as I recalled the thoughts and emotions that had sent me into a spiral – that threatened to do so again. "Kazimir told me during the opening ball that his father, Kriztof, Zekari, and Kirigin all died the night I was taken from the Night Realm. After he and Ruslan fought and we finally returned to our apartment, I just lost it. I couldn't hold everything in anymore. I thought when I saw them side by side I would know... and I didn't. I am more confused than ever before, and the reality of the prophecy set in... It was a lot all at once."

Unbidden, tears spilled out of my eyes and down my cheeks. I quickly wiped them away with the back of my fur-lined glove.

"What else?" he prodded.

"I'm so on edge right now, like the slightest noise will startle me, and the feeling of being watched and not seeing who is watching me makes it hard to relax," I continued. "I feel like I'm back in the cave all over again."

Until those words slipped out, I hadn't realized that was truly what I was feeling. Another wave of panic washed over me, and I gripped the reins tightly in my hands. Mistik stopped, shifting nervously beneath me as she sensed my rising terror. Zuriel pulled Twilight to a halt, then hopped off the mare and rounded to my side.

Without him needing to say anything, I dismounted, legs trembling beneath me as I leaned into my mare for support. She pushed back into me, giving me her strength. Mistik snorted at Zuriel when she couldn't turn her head to see me, and with a small smile, he sidestepped and allowed me to wrap my arms around her neck. Burying my nose in her horsey scent grounded me, and I cracked an eye when Zuriel cleared his throat.

My Angel cousin crouched so we were at eye level, his icy blue eyes capturing my own and forcing me to see him and not the darkness crawling from the back of my mind.

"You are still trying to survive," Zuriel stated, not a hint of doubt leaking through his tone.

"But I'm not," I protested. "I have food, warmth, power, love... everything I should need to feel safe. But I don't."

Zuriel shook his head, his white hair falling from behind his pointed ears. "From the time you left the cave, you were on the run from your pursuers and toward a world you never truly knew. Then you came to the Iron Realm, and you lived in fear of Rares and King Azim and what they wanted to do to you until only a few days ago. That, sweet cousin, is still surviving, whether your basic needs are met or not."

The Angel blurred before me, and I blinked rapidly, trying to dispel the saltiness from my eyes. "How do I feel safe, Zuriel?" I asked, my voice no more than a whisper. Mistik dipped her head and dug it into my back, then rubbed it up and down as if she were trying to soothe me, too. I released a watery laugh.

"I told you once before that the only way out is through. You must feel it all to let it go. You must feel it and then replace it with something stronger, more powerful. I know Drazen has also told you that you must let go of your emotions while fighting and be fully present with what's in front of you. Until you can do both of those things, you'll never truly be free."

I buried my face in Mistik's mane again, unable to meet my cousin's intense gaze any longer. "It hurts so much. I can't feel it. It will consume me."

"Izidora, you are stronger than you know. Right now, the pain might seem endless, but I've lived for more than two thousand years. Trust me when I say that feelings are not forever."

Snow crunched beneath Zuriel's boots as he walked away, and when I opened my eyes, I saw him pulling a familiar-looking necklace from his jacket pocket. The amethyst on the long chain glinted in the sunlight, and without thought, I reached out for it.

"I found this in the training room after Ruslan moved you

both away from there after his altercation with King Azim. I think it's time you put it on again," Zuriel said quietly.

"There's more?" I asked, hope filling my chest with butterflies. Seeing my mother again with the Goddess and my father hadn't been enough, and I'd promise the Goddess I'd choose immediately if she'd let me embrace my parents one more time.

"No," he sighed, looking older than his millenia of life. "But with your level of distress, I thought you might find comfort in it."

I wrapped my palm around the stone, then tucked it away, not quite ready to delve back into my mother's memories. Silence stretched between us, only a light breeze lifting our hair and whispering in our ears.

Finally, Zuriel said, "Walk with me." Tucking his hands behind his back, he ambled forward, leisurely, and I followed, leaving the horses to stand in the snow. The world around us was still, and with the sun caressing my face, a modicum of peace settled over me.

We strolled for a few minutes before my cousin glanced my way. "I fought in the great war between the Angels and Demons. Nowhere in Keleti was safe by the time I was forced to join the fight. But in the years before that, it was hard to sleep at night. No one knew when the enforcers would come to conscript us, or if our city would be raided by the Demons. I was young then and thought I knew everything about the world, as all younglings do. It was decades, centuries maybe, before I realized that even though the war was over, the fear of it still lived inside me.

"Honestly, it was only after I lashed out at Ithuriel that he sat me down and had the same conversation with me that I am about to have with you. We both lost so many we loved during that war, and I was so wrapped up in my own pain that I forgot he suffered too. But he handled it much better than I did. I pretended everything was fine, went on living my life, burying myself in task after task, never giving myself time to think or to really *feel* what happened. Until I snapped after a small disagreement that should have been nothing."

Holy shit, Zuriel was describing exactly what was happening to me.

"That was when Ithuriel forced me to be still, to talk about what happened and how I felt about it. And not in the 'recite what happened to me' way that you did when we first met. But to truly open myself to the depths of my pain and process it in a way that made the memories less acute."

My throat thickened, and I tried to swallow down the emotions knotted there. "Did it help?"

My cousin nodded slowly. "It did, eventually. It was fucking hard at first, to feel it while I was speaking of it rather than detach myself from what had happened. But in order to heal, the full integration of mind, body, and soul is necessary."

I watched my breath fog the air in front of me as I exhaled long and slow. "Then I want to do it. Can you help me?"

"I can do my best. Ithuriel was gifted with a different mind magic than you or I that lent itself better to these types of situations, but his instructions still live on, even though he does not." Zuriel offered a sad smile as we spoke of my father, his uncle, who had been like a father to him.

"When can we start?" I asked. If this method could help me let go, figure out the right choice, and empower me, I did not want to wait.

"Do you feel comfortable doing it out here?" He gestured to the nearly barren landscape around us. There were no Fae in sight, and only the sounds of the horses and other farm animals reached our ears.

"Yes," I confirmed, striding to a few misshapen rocks large

enough to sit on and clearing them of snow. Zuriel joined me, settling himself cross-legged before taking a deep breath.

"First, we need to establish some rules. Number one is that I will not share anything you say to anyone unless you specifically ask me to. Number two is that you must tell me if you need to stop at any time."

"I will," I promised him.

"Good. You need a few grounding phrases, too. I know you already have a few that you prefer, so say them aloud for me now," he instructed.

Nodding, I said, "I am safe. I am an insidious bloom. I am strong. I am powerful. I will not be afraid."

"The first is what we shall work on today. Safety," he began, "is essential to healing. Until you feel safe in your skin, in your environment, in your relationships, nothing else will change, no matter how hard you work to change it."

"But I am safe, technically," I frowned.

"But your *body* does not feel safe. That is where the holistic integration comes in. In your mind, you know you are safe. But in your body, in your soul, do you truly feel safe?" he queried.

I opened my mouth to speak, but he cut me off with a shake of his head. "Tune into your body. Think of being in danger, and see where you feel it."

Nodding, I closed my eyes, scanning like I would to find my magic. I bypassed the well, instead thinking to myself 'I am not safe.' A flare of tension in my low belly immediately caught my attention, but the sensation did not stop there; it grew throughout my torso, wrapping my chest in a vice and tensing my neck and shoulders as if I were prepared to fight for my life. I sucked in a sharp breath.

"Good, Izidora," Zuriel murmured, "focus on the feeling. What comes to your mind first?"

Whips.

Chains.
Cold.
Fetid meat.
Blood.

"So much," I croaked, panic clawing its way up my throat.

"Cross your arms over your chest, resting a hand on each shoulder. Then tap one side, then the other," Zuriel said, and I did as he instructed. The tapping back and forth was rapid and desperate, and even more flashes of memory started to appear.

Tears overflowed freely, and I didn't bother trying to stop them, not when it felt like I had turned on a faucet and the pressure of the water departing me felt freeing in the strangest way.

"You can speak your memories out loud, or keep them to yourself, the choice is yours," Zuriel murmured. "Keep focusing on the feeling in your body, either way."

I managed to nod, then a vivid yet hidden memory burst unbidden from me. "I was young, so young... I had a caretaker, she was so kind and loving. And then one day, they dragged her away from me. The guards pinned me to the wall, locking the iron manacles I always wore around my wrists and ankles to heavy chains attached to the stone wall of my room. I-I heard them tell her I had become defiant in her care, and that they needed to break me now. She begged them for a second chance, and even over my own sobs, I heard them say no. Then there was a scream, and then nothing. They-they killed her."

The ache was so acute, like a knife was being plunged into my body and continually twisted, but I kept tapping, kept feeling, even as my breath came faster, shallower, and my tears carved a river down my cheeks.

"Keep breathing," Zuriel encouraged.

Dragging in a deep breath, I continued. "I was so scared. I felt so alone. The guards had mostly left me alone until that point, but she always acted as a buffer between them and me.

Without her... without her, they started to hurt me. That was the first day I was whipped. It was just one lash, but I was terrified. The chains–" the panicked sensation rose within me, and I had to breathe harder, tap faster, "the chains were shortened, and they ripped open my tunic. I screamed, I pleaded, I cried, but it was no use. I can still feel their fingers on me as they tore the shirt." A tightening sensation across my back had me biting my lip to stop from crying out. "The whip..." The lash felt as fresh as it had when it landed across my back for the first time. "That wasn't even the worst time. They only hit me once. But I still feel it so acutely."

"Keep the focus there, and keep tapping. Breathe," Zuriel said gently.

I did, allowing myself to *feel* every bit of the sting, the utter terror as I waited for the whip to fall, and the anguish that I no longer had the only person who loved and cared for me there to protect me. My muscles bunched and tensed as I relived the moment over and over and over; all the while, Zuriel encouraged me to suck down sharp, icy breaths. The air in my lungs was the only thing grounding me to the present moment as I confronted that fateful day.

"Now, we're going to rewrite that story. How is your younger self saved from this situation?" Zuriel prompted. "Visualize every last detail."

Without hesitation, I replied, "I'm there. The female I am now, not my younger self."

"Keep going," Zuriel encouraged.

"I throw myself in front of her, taking the strike so she doesn't have to. I catch the whip in my hand and yank the male forward. Then I burn him alive with my fire." The tapping continued, but with a vigor that shifted from despair into confidence. Suddenly, the terror that had tears spilling from my eyes morphed into something different, something not quite like absence of pain, but the pain of the memory was no longer like a hot knife slicing through me. "I run to her side, unlock her chains, and then we race away from there together. I fly her to safety, and we find a place to live where no one would ever hurt us again."

"And where is that?" Zuriel asked.

The name immediately popped into my head, nearly stealing my breath. It wasn't a place, but a person. "Somewhere far, far away," I said, since neither the Night Realm nor the Iron Realm felt like appropriate destinations.

"And what would you say to her once you had gotten her to safety?" Zuriel prodded, redirecting my thoughts.

"That we were free. That I would love her and take care of her. That I wouldn't let anyone hurt her ever again." My voice cracked, and a fresh waterfall spilled from my eyes.

That's all I'd ever wanted anyone to say to me.

And Kazimir had, when the Nighthounds rescued me. I believed him then, too. But it was a half-truth, and he'd broken my trust when I learned of it.

"Where are your thoughts now?" Zuriel asked, as if sensing my shift in focus.

"Kazimir," I gritted out, my arms tightening almost protectively over my chest.

"What about him?"

"I thought I was safe because he said those exact words to me when he rescued me. I guess I was safer than I had been, but when I came to the Iron Realm, I learned that wasn't necessarily true." My words held a hint of bitterness.

"In what way?" Zuriel asked, his head cocking slightly to one side.

I gritted my teeth as a fresh wave of anger rose from within, protecting the hurt that was still so raw. "I trusted him to tell me the truth after everything I had been through. After everything I told him. But he manipulated me. He told me I would be a better ruler than King Zalan, which I think is true, but he told me that to maneuver me for his own gain: being king himself and being with me. I can't excuse the half-truth of that, not when I let my guard down for him, not when I let him get close to me."

My vision blurred, and I clenched my teeth, anger at myself rising from somewhere unknown. "How could I have been so stupid, just blindly trusting the first people who showed me kindness after everything that I suffered? After everything I went through, all the abuse, how could I have been so foolish as to let all the lessons I'd learned about surviving disappear into nothing?" The tapping on my shoulders quickened as more self-loathing broke through the hurricane of emotion whipping through me. "How could I have been so blind to his intentions? How could I have trusted him? Any of them?"

"How could you have known any better?" Zuriel murmured, breaking my tirade.

"How could I have known anything?" The words broke out of my throat like shattering glass, nearly mirroring the sensation stabbing into my heart. Hot tears spilled down my cheeks, steaming in the cold air, and I sucked in a lungful of it, welcoming the burn it offered to soothe the tidal wave of pain that threatened to drown me. "Everything I thought I knew... Every *fucking* day I'm learning something new, that challenges what I used to think, what I used to think I *knew* with certainty. I feel *powerless* because of how much I don't know, and the understanding that there is so much I have to rely on others for. How can I know that anyone is telling me the truth about anything?"

My voice had risen to a fevered pitch, but Zuriel was as calm as ever as he sat motionless and listened to me. "What do you think your mother would say to that question?"

The amethyst in my pocket warmed, as if my mother were

with me then, encouraging me to surrender the pain and find my way out of the darkness. "I think she'd say that I need to trust myself more than anything," I whispered, and with those words, some of the ache abated. "I think she'd tell me to look for the intentions of the person I'm speaking with, and if I find them to be good, then I can trust them." Another statement that caught the breeze and swept away my inner turmoil. "I think she would tell me I am smart enough to figure things out for myself." The words spilled rapidly from my lips. "I think she'd tell me she loves me and that I have many people who can support me now, that I don't have to do it all on my own."

Zuriel.

Liliana.

Drazen.

The other Félvér.

And most of all, Ruslan.

My tapping slowed, then stopped, as I realized the emotions that had sunk their claws into me at the beginning of our session no longer clung to me. Blinking rapidly, my lips dipped into a frown, and then my brows followed. "What–" I patted myself as if I were searching for something that was no longer with me.

"How are you feeling, Izidora?" Zuriel asked, hiding a smile.

Lighter.

Breathing easier.

Unburdened.

Less fractured.

"Holy fuck," I whispered, my hurried movements ceasing. "Is this what it's supposed to feel like?"

Zuriel nodded slowly, and a choked sob rose from within as the realization settled over me. "It's like it was never there at all," I murmured, fresh tears coating my lashes and a wide smile breaking across my face. "It's like I was wearing a heavy jacket and suddenly I no longer need it. It's like this weight has been lifted from me, and I no longer need to carry it. Oh my Goddess, Zuriel, is this really possible? It's not just going to come back in an hour?"

"This is possible, Izidora. The more you continue to do it, the more you will feel settled and whole in your body," Zuriel noted. "Though, you will feel raw and more emotional while this work continues. The little things will continue to trigger you, and you might find it more difficult to rein in your emotions. It's especially important that you continue to focus on shielding from everyone else's emotions, so you don't get them confused with your own fresh ones."

I closed my eyes for a moment, sinking into the feeling of ease in my body that I'd never possessed before. It was as if the shattered pieces of me had been restored to their original pristineness, the crack never there to begin with. When my mind returned to that fateful day when my caretaker was dragged away from me, terror no longer speared its cold embrace into me; instead, I watched the scene unfold as if it were happening to someone else. My body did not react with the instinctual need to fight or to flee, but remained grounded in the present moment, the rock I sat on digging into my butt and the tip of my nose turning cold.

If this was possible after a single session over a single memory, what was possible with more?

"Thank you, Zuriel," I said, leaping forward and embracing my cousin.

"You are welcome, Izidora," he replied, returning the hug.

I was simultaneously giddy and exhausted when I pulled away. The Angel glanced overhead, then around us, where smoke billowed from chimneys and doors began creaking open. "I think it's about time that we return to Ryza Citadel. Do you need a few minutes to collect yourself?"

"No," I answered, then hopped down from the rock, my legs

protesting momentarily as the blood returned to them. I wiggled my toes in the fur-lined boots Ruslan had gifted me, savoring the warmth they provided, then trekked back to Mistik and Twilight, the snow crunching with every step and pulling a giggle from my chest. My mare snorted and then bumped me with her nose when I greeted her, in much better spirits than when I had left her before. Her eyes seemed to sparkle with the change in me, and she nuzzled into my jacket as I petted her dappled hide.

"Zuriel, I just can't believe it," I repeated when we mounted the horses and turned them toward the city.

An amused chuckle was his response. "It makes me happy to see that you are feeling better. I am glad I could help."

My throat thickened. "You have, so much."

This session hadn't fixed me by any means, but it had begun stripping away the barriers that prevented me from processing and healing from all the trauma. I would do whatever it took to have the freedom I so desperately craved, even if the path toward it was as painful as everything that had already happened. Steeled in my decision, I dried my eyes, lifted my chin, and returned to the citadel with my head held high.

13

LILIANA

My head pounded. Or was that the door? I groaned as I pushed myself upright. Nope, definitely both. "Endre, go get the door," I moaned as I flopped back against the pillows. The pounding sounded again. "Endre," I smacked his side of the bed, only to find it empty.

"Liliana, do you want to miss the spa day or not?"

Was Domi's voice always this shrill?

"Coming!" I shouted, then groaned as the sound sent shooting pain through my ears and into my shoulders. "Fuck me," I swore as I slid from the bed, my head fuzzy and mouth dry. I stumbled to the bathroom, yelping when the bright light hit my eyes. My head felt like I was being stabbed repeatedly. I gulped down water from the basin, my thirst nearly unquenchable, then took in my appearance. My hair and makeup were a mess, lip stain smeared across my cheek, black circling my eyes. I washed my face quickly in the sink, removing all trace of color, then combed my fingers through the mess of waves that clumped together. I found a loose tunic and leggings on the floor of the bathroom and yanked them on quickly as another knock sounded on the bedroom door. My jacket rested near the foot of the bed, and I grabbed that too, shrugging it on and fastening it quickly.

"Almost ready!" I called as I burst into the room, bringing the sun with me. There was no sign of the males, and my fuzzy brain reminded me that they'd gone out for a hunt this morning.

"You were out late again last night," Domi observed as she led us from the apartment and out into the hallway.

"Yeah, we went out with Slavian and Anton again."

Domi snorted, "That much is obvious. You reek of them and–" she sniffed the air around me, "herbs?"

"Don't judge, Domi, these were the best I'd ever done. You and Kaztar should come another night. But fair warning, their club is very, very indecent. But *so* much fun," I drawled.

"Alright, tell us all about it when we get to the spa. Right now, we are running late."

"Sorry about that. By the way, what time is it?" The halls weren't overly busy, nor were they overly empty, and I honestly struggled to know which way was up or down as my head swam with another sharp turn.

"Mid-afternoon, almost two. We are supposed to meet Queen Immonen and Izidora in the courtyard so we can all ride together. Queen Viktoria is not feeling well, so she won't be joining us." We rounded a corner and found Immonen waiting for us in the hallway outside the Crystal Realm's apartment.

She pressed her lips together, suppressing a smile when she saw my appearance. "Another long night?"

"There were plenty of long parts about it," I said suggestively, and the females burst into laughter as we fell in line and strolled toward the citadel's courtyard. I liked both of them immensely, and we'd bonded during our time together as the only females in our traveling party. We trained together, laughed together, gossiped together, and I fervently hoped that Izidora would slot perfectly into our little group.

I winced as we entered the afternoon sun, finding a carriage waiting for us. Izidora stood in front of it, petting the horses' noses while Ruslan casually watched her and then us as we approached. The hairs on the back of my neck rose as I fell under his gaze, his whole being reminding me of a predator that enjoyed playing with its food before going for the kill. I could not deny how damn sexy he was, though. He was huge, muscles rippling beneath his thick, albeit skin-tight clothing. Tattoos peeked from every opening in his jacket, and his eyes were mesmerizing. Truth be told, I would have spread my legs for him too, if only to have one taste.

"Queen Immonen, Ladies, I have set you up at the Iron Mountain Spa for the afternoon. Pick whichever treatments you'd like – on me," Ruslan smiled at us, his demeanor more relaxed than I'd seen before.

Immonen dipped her head to him. "Thank you, King Ruslan, that is most generous. We promise to have lots of wine and pampering."

Ruslan held out his hand to Izidora, who eagerly rejoined him. He swooped her in for a long kiss, then rested his forehead against hers. "I'll miss you, my sprite," he breathed. For a moment, I saw the love he had for her, his words ringing sincere and true in my ears. He softened with her in his arms, even holding her hand until the last possible moment as she climbed into the carriage. With a parting glance in his direction, I followed her inside the warm and cozy space, Domi and Immonen behind me. Once the four of us settled, the carriage pulled away and we descended into Radence.

Izidora watched Ruslan disappear from view, then turned her attention to the rest of us. She looked me up and down for a moment, then asked, "Why do you look so awful?"

I scoffed. "It's nice to see you too."

"She didn't come in until nearly dawn this morning – again," Domi tsked.

Tattletale.

"Apparently it was a long night," Immonen said suggestively.

"Another trip to Steel? Do tell, Liliana." Izidora turned to me, waiting for me to spill all my secrets.

"Later, I promise. It is a tale that cannot be interrupted. Where is the Iron Mountain Spa anyway?" I fanned myself, trying to quell the nausea rising from my belly as we hit a bump in the road.

"It's on the far side of Radence, close to the mountains, I think," she responded.

"You haven't been there yet? How rude of King Ruslan to not treat you. But don't worry, we'll make up for it today," Immonen laughed.

A hint of a smile spread on Izidora's lips as she suppressed a snicker. "He treated me to a massage himself."

"I hope he was naked when it took place," I sighed. Ruslan was *very* easy on the eyes, more so than any of the Nighthounds, in my opinion. Izidora seemed genuinely happy with Ruslan, and the way he looked at her before we entered the carriage told me he felt the same. Izidora was my best friend, and all I wanted was for her to receive the love she deserved. Kazimir, in my opinion, wasn't capable of giving her that any longer. He had changed since the night he lost Izidora and his father, and at the rate he devolved, I worried for his sanity. He was not the stable friend of my brother's he used to be.

"Very, very naked. It was hard to relax." Izidora burst into laughter, and we all fell into it with her. We drifted into a light-hearted conversation as we rolled through Radence, the Agrenak Mountains growing closer and closer.

I was the first to hop out when we rolled to a stop in front of a long, gray stone building with large windows that revealed a serene interior. The entrance doors opened from the inside, and a female with a tight updo greeted us warmly.

"Welcome, Your Highnesses, we are so pleased to host you today. We've cleared the schedule so you have the whole spa to yourselves for as long as you'd like it. Come, let me show you inside."

A lightly scented breeze wafted in our faces as we entered the airy space. The click of our guide's heels on the polished stone floor was the only sound other than bubbling water, the silence peaceful instead of unnerving. We descended a wide staircase and turned right into a long hallway where the humidity rose with each step we took. Finally, we arrived at a large grotto where natural hot water bubbled from the earth and filled a deep soaking pool. The shallower end held four beds piled with linens, and close to us, lounge chairs and a table laden with wine, fruit, and cheese beckoned us to relax and unwind.

Our hostess poured a glass of sparkling white wine for each of us, handing them out in turn. The glasses already fogged and sweated in the humidity of the underground cave. "Robes are laid on the chaises for each of you, though feel free to dress to your comfort level. We'll be back in an hour after you've had time to soak and decide on treatments. Ring the bell if you need anything before then." She curtsied to us, then quietly closed the door behind her.

"To us!" Immonen cheered, clinking her glass against all of ours before taking a sip of the bubbles.

"To us!" we replied in unison.

The wine was perfectly chilled as it slid over my tongue. The alcohol beat back my hangover, and I nearly sighed with relief, deciding to down the rest of the glass. I smacked my lips when I finished, savoring the fruity taste left over there.

Setting the glass aside, I lifted one of the fluffy robes, rubbing the fabric against my face. The softness of it was much more inviting than my stiff leather clothing, especially as the humidity caused little flyaway hairs to cling to my face. Stripping quickly, I tossed my discarded clothes on a chair, then slipped the robe over my shoulders and tied it at my waist.

Domi floated a green bottle of wine in our direction using the silvery tendrils of her magic, picking up our discarded glasses along the way, and we each accepted the empty glass that hovered in front of us. She maintained her magic as she uncorked the bottle, then used it to pour a hefty measure of the bubbly liquid for each of us.

"Show-off," I teased her, and she winked at me before her magic disappeared.

The four glasses clinked and we sipped from them, savoring the fine wine. My brain immediately thanked me as more alcohol hit my stomach, relieving at least some of the headache and malaise still clinging to me. When my stomach growled moments later, I snickered, then grabbed a plate and piled it with cheese, fruit, and bread before settling on a lounger and picking up a handwritten menu of treatments.

Domi and Immonen carefully removed their jewelry, placing it strategically on an empty table far away from the water, then stripped out of their clothes, entering the pool fully nude, glasses in hand. Izidora looked between them and me, chewing her lip as if she were trying to decide what to do.

"Get naked and grab a robe!" I called, realizing that this was her first experience like this, and I'd left her clueless as to how to proceed.

With a giggle, she stripped, threw on a robe, and joined me for a quick snack.

"Sorry, I'm not sure how all of this works," she admitted, her gaze downcast as she picked at her food.

"Hey, no need to apologize. We've been apart for so long I've forgotten that you didn't grow up with things like this," I reassured her. "We'll hang out here for a bit, maybe soak in the water, and then when we're ready for massages, we'll just ring the bell and let them know. Today is all about us and relaxing."

"Thank you," she breathed, her shoulders dropping away from her ears. "But first, I need advice, Liliana, now that we're away from all the tension and noise at Ryza. I'm so lost and confused."

I glanced toward the deep end of the grotto where Immonen and Domi were chatting and sipping their drinks. "Whatever you're going to say needs to stay between us. I love Immonen and Domi, but with everything going on, it's best that we only trust each other with this, okay?"

Izidora nodded and swiped a juicy berry from my plate, and I made a noise of protest before shrugging and downing more wine.

"I am half Angel," she began, chewing slowly.

"I know." I put my hand on her arm, reassuring her that her heritage did not bother me.

She swallowed the rest of the fruit, then sighed. "Okay, then I can skip ahead. There is another Angel at the Iron Realm, Zuriel, who was present the day the Goddess's Prophecy was spoken over a millennia ago. You saw him at the archery competition. We're related. His uncle was my mother's mate – my real father. But he told me when the original prophecy was spoken, it was delivered in an old language. In our modern tongue, the meaning was misinterpreted. It called for two mates, which is why I have to choose."

I sipped from my wine, needing it to steady me. "Go on," I encouraged.

"Honestly, I didn't know what to think, until Zuriel gave me a necklace enchanted with my mother's memories. When I put it on–" she paused, looking to the ceiling as her throat worked. I stroked her arm soothingly. That must have been life-changing for her, to hear from the mother she never knew. "When I put it on, I fell into moments of her with both Ithuriel and Zalan. King Zalan was so awful to her. And I felt what she felt for Ithuriel. At the end, she told me what a male should be and what a male should not be.

"I told Ruslan I needed time to decide. I wanted to see Kazimir again, to see which of the two was the better male. Because the fate of our world rests on who I pick, and the burden is so heavy." She took a drink, steadying herself. "But when Kazimir rode up to the citadel, I sensed he was different. He was not the male I left. He was," she paused as if she were searching for the right word, "sinister, almost reminding me of the guards in the cave."

Another sip as she recalled the horrific memories she carried.

"In the receiving line, he was so unnecessarily cruel. And then he called Ruslan a rapist and stabbed him. The Kazimir I knew would never have acted that way. But when we went out on our date and he returned Mistik to me, the old Kazimir broke through, and it sparked this tiny hope in me, despite the obvious warning signs."

I rubbed circles on her back as tears welled in her eyes. She dipped her chin, and with a shuddering breath, continued. "I am also an empath, so I feel *everything*. So deeply. A few nights ago, I slept and dreamed of them – my mother, my father, and the Goddess. I got to embrace them–" A sob wracked her petite frame, and I pulled her into my arms. My best friend had been through so much, all on her own, and my heart hurt for her.

She pulled away when she was ready to speak again. "You don't know Ruslan very well, but I do. We understand each other in a way that no one else can. He grew up parentless, just like me. He did what he had to do to survive, just like me. He struggles with his emotions, just like me. And that understanding means everything. He is afraid of being abandoned, just like me. He has his darkness, yes, but he follows my light. Our pain dances together and creates something beautiful. I want to choose him, but with the weight of the decision... I don't know. I guess I am fearful of making the wrong choice."

Izidora's voice broke, and then she shattered, tears flowing faster and harder than the small waterfall at the back of the grotto. I clutched her tighter to me, and her hands fisted my robe, clinging to me like she needed someone to save her from the demons that plagued her mind and the impossible decision that lay before her. My eyes burned, and not from the scented steam of the mountain's water. Guilt also settled in my belly, as I knew information that would help her make this choice, but would imparting it sway her in the wrong direction?

That was the thing about prophecies: they were all so vague and open to interpretation. And if I were the one who forced Izidora on the wrong path, what kind of friend would I be? Her burdens were already so much, I couldn't add to them.

So I sat in solidarity with Izidora, allowing her the space she needed to feel and process without pressing my opinions on her. Because the last thing she needed at that moment was to feel pressured by me to choose one way or another. How was anyone supposed to know what was light and what was dark until after the fact? Everything in this life existed on a spectrum of gray, and even then, how could anyone be certain of the shade unless it was held up against another?

"Izidora, you are so incredibly strong to go through all of this on your own. And you have empath magic – such a rare gift. You are the perfect person to wield it," I murmured after a few moments.

"I only want to do what is best for everyone around me. I

don't want to plunge the world into chaos because I'm being selfish in my decision," she sniffed, lifting her head from my chest and revealing her watery, red-rimmed eyes.

"Well, someone has to take care of you, and it sounds to me like you could use a friend no matter what. You will always have that person in me, Izidora, no matter who you choose." I smiled at her through my own blurred vision.

She threw her arms around my neck and sobbed. "I thought you wouldn't want to be friends anymore after I told you I thought Ruslan was the right choice."

"Females first, always." I meant every word, and I hugged her back. "You are my friend, my best friend, and no male will ever change that."

"Thank you." Her laugh was hoarse and thick. "If Kazimir had someone else, I wouldn't feel so bad. Honestly, it would make this choice easier."

I pressed my lips together, debating revealing what he had been up to during each night since we'd arrived in the Iron Realm. Finally, I sighed. "He's been going to Steel too, and participating."

She nodded. "Well, I have been fucking Ruslan, so it's not like I should expect him to stay celibate."

I offered her another firm squeeze. "It's okay if you feel hurt by his actions."

She paused for a moment, the corners of her mouth momentarily dipping into a frown. "That's the thing, I don't. If I end up choosing him, we'll be on equal standing, having both been with others since we parted. If I don't choose him, there's hope that he can move on with his life." She swiped at her eyes with the backs of her hands, shaking her head and clearing it. "Thank you for listening."

"It sounds like you needed to talk. I missed you so much," I whispered to my friend. My hand rested on her shoulder and I gave it a light squeeze.

"Goddess, I did," she sighed, shoulders slumping inward. "No matter what happens, will you promise to stay with me?" Her eyes pleaded with me to say yes.

"Absolutely. I can give males hell from anywhere on this continent," I laughed, looping my arm through hers and then touching my temple to her shoulder. After a moment, I rose, pulling off the white robe and tossing it to the side, Izidora following my actions. We joined Domi and Immonen in the water, and I groaned as the heat enveloped me and chased away the chill of the Iron Realm. I brought along a menu to read from while the steam soaked into my every pore. I pointed out and explained the different options to Izidora while we sat, and eventually, Immonen insisted we get one of each type of treatment so Izidora could try them all. Once our decisions were made, Immonen rang the bell, and not a minute later, the female attendant reappeared. We relayed our choices, and she promised to return momentarily with supplies and body therapists to treat us.

"Okay, Liliana, you have to tell us what happened last night. I need a lighthearted topic," Domi chuckled as we each settled on the tables in the water.

"It's not quite a lighthearted topic so much as a long-dicked topic," I sniggered, flipping onto my front as the female rubbing mud all over me worked her way down my back.

"I simply must hear this story," she insisted, and we shared a laugh as I launched into the tale of Steel and the wildness of the previous nights. Many gasps and flushed faces filled the underground grotto as we were pampered, each passing moment pushing me into a deeper relaxation. Izidora, too, finally relaxed, and that was the happiest moment of them all.

14

BÉKE DAY FOUR

The whip cut through the air, and my eyes slammed shut, then burst open as pain split my back, tearing a cry from my lips. All I saw was darkness, and as my nails scratched at the rough rock under them for something, anything, to hold on to, a flash caught my attention. Lightning rent the air, crackling in every direction and casting a flash of brightness over the world around me. I caught sight of my reflection in a mirror perched so close I could touch it. With a trembling hand, I reached for it, and the moment my fingers made contact with the cool surface, I was plunged into darkness once more. A heartbeat later, the whip sang again, followed by a cry of pain as my back bowed. Lightning flashed, and this time, I was ready to face my assailant. But the mirror offered nothing other than my tear-streaked face. I grasped at it helplessly, watching myself fade away as inky blackness blotted out the world once more. I knew what came next, and in a panicked rush, I leaped forward, trying to shatter the mirror with my head and arm myself with its shards. But the reflective surface did not crack; instead, I was falling, falling, falling, *until I was afraid not of the lashes across my back but the impact that came with hitting the ground at full speed. "No!" I cried out—*

The echo of my nightmare rang in my ears as I bolted upright, grasping for something to hold onto, to stop me from plummeting to my death. My chest heaved as I blinked, the bedroom at Ryza Citadel coming into focus around me. Soft light spilled beneath the heavy black curtains pulled across the wide windows, and a moment later, Ruslan burst through the door, a wild look in his eyes.

"Izidora, are you alright?" he asked, rushing to my side, his eyes raking across my naked, heaving chest and the sheets pooled at my waist, not with hunger, but with worry.

My teeth sank into my bottom lip, and I nodded, blowing out what little breath I had. Ruslan clearly did not believe me, because he crawled into bed behind me and pulled me flush against him. His arms caged my torso, and his legs tucked against mine until there was no possible way for us to be more connected. "Nightmare?"

"Yeah," I half-whispered, half-sobbed. "The whips..."

Ruslan's arms dropped from my chest, instead coming to rest on my tense shoulders. Light circles of his thumbs there helped ease some of the lingering tension from my dream, and I leaned my head back, resting it against the steady rise and fall of his chest.

"How do you cope with them? You never wake me up screaming like I do to you," I murmured, letting my eyes close again.

"Mine aren't as bad as yours, not anymore at least." He paused his strokes, then gingerly directed me to lie on my stomach in front of him. I followed his direction, turning my head to the side so I could see him as he began a slow massage of my legs. "It took years for them to come less frequently. Now I mostly have them when I am stressed." He frowned, then shook his head and continued up toward my ass. "That's what woke me up this morning. I tried not to disturb you. You were worn out last night, and I wanted you to rest."

"Zuriel said that I might feel more emotionally raw and drained after what we did yesterday," I sighed, nearly groaning as Ruslan dug into a particularly tough knot in my lower back. Despite the hour spent soaking in the grotto, mud wrap, and massage the previous day, I still couldn't relax and let go of the tension lining every fiber of my being.

"But it helped?" he questioned, all serious as he took care of me.

I nodded, my cheek brushing against the soft blanket covering the bed. "It was incredible, feeling the terror just... melt away. I didn't know how much it weighed me down until it was gone."

Ruslan reached my upper back, and this time, I did moan at how amazing his fingers felt digging into the muscles there. "I have something for you," he started, trailing off as he focused on my shoulder.

"Do you?" I asked, my voice tilting lighter.

"Something that will make you feel safe, strong, and power-ful," he promised, finishing his ministrations and shuffling us around. The bed dipped, then sighed in relief as his massive frame strode away from it and back into the living space. I pushed myself to a sitting position, then slid off the bed and pulled on a large tunic that belonged to Ruslan, the fabric kissing my mid-thigh. One sleeve was rolled halfway up my forearm when he returned, holding several velvet cases that reminded me of the one that contained Liliana's bow.

He tsked when he noticed my attire. "As much as I love to see you drowning in me, sprite, I need you to put on something that actually fits you. Dress like you would to spar."

I quirked a brow in his direction, but did as he bid, rifling through a few drawers and pulling on my favorite leather pants and a tight-fitting tunic that I wore beneath my training gear. "There," I said, presenting myself with a sweep of my hands.

Ruslan placed the velvet boxes on the bed, then moved to open the largest one. Two snaps flipped open, and then the lid lifted of its own accord, revealing armor the color of the sides of the Agrenak Mountains when they weren't covered in snow. My eyes widened as I took an involuntary step forward, drawn in by the exquisite craftsmanship. The metal was not thick and heavy like many of the Félvér wore, but rather made of tiny, overlapping pieces that reminded me of the hint of black scales that dusted Ruslan's torso when he shifted into his Dragon form.

"I had these pieces made especially for you. The metal will protect you more than the traditional leather armor of the Night Realm, but it is just as light. No arrow will be able to pierce the metal, and it would take a significant strike to break the scales apart," Ruslan explained, lifting the piece away from the cushioned interior and holding it out to me. "Arms up," he ordered, and I lifted them overhead, allowing him to settle the new armor over me.

It spilled across my torso like silk, hugging my curves without being restrictive. When my arms dropped to my sides, I found that the metal moved and flexed with me, not inhibiting my dexterity in the slightest. "What about my wings?" I questioned, glancing over my shoulder in hopes of seeing holes in the back.

"Magically enhanced to allow them to burst through," Ruslan smirked, eyes glittering as he drank in my form. "Unfortunately, I can't do anything to protect them against attack, so you'll have to pay attention to them. I know you are more than capable of doing that, but I will always be watching them too. "

I nodded, then tapped into the crystal wrapped in white flame and moonlight in my chest, bringing the white, feathery wings into existence. My muscles didn't even protest as they settled behind me, and I strode to the full-length mirror, fluffing them proudly as I admired my new armor. The tips of the largest feathers arced toward the ceiling above us, and the light that filtered through the windows caught and reflected off their diamond-like surface. Then the light caught on the new chest plate, and I took a step closer, squinting at the small pieces of metal hammered together. "Are those roses?" I asked, my mouth falling open in awe.

"For my insidious bloom," Ruslan hummed, coming to stand behind me. Warmth filled my chest from the certainty that everything he'd done for me was to help me blossom into the strong, powerful female I was becoming.

Ruslan reached around my waist, finding leather straps along my hips and pulling them taught before tying them and tucking them away. I turned to the side, still absorbed in the fine details of the metalwork, causing him to duck out of the way of my wings. He chuckled and strode to the bed, where more unopened cases sat.

"There's more," he said, and I waited patiently for him to produce the next surprise.

When he returned to the mirror, he held up a pair of etched metal wrist covers, with long-stemmed roses displaying deadly thorns running up the middle. A smile spread across my face as I held out my arms and allowed him to secure them in place. "These are incredible," I enthused, turning my arms over and admiring them from every angle.

"I selfishly bought these for you so that I knew you'd be safe, but I think after the past few days, you need that too," he murmured, planting a kiss on my neck before backing away. Tears pricked my eyes, and I drew a long breath, holding it for a moment before blowing it out again.

"I do."

When he returned this time, he held armor for my legs, the top half similar to the interlocking roses that covered my torso, while the bottom mirrored the engraved metal with long-stemmed thorny roses on either side of my calves. Ruslan knelt before me, securing the bottom first, then lacing up the tops at the back of my thighs and securing them using the strings he'd tucked away earlier.

I smoothed back his dark hair, running my nails along his scalp and eliciting a groan. His eyes were hungry when he rose, towering over me. "There is one other piece to complete the ensemble," he purred, tucking a wayward lock of hair behind my ear. "Well, technically two."

The last velvet case remained unopened as he brought it to me, and I reached out a tentative hand, flicking one lock, then the other, and opening the maw of the box. My jaw nearly hit the floor when I beheld what was inside. A cushion nestled twin swords of dark iron-gray metal, short enough for me to wield both simultaneously. It wasn't the swords that caught my eye, but the glittering round garnets set into each hilt. Their color was a deep red, rich enough to be freshly sown blood, and around them was a ring of tiny obsidian stones, circling the massive gems in a protective embrace. I lifted one, then the other, from the box, finding them surprisingly light. When the sun caught the blades, I noticed the roses inlaid in a silver metal there, nearly invisible until the light caught it. I grinned at the meaning. No one would see them until my blade already arced for their neck.

Ruslan's thoughtfulness melted my heart, and as I returned my attention to him, I couldn't help the love that spilled from deep within me. "Thank you," I managed to whisper, momentarily overcome.

"The High Priestess will tell you that the garnet surrounded by obsidian will protect you in battle and help you channel your emotions in a manageable way," he said with a shrug. He stepped toward me, careful to dodge the blades that slowly dropped to my sides. His fingers twisted in my hair, supporting my head as he tilted it up at him. "Believe what you want, but I won't take any chances with your safety, whether you choose me or not. And you deserve to feel safe, Izidora. I hope this armor can give you a semblance of that while you continue to heal."

My throat thickened, and a lone tear tracked down my cheek. Ruslan's rough thumb swiped it away before it reached my chin. "I love you," I said around the thickness in my throat.

"And I love you, sprite," he murmured, dropping his lips to mine and capturing them in a searing kiss – one that spoke of just how much he cared, how much he wanted me to be safe, and how much he wanted *me* to be the one to give that safety to myself.

"Wear this to the competition today," he requested when he finally released me. "And wield those swords with all the fierceness I know you possess."

The smile I flashed at him was both feral and saccharine. "They won't see my thorns until it's too late."

"That's my sprite," Ruslan purred, hands roaming shamelessly over my body before he pulled me into him again and kissed me roughly.

Laughing, I broke away and carefully tossed my new swords onto the bed so my hands were free to roam his body as well.

"As much as I would love to stay with you and strip you out of this armor I so painstakingly secured you into, I have some matters to attend to," Ruslan groaned, resting his forehead against mine.

I chewed my lip, causing his eyes to darken. A hand slipped between us as he tugged it free. "Later," he promised, the raspiness of his voice heating my low belly. With a sigh of protest, I relaxed my grip on his tunic and he stepped away, quickly dressing himself in more formal attire to leave our apartment at Ryza Citadel.

"I suppose I can go find Liliana," I said, my voice lilting up as if that wasn't the only other plan I had for the day. I had missed my friend so much, and after she'd sworn to stick by my side the previous day, I wanted to waste no more time catching up.

"You should. But don't get into too much trouble. I've heard now just how wild she can be," Ruslan teased, and I grinned back at him.

"No promises," I sang, untying the armor and arranging it carefully across the bed.

"Think you can put it on by yourself later?" Ruslan asked, slipping the Iron Crown over his brow, the final piece of his kingly attire in place.

"I believe in myself," I laughed, then tugged on a warm fur jacket over my tunic, preparing to depart with him.

We walked hand in hand out the door and down the spiral staircase, only parting when Ruslan had to go right toward his office and I needed to go left to the dining hall where breakfast was underway.

"I'll see you later, sprite," he murmured, planting a kiss on my forehead and then striding away. I was so focused on the thoughtful male who only wanted to see me safe that I didn't hear my friend approach.

"You know I hate you just a little bit for how sweet he is to you," Liliana joked, and I startled, throwing up a shield of white magic around myself on instinct.

"Oh my Goddess, you scared me," I gasped, spinning to face her, clutching my chest and sucking down a breath. My magic dissipated like smoke in the wind, revealing my friend.

"Sorry," she said, looking sheepish. "Didn't want to disturb your moment." She flicked her chocolate brown hair over her shoulder, then looped her arm through mine. "Now, what are we going to do until the sword competition?"

I laughed, glancing down the hall one last time, then said loud enough for Ruslan's keen Dragon hearing to pick up, "Cause trouble."

15

RUSLAN

Béke Day Four

"Rares." My tone was clipped as the old Mage hobbled into my study. The male responsible for the creation of the Félvér settled into a high-backed chair across from me with a piercing glare. The two of us held no affection for each other, and Rares was especially dangerous for me since I'd shut down his breeding program and his experiments to please Izidora. Her distaste for it matched my own, but it gave me the perfect excuse to do something I'd wanted for a long time, something that had not been possible while my father was king. Which was why this conversation needed to happen. Rares's oath may have been to the Iron Crown, but that did not mean he was loyal to me.

He tapped a gnarled finger on the wooden arm of the chair, waiting to hear the reason I'd called him to my study. A smirk played across my lips as I leaned back in my plush chair, kicking my boots up on the polished mahogany desk that once belonged to my father and sipping from a glass of amber liquor. "I need you to swear another oath."

The wizened Mage snorted. "Absolutely not."

Tipping the last of the whisky into my mouth, I dropped my feet to the floor, leaning my elbows on the desk as I scowled at the male who had been directly involved in my parentage. "If you do not willingly comply, I will be forced to compel you."

"The only way you can compel me to do anything is if your life is on the line. And even then, I'd fight the compulsion rather than save your life, Ruslan," he hissed.

I raised a sharp brow. "Do you think I am above taking myself to the brink of death to force you to surrender? After all, you've taken me there so many times already, death is almost like an old friend."

Flashes of Rares's torture from my childhood surfaced, haunting me with twinges of mental and physical pain. I cracked my neck from side to side, banishing those images as I waited for the Mage to respond. "That was not a rhetorical question, Rares."

"No, I do not think you are above it," he gritted out through yellowed teeth, his fingers curling like knobby tree limbs.

"Good. Then you know where we stand. You will swear an oath to me, right now, to never harm Izidora and to protect her life with yours, as you do mine."

Rares's lips pressed together as if he were trying to hide a sliver of amusement. "So she accepted your mate bond then?"

Heat billowed across my body, and I was on my feet in an instant, glass shattering under my fist. "She does not need to accept the mate bond to receive that kind of protection."

"And if she chooses Kazimir? You won't go to war to fight for her?" Rares scoffed, leaning back in his chair and crossing his arms.

I threw my head back and released a manic laugh into the space, the wildness in the tone filling the air with a crackling energy. "She will not choose him, Rares, and not because of that enchanted ring I had you make. She will choose me because I am the right choice. But if we go to war, it will be Kazimir's fault."

The Mage's wrinkled face lost all signs of amusement at my abrupt change in mood. "So you didn't give it to her then."

"No. And now that I know you can make such an object, I want to prevent you from using that power on anyone else. So you will swear this oath to me, right now, or I will force you to, and you won't like the consequences after I am brought back from the brink of death."

Rares's lips and knuckles were white from his restrained fury, and with a string of curses, he pushed to his feet, using the desk to brace himself as he kneeled before me.

"Repeat after me, Rares," I commanded, then spoke his oath not to harm Izidora and to protect her with his life, adding in a clause about using enchanted jewelry at the sole discretion of the ruler of the Iron Realm. Once he finished his oath, the tendril of magic that stretched between us snapped and thickened with his new directives. Then, I dismissed him. "You may go, Rares. See to it that the entertainment portion of Béke is handled."

The "fuck you" he muttered under his breath on his way out the door was audible to my Dragon senses, but I let it slide when I noticed Drazen perched on the threshold of the door. "What is it, Drazen?"

The male sauntered in with a dark smile, resting his armored forearms on the back of the chair Rares had just occupied. "I got the last one."

Fuck, yes.

Drazen had been searching for every male who'd had a shift in the cave where Izidora had been chained since the moment we returned to the Iron Realm, slowly gathering them for me to carve up and kill as vengeance for my mate. I wanted it to be a group execution, so each male watched his comrades die slowly around him, heightening the delicious scent of fear when each knew his end was near. Their pleas for mercy would be my music as I peeled the flesh from their skin and watched the life fade from their eyes.

It would be my greatest gift to Izidora yet.

"Have you taken them all to Vasvain?" I asked, leaning back in my chair and drumming my fingers together.

Drazen shook his head. "Not yet. They all remain in the dungeon. With Béke going on, I didn't want to risk moving them without your permission."

I weighed my options. With Drazen and me participating in each competition, we couldn't move them while everyone was preoccupied. And since only the two of us knew of this plan, I couldn't ask anyone else to do it. We'd have to wait until the dead of night to move them to the cave where Izidora had been chained. It would be poetic that we'd slaughter them there like the pigs they were. "Tonight, we'll take them there," I concluded, "and keep them alive enough for the next few days – I want to kill them myself."

"As you command," he said, pushing off the chair. "Are you almost ready for the swords competition?"

I rose from my chair, cracking my knuckles as I strode toward Drazen. "We can go together. Izidora is off with Liliana somewhere, and I know she won't miss this competition, not after how hard she's been training."

Thankfully, my magic was brimming, and muttering the spell that moved us through time and space to a hidden spot near the competition arena was effortless. Drazen and I emerged from the nondescript building to an overcast day that threatened to douse the Iron Realm in snow. Already, the seating was packed, and the singular range that had been erected for the archery competition had been broken down into three separate sparring rings in preparation for the swordsmanship competition. Unlike the archery competition, there were classes based on sex and size, and each had its own bracket.

The stage waited for me, and as I ascended the stairs, I surveyed the competition sprawling before me, spotting Izidora, Liliana, and Queen Immonen strapping into armor off to one side. Izidora's armor gleamed despite the lack of sun, the lightweight metal fitting her like a glove. Her eyes shone like gemstones when I'd presented them to her that morning, and the memory of her unfiltered joy eased the ache of her absence from my chest.

I could never get enough of her.

Taking my seat, I turned to Queen Viktoria, the only monarch not participating in the events. "Queen Viktoria, you look lovely today."

My compliment was not insincere; the queen's beauty was striking, her dark skin stretched over high cheekbones and sharp eyes that missed nothing. Even bundled in furs, she did not lose her vibrant style, and the orange headdress she wore today was like a beacon among all the gray.

"King Ruslan," she trilled, "you flatter me."

"Not at all, Your Highness. If the babe is a girl, I hope she takes after you."

The queen threw her head back and laughed. "I do too. Can you imagine what Geza would look like as a female?"

King Consort Geza had stepped into the first ring with Savich, and as they squared up, I tried to imagine the muscled Day Fae as a female. "I cannot," I admitted with a wry grin. "If she does end up looking like him, it might be best to secure a marriage contract for her while she is still a child."

Queen Viktoria smacked my arm as she cackled with amusement. "Are you trying to tell me something, King Ruslan?"

"My mate is not pregnant, Queen Viktoria. That I can assure

you. In fact," I dropped my voice and dipped my head toward her, "Izidora had never had contraception until she arrived in the Iron Realm. I was shocked to learn that Kazimir had not offered it to her despite their intimacy."

The queen of the Day Realm sucked in a breath and shook her head. "After everything that poor child has been through..."

Despite Izidora's wise soul, she was, in fact, barely an adult – something I frequently forgot as I interacted with her. To me, it felt as if we'd been together for years instead of months, and she was as familiar to me as my own reflection. She'd always been part of me, and I'd always been part of her, and we would continue to be, even beyond this lifetime.

"And now she must make a nearly impossible choice between the two of us, with the course of history depending on the path she chooses. Obviously, I want her to choose me. She is my soul, my fire, my reason for breathing. But if she were to choose Kazimir, I would have to let her go for the sake of the world. I only wonder if he would do the same."

Planting the seeds of doubt in Queen Viktoria's mind seemed to be working, for she hummed her agreement. But the way she pressed her lips together told me she knew more than she let on. Clashing steel drew our attention, and I whipped my head to the three sparring rings, where King Consort Geza and Savich fought fiercely, their blades locked between their chests. But Savich was slow in his metal armor, and the king of the Day Realm shoved him off and circled away, swinging a heavy blade toward Savich's abdomen. The tip of the blade grazed against the Félvér's armor, earning the Day Fae five points.

The timer had yet to run out on the round, and I trailed my gaze across the two other rings. A pair of Iron Fae I did not know battled in the center while High Lady Domi fought a Félvér female at the other end. The females' bout ended before all the sand fell to the bottom of the glass, the Félvér catching the Night

Fae female off guard and sending her to her back. King Consort Geza bested Savich a moment before the sand ran out, while the pair in the middle had to be judged on points.

"Your husband is an incredible fighter," I commented to Queen Viktoria as Geza's hand was raised in the center of the ring, and he clapped arms with Savich before they both exited.

"Why do you think I married him?" A smile tugged at the corner of her mouth, but her eyes never left him.

"Fair enough," I replied, leaning forward on my elbows as Izidora stepped into the ring with Queen Immonen. The queen of the Crystal Realm was waif-like and tall, and she held a thin rapier that extended her reach. Izidora boasted the two short swords I had gifted her, their hilts inlaid with garnets and obsidian. The flash of silver roses carved into the blades caught my attention, and an impish grin spread across my face.

My insidious bloom.

Izidora did not call white flame to her blades, and for once, I was grateful. Her power was unique, and I did not want her to become a target, not with so many unknowns and eyes on her at the moment. The other two rings were forgotten as the sand was turned, signaling the start to the next round, and Izidora waited patiently for Queen Immonen to make the first move. The Crystal Realm was not known for producing warriors, and it was immediately clear to me that Queen Immonen was no exception.

Izidora danced around her long, thin blade, parrying it as she stepped in and around, swinging her new swords in a flurry of activity designed to off-balance her opponent. Even from this distance, I could see that light danced in her eyes as she threw herself into the fight, and my blood heated as she executed each move with precision and speed like we'd practiced daily since we arrived in the Iron Realm. The glass was still nearly filled with sand when Queen Immonen yielded, and a wide grin stretched across my face, reflecting the one my mate wore.

"She is an incredible fighter," Queen Viktoria commented, patting my hand.

"She works hard at everything she does," I replied. "I've never met anyone with so much enthusiasm for life."

"Neither have I," she mused, pulling the fur shawl tighter around her as a cold breeze blew through the arena.

The wind picked up a few stray chestnut hairs that had fallen out of Izidora's braid as her hand was raised. Our eyes locked, and I shot her my best 'I am so proud of you' smile. She blushed a pretty shade of pink before her hand was dropped. Then she hugged Queen Immonen, the two of them chatting the entire walk out of the ring.

As the next class of competitors was called, I bid Queen Viktoria goodbye. I strode toward the matchmakers, scratching at their papers and shouting at contestants, trying to organize the chaos of the matches.

"King Ruslan Drakkar of the Iron Realm!" one of them called, half-standing and scanning the gathered group of males all roughly the same size.

"Here," I stated, pushing through and stepping up to the table.

"And High Lord Viktor Adimik of the Night Realm!"

The male on his right shouted, "High Lord Kazimir Vaszoly of the Night Realm and General Drazen Fedir of the Iron Realm!"

Fuck.

Silence fell over those around us, and the thread that tied Izidora to me vibrated with anxiety. Even though I couldn't see her, I knew she was somewhere nearby, heart racing.

The rest of the matchups were read, but I did not hear them over the roaring fury in my ears. My hand tightened over the pommel of my swords as Kazimir and Drazen, along with two other pairs, stepped into the rings.

I didn't trust the Night Fae not to fight dirty, especially with Drazen. But Drazen carried his 'I don't give a fuck' attitude right into the ring, squaring up to Kazimir with a bored expression on his face. When the sand turned over, Kazimir sprang forward, his emerald pommel flashing as he thrust his sword straight up the middle. Drazen sidestepped, twirling the hilt of his weapon over his hand before parrying Kazimir's next strike. Veins of lapis lazuli ran through Drazen's sword, matching his wings, and the stone glittered as it met the solid steel of Kazimir's blade. They fought in a flurry of strikes, and all eyes were on them, the other two matches forgotten as they battled for control of their ring.

Drazen's strength was subtle, unlike Savich's, and he managed to land a series of heavy blows that had Kazimir backing toward the fence. Sweat poured from their brows, but Drazen's bored expression never fell, despite the obvious strain as they fought.

Come on, Drazen.

I needed my cousin to win, not only for the Iron Realm's overall score but to prove a point. The Night Fae might think they could show up and take Izidora back with them, but it simply wasn't happening.

Kazimir faltered, and Drazen lunged for a yielding blow, only to release a harsh curse as he stumbled over something in the flat, packed-dirt arena. I pressed closer to the fence separating us, eyes trained on the spot where Drazen had been moments before, and I swore a snake lay in the dirt. Squinting, I blinked and looked again, only for that black line to disappear. Drazen had recovered, and the scrape of metal drew my attention to the two males again.

The sand was nearly empty, and my heart pounded in my chest in time with the furious strikes Drazen landed, the very last knocking Kazimir's blade from his hands. His eyes darted to the glass, then back to my cousin, and I knew he debated how long he could hold this position without yielding so that the round was judged on points. But Drazen already knew, and with the speed gifted to Félvér, he pinned Kazimir against the fence with his blade at his throat, leaving him no choice but to yield.

Kazimir spat out the word like it was poison, and Drazen stepped away, maintaining his nonchalant demeanor. Kazimir hurled more words at him, and they were enough to have the half-Dragon spinning on his heel and stalking back to Kazimir. Drazen's face was a breath from the Night Fae's, and his expression was pure fury.

"You're a fucking cheat, Kazimir. I know you used magic against me, and yet you still lost," Drazen scoffed.

Kazimir shoved Drazen away, his expression darkening. "You're just a mongrel playing at nobility, Drazen. Take your filth and crawl back into the hole you came from."

The two stepped forward again, poised to strike with fists before judges entered the ring and separated them. Drazen's normally cool facade was utterly cracked as he passed me, and I tried to grab him by the shoulder, but he shrugged me off and kept walking. I made to follow him, but my name was called.

My jaw flexed and my knuckles cracked one by one as I entered the ring. Viktor had already taken his place, and the crowd around us was silent as we squared up. Slowly, I drew my sword from its sheath at my side, the deep obsidian veins crafted into the lightweight metal giving it a sinister, threatening appeal. The deep red garnet set into the hilt was the color of freshly drawn blood, and it flared with energy the moment my palms gripped the metal.

The world fell away as my focus honed in on the Night Fae in front of me. Viktor was tall and stacked with lean muscle, but his leather armor was no match for the lightweight metal I wore. The Iron Realm had been hard at work crafting stronger and lighter metal for a century, and in my lifetime, we'd succeeded. Viktor, like most of the other Fae, probably assumed my armor would slow me, and a small smirk formed on my face as I waited for him to underestimate me. Besides, I was the most powerful Félvér to have ever lived, and even the Goddess couldn't save him from my wrath.

The sand turned over, and Viktor struck first.

His sword speared toward my middle, and I easily parried it away, sidestepping and returning with a slash at his legs. Viktor jumped backward, the tip barely grazing his thigh, before planting his foot and pushing forward, using the momentum of his retreat to swing his blade up toward my chin. I slipped to the side, the song of metal whispering in my ear, then met his sword with my own as he retracted.

Both of us pressed into our blades, trying to force the other to back off first. Sweat beaded his forehead, and I grinned, not even the slightest hint of fatigue gracing my body.

"Guess us *mongrels* could teach you Fae a thing or two about fighting," I purred, sending Viktor stumbling backward with a mighty shove. Without waiting for him to recover, I launched an attack, my sword moving faster and faster with each subsequent strike. The force of our blows reverberated up my arm, but I had trained my whole life to be a weapon, and there was no way I was losing this match.

"Guess you could teach me a thing or two about torture, too," Viktor snapped, finally planting his foot and putting energy into pushing me backward.

I laughed, a manic, crazed sound that had my blood singing. "If only you knew."

Feinting an arcing strike, I flicked my wrist at the last second and sliced into Viktor's forearm, causing his fingers to flex around his blade, nearly dropping it before he recovered, only holding it with a single hand. Blood streamed down his arm and onto the dirt beneath our feet, but he did not complain.

The sand in the glass was halfway gone.

"I was there when we rescued her, you know," he hissed, lunging for me.

"And I remember your smell from when I arrived hours later," I sneered, swinging my blade, only to pull it at the last moment and blast him backward with a kick to the stomach.

The air whooshed from his lungs as he stumbled, surprised by my change in tactics. His blade barely clanged against mine as I struck again. With a rough flick of my wrist, I finally disarmed him, and he held his hands in surrender.

"I yield," he grumbled, his eyes harder than rock as he surveyed me.

I didn't bother to offer him my hand, merely spun on my heel toward the center of the ring, where the judge raised my hand in victory.

As I exited, movement in the crowd caught my eye, and Izidora pushed away from the fence and raced toward me. A grin split my face as I caught her in my arms. Sensing eyes on me, I looked up and over Izidora's head, discovering Kazimir and the Night Fae standing together and watching our every move.

Izidora whipped her head around too, finding them, and her face pinched with disgust. She tugged on my hand, clearly not wanting to engage with them as she led us away, toward Zuriel and the Demons who waited patiently for their names to be called. It was a small victory, but one that I relished immensely.

There was no need for me to shower Izidora with gifts and words of affirmation to win her over when Kazimir made an ass of himself at every turn. My mate deserved to be taken care of in every way possible, and I intended to do so for the remainder of my years. Izidora would not leave me, and I repeated the phrase over and over, once again hoping that eventually, I'd believe it.

16

KAZIMIR

Béke Day Four

The way Izidora looked at Ruslan after she won her division at the swordfighting competition nearly unleashed the sinister beast that lived inside my chest, wrapped around my moonlight magic like a parasite. It whispered sweet nothings in my heart, promising revenge and my mate, yet every time I gave into its siren call, I ended up worse off than I was before.

Should I have provoked Drazen? Perhaps not, but that beast was out for blood, and I was pissed that I had let the male best me in a competition I should have won handily. The Iron Fae mongrels were no match for me, not with this dark magic, but I couldn't show my hand – not yet. The sweet secret held in my chest might have cost me the battle, but I would win the war.

Izidora and Ruslan slipped away after the competition, and amid all the chaos of the crowd, I called on that darkness, mixing it with the moonlight in my chest and rendering myself invisible. My footsteps were muffled as I followed them through the halls of Ryza Citadel, up the spiraling steps of a tower, and down a hallway to a terrace that overlooked Radence. It was large enough to hold fifty Fae, and in the center, flickering candles surrounded a pile of furs. I pressed myself against a wall on the back of the terrace as Izidora's aquamarine eyes scanned the expanse, though I knew without a doubt she could not see me.

Ruslan's hand was on Izidora's lower back as he led her to the wine glasses and bottle of deep purple liquid that waited for them, along with some sort of chocolate dessert. "I know we have to stay here for the feast, but I still wanted to have special moments alone with you." Ruslan spun her to face him, and she melted into his body.

"You are so thoughtful, Ruslan." She stroked the spot between his brows, smoothing the crease lining it. "You have nothing to fear. I love you."

Her words were like a stab to the gut.

"You are my light, sprite, my path out of the darkness. I love you more than life itself." Ruslan tucked a stray strand of hair behind her ear, smoothing the flyaways down with the palm of his hand. "Did you hear what Kazimir said to Drazen?"

She nodded. "Kazimir called him a mongrel."

Ruslan growled, and I didn't feel the slightest bit guilty about my words. I was, however, curious as to how Ruslan would respond. The male cracked his neck, and Izidora grasped his hands, running her thumbs over the back of them until he blew out a breath, his shoulders dropping. "Thank you," he muttered, pulling her into his chest and dropping a kiss on her pink lips.

Bile rose in my throat, and my nails dug into my palms so hard that the metallic tang of blood filled my senses.

Ruslan's nostrils flared, and he jerked his head away from Izidora, scanning the terrace like she had moments before. But Izidora drew his attention again when she moaned, reminiscent of the ones she made while I was between her thighs, as she bit into the chocolate. "Cedomir has outdone himself yet again." Ruslan huffed a laugh into her hair as he kissed the top of her head. Then he tasted the dessert himself, mimicking her moan with his own.

The smile she flashed him made my heart ache with an acute intensity I hadn't felt since the day Ruslan ripped her from my arms. This moment between them was so intimate, so easy, and everything I wanted with Izidora.

Why couldn't she see that I was the better choice?

I had to show her, but she hadn't let me close enough to ask since our second day here. At dinner, I would force her into a conversation, and this time I would not lose my temper. She was mine, and if I could only hold it together long enough to get her to accept the bond, we could forget this shitshow and leave everything behind.

Ruslan seated himself behind Izidora and pulled her into his lap, cradling her in his arms as they looked upon the jagged peaks in the distance. He said something in her ear, eliciting a breathy gasp, and my cock hardened at the sound. Memories of all the times Izidora fell apart around me, how her walls milked me as she came, flooded my mind, begging me to snatch her from his arms and take her to my bed.

But I had to watch as Ruslan trailed his fingers along the seams of her armor, stripping off piece after piece and exposing her wool tunic and leather leggings to the cold air that blew through the Iron Realm like a bane. She snuggled into his chest, stealing warmth from him, and I ground my teeth together as she said, "You take such good care of me."

I took better care of her. I was the one who brought her back from the brink.

After everything I did for her, she dared reject me for this male who didn't have to pick up the broken pieces like I did. Izidora was where she was because of me, and if I hadn't spent so much time teaching her magic, ensuring she was learning about the world, learning how to fight, she'd be nothing.

She. Was. Mine.

That black magic surged in my veins, and if I hadn't already been clenching my teeth so hard, I would have growled as the darkness took over. With every ounce of self-control I had left, I called my wings to me and shot into the air, away from my mate and toward a place where I could let the beast within me loose, if only to vent the boiling steam it created with its desires.

BÉKE DAY FIVE

RUSLAN HAD BEEN SHOWERING Izidora with gifts and affection, and two could play that game. The morning before the strength competition, I convinced Izidora to go with me to a place I'd spotted as I flew to the mountains the previous night to blow off some steam.

Izidora and I were better when we were *doing* something together, and I would show her just how great we worked as a team. The dance studio was on the outskirts of Radence, though I hadn't told her where we were going when we met in the stables, only that it was a surprise. Astride Mistik, she seemed less tense, as if the horse's familiarity lulled her into the ease we had as we rode through the Night Realm. I congratulated her on her victory at the swords competition, though I left out my distaste that she had chosen neither the Night nor Iron Realms to represent at Béke.

At least she hadn't picked a side.

There was still hope for me.

Pulling on Fek's reins, I slowed him to a leisurely walk in front of the stone building with large windows that let in the soft morning light. Mistik stopped alongside us, and Izidora dismounted with the ease of a female who had been riding for her entire life. "What is this place?" she asked, eyes roaming over the small building.

"I have arranged for us to have dance lessons. With the masquerade coming up in a few days, I thought it might be fun to learn some of the Iron Realm's traditional dances," I said, taking Mistik's reins from her and hitching our horses to a post alongside the building.

When I glanced up from my work toward Izidora, her lips were pinched, and her eyes held a level of wariness I hadn't seen since the first days we had together. The sight of that ripped me to shreds, and I couldn't lie to myself and say that it wasn't entirely unwarranted. She had asked me to be gentler with her when we last danced, but I was so caught up in seeing her that I did not listen.

The binding magic slumbered in my chest after I'd beat it into submission the previous night, sending dark tendrils flying in every direction among the snow-packed trees in the mountain closest to Radence until my body trembled from exertion and the wicked magic no longer begged to be unleashed.

I took a slow step toward her, hoping she wouldn't bolt around me and clamber up Mistik to escape the date I had planned for us. "I promise I won't hurt you, Izidora. You know I'm not like that."

She blew out a breath, but her aquamarine eyes did not melt for me like they once had. "If you do, I will cut your balls off." Her normally bright voice was serious and carried no hint of teasing.

"Understood. Shall we?" I hovered a hand out toward the door, directing her to enter first. She threw a look over her shoulder, then pushed through the wooden entrance, unveiling an open space with wall-sized mirrors and polished wood floors.

A pretty dark-haired female, the same one I'd spoken with the previous night, greeted us. "High Lord Kazimir, so good to see you again. And this must be Princess Izidora." She dipped into a quick curtsey. "I am Iskra."

"So nice to meet you, Iskra. Are you Fae or Félvér?" Izidora smiled at the female with all the warmth she'd kept from me.

"Félvér. How did you know?" Iskra blushed, and I ground my teeth. Of course, she was Félvér.

Were there no pure-blooded Iron Fae left in this Goddess-forsaken place?

"You look like you might carry a hint of Shifter. Some sort of bird if I had to guess?"

"You are correct. My father is part Eagle Shifter. Must be why I love ballet," Iskra grinned. "But enough about me. High Lord Kazimir said you wanted to learn some steps to traditional Iron Realm dances." She glanced at both of us, dressed in casual yet warm clothes. "I'll take your cloaks, and then we'll meet in the center of the space."

I shrugged out of my furs, handing them to the female and following behind Izidora as she blazed a trail to the middle. That tug begged me to close the physical and mental distance between us, but I bided my time, knowing we'd be forced together during the steps of the dance soon enough.

"Great, here's how we will learn. I'll demonstrate the first few steps, and then you will try until you've got them down. Then we will add on, repeating the process until you can twirl about the room on your own. I'll hum the tune as we go along." Iskra proceeded to teach us the steps, a simple series where Izidora and I walked side by side, hands clasped at shoulder height. Her hand was tense in mine, and the stiffness ran all the way through her body as she held me at arm's length. We mastered the first part in minutes, and Iskra walked us through the next steps, which involved a tug and a twirl with Izidora landing against my chest.

Heat surged through me at the thought of our bodies being flush, though it was obvious from the coolness in Izidora's countenance that she was less than enthused about the steps. After our third failed attempt, Iskra cut in. "The Iron Realm is a sensual place, Your Highness. Relax your body and let it glide through the air."

"Thanks," Izidora said, her voice clipped. She drew a breath, then blew it out slowly, dropping some of the tension that held her straighter than a freshly forged sword. "Let's try again."

When we grasped hands at the top of the dance floor, I gave her small hand a reassuring squeeze. "You are doing so well, Izidora. We'll get the steps."

She ignored me as Iskra hummed the tune, and our first few steps were flawless. When the tune switched, signaling the first tug, I pulled Izidora toward me, throwing her across my body as she spun on her toes, her body light and loose. Once she'd unspiraled completely, I reversed her direction, sending her twirling into my chest. Her untethered palm landed just above my heart, and it gave a heavy beat as if it knew she touched there. That tug tightened us together, seemingly of its own accord, and for a moment that icy exterior Izidora had tried so hard to maintain melted and I saw the depth of her pain.

The moment was broken by Iskra's claps echoing through the empty space. "Well done! Let's practice the next steps." Iskra replaced Izidora, demonstrating the hand placement for the rest of the dance, as well as the next ten steps that sent us diagonally across the space. "Now, from the top!"

Izidora and I clasped hands at shoulder height, walked forward, executed the tug and twirl, and the moment Izidora landed against my chest again, that bond we shared became insistent. My hand found her hip while the other held her tiny hand, and her free hand pressed against my chest, searing into my skin beneath my tunic.

The tune changed, and I guided her along, making sure my resting hand was not hurting her like it had last time. The steps that took us across the open space were slow and sensual, legs and torsos brushing as the space between us became nonexistent.

"You're so beautiful, Izidora," I whispered as we reached the end of our first diagonal, cutting back in the direction we came.

A blush spread across her cheeks, and she looked up at me through dark lashes as we crossed the space, though she said nothing. Before our next switchback, I spun her again, this time directing her back to land against my chest, and I splayed my fingers across her belly as we blazed a slow path across the room.

Pebbles broke out across the skin that was visible around her tunic, and my heart pounded into her back as we continued our dance. We switched directions, and her breath hitched as my large palm dipped lower on her opposite hip. "You fit in my arms perfectly, like you were carved from stone just for me," I murmured, dipping my head so the words brushed over her ear.

The shiver that went down her spine stopped at my groin, heating it in the best way, and by the way she pressed back into me, I knew she felt my desire for her. I wanted more, so I kept going. "The first day I saw you, I knew you and I were meant to be together. The way I raged for you when I saw you in chains, the anger I felt when I learned you were not given your name, the grief that I felt when you backed away from me in fear. I promised myself that I would show you how to live."

The air froze in her lungs as I spun her again, and her head tipped up to look at me. Iskra's humming melted into the background as it became only Izidora and I dancing. "I'd fight the Fates with nothing but my fists to save you, Izidora. I promised you that I would protect you, that I would never see you chained again. I fell into darkness to get to you, and now that I'm here with you again, I'm starting to see the light."

She lifted a single brow over her gem-like eyes. "Are you?"

"It helps when you are near, like this. When we are apart, I am crazed for you, dying for even a taste of you." I dropped my head so my lips hovered a breath from hers. "Mate bonds are a powerful, ancient magic that defy all logic, all reason, all sense. They surpass any other type of magic one may possess, and mates often die of broken hearts when their other half dies before them."

We reached the opposite side of the dance floor, and I spun her again, my erection digging into her back as we glided across the polished wood. "I'm so sorry I hurt you before, my love. I have been out of my mind with worry for so long, I overreacted to your presence. How could I not? You are not only my mate, but also the most incredible female I've ever met."

"Kazimir..." Izidora whispered, melting into my embrace. My fingers dipped lower on her belly, nearly brushing the apex of her thighs, and our bond turned into an inferno.

"You are like the stars that shine over the Night Realm, glittering and enticing in their otherworldly beauty, and I could spend hours gazing upon you and never tire of the view." My nose brushed behind her ear, and I inhaled her rosy scent. Brushing my lips against the sensitive underside of her jaw, I said, "You smell like a garden of roses, but not just any rose. Roses of the purest white, so light that you think you are in the Goddess's garden."

My words seemed to be working, and I prayed that Iskra did not stop humming as we switched to face each other once again. My hand that was splayed across her belly had moved to her hip bone, but as we glided away from our instructor, I slipped it between us, cupping her center and devouring the flush that rose to Izidora's smooth skin. "And your taste – it is like honeyed wine, so sweet and intoxicating."

Her dark lashes fluttered, and she did not move away from me or tell me to stop. I rubbed a circle over her clit, and her legs widened in our dance, allowing me more room to rub her the way I knew she liked. I traced her seam through her leather pants with my fingers, wishing there was less fabric between us. "You are my beautiful rose, my shining star, my beacon home. I love you, Izidora."

And with that, I took the most painful step back of my entire life.

"Splendid!" Iskra clapped her hands together, applauding our dance.

Izidora's cheeks were pink, and her lips were parted as if she were trying to catch the breath that had been stolen by her arousal. Hints of buds appeared on her chest, and I knew I'd gotten under her skin.

"Our next dance is even more sensual, and after the way the two of you finished the last dance, I know that you'll fly through this one."

With arms and legs intertwined, wrapping around one another only to break apart and be pulled back together, we undulated against each other, ratcheting up the tension between us. Each brush of her soft frame against my muscled one only made my dick harder, while each sensual caress across her torso sent pebbles across her skin, blowing out her eyes until they were nearly black.

Fucking fates, this was what I'd needed with her from the start.

Izidora did not need to return my affection with words of her own; she showed me with every willing brush of her body against mine that Ruslan did not have her heart secured in the palm of his hands.

How would he feel when she rode up smelling of me?

The image of him scenting me on her pleased me more than I should have allowed. Our bond tugged at me for more, and after the next dip of Izidora over my arm, I captured her mouth in mine, tasting those perfect pink lips as she sighed and arched into me. My tongue pressed against them, begging for entrance, and she relented, her own tongue weaving with mine as I deepened our kiss. Heart galloping, I clutched her to me, ignoring the tune and the steps to the dance as we stoked the embers of our love into an inferno.

The chasm that had opened between us during our time apart disappeared as she melted into me, her hands clutching onto me like I was her hero, her savior, once more. "I want all of you, Izidora," I breathed, breaking our kiss.

Izidora's lashes fluttered against my cheeks. "We have an audience."

"I don't care. I only want you." My lips fell to the place where her neck met her shoulder, and I grazed my teeth over the sensitive spot.

She gasped, head falling back and spilling her chestnut locks along with it. My eyes flicked up to see Iskra disappearing into a room in the back, and I silently thanked her before returning my attention to my mate.

Snaking my arms around Izidora's waist, I lowered us both to the floor so my muscled body pressed her into it. The cage I created for her with my arms was intentional, because I had her where I wanted her, and I was not letting her go. She was mine.

I rolled my hips against hers, letting her feel every inch of me that wanted her. The sound she made was breathy and wanton and sent a wave of heat to my groin, causing me to grind into her again. My lips captured hers in a bruising, demanding kiss, and she fell into it, arching off the floor to close the distance between us.

With one hand, I unfastened my pants, gripping my shaft

and pumping a few times to relieve the ache there. "You are mine, Izidora." I found the laces of her pants, pulling them apart until I had room to slip a finger against her skin, then worked my hand down to cup her core. The wetness there soaked my hand immediately, and I growled my approval. "So fucking wet for me already."

But then the door to the studio banged open, and I tore my gaze away from Izidora to see who dared intrude on our moment together.

17

RUSLAN

Béke Day Five

I was fucking weak. I hated myself for following them to the dance studio, watching as Izidora melted into Kazimir. But that fucking voice in the back of my mind screamed at me that this was the moment she was going to abandon me, and I caved to the fear. I'd tried so hard, and still fucking failed to let her have the space she needed to make her decision. I just loved her so much, and her leaving me would break me in a way that was irreparable. No matter how much logic I shoved in my brain, that fear screamed louder, until it won out when Kazimir bent her to the floor and loosened her pants.

I was on him in a second, ripping him away from her with the force of the fear driving my actions. Izidora scrambled to her feet, backing away from us as Kazimir swung at me, driving a hard fist into my stomach. "You bastard!" he shouted, shoving me back.

Regaining my footing, I raised my fists, waiting for Kazimir's next charge. On cue, he shot toward me, and I changed my level, his fist flying over my head as my arms wrapped around his waist and locked together. Squeezing, I lifted him off his feet and slammed him into the floor. The wood was unforgiving against my knees as I followed him to the ground, pulling my fist back in preparation to strike.

"Stop it!" Izidora screamed, and a blast of white light blinded me as it knocked me away from Kazimir. My opponent shot to his feet, his eyes fully black and rage written on his features, only to be met with the same reaction from Izidora.

"Who do you fucking want, Izidora?" Kazimir snarled, chest heaving and fists clenched, no doubt mirroring my own stance. "It's obvious Ruslan can't handle the thought of you choosing me, otherwise he wouldn't be here."

"I can say the same for you," I growled, taking a threatening step forward. "You fucking stabbed me. Called me a rapist."

"Shut the fuck up, both of you!" Izidora snapped. I tore my attention from Kazimir to her.

"You," she pointed a jabbing finger at me, "were supposed to give me space to make my decision. And you," she turned her ire on Kazimir, "have been cruel since you set foot in the Iron Realm. Maybe I should choose neither of you and doom us all. How about that?"

Izidora practically vibrated with rage, white flames licking through the beautiful blue of her irises, and I'd never been harder in my life. This was the fire I had been missing from her, and, fuck me, I wanted her to spew more. I raised my hands in supplication. "I'm sorry, sprite. I am struggling, and I let it get the better of me."

Kazimir made no move to appease her; instead, he shot me a look that was so sharp it could have killed. Nothing got by my sprite, and she hissed at him. "And what about you? What do you have to say for yourself?"

With one last dagger-stare, he returned his focus to Izidora.

"I've been hurting too, for months, while you were here with him."

She quirked a sharp brow at him, dissatisfied with his answer. "And?"

"And... I'm sorry for being cruel to you. I shouldn't have hurt you because I was hurting." Kazimir ran a hand over his face, some of the emerald color returning to his eyes. I narrowed my own on him, suspicion settling heavily in my gut.

What sort of magic was this?

Izidora blew out an annoyed breath, crossing her arms over her chest. "Was that so hard?"

"I am a proud male, Izidora. You know that." Kazimir's words were defensive, and flames danced in her eyes again.

She opened her mouth to say something else, but I redirected her attention away from him, not because I didn't want to see her rip him to shreds, but because my fear still hadn't abated. I had fucked up, again, and needed to know if it was the end for me.

"Where do we go from here?" I asked, my voice coming out more level than I thought it would.

She chewed her lip, eyes bouncing between the two of us while she considered. The moment an idea crossed her mind, I read it in the sparkle of her eyes. "I want to try something. But I need your word that you will not harm each other in the meantime."

Satisfaction curled through me as I realized what Izidora wanted to do. She'd spent enough time with Liliana recently that the guess was right there for the taking. Glancing at Kazimir, I tried to read his expression and gauge his reaction. He was guarded, but a hint of curiosity peeked through.

"She wants both of us at the same time," I stated, since he wasn't grasping the concept. He turned his attention on me, lip curling back from his teeth.

"She is mine, why would I share her with you?" he snarled.

The derision in my snort was not lost on Izidora, who shot me another sharp look. I held back what I truly wanted to say to Kazimir, and instead addressed my mate. "If this is what you want, then I will promise not to hurt him. I'd do *anything* to make you happy, sprite." With my last statement, I dragged my eyes to Kazimir, daring him to deny Izidora.

As much as I hated the male, I loved Izidora's fire, and watching her stand up for herself and tell us what she wanted for a change set my blood racing. If he couldn't put aside his selfish feelings for her sake, that would make me the clear choice.

"I promise not to harm Ruslan while we are pleasuring you," he finally grumbled, running a hand over his face.

"Good," she said, squaring her shoulders and lifting her chin.

Taking a slow step in her direction, I rasped, "Tell us what you want us to do."

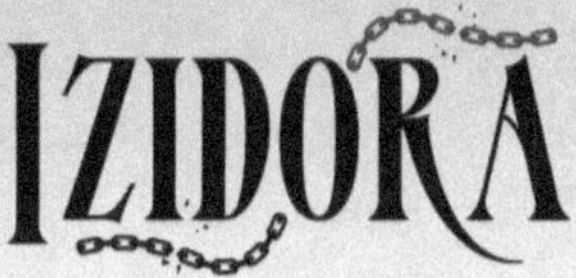

18

IZIDORA

Béke Day Five

Looking at the males side by side triggered an idea that would even make Liliana blush. After all, this was what I had wanted prior to Kazimir arriving – to be able to measure them side by side and see who was the better choice. My core heated the longer I thought about it, and I decided to voice my desires.

"Tell us what you want us to do," Ruslan rasped, taking an involuntary step forward.

Grasping the hem of my shirt with both hands, I tore it over my head and tossed it aside, revealing the lacy band underneath. "Kiss me," I told Ruslan, grabbing Kazimir's shirt and hauling him to my backside. "Touch me."

As I stood between the two males, the two bonds screamed their appreciation, flooding my veins with heady lust and intoxicating me with the promises of the orgasms they could deliver. Kazimir's rough fingertips skimmed my sides while Ruslan captured my mouth in his. I immediately opened to allow him access, and his tongue slipped inside, swiping at mine until he stole all my air. Kazimir's hands began kneading my breasts, brushing against my hard nipples and eliciting a moan. His erection dug into my back, while Ruslan's pressed in from the front, and I was drowning in their desire for me.

Kazimir swept my hair off my shoulder, blanketing it in kisses and nips, then Ruslan wound my long locks around his hand and tilted my head back to give them both better access to me. They worked my mouth, neck, and shoulders in tandem, teasing, licking, sucking until I was certain my arousal would drip to my ankles before I found relief.

Breaking away from Ruslan's lips, I spun in their arms to kiss Kazimir, tasting amber as I did so. Ruslan's hands traced a map across my stomach and to the undone laces of my pants, loosening them further so he could slide his hand lower. "Fuck, you are drenched," he moaned when his fingers brushed against the lace covering me there, pushing it aside to stroke my center. My breath caught in my chest as I broke my kiss with Kazimir, groaning as he wet his finger and trailed it to the sensitive bundle of nerves at the apex of my thighs.

Kazimir's hands yanked at the lace binding my breasts, yanking it over my head and tossing it to the side, where it joined my discarded shirt. With my nipples freed, he knelt, sucking them into his mouth one by one. I groaned, threading my fingers in his hair and scratching his scalp, pushing him into my breasts in a silent ask for more. His teeth replaced his lips, and I hissed as he scraped them across the hard peaks.

Ruslan's fingers dipped lower, stroking my slit, and my whole body was alive with sensation. "Take them off," I managed to pant between waves of pleasure. He wasted no time in ripping my pants down to my ankles, and I braced myself on Kazimir's broad shoulders as he tore my shoes from my feet, followed by my pants. Ruslan captured me against him as Kazimir tossed his shirt aside, revealing the colorful tattoos across his chest.

"Drink from her," Ruslan commanded, lifting me higher so I was forced to stand on the tips of my toes, legs spread wide. Kazimir's emerald eyes cut sharply toward Ruslan, but he dropped to the ground beneath me, his fingers digging into my thighs as he parted them wider.

His nose trailed up the inside of my thigh, his hot breath dusting across my even hotter core. "You smell divine," he crooned before his tongue flicked out and tasted me.

"Oh," I whimpered, caged against Ruslan's body while Kazimir's tongue slipped inside me.

My thighs trembled from my precarious position and how close I already was to coming. Ruslan must have scented my arousal because he whispered in my ear, "You think you can handle two cocks in your pretty little holes?"

"Yes," I panted, my body winding up to the point of breaking. My walls fluttered, and Kazimir groaned against me, removing a hand from my thigh and using his fingers to replace his tongue in my core. His mouth latched on to my clit as he began pumping two fingers in and out, and I shamelessly rode his face, chasing the release that was mere moments away. "Oh my Goddess," I gasped as I broke apart, my walls sucking Kazimir's fingers deeply and throbbing with need even though I was already coming. My orgasm did not leave me satiated in the slightest, and I wanted – needed – more pleasure.

Kazimir removed his fingers from me, rising to his feet and holding them out. "Suck."

Ruslan gripped my jaw with his free hand and forced my lips open, allowing Kazimir entrance to my mouth. I used my tongue to clean his fingers, moaning at my own taste. Ruslan passed me to Kazimir, and as my legs almost gave out, I was grateful for the support. He yanked his tunic over his head, kicked off his boots, and removed his pants until he bared himself to me, his cock painfully hard and dripping. My eyes roamed the dark tattoos covering his torso and arms as he stroked himself.

Kazimir growled and pushed me to my knees. "Suck his dick while I fuck you from behind."

"Crawl to me," Ruslan ordered, lowering himself to the floor. The wood was hard on my hands and knees as I slinked toward him, swaying my hips for Kazimir behind me. I heard Kazimir's clothes hitting the ground in rapid succession, and by the time I'd gripped Ruslan at the base and lowered my lips to his head, Kazimir was pressing against my entrance.

With a groan, I sucked him into my mouth, and Kazimir pushed into me, filling two of my holes with their massive cocks. Every nerve was alight as my tongue swirled over Ruslan's velvety skin and Kazimir stretched me. Ruslan wrapped my hair in his fist, getting it out of the way so the two of them could watch me bobbing my head up and down, coating him in my saliva.

"Such a good fucking girl, taking my cock to the back of your throat," Ruslan praised as he pushed my head lower until my nose brushed his abdomen. I gagged as he lifted me by my hair, the motion forcing me to suck him deeper before letting him go. The groan that left his lips was primal.

Kazimir's pace was slow and unhurried, sliding in and out from base to tip over and over, driving me wild. I wanted more, harder, and faster. I pushed my hips back into him, silently asking for more since my mouth was otherwise occupied. His fingers dug into the muscles of my ass, and he picked up his pace, slamming me forward and down onto Ruslan's cock. I tried to relax my throat around his length, but with the way my core tightened, I couldn't help but pant around him as my body trembled with the need to come.

"She's getting close," Kazimir grunted from behind me, his skin slapping against mine as he quickened his pace.

"Is that right, sprite? Are you going to come with my cock in your mouth and his in your cunt?" Ruslan grinned, shoving me down harder.

"Mmm," I managed, my brows pinching as I teetered at the edge. I was so deliciously full, and my nostrils flared as I tried to focus on the dick in my mouth. But it was no use. With a strangled cry, I broke apart, releasing my mouth from Ruslan as Kazimir rode me harder, forcing my spine to arch as he dragged out my pleasure.

My eyes rolled into the back of my head, and with a sharp tug on my hair, Ruslan commanded, "Look at me while you come."

Barely managing to open my eyes, I did as he asked, though my vision was blurred with the tears left over from having him so deep in my throat.

"You are so fucking sexy when you fall apart," he said, and with one last shudder, I came down from the heaven they sent me to.

But I wanted them to drag me to hell. "I want both of you. At the same time," I panted.

"Then you'll have to get my cock wetter," Ruslan purred, directing me back to his hardness. Kazimir gathered the arousal coating my thighs and brought it to my puckered hole, causing me to jerk with pleasure as the sensitive area was awakened.

I allowed the drool to fall around Ruslan's cock as I licked and sucked, pushing back into Kazimir's fingers as he stretched my ass. "Did he take you here?" Kazimir growled behind me.

"Like the good little girl she is," Ruslan responded for me, a challenge in his tone.

Through blurred vision, I watched his signature smirk spread across his face, and with the way Kazimir's fingers pushed into me, I could tell he wasn't happy with Ruslan's answer. The tension between them, the desire for me rolling off of them, and the way both fought for me sent a new wave of wetness gushing from me. Never before had I felt so wanted, so needed, and the power from it was fucking exhilarating. I whimpered as he inserted the digit to the last knuckle, circling it around and rubbing it against his dick that was still inside me.

"I think she's ready," he stated, pulling out and leaving me empty.

With a gasp, I released Ruslan, who gently pushed me back until I sat on my heels. Kazimir settled himself on the ground behind me, and I turned to face him, gulping as I realized both their erections were about to fill me. As much as my heart pounded at the thought, my pussy throbbed even harder, and I crawled to him, positioning myself over Kazimir so I could slide down on his length. He released a guttural groan as I seated myself, circling my hips a few times to get the friction I needed on my clit.

Ruslan's knees hit the hard ground behind me, his hands finding my lower back and pushing me down onto Kazimir's chest. Bracing my hands and knees on the hard floor, I took a deep breath, trying to relax as Ruslan spread my cheeks. "Distract her," Ruslan said to Kazimir, who wasted no time yanking my lips to his.

His tongue invaded my mouth, brushing against mine, and I was lost in the moment as he diverted all my attention to the next position of our dance. His free hand found my aching nipples, tugging them and eliciting a gasp as pain mixed with pleasure.

Ruslan's cock pressed against my hole, slowly working its way in. A finger dipped down between my thighs, gathering more wetness and smearing it around as he pushed deeper. Pure ecstasy flooded my veins as he stretched me, and every nerve was alight with sensation as the males played with every sensitive area of my body.

Except for one. Bracing myself, I slipped a hand between Kazimir and me, finding my clit and rubbing it. The extra sensation heightened my arousal, allowing Ruslan to slip deeper into my ass. "Oh fuck," I whimpered, my hand working faster.

Kazimir began slow thrusts upward, moving his hands to my hips to hold them in place while I circled my clit. "You're so fucking tight," he groaned, digging his fingers in so hard I knew they would leave a bruise.

My knees banged against the hard ground as both males increased their pace, timing their thrusts so I was never without sensation. That only made me wetter, and soon, Ruslan was fully seated inside me. The fullness was indescribable, and my mind completely blanked of everything but the carnal pleasure they delivered.

There was no choice, no mates, no prophecy. Only the incredible feeling of being thoroughly fucked.

Ruslan yanked my hair back, forcing my back to arch and take both of them deeper. Kazimir dropped his hands from my hips, bracing himself on the floor and sucking a nipple into his mouth, using his teeth to tug it harder.

My core throbbed around them, wetness gushing and making the studio echo with slick sounds as we moved together. Sweat dripped between us, and the smell of sex was nearly overwhelming. But I did not want to stop; I wanted this to last forever.

"More," I begged, though for what, I did not know.

The two fucked me harder, thrusting from beneath and behind to fill me to the brim, and Kazimir moved my hand away, replacing it with his. It was all I could do to hold myself upright as they fucked me, delivering more pleasure than should have been possible.

"I'm... going..." I panted, shaking like a leaf with the force of my impending orgasm.

"Come for us," Ruslan commanded, giving me my head back as my spine arched and my scream shattered the other sounds around us.

"Fuck, fuck, fuck!" I chanted as wave after wave of pleasure crashed through me, my core tightening around them. My nails scratched against the polished wood floor as I grasped for purchase, needing something to ground me as I was vaulted to the stars.

"That's it, milk our cocks," Kazimir growled, his fingertips working furiously over my clit. His thrusts grew erratic, and with a strangled groan, he coated my pussy in spurts of hot liquid.

He throbbed inside me, joining my fluttering walls as Ruslan continued to fuck my ass, gripping my cheeks and leaving his own set of bruises as he came with a roar.

No one moved for minutes as we all returned to our sweat-soaked bodies, panting with exertion. Finally, Ruslan shifted out of me, hooking me under the arms and hoisting me from the ground. My knees screamed as I straightened my legs, and as I glanced down at my body, I discovered a trail of bruises around my hips and a massive one marking either knee.

Ruslan spun me to him, kissing me deeply as Kazimir pushed off the ground and joined us, stealing me from Ruslan for a kiss of his own. Breaking away from both of them, I stepped back and admired their naked forms.

"Satisfied, sprite?" Ruslan asked with a smirk.

Sleepiness pulled at me, and I nodded. "I think I need a nap now."

"I'll take you home, " Kazimir offered, stepping forward, but Ruslan cut him off with a hand to the chest.

"Let her choose who she wants to go with," Ruslan said, his smoky grays swirling with black fire. Kazimir swept his hand off his chest and took a menacing step toward him.

"I may have promised her to play nice while we fucked her,

but I made no such promise for after." Kazimir's emerald eyes turned completely black without even the whites left in them, and that sickly aura that had surrounded him since his arrival returned with force. His fingers flicked across each other in the way I knew he called his magic, and on instinct I tapped into mine, sending it in his direction and siphoning away his anger, one tiny tendril at a time.

Ruslan bared his teeth at the challenge, and I swept my empath magic in his direction, pulling with everything I had to get them to calm down before they hurt each other. My decision was hard enough without them at each other's throats. But I did not like the energy rolling off of Kazimir or the sickly way it tainted my own as I worked.

"Ruslan can take me home since I don't think I can ride. Can you bring Mistik back with you?" I asked Kazimir, hoping the mix of my siphoning their emotions and asking him to do something for me would appease him.

He ran a hand over his face, the emerald color returning to his eyes, then nodded. "I'll take good care of her, like I did on our ride here from the Night Realm."

We pulled on our clothes in a hurry, and it wasn't until Ruslan and I called our wings to fly home that I realized Iskra had disappeared and never returned. My cheeks flamed at the thought of her hearing what we did, but at the same time, my pussy clenched. The Iron Realm certainly had brought out a sexual side of me I never knew existed – or could possibly exist. The power rushing through me from commanding Kazimir and Ruslan to pleasure me was something I never imagined for myself either, and I flew even higher on our return journey from that feeling alone.

19

RUSLAN

Izidora was exhausted when we returned to our suite at Ryza Citadel, and without question I took her to our bed, tucking her worn-out body into the warmth it offered and curling around her to offer my heat. My Dragon senses smelled Kazimir on her, and I gritted my teeth, anger rising both at myself and at the male who challenged me for Izidora.

How far would things have gone if I didn't stop them?

Izidora needed to make her own decision, and I was trying to give her the space she needed, but fuck, that voice whispered in my ear that she was going to choose him and I'd caved. I just loved her so much, and I was terrified of losing my one shot at unconditional love, where I'd never have to worry about someone leaving me because I fucked up or wasn't enough for them.

But I had fucked up, and I knew it. Though I'd gladly break my promise to her again to bring out the spitfire inside her, because that was the sexiest damn thing she'd ever done. That was who she truly was, who she deserved to become, and I was so fucking awed witnessing it unfold. She needed to know it was safe for her to let it rise to the surface, and I planned on lighting that path forward for her.

Izidora released a soft sigh, sinking deeper into my hold, and I immediately tightened my arms around her, needing to bury her inside me and imprint her on my soul. There was no way to get close enough to her, and I ached for her every second of every day. It was driving me insane, these feelings for her, and no amount of secret sessions punching the shit out of the bag slaked the anguish swirling inside me.

"I'm sorry, sprite," I murmured into her hair, my breath releasing a whoosh of rosy scent from the strands and into the air. "I broke my promise to you."

"Yes, you did," she said, though her voice was soft and contained no anger. She spun in my arms, her bright blue eyes sad as she drank in my raw expression.

"What do you need right now?" I asked, releasing a hand from her lower back to smooth her hair away from her face.

"Nothing anyone can give me," she admitted. "I'm so exhausted. My mind is spinning out of control, worrying that I'll doom us all if I make the wrong choice. I thought choice was what I wanted, but with the weight of the decision, I just wish the Goddess had chosen for me."

It was then that she revealed the weariness in her eyes, the truth to all the nights where I'd rolled over and tugged her closer as she tossed and turned, nightmares tearing her from sleep more often than not. "I will do better at reining in my own emotions. I've told you before and I will remind you now that I intend to spend the rest of my life making up for all the wrongs done to you, my own included. I will not add to your burden now by forcing you to use your magic on me because my fear of you choosing him is out of control."

"Thank you," she whispered, her eyes brimming with tears.

"You are the light that cuts through the dark and shows me the way forward. My every breath belongs to you, now and forever. And as I lay dying, my last thoughts will be of you."

She buried her face into my chest, and I held her there, rubbing soothing circles across her back until her heart ceased racing and her breaths slowed. It wasn't long before she succumbed to her fatigue, and I refused to move as she finally found rest. She was my everything, and it was my duty to ensure she was taken care of in every way possible. I'd lay down my life for her, stay awake all night if that's what it took for her to sleep, and go without food or drink to see her survive.

Deep down, I knew she would choose me in the end. It was the waiting that was killing me.

20

IZIDORA

Béke Day Five

"He was saying all the right things," I told Liliana as we dropped our horses off in the makeshift pen to one side of an arena that had been erected on the outskirts of Radence. Drazen had cleared this spot of snow, again, while a smattering of small arenas and roped-off areas marked the zones for each strength competition. A grandstand stood opposite us, filled with residents of the Iron Realm who had turned out to watch the competition. We'd have to pick a spot and cycle through each game until we'd finished them all.

"So what happened?" Liliana asked, sweeping her long braid over her shoulder.

We stopped at the nearest event table and gave our names before getting in line. "The dances were so sensual, I got caught up in them. We were kissing, and then he laid me on the floor. Ruslan showed up, and..." I trailed off, core flaming along with my cheeks at the memory. "They fought, then the three of us fucked. It was incredible, but after, Kazimir challenged Ruslan, and his eyes went pure black like there was not a bit of white left in them. I managed to siphon away some of whatever that was, and when he came back to himself, he acted like nothing had happened."

"First, that's hot as fuck and I expect more details later. Second, what the fuck," Liliana cursed, shaking her head at the ground. "Endre definitely knows what is going on with Kazimir. I will force it out of him. You need to know what you are choosing, Izidora."

I blew out a breath. "No kidding. I have a fucking headache constantly from the thoughts circling in my mind, and when I do manage to sleep, I'm torn back to reality by nightmares of what happens if I choose the wrong one. The sex was incredible and empowering but it didn't change any of my feelings."

Shouts rang out around us, and I craned my neck around the large males in front of us to glimpse what caused the commotion. Savich had hefted a boulder the size of three of me over his head, and sweat poured down his burly frame as the seconds ticked by. "Please tell me we don't have to lift that boulder," I groaned.

Liliana snorted. "We have to lift a boulder, but not that one. I think it weighs more than you, me, and Domi combined."

The aforementioned female pushed through the line of participants to rejoin us, glass bottles clinking in her arms. "Thank the Goddess, I really need a drink after what Izidora just told me."

Domi lifted a perfectly shaped black eyebrow, her eyes dancing with curiosity. "Oh? And what's that?"

Liliana used her silvery magic to pop the cork out of a bottle of red wine, then tipped it back and chugged. She released the lip with a sigh, wiping her mouth with the back of her hand. She handed the bottle to me before saying, "Kazimir's done some shit again."

Domi rolled her eyes, using her magic to uncork the other bottle. We clinked the lips of our wine bottles together before we both drank down greedy gulps. The red wine carried a hint of spice and smoke, and I licked my lips for every last drop before passing the bottle back to Liliana. It was bitterly cold and overcast, and the alcohol brought some warmth back to my veins.

"Lately, I am beginning to question what Kaztar sees in him. I know he saved them from that avalanche, but the way you talk about him, Izidora, makes me question which side is the real Kazimir," Domi murmured after a long moment.

"I've known him my whole life, and the side Kaztar likes is what I've seen up until the last few months. Maybe losing you broke something in his brain," Liliana offered.

"Whatever happened to him doesn't change the fact that I still have to make this fucking choice," I grumbled, tucking my fingers into my armpits to keep them warm. Someone's attention fell over me, sending a shiver down my spine, and when I glanced over my shoulder, Ruslan's smoky eyes bored into me from where he sat with Queen Immonen and Queen Viktoria on the raised platform, surveying the event. The females were bundled against the cold, and a row of braziers sent sparks into the air around them, offering what small reprieve they could.

My stomach dropped at the sight of the worry in his eyes, and I grew even colder than before. Domi nudged me with her elbow, offering me her bottle of wine. I accepted it gladly and took a long swig, wiping my mouth as we took a few steps forward. The other contestants had finally finished their round with the boulders. "From everything you've said, it sounds to me like Ruslan is the one you really want. You talk about how he understands you and sees you and that's all you've ever wanted, if that helps anything."

"But what if the male I love is the wrong choice?" I whispered my deepest fear into existence, hoping that this choice of light and dark wouldn't cause me to lose everyone I cared about.

Liliana grabbed my hand and gave it a squeeze. "Why does there have to be a right and wrong, or a good and bad? The prophecy doesn't say 'if you choose the wrong one we're all fucked.' It says 'there is a choice' and that 'kings will fall and rivers will run with blood.' The fate of the world part is what people have interpreted."

For a moment, I considered if she was right.

"Prophecies are never *that* straightforward," Domi interjected, snuffing the spark of hope Liliana's words had given me.

"If someone could just decide for me that'd be great, thanks," I groused, setting the bottle in the dirt before walking to a boulder that looked light enough for me to lift. Liliana walked to one further down the line, and Domi selected the one beside me.

A whistle sounded, and the three of us, along with a few males past Liliana in the lineup, lifted the stones as high as we could, dropping them as soon as we had managed to hoist them overhead. Everyone passed the first round, so we stepped to the right, waiting for the signal to lift the next-largest boulder. Between the wine and the weight, sweat bled from my every pore, and after five more lifts, my shoulders gave out. I joined Domi on the sidelines, waiting for Liliana and the others in our round to finish.

Two males succumbed to the heavy stones after the next whistle, and although Liliana remained in the round, she was far behind King Consort Geza, who hefted the largest stone that Savich had struggled under. Thankfully, we were judged by the same classes we'd been given during the swords competition, otherwise, we females would have been – unfairly – at the bottom of the leaderboard.

Both Liliana and King Consort Geza failed to lift their stones fully over their heads, which ended our round. Domi and I jogged to catch up with Liliana as we headed to our next station – throwing spears. "Great work, Lil," I said, offering her what was left of the bottle of wine.

She took it, tipping the purple liquid into her mouth. "I can't feel my fingers anymore," she laughed. "If you do choose Ruslan, we've got to get away during the winter months. It's too damn cold here."

"I'd love to go to the beaches in the Day Realm. From what Queen Viktoria has told me, the water is crystal clear and you can see fish swimming around your feet!" I exclaimed.

Liliana's laugh was light and airy. "Tell Ruslan you want to go, and I'm sure he will make it happen."

The thought of Ruslan lit me up, and that thread that tied us together hummed as we approached the stage where he lounged. "Sprite," he called from his makeshift throne. "You've gotten so strong."

Heat rose to my cheeks as I smiled shyly up at him, batting my lashes. "I had a good teacher."

His grin was roguish and made my stomach flutter. "Good luck with your other rounds."

"He has such a cute nickname for you," Liliana sighed. "I wish Endre would step it up a notch. You get gems and horses and armor and sweet words, and I get... sex."

Domi and I snorted simultaneously. I opened my mouth to retort that I also got sex, but a tug around my middle tore the words from my mouth as we found Kazimir, Endre, Viktor, Vadim, and Kaztar stepping away from the spear-throwing range.

Shit, shit, shit.

Kazimir's eyes flashed black like they had when he'd been in Ruslan's face that morning, and the males all stiffened around him when they noticed our approach. I was stuck halfway between my two mates, and once again I felt like I was being ripped apart as the string that tugged me to Kazimir forced my feet forward and the thread that bound me to Ruslan tautened and pulled me backward.

Why couldn't I just make a fucking choice?

This feeling of being torn was exhausting, as was constantly draining my magic to shift and block the emotions of everyone around me.

I shoved away all the feelings screaming for my attention and focused on putting one foot in front of the other. Liliana sauntered up to Endre, running her fingers along his chest and down his arm, causing his throat to bob as his peridot eyes traced her every movement. Then she patted his cheek and shouldered past him, lining up at a station where a young male was laying out spears. Endre's eyes followed her as she went, and it wasn't until Vadim pushed him that he followed along behind Viktor and Kazimir, whose aura swirled with that oiliness once again. Kaztar planted a chaste kiss on his wife's cheek before following the rest of the Night Fae toward the station set up for tug-of-war.

After we'd finished throwing spears, the three of us wandered to the leaderboard, where our names and event scores were seared into the smooth stone with fire magic. I quickly checked the ranks of my Iron Realm friends – Drazen, Zuriel, Savich, and a few other of our personal guards – before my attention snagged on Kazimir's rank. He outclassed Viktor, Endre, Vadim, and Kaztar in every event, some by quite a margin. My brows pinched together as I reexamined the scores, certain there must have been some mistake.

Kazimir was tall and strong, but he was by no means the biggest male competing. His stone-lifting score was nearly that of Savich and King Consort Geza.

There was no way he could possibly be that strong.

My stomach tightened, and somehow I knew that it was related to that sinister aura that surrounded him and the darkness that flashed in his eyes.

Liliana interrupted my inward spiral with a tug on my arm, leading me toward the sand pit where a thick, brown rope stretched between two males. I groaned internally as we settled along on the sidelines, not happy with having to watch the Night Fae compete while we waited for our turn. Away from the other contestants, we passed the last of the warm wine between us, letting it chase the chill from our fingers.

The Night Fae stood off to the side, stripping out of their tunics and tossing them aside as they prepared to flaunt their strength. Sweat rolled off all of them, steaming against the cold air, and I couldn't help the heat that pooled in my belly as Kazimir's trunk twisted and flexed, showcasing the ink decorating his broad chest. As if he felt my attention on him, he glanced in our direction. His emerald eyes were clear, though they were filled with longing. I averted my gaze, instead focusing on the end of the battle in the sand, where an Iron Fae I did not know plowed face-first as one of the Day Realm's High Lords claimed his victory.

Whoops and cheers filled the air as High Lord Domon stretched a hand out to help his fallen opponent, and the two embraced quickly once the male rose from the sand. The match officiant called for the next competitors, and Kazimir kicked off his boots and entered the pit. "You got this, Kazimir!" Viktor yelled from the sidelines, and Vadim wolf-whistled, causing Kazimir to flash him a smirk before turning to face his opponent.

Artur, Drazen's second in command, approached the thick, red mark toward the end of the rope and hefted it, red Dragon scales flashing across his forearms before disappearing. I had sparred with Artur numerous times, and in each bout, his expression never changed, giving me an unnerving sense that he was toying with his food before going in for the final kill. He carried that same energy with him now, his dark eyes impassive and jaw held loosely as Kazimir lifted the opposite end of the rope.

The tension between the males was more than just the length of rope stretched between them, and the sneer Kazimir wore when he realized Artur was Félvér lasted only a moment, but I made note of it. A whistle pierced the pit, and Artur yanked with all his might, sending Kazimir stumbling forward before he planted his feet and recovered.

Drazen and the other Félvér began shouting words of encouragement at Artur, while the Night Fae did the same for Kazimir. The sand stirred beneath each of their feet as they scrambled for purchase, alternating between leaning backward and forward and shifting their weight around as they tried to gain the upper hand. Both males' forearms strained with the effort, veins and tendons popping as they gripped the thick rope with both hands.

"You've got to admit, this is a nice view," Liliana joked, flicking her hair over her shoulder.

Domi snorted in response. "I won't say no to shirtless males showing off their physical prowess against one another. If Kaztar wins, he'll definitely get a prize tonight."

It was my turn to snort. "You'll ride him better than any of your horses?"

"Exactly," Domi grinned, her green eyes roaming over her husband's bare chest across the sand. He winked at her, then returned his attention to the game.

Artur had been dragged forward, nearing the center mark. His dark eyes were hard and his mouth was set in a firm line, showing more expression than I'd ever seen him display before. Drazen and the others screamed as the mark closed in on him, the competition between Night and Iron reaching a new peak. Ruslan's raspy voice rose in the distance behind me, as if his whole focus was on this match.

If Kazimir won this, would there be an all-out brawl?

It was no secret at that moment that there was tension between the two realms, and even more so between my two groups of friends. And it was all because of me.

Guilt slammed into me as if I'd dropped one of those heavy stones on my stomach. I was the cause of the tension, and I was only making it worse by not making a choice. But I knew, deep down, that the moment that choice was made, the consequences would be outside of my control, and once the ball was rolling, there would be no stopping it. I was delaying the inevitable, and the longer it continued, the higher the stakes would be – the Goddess had told me as much when she appeared to me in my dreams only a few days before.

The Fates seemed to be toying with me too in this moment, showing me exactly what would happen no matter who I chose. The animosity had only risen since the start of Béke, and without a doubt, there would be a war once it was over. Ruslan and Zuriel had wanted to avoid a war like the one that broke out between the Angels and Demons millennia ago, but with each passing day, it seemed unavoidable.

Whether the Night Realm had brought an army to the Iron Realm's doorstep wasn't a question I had yet asked, and I doubted the two females would tell me even if I did. Liliana's loyalty may lie with me, but she wouldn't put her brother or Endre in harm's way either.

A roar snapped me out of my thoughts, and we jumped to our feet as Artur's arms shook from the effort of holding on to the rope, drops of blood slipping from between his fingers and colliding with the sand. Kazimir took one step back, then another, pulling Artur with an ease that should have been impossible given how long their battle had lasted, until finally Kazimir yanked the rope toward him, his biceps flexing with the effort. Artur stumbled over the center line, defeated.

Those emerald orbs flashed to me, seeming to dance with amusement at my shocked expression. His torso shone with sweat, and as he dropped the rope, his back muscles flexed in the most delicious way. I shook my head, trying to rid myself of hungry thoughts.

It's just the bond and the fact that we fucked earlier.

Artur shot to his feet, not bothering to acknowledge Kazimir's victory, and stomped to the sidelines, rejoining his unit and binding his raw and bloody palms. Kriath, an Eagle Shifter Félvér who was part of our personal guard, stalked forward and squared up with Endre at the rope. The air was so thick with tension that I could have sliced into it like cake. Heavy footsteps closed in behind me, and I glanced over my shoulder to see Ruslan carving a path straight toward me. His iron-gray eyes swirled with black fire, and his jaw was clenched tight as he snatched me into his chest, snaking his arms around me like a vice. Kazimir's attention turned from his friend to us, and his lips curled back, baring his teeth at Ruslan in an obvious challenge.

The thread that tied me to Ruslan vibrated with nervous energy, wrapping me in an embrace that set my teeth on edge. Drawing a deep breath, I reached out to Kazimir's mind with my magic, siphoning away his rage, while my physical connection to Ruslan allowed me to do the same for him.

But I didn't stop there. I pushed soothing emotions out around me like I was making a ripple in a pond, and one by one, the males crowding the sidelines relaxed, shoulders dropping, arms uncrossing, and breathing evening out. If it weren't for Ruslan holding me up, I might have collapsed by the time I was finished.

"Sprite, are you alright?" Ruslan bent his head to whisper in my ear. "I felt you take away my anger again."

"I'm a bit tired now. I've been using my magic more than I should be, and I keep forgetting to clear."

A hand flexed across my stomach. "You have to clear, like Zuriel said. I can't lose you because you overextended your magic. I came so close," Ruslan's voice broke on the last word, "to losing you to burnout. I cannot bear to go through that again, to watch you suffer like that again."

"Then can you try to ease some of this tension between the Iron and Night Realms? It's killing me to keep trying to keep the peace through my magic," I snapped, my exhaustion and stress seeping into my words.

Ruslan glossed over my tone as if it wasn't there, and for that I was grateful. "I don't think there can be peace between us, at least not until you've chosen," he murmured, arms tightening slightly before relaxing. His words echoed my earlier thoughts, and I could only nod in response. "But I do have another gift for you."

"Oh?" I said, my eyes still on Kriath and Endre slipping through the sand.

"Tonight, I will show you. I hope it will help you feel better." Ruslan planted a kiss on the top of my head, and I sighed, leaning into his embrace and burying myself in the scent of cedarwood and vanilla.

He remained there with me, holding me upright until all the males had finished their matches. The Night Fae had won every match, except for the one where Viktor battled Drazen for control of the rope. No fights broke out, thanks to my earlier intervention, but I was exhausted and unsure if I could push myself through the tug-of-war match against an Iron Fae female. She was much taller than me, her long frame cut with muscle, and from the looks of it she might have been a warrior.

"You've got this, Izidora!" Liliana cheered from the sidelines where she stood next to Ruslan. He shot me a knee-weakening smile, and I squared my shoulders and faced my opponent. Kazimir's attention sent a shiver down my spine, and I tried my hardest not to look at him, only to have my bond force my hand. Those emerald orbs blazed with lust as I hefted the rope, my newly built muscles straining under the tension.

Insidious bloom — don't show your thorns until it's too late.

The whistle signaled the start of my match, and I pitched forward, my lack of focus causing me to lose ground. I gritted my teeth and dug my heels in, arms screaming in protest as I anchored myself in place. The female across from me was already panting with effort, leaning back so far she was nearly parallel with the ground. After watching five matches in a row, I knew that meant she was nearly immobile, so I switched tactics.

My trick had to be executed perfectly, otherwise I'd land myself straight over the center line. With the rope still gripped tightly in my hands, I straightened quickly, sending the female stumbling back, and before she could regain her balance I dug my feet into the sand and yanked with all my might, sending her veering in another direction. A strangled cry escaped my lips as I held on and backstepped, pulling her and the heavy rope toward me. The tendons in my hands popped around the rope as I readjusted my grip.

I was going to win this.

Liliana screamed at me to keep going, and Ruslan roared his approval as I managed to drag my opponent forward another step. My arms trembled under the strain, and my legs wobbled as I continued to battle for control of the pit. With one last ferocious tug, I pulled the rope toward me with everything I had, and the female stumbled across the line.

The rope hit the ground a moment later, and I collapsed to my hands and knees, chest heaving and my whole body shaking from the effort. "Thank fuck," I panted into the ground. Despite all odds, I had pulled through and won. The victory filled me with a sense of accomplishment that had been absent while I drowned in a sea of self-doubt.

Ruslan captured me in his arms the moment I pushed to my feet. "You were amazing, sprite. I am so proud of you." His words were a salve, soothing the acute ache that was like a permanent scar on my soul. Ruslan understood that pain, that angst of always having to prove myself to obtain the love and approval I wanted, and his understanding of my need to hear those words despite the obvious evidence of my victory meant more than he knew.

I pulled away from him, reaching up a hand to cup the back of his neck and bring his lips to mine. When they connected, my body lit up like it never had before, and his large hands pulled me flush to his body, tipping me backward and deepening our kiss. Whoops and whistles sounded around us as his tongue danced with mine, and I smiled through our kiss because it felt so right.

Being understood was like bathing in the light of a new dawn, the warm rays caressing each part of me that I thought needed to be kept hidden. Being understood, being loved by Ruslan, was like walking into warm darkness, where all walls were free to fall away, where all layers of self-preservation were shed like scraps of fabric, and where I could be unequivocally myself. As we kissed, the fog of doubt drifted from my mind, revealing the truth that lay beneath it.

Ruslan was the right choice.

21

KAZIMIR

BÉKE DAY FIVE

Watching Ruslan and Izidora wrap themselves around each other in front of the entire fucking arena set my blood on fire. The sweat that dripped off my body was nothing compared to the heat burning in my chest, where the twisted binding magic roared to life. The bond I shared with Izidora tightened as I pulled on it, desperate for her to look at me, to *feel* me. But she ignored it, smiling instead at the king of the Iron Realm.

If it was a king Izidora wanted, I would make that happen.

My teeth nearly cracked with the force of my gritting them, and I stalked away from the tug-of-war ring, snatching my shirt off the ground in the process. The cold air slapping my face did nothing to soothe the tightness in my chest and neck, and it took every ounce of my self-control not to unleash ropes of pain on every single fucking person in attendance.

Red and black coated my vision until I found myself standing in front of the leaderboard, my name higher than all the rest. A wicked grin split my face as I realized I had won the entire event, and quite handily by the number etched beside my name. Thanks to my binding magic, I was stronger, faster, and more powerful than I had ever been.

The discarded tunic clung to the sweat on my skin as I pulled it over my head and walked to the nearest stand serving hot drinks. The scent of spiced cinnamon reminded me of Izidora as the tender handed me a mulled cider.

With all my might, I locked away every emotion raging inside me, focusing on the taste of the cider over my tongue as I waited for the rest of the contestants to finish their events and return to the stage.

An idea started forming in my head as I watched the Fae from afar, and by the time everyone had gathered around the stage, it was a full-fledged plan. My friends sauntered up beside me, drinks in hand, as Ruslan began to speak.

"The strength competition has concluded. The Iron Realm offers a prize for the individual winner of each event, as well as an overall winner." He paused, sweeping out a hand for a dozen servants to bring the prizes forward. Each velvet pillow cradled gems, metalwork, and fine fabrics, a testament to the wealth the Iron Realm could so carelessly toss away.

An officiant stepped forward, handing Ruslan a folded piece of paper. An excited tension hung in the silent air as he opened it. His expression darkened, and his fingers tightened over the paper. It was gone in a flash, and he lifted his head, plastering an easy smirk across his face.

"The first winner is High Lord Kazimir Vaszoly of the Night Realm." He spit out the words like they were poison, but his tone was lost among the claps and cheers.

"Go!" Viktor said, clapping me on the shoulder and shoving me forward.

I allowed a smile to reach my lips, but my eyes were hard

and cold as I ascended the stairs to the stage and crossed to the center where Ruslan and the servant touting the prize waited. The metalwork on the faceplate meant to protect a horse's head was exquisite, and the spikes sticking out of it brought images of Fek racing into battle against the Iron Fae to the forefront of my mind.

I accepted it, then waved to the crowd, acting like the king I was about to be. The beast thrummed in my chest when the king of the Iron Realm drew near, whispering to me to throw out those thick black ropes and choke him until he could no longer breathe, then rip the Iron Crown from his head and place it on my own.

I shoved it away and allowed the cheers that greeted me as I showed off the piece to soothe the need to be seen and appreciated for the hero I was. I loved every moment of attention they threw my way.

Ruslan held up a hand, bringing silence once again. I turned to leave, and with a gloriously pained grumble, Ruslan said, "Don't go anywhere." Clearing his throat, he said louder, "High Lord Kazimir Vaszoly has won every prize. He is the overall winner of this Béke's strength competition."

The Night and Crystal Fae erupted with excitement, and I met Ruslan's eye in a clear challenge. Hatred blazed in them, no doubt because I'd embarrassed his entire realm in the span of a few hours. I held a deferential smile as he handed me prize after prize, ensuring the crowd – and Izidora – saw my graciousness. I thanked him loudly over and over again, commenting on how fine the prizes were.

By the time the last one was piled at my feet, I thought Ruslan might unleash the claws he'd shown us the other day and swipe at my throat. Instead, he faced the gathered Fae. "This concludes the day's events. Tomorrow, we will race around these arenas on horseback. I wish you all a lovely evening of cele-bration."

The sound of laughter and footsteps echoed around the valley as the onlookers exited the stands and the competitors congratulated each other and embraced. Ruslan stalked from the stage, the servants and officiants following closely behind him, though the queens remained seated, waiting for their husbands. Endre, Viktor, Vadim, and Kaztar ascended to the stage behind the two kings.

"Congratulations, Kazimir," Kaztar said by way of greeting before scooping an armful of prizes.

I shrugged, acting as though I was humbled by my own obvious prowess. "Thank you, Kaztar. Your encouragement helped me carve the path to victory."

He snorted in response. I helped my friends carry my winnings to our horses, securing the metal plate over Fek's bridle. He looked as fierce as I'd imagined, and as I mounted him I fell into fantasies of destroying the Iron Realm once and for all.

But it was not the time to overextend my imagination on daydreams; I needed to set my new plan in motion.

I released a heavy sigh, allowing my shoulders to slump as the five of us rode along the path back to Ryza Citadel. "I don't think Izidora will choose me."

Viktor and Vadim shared a look that made me think they agreed, but Endre butted in with reassuring words. "You don't know that. There is still time."

Dropping and shaking my head, I said, "After the way she kissed him at the tug-of-war, I don't think there is time for me anymore. I'm too late. I just don't want him to become king of the Night Realm too."

Kaztar pulled his horse up, stopping our procession. "Hold

on. We cannot allow that to happen. I will not put my realm in the hands of that madman. If you truly think that Izidora choosing Ruslan is inevitable, we must act quickly. Izidora was never crowned, nor did King Zalan name her heir apparent. The line of succession remains open."

If not for the thick cloak covering my smile, Kaztar would have seen that I'd maneuvered him right where I wanted him. Clearing my throat and swiping at my eyes, I lifted my gaze to meet his. "What do you suggest? We can't get a raven to Este Castle fast enough to make a decision, and I'm almost certain High Lords Valintin and Luzak would vie for the throne again."

The five of us had formed a circle, facing each other on our mounts. I glanced from friend to friend, hoping none could see through the act. But I was good at hiding my true feelings when I wanted to, for none of them knew the level of obsession I had with Izidora prior to us finding her. Viktor's dark brows were pinched over his sage eyes, and I knew him well enough to know he was analyzing every possibility. "Our fathers have given us full autonomy to make decisions on their behalf. We don't need to send a raven to Este Castle when we have a majority here."

"That is true," Vadim said, "but if one of you is to become king, that would take you out of the running, evening out the vote."

A small smile tugged up the corner of my lips. "Before we left Este Castle, I spoke with Endre and Viktor's fathers about moving House Arzeni up once Izidora and I married, since House Vaszoly's seat would be open. They agreed."

Vadim's evergreen eyes shone for a moment before he smoothed back his long, dark brown hair piled into a bun on the top of his head. "But House Vaszoly is still a High House at the moment."

Kaztar interrupted him. "I see what you're saying, Kazimir.

We could elevate Vadim to our level, knowing that one of us would be king, to provide a fair vote. I like it."

"Precisely," I agreed. "The ruling of the Night Realm is being handled by your fathers at the moment, and there's not much they can do here or we can do there." I dropped my voice low so only they could hear. "The Iron Realm still invaded our sovereign territory, and regardless of Izidora choosing me or Ruslan, that cannot go without a response. We need a leader who can get us the justice we deserve."

"Fuck yes," Viktor said, his eyes flashing with excitement.

"I agree completely, Kazimir," Kaztar grinned. "After you saved us from the avalanche, I think you should be king. I trust you with my life, and I trust you to lead me in battle. You are the leader of the Nighthounds, and these males have always looked to you for guidance. So long as you can contain your... new magic, you'd make a fine king."

Fucking Fates, Kaztar said everything I needed him to say.

"Kaztar, you flatter me. I was going to suggest that you should be king. After all, House Rass ruled before House Valynor," I responded, hoping I sounded humble.

"You forget that House Vaszoly ruled between the two," he chided, then he looked to Viktor, Vadim, and Endre. "What do you think? Should Kazimir be our new king?"

The wolfish grin on Vadim's face preceded his confirmation. Viktor needed no further convincing, though Endre's peridot eyes held a hint of something I could not place. "I don't know who else could lead us like Kazimir," Endre finally said.

I dipped my head, feigning humility at their decision. "I don't know that I could possibly rule an entire realm, especially since I was not trained for it. But with you all by my side, we will make the Night Realm, and all of Északi, a better place."

"All hail, King Kazimir Vaszoly of the Night Realm," Kaztar

cheered, and Vadim released an answering whoop of excitement.

"Welcome to the High Houses, Vadim," I laughed, saluting my friend.

"Think I can get even more pussy tonight at Steel now that I'm a High Lord?" He waggled his eyebrows, sending our group into a fit of laughter.

Endre rolled his eyes, then turned his mount back to the road. "Probably some dick, too," he called over his shoulder. Vadim and Viktor dug their heels into their mounts' sides, trying to catch Endre, and the three of them squabbled while Kaztar and I hung back.

"Thank you for your support, Kaztar. I want you to know that I do consider you a friend and an essential part of our group."

The male was quiet for a moment, the silence between us filled with the clopping of hooves and indistinct arguing ahead of us. "I'm sorry you didn't get Izidora back, Kazimir. If Domi had chosen another male over me... I don't know what I would have done. I will forgive you your outbursts because I cannot imagine the pain you are in. Let's get the rest of this feast over with, and then we'll get vengeance for the Night Realm and for you."

"How should we announce the change in leadership?" I asked him. "Unfortunately we do not have the Night Crown with us."

Kaztar snorted. "We're in the Iron Realm. Go have something made. Something that looks like a big 'fuck you' to Ruslan and will make Izidora regret her choice."

"She hasn't officially chosen yet, but maybe my newfound status will sway her. Then it might even be a win-win," I shrugged.

"Brilliant, Kazimir. Let's leave them to their argument and go find a jeweler to make a crown fit for the king of the Night Realm," Kaztar grinned, his horse picking up speed as he sensed his rider's excitement.

I allowed him to lead us in the direction of Radence, all the while biting back the smile that threatened to reveal my victory.

I was King of the Night Realm, and I would get what was mine.

INTERLUDE

Light hair fanned out across the pillow as the female laid flushed and waiting for the chiseled male before her to strip. His emerald eyes glinted with a hint of something sinister as he watched the rapid rise and fall of her bare breasts. "Hands above your head," he instructed, pressing a knee into the mattress and causing it to dip.

She did as he bid, gripping the pole of the wooden headboard with both hands. Moments later, they were restrained by silvery cuffs of magic, rendering her unable to move them. A giggle escaped her lips as the male drank in her naked form, his cock bobbing as he made his way to her center. Bracing his hands on either side of her head, he dipped his own to her neck, nipping at the fluttering pulse and growling when he felt its erratic beat. "Are you ready to play?"

"Yes," she breathed, arching her back off the bed and brushing her hardened nipples against his chest. She was immediately pinned against the bed by a hand on her throat and another on her hip bone, eliciting a shocked gasp. He rested his hand around her delicate throat, loving the way it worked beneath him as she struggled to breathe, struggled to knock him off with her hands pinned above her head.

Only when her lashes fluttered did he release her, and she drew in a gasping breath. He ran his nose along her neck, kissing and sucking where moments ago he had been choking. Backing away from her, he shoved her legs apart, using his magic to pin her ankles in place so she was bared to him completely.

Before she could protest, he dropped between her thighs, using his tongue to part her folds and finding her wet and wanting. She moaned, a deep, reverberating sound that pressed into his jaw as her thighs began to shake. Gripping them hard enough to bruise, he forced them further apart and himself further inside, moving his tongue from her folds to her clit and nipping harshly.

"Goddess!" she screamed, arching off the bed at the bite, but the male's rough hands pinning her legs and his magic pinning her wrists and ankles did not allow for much movement. He soothed the ache with flicks of his tongue, and she relaxed backward once more.

"You've got to be prepared for all of me. Be a good girl and come for me while I fuck you with my fingers," he said before shoving two into her dripping center.

She was tight in all the right ways, and he moaned to himself at how good she was going to feel around his cock. It didn't take long for her to orgasm, not when his fingers and tongue found the right rhythm and the tension between them was palpable. The whole night, she'd flirted with him, sat on his lap, and trailed her fingers along his shoulders and jaw. His brothers-in-arms were jealous when she invited him to her room in the large manor home they currently occupied. He had shot them a salacious wink as he left them behind.

"Kazimir!" she cried, her walls pulsing around his fingers,

and he withdrew them immediately, pushing off the bed and lining himself up with her entrance before she'd even come down from where she floated.

"Time to give you what you want," he growled, seating himself to the hilt and landing with hands braced on either side of her head. His thrusts were brutal and punishing, and a slapping sound filled the room, along with his heaving breaths.

The female was totally at his mercy, and his dark desires wanted to play that night. She whimpered and moaned as he spread her open, his cock licking every inch of her inner walls. His pounding was so relentless that the bed rocked rapidly, creaking under the ferocity of his pace. Craning his mouth to the crook of her shoulder, he bit down, drawing a hint of blood from her skin and leaving a purple bruise in his wake.

"So fucking good," he praised as she continued to take him. Moving his way down her shoulder, he imprinted more dark marks with his teeth, and she tensed beneath him.

"That's starting to hurt," she whimpered.

"You can take it, Izidora," he shot back, moving a hand to her throat.

"That's not my–" she protested before he cut off her air.

His spine tingled, balls tightening in preparation to come, and with his thrusts growing erratic, he pulled out of her. "Fuck, Izidora," he groaned again, coating her belly and chest in his seed while her lashes fluttered against her high cheekbones.

Releasing her throat, he returned his fingers to her core, fucking her with his hand until she came moments later, wetness gushing everywhere. The female's breasts heaved, and her face and chest were fully flushed as she eyed him with a mixture of lust and confusion. He left her on the bed, cuffed with his magic, until he was fully dressed. From his pocket, he pulled a small bag of coins and plopped it on a bedside table.

"Tell no one about what happened between us," he

instructed, striding for the door. Only once he was about to reach for the handle and open it did he banish the silver from her body, slipping into the hall and jogging down the stairs toward the sound of merry voices that carried through the manor.

Once he'd slipped back into the party, he sought out his brothers-in-arms, finding three out of four of them waiting near where he'd left them. The one with shaggy hair and a beard clapped him on the back when he broke their circle. "Nice work, brother. She looked delicious."

"Where's Kriztof?" the emerald-eyed one asked.

"He found himself a pretty Crystal Fae to take upstairs, too. If it weren't for Cazius watching us like a hawk, we'd have joined you two," the other shrugged in reply. "He really wants us to work this year's crowd at Béke to find some leads on the lost princess."

It had been sixteen years since she had been kidnapped, and new leads were few and far between. "Let's go see what we can find," the emerald-eyed one sighed.

The four companions slipped into the crowd, their masks giving them the perfect cover to strike up a conversation with the Fae in attendance. They were all smooth talkers after years of coaxing secrets from unwilling mouths, though their efforts were not fruitful that night – at least not in finding information on the lost princess.

II

THE CAVE

22

RUSLAN

Béke Day Five

Thirteen males waited for us in the cave where Izidora had been chained. Drazen and I had rushed from the strength competition to move them while the streets were still packed and Fae and Félvér busied themselves with food and drink. These thirteen were all pure-blooded Iron Fae, and I had no qualms about killing them – not that it would have stopped me had they been Félvér. These males had raped and scarred my mate, and they would not live to see another day.

Under the cover of darkness, Izidora and I slipped from a hidden exit of Ryza Citadel and onto the streets of Radence. The night air was like a slap to the face, and I knew without a doubt that by the time we returned in the morning the ground would be covered in snow. The cloak I had gifted Izidora was pulled tightly around her, the rare white fur trapping every bit of heat she needed to stay warm.

Maybe I should see if Rares has a way to fix that rib of hers that always aches in the cold.

"Let me know if you need to stop and warm up, sprite."

Her aquamarine eyes shone up at me from beneath the steel gray hood of her cloak. "I'll be fine. Where are we going anyway?"

I steered her down a side street, toward a nondescript building a dozen blocks away. "Do you trust me?"

She stopped in her tracks, somewhat hidden in the shadows between two stone buildings. "You're making me nervous. What is going on?" She chewed on her lip while she waited for my reply.

I cracked my neck, then blew out a long, slow breath. "Do you remember my first promise to you?"

Her brows furrowed as she stared up at me. "That you'd spend the rest of your life making up for the pain I'd endured?"

I nodded. "This is one of those ways I am making it up to you." I snatched her arm and continued leading her toward the building. "But I need you to trust me. I know this isn't going to be easy for you."

That thread that tied us together hummed at our proximity, but I wanted her closer. I wanted her to know I would burn this fucking world down for her, and that she was the light in my life. But before the night was over, she was going to descend into the dark with me. Our inner demons would be let out to play, and Izidora would reclaim some of that power that had been stripped from her at the hands of those males.

The arm I was holding onto drifted from beneath her cloak to wrap around my waist, and I released it, pulling her closer instead as we neared the building. "I love you, sprite."

"I love you, Ruslan." Her voice was as soft and silky as the open sky above us.

The heavy iron doors were unlocked, and I pushed one open a crack, just enough to allow Izidora and myself to slip through them into the darkness beyond. Izidora threw bubble lights into the air, and they scattered, illuminating the space around us.

The entrance to the tunnels beneath the Iron Realm looked like any other warehouse in the city, save for one key difference – an intricate metal box in the center of the space holding a wheeled contraption on rails.

"What is that?" Izidora breathed, circling the box, her curiosity piqued.

"It's a cart like the miners use to enter the mountains in the Iron Realm, but this one has been modified to carry people instead of gems. It has straps so you won't fall out when we move with magic," I explained, joining her beside the cart and placing my hands on her shoulders. She leaned into my touch, and my heart leaped at her affection.

She was so close to accepting our mating bond.

"And where does it go?"

"To Vasvain."

The air around us dropped a dozen degrees, and Izidora went deathly still and utterly silent. My keen Dragon sense picked up on her racing heart, and the scent of her fear filled my nostrils. I spun her to face me, then crouched down so we were at eye level. Her beautiful jewel-like eyes were wet and filled with trepidation, and the shallow rise and fall of her chest showed me exactly how close she was to falling apart.

"Vasvain?" Her voice was barely a whisper, and her pink pout began to tremble.

My hands massaged her shoulders as I tried to soothe her. "When we face our fears, they no longer have power over us. That is where true freedom lies, in the space after fear." A lone tear fell from her eye and trailed down her cheek before I caught it with my thumb. "The first time I saw that spark of fire in you, I wanted to grow it into a wildfire that consumed everything in its wake. Day after day, I've watched you step into that inferno and stoke it even higher until you've become a force to be reckoned with."

She drew a serrated breath. "So we're going there so I can face my fears?"

"Izidora, we are going to return to Vasvain so you can reclaim all the power you lost at the hands of the males who abused you. I tracked down every last one of them, and they await us in the cave where you were chained, ready for you to kill them."

Her mouth popped open, and she blinked at me for a few moments before regaining her composure. "You really did that?"

"I would do anything for you, sprite. I'd burn this whole fucking world down to avenge you and enjoy every moment of suffering I inflicted. You are *everything* to me, Izidora, and I fucked up by not checking on you all those years you were kept there. But now, I get the pleasure of helping you become powerful on your own, so you never have to suffer at the hands of another male again."

The words poured out of me with such conviction that Izidora threw herself into me as they dried up, her mouth more desperate for mine than I'd ever felt before. I welcomed her touch, her tongue, her nails scratching my scalp as she arched into me, needing to be closer. I unclasped the cloak from her neck and let it fall to the floor alongside mine, keeping her warm with my body heat as I crushed her against me. The scent of her, the feel of her, the taste of her, was enough to drive any male mad, but I would gladly lose my mind if it meant her being mine.

Izidora pulled away, breathless, pupils blown out as she stared up at me. "I don't have any weapons."

"I have everything you need already there." I nipped her bottom lip as I kissed her one last time, then directed her to the cart. She hopped onto one of the front seats, then looked at me expectantly. The wood was smooth beneath my fingers as I climbed in beside her, pulling a fur over our laps. I strapped both of us in, ensuring the blanket was secured too, before tapping into the well of black fire that slumbered in my chest.

"It's a long journey, and we need to move quickly. I know you don't like going fast, but I promise I've got you." Draping an arm over her, I pulled her into my chest. Her arms circled my waist, and she leaned into me a moment before I lowered us onto the track beneath the city.

The metal rails lined up with a loud clack, and all that was in front of us was darkness. "If you want to throw up your bubble lights, you can. It might give you something to focus on as we go. Ready?"

"Ready," she breathed, her petite body tense against mine. A halo of little white lights surrounded us, brightening the space and revealing two parallel lines that seemed endless as they disappeared into the distance.

"Hang on," I warned, then pushed my magic out, sending us flying down the tracks at a breakneck pace. Izidora released a small scream, but as the moments passed and we did not crash, she quieted. My thumb stroked her shoulder as I held her, and I did not object to how tightly she clung to me, her small hands fisting my clothes and gripping me like I was her lifeline.

The pace was too fast for us to speak, wind whipping in our eyes and ears as we rushed beneath the earth. After a few minutes, other tunnels began to flash by on our left and right, leading to other parts of the Agrenak Mountains. The Iron Realm had been preparing for a continent-wide war since the last one, digging this massive network of tunnels that only those gifted with earth magic could use.

And the other realms had no clue.

Within a few days, tens of thousands of soldiers could travel from the Iron Realm to the outskirts of the Crystal Realm, Night Realm, and Day Realm, with dozens of caves dug into the deepest parts of the mountain range filled with supplies and places to rest and recover. The cave in Vasvain where Izidora was kept was one example of this entire hidden network.

There was no doubt in my mind these tunnels would be put to use in the coming months, especially if Izidora chose me. Kazimir had tried and failed to win her back, and after his display over the last few days, I knew he would wage a war merely because he needed to feel like his dick was still big.

Izidora's empath magic could have swayed the rulers of the Crystal and Day Realms to our side without bloodshed, but Kazimir and the Night Realm's obsession with my mate would leave rivers running with blood across Északi.

The lack of a communication network across this vast continent would make surprise attacks easy for the Iron Realm, and we'd be able to wipe out entire armies before they knew we were already upon them. Once Izidora and I were installed as rulers over all of it, the Félvér, Telivér, and Fae of all races would be free to live where they wished, and with the powers of the Mages, I'd be able to seamlessly communicate with all the nobles across the realm, keeping the peace from the palace I'd built for Izidora.

Lights in the distance signaled our arrival at the first stop where we'd need to change tracks toward Vasvain. I slowed our pace until my ears echoed with the silence of the lonely mountains. Izidora's small fingers untangled themselves from my clothes as we crawled to a stop. She shook out her hands as I lifted mine to manipulate my magic, guiding the square of earth beneath the cart to turn before rolling the cart forward and resetting the stone. Eternal flames burned around us, magically enhanced to never go out, and I allowed Izidora a few more moments to gather herself before pushing down the next set of tracks.

"How far do these tunnels go?" she asked, her eyes

wandering over the rough stone tunnel and the torches that cast deep shadows around us.

"Everywhere under the Agrenak Mountains," I replied, easing us forward and allowing her to ask the questions I knew still swirled in her beautiful brain.

My curious little sprite.

"Really? How long did it take to build them?" She tucked a lock of chestnut hair behind her ear as the wind whipped it about.

"Nearly a century." I wrapped her up beneath my arm again and turned up the speed.

"And I'm assuming the other realms have no idea?" she shouted, her words ripped away by the roaring of the wind as we flew along the tracks.

I nodded, increasing our pace. Izidora's white bubble lights winked out, bathing us in black before she brought them back to life, making them dance in the darkness in front of us. Those pinpricks were our only guide, and it wasn't until more eternal flames appeared in the distance that anything other than Izidora's light and the endless void filled the space around us. Slowing once more, we rolled to a stop in the middle of an open space. The area on either side of the tracks had been carved high and wide with enough space to fit several hundred soldiers. Off to one side, pushed against the stone, there were a few carts like the one that ferried us here, and next to them was a pile of unlit lanterns and sacks of grain.

On the opposite side, a heavy iron door waited, silent and solemn. It was as if it too knew the magnitude of this moment. After all, it had witnessed me and Drazen drag Izidora's former captors, in chains, from these very tracks to the peak of the highest mountain in Északi.

I parked the cart on the tracks, since we'd be using it again to return to Radence, and hopped over the side, reaching my arms up to lift Izidora from it. Her nails dug into my shoulders as she balanced herself against me, and when I placed her gently on the ground, she did not release me immediately. I slipped my hand in hers, giving it an encouraging squeeze as we walked toward the looming door. The smell of her fear increased with every step forward. Fear was not the only scent that filled my nostrils; excitement blended in, creating an intoxicating mix that pulled a smirk to my mouth.

I flattened my hand on the smooth metal, and with a scraping groan, it slid open, revealing the slab of stone that would carry us thousands of feet upward. We paused on the threshold, and beside me, Izidora sucked in a shuddering breath.

Turning to her once more, I leveled a serious gaze on her. "These males will not hurt you, Izidora. I will be with you the entire time. You are not alone, and you will never be alone again. It's time to be free."

Izidora nodded once, a firm, determined gesture. Then she braided back her hair, revealing her bright, aquamarine eyes that held so much love. She was the most exquisite female I'd ever laid eyes on, and in that moment, a fire burned in her eyes that made me proud to be her mate.

"I love you, sprite. Step into the darkness with me."

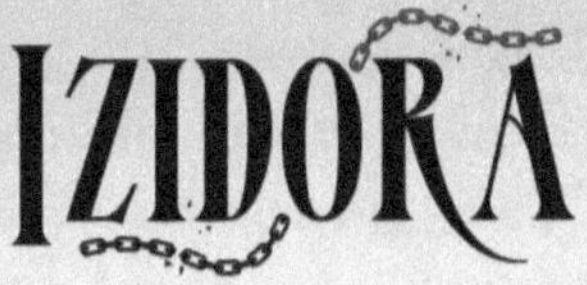

23

IZIDORA

Béke Day Five

When Ruslan had told me on our first day together that he would avenge me, I didn't believe him. I had thought his words were all a ploy to manipulate me into becoming a weapon for his use, but during our time together, Ruslan had shown me over and over that when he said he would do something for me, he meant it. I wholeheartedly believed him when he said that he'd die without me and burn the whole world down if that was what I desired.

Ruslan's love for me was the wildfire he wanted to bring out of me – all-consuming, never-ending, and filled with heat. His smoky eyes danced with black flame, and the darkest parts of him hummed just beneath the surface of his skin, ready to play.

"I love you, sprite. Step into the darkness with me."

And for once, I let go of my light and did just that. I grasped his outstretched hand and stepped into the lift with him. "I love you, Ruslan. You are the dark to my light, but tonight I want to be consumed with darkness – with you."

A tug on my arm pulled me into him, and he captured my lips in a bruising kiss as the iron door closed on us and the lift began to move. Ruslan's power was mighty, and it never ceased to amaze me how he could use so much of it while being wrapped up in me. His teeth nipped my lower lip, and I whimpered as he drew blood. His tongue lapped it away a moment later, the metallic taste coating both our mouths as he deepened our kiss. Fire pooled between my thighs, and I forgot all about us hurtling upward as his hands gripped my ass and pulled me off the ground. Wrapping my legs around his waist, I allowed him to hold me tighter, and a hand yanked my long braid back, tilting my head up and exposing my neck.

A trail of kisses left shivers in their wake as he made his way from my jaw to my ear and down to my exposed collarbone, stopping to suck on my pulse point along the way. "When we're finished killing them, I will fuck you senseless," Ruslan growled at my neck, and my thighs clenched together around him at the promise in his words. I rolled my hips against the hard planes of his stomach, and his large hands lowered me so I was flush against his hardness. "You get me so fucking hard, especially when I see that spark of fire in your eyes. You are so fucking perfect for me, hand-crafted by the Goddess herself."

The words went straight to my core, and it throbbed with need. Ruslan dragged me up and down his length, and the friction through our clothes barely eased the desperation vibrating in our bond to be closer. His forehead touched mine, and the corner of his mouth twitched up as he continued to grind against me, eliciting whimpers and a flush across my face.

"We should ride the lift like this every time," I managed to say, and his grin widened, eyes flashing with wicked desire.

"That can be arranged," he replied, his tone leaving no doubt that he meant it.

We slowed our ascent as we approached another iron

door, and I was suddenly breathless and dizzy. Ruslan seemed to sense this, and a strong arm wrapped around my back and held me in place as he turned to open it. Trepidation clenched my stomach as the door slid open with a heavy groan. We emerged into a domed room, the center occupied by a large hearth with tables surrounding it, some laden with dishes and cookware and others with blankets and other supplies.

"We can sit here until you regain your breath. The change in altitude was fast, and the air is much thinner up here." Ruslan carried me to a table with blankets, pulling out two chairs and placing me in one before wrapping me in the thick wool and rubbing my arms to bring some warmth into them.

But his touch couldn't chase the chill that settled over me, as if my body knew exactly where we were, despite never having laid eyes on the space.

"Is this…" I trailed off, mind still trying to process what I was seeing.

"Where you were kept? Yes."

The walls were lined with more of the same strange flames from the tunnels beneath the mountains, giving light to a space that was antithetical to the darkness where I had been chained. Down a hall, wood doors stood ajar, and in the closest room there was a bed and a small dresser, presumably where the guards had slept.

"I want to know everything that happened to you here. I want these bastards to feel the full force of my fury, and I want to make them pay for every last thing they did to you," Ruslan growled, placing his hands on my knees and leveling me with the most violent, serious expression he had ever offered.

Though it had only been months since I'd last been in this cave, it felt like a lifetime. So much had happened since the day Kazimir and the Nighthounds appeared in the darkness like

Goddess-sent saviors. The female who came of age that night was fearful, untrusting, ignorant, and powerless.

But my time with them had not been as true as I had once thought.

Kazimir had lied to me, manipulated me, and after seeing him again in the Iron Realm, I understood there were parts of him that had been kept hidden away – purposefully. I had trusted him, trusted all of the Nighthounds, thinking that anyone who claimed to have spent so long searching for me only had my best interests at heart. While the other Nighthounds may have, Kazimir did not. Kazimir had thought of only himself, and what I thought was infatuation was only obsession – and not of the type that made me feel safe and secure any longer. Mates may have had an extraordinary connection that made them closer than any two who naturally chose each other, but Ruslan had proven that there could still be a healthy balance to it, one that Kazimir did not offer, or know how to offer.

Kazimir may have helped me trust again, he may have shown me how to be powerful, but it was I who claimed that power for myself, who worked so hard every fucking day to rise above what had happened to me, and who chose to live instead of survive.

I was no longer a victim; I was an insidious bloom, thorns hidden beneath a pretty exterior, with a wildfire inside, ready to be loosed upon anyone who dared hurt me again.

I was a powerful Félvér, and I would bring the whole continent to its knees before me.

But first, some males needed reminding that they could not fuck with me and live to tell the tale.

So I opened my mouth and spoke every vile action and cruel comment into existence, unburdening myself to my mate. I recounted the faint memories of a kind caretaker who gave her life for me. I gritted my teeth and forced out the memories of my subsequent keepers and their visits, during which they forced me to recite poetry, to become elegant, eloquent, and intelligent in preparation for my noble role. I told him how I never believed them, because the moment they left and banished the light they'd brought with them, the worst of the guards would slink into my cave and whisper the opposite words into my ear, and then whip me if I fought them in any way. Then days later, the nicer ones would appear with treats, fresh clothes, and apologies on their lips. The cycle repeated itself, and I marked the endless passage of time by the arrival and departure of the females and the few hours of sound sleep I managed.

While I spoke, the air around us simultaneously chilled and heated with Ruslan's unbridled fury. He had to remove his hands from my knees, and by the way they gripped his own, I knew he would leave deep, purple imprints there. The way he vibrated with barely restrained anger would have once frightened me; now it made me burn for him in the best way, and I knew without a doubt he would go to the ends of the earth to avenge me.

Despite his own rage, he knew and understood this was something I needed to do.

Shucking off the blanket, I pushed to my feet and looked at my mate. "Where are they?"

I was ready to take my revenge.

"Chained to the wall they kept you on," he replied, rising smoothly to his feet. "Though there will be light while we kill them. I want to see the looks on their faces as they die."

From my time chained there, I knew they could hear every word that cut through the deathly silence of the cave. "Then we'll have to blind them one by one so they know what it is like to be kept in the dark."

Ruslan's expression turned feral, a darkness flashing in his eyes that made my toes curl. "So wicked, sprite. Who knew something so pretty could be so deadly." He placed his hand on the small of my back, guiding me away from the large living chamber and down a hall lined with torches. After a minute, the first place I ever saw beyond my wall appeared up to my right, the natural opening of the cave revealing the black of night beyond. The walls glittered in the firelight just like I remembered, the black stone creating a rough arch that disappeared into the darkness above. I paused mid-step and turned toward the mouth of the cave, faint childhood memories drifting into those of the night of my rescue.

Endre unlocking my chains. Kazimir scooping me into his arms. The free fall as we flew away from the cave. The smell of amber that filled my nostrils as I clung to him. The brilliance of the stars overhead, and the jagged, snow-capped peaks all around me.

A gust of cold air slapped my face as I reached the entrance, the overhang stopping only steps before a lip of jagged rock. The moon was full and at this altitude, it looked close enough to touch if I reached out my hand. A million twinkling stars gazed upon me, caressing me with their light among the endless dark around us. The view was breathtaking, and when Ruslan joined me, he wrapped his arms around me protectively.

"The day I arrived to take you home, I stood in this very spot, gazing over the peaks and wondering where you had gone. I thought I knew then what love was, and what a mate bond should feel like, but I was irrevocably mistaken. We haven't even accepted the bond yet, and I know that my heart would shatter if we parted. My life is yours, my heart is yours, my soul is yours, and without you, I am nothing. You are everything to me, sprite, and there are not enough words to express the depths of what I feel for you."

I tried to picture Ruslan standing here on his own, looking down at the world below. The male who came to Este Castle to take me to the Iron Realm was so different from the one safe-guarding me now. Ruslan still held his cocky attitude and ruthlessness, but somehow he had softened, especially with me. I loved when he grabbed me like he'd never let me go, kissed me like I was the air he needed to breathe, and caged me beneath him while we moved together. He made me feel safe enough to let go and trust that he would take care of me; he never made me feel trapped and powerless.

"We're both so different than we were that night," I murmured, taking one last look at the star-dusted sky.

Ruslan kissed the top of my head. "And better for it."

I slid my hand into his, and we retraced our steps, entering a hall with fewer torches, the end of it disappearing into an endless black. Tingles raced across my body as we stepped beyond the firelight, from both anxiety and adrenaline. I was returning to the place where I had been endlessly abused for countless years, and my every nerve was alight with anticipation.

And I was not alone.

Ruslan's hand tightened around mine as if he could sense the direction of my thoughts, and with his free hand he called black flame to his palm to light the way. A serrated breath passed my lips, and I called white bubbles of light to my hand, then threw them into the air around us, lighting the path to the males who had abused me.

As we crept along the hall, muffled whimpers and the smell of urine reached my senses, along with the occasional scrape of iron against rock – a sound that would always be familiar to me. A chamber opened on our left, and I froze on the spot, heart hammering wildly as my magic was swallowed in the void only a few feet ahead.

This was it.

I took a tentative step forward, and then another, pushing myself through my fear of returning to this spot.

What if this had all been a ruse, and I was about to be chained again?

The thought stopped me in my tracks, and Ruslan hesitated only a moment before folding me into his chest and stroking my hair and back. "Shh, sprite, I've got you." I didn't realize I was crying until the fabric of Ruslan's tunic became wet beneath my face, and I forced myself to breathe. "You are so brave."

He continued to stroke and whisper words of encouragement to me until I felt calm enough to break from his embrace. I swiped at my eyes, then opened them to the sight of a hundred candles and lanterns scattered around the space, casting light around the cave where I had been chained, raped, and abused. Ruslan's black fire was intimidating, but I wanted to leave my own mark on the minds of these males, so I swapped each black flame for ones of brilliant white, so bright they were nearly blinding.

Thirteen males were chained and gagged, lined up side by side against the rough-hewn wall that was more familiar than my own face. Most were covered in dirt or blood or both, with scraggly hair and beards on some, while others lacked the layers of grime.

"How long did this take you?" I asked Ruslan as I stalked along the line of males, examining each of them closely as I passed, finally looking upon the faces of those who had hurt me.

"Too long," Ruslan hissed, squatting next to a leather wrap and unfurling it to reveal an array of gleaming metal objects. They glinted in the white light cast by my flames, nearly as bright as Ruslan's iron eyes as he plucked a wicked-looking knife from the leather. The male closest to him whimpered at the sight of the serrated blade, his eyes going wide with fear as Ruslan stalked toward him, flipping the blade over and over in his hand. The slice of the knife through the air sounded more like a death knell.

"You want them to know what it's like to live in darkness, like what they did to you?" His raspy voice held all the wickedness he showed to everyone but me, and the heat that pooled low in my belly was nearly shameful.

Ruslan stopped in front of the first male in chains and caressed his cheek with the sharp blade. With a few tentative steps, I joined them, gazing down on my former captor trembling with fear, a tear tracking down his cheek and ghosting over Ruslan's blade. The smell of the unwashed males hid most of their scents, but the musky odor of the males who'd raped me was a scar on my mind just like the scars on my back from their iron-tipped whips. The blade paused just below his eye, and the one beside him widened his eyes as he waited to see what would befall his comrade. Down the line, the pathetic bastards trembled, and some even began pleading with us through the thick gags that robbed them of words.

"I do."

My words were the permission Ruslan needed to carry out his task, and without warning, he sank the blade into the male's dark eye. He screamed through his gag, muscles of his neck straining as he fought through the pain of Ruslan twisting the knife around in his eye socket, sending blood cascading down his cheek. As quickly as he entered, he yanked the blade back and plunged it into the other eye, permanently blinding him.

My stomach churned at the sight, but I held firm, needing to see this vengeance carried out. The male slumped forward, chest heaving, once Ruslan had finished with him, and the river of ruby running from his eyes began carving its path into the stone floor. One by one, Ruslan repeated the process, blood coating the faces of these males who had raped and abused me while chaining me in darkness. The metallic scent was nearly overwhelming when mixed with the smell of excrement, and I had to breathe through my mouth as my former prison filled with the noxious fumes.

Their screams were nothing compared to the ones I'd made, ones that left my throat raw until I learned to hold them back and float my mind anywhere else. Ruslan had not even breached the surface with what he planned to do to them, of that I was certain, and I hadn't yet gotten a turn of my own.

Locking down my empath magic, I steeled myself against their anguish, not allowing their emotions to become my own, not when exacting pain in kind for what they had given me was so high on my priority list.

They had no mercy for me, and I would have no mercy for them.

Stalking to the roll of instruments, I selected a thin knife that looked like it would draw shallow cuts without killing them. These males would die, but I wanted to drag it out like they had so often done to me when they split open my back. "Strip them," I ordered, glancing up from my weapon to Ruslan, whose sinful smirk held no objection.

"What my mate wants, she gets," he crooned, crossing the length of chains that bound my former captors to the wall of this prison and selecting one of them at random. The guards around him all jumped, sending a tinkle echoing through the chamber as their irons shifted. Ruslan moved up and down the line, never giving them a chance to figure out who his next target was as he stripped them bare, leaving as much skin as possible exposed for me to carve.

The whimpers and pleas from the blinded males fell on deaf ears as I followed Ruslan's game of psychological torture and selected one simply because he smelled like one who had raped me until I nearly fainted from blood loss. Carefully stepping over his bindings, I raised the knife a breath from his back, watching as the hairs stood on end and goosebumps broke out across his flesh like a plague. He knew I was there, and he trembled with anticipation, ignorant to what pain I planned to inflict upon him.

And that was the sweetest revenge of all.

A slash drew a shallow cut across his shoulder that bled immediately, hitting at just the right angle to draw the most blood. His back arched, much like mine had when they'd whipped me, desperately trying to move out of the reach of my blade as I carved him like a roast.

Pathetic.

My former guards held none of my inner strength, for even I knew when their actions were inevitable and that lying down and biting my tongue were my best options for survival. Yet they still pleaded through their gags, veins in their necks popping from the effort, sweat rolling off of them as I not-so-accidentally caused their chains to clang while I navigated the space around them, delivering a shallow slice here and there.

The blood that spilled down their backs was not enough to atone for everything they had done to me.

I stopped at random among the males, carefully picking my way among the iron until I could lean down and whisper in his ear. "What would you do to stop the pain?" I asked, barely recognizing the sound of my voice when it was filled with teasing malice.

"An-an-anything," he whimpered around the gag, garnet tears tracking over his jowls.

I threw my head back and laughed, the manic sound echoing off the domed ceiling of the hewn cave. Every one of them jumped, sending a sick satisfaction up my spine.

"It's funny that you say that," I purred, resting the sharp tip of the blade on his shoulder and lightly tracing it across his chest as I rounded to his front. "Because no matter how many times *I* begged, you never did." The tip rested between two of his ribs, and I shoved it through the muscle. A cry ripped from his throat, short-lived as the air fled his lungs. He wheezed, thrashing against his bindings as he slowly began to suffocate.

Ruslan's face glowed among the white firelight, watching me with a dark heat as I worked my way down the line again, enjoying every moment of torture I delivered to the guards. "You're so fucking good at this, sprite. I want to see more of your darkness."

He held out what looked like clawed prongs, and I accepted them, threading my fingers through the holes and snapping them open and shut with a sharp click. "What are these for?"

"Take a wild guess," he drawled, as if we didn't hold thirteen – now twelve lives in our hands.

A slow smile spread across my face as I realized what they were meant to do. "Well, then, I'll definitely be needing an assistant."

Ruslan kept his steps light, hiding his approach from the male on the far end, the one I hadn't carved up quite as much as the others. Shock turned into a muffled scream as Ruslan dragged him to his feet, his empty eye sockets looking toward the endless ceiling above as his head was yanked back. Snapping the clawed instrument open and shut, I descended on the standing male, soaking in the pleasure of knowing the others were on edge, unable to see what was happening around them.

I circled to the male's ear, standing on my tiptoes so I could whisper in it. "I killed one of your comrades that came after me by cutting off his dick and balls. I wonder how long you'll last before you bleed out?" I ripped his gag away as I stepped back, wanting the full effect of his scream as I clamped the sharp ridges around his balls and ripped.

The shriek that left his lips remained in this world long after he did, the acoustics of the room giving it life as it bounced from stone to stone and out the mouth of the cave, wrenched away by the night wind. His listless body crumpled to the ground as

Ruslan released his hair, and the eleven living males sobbed, shook, and shouted as we coordinated our next target. The first victim of my back painting was looking paler by the moment as his blood mixed with that of the others on the floor, and I jerked my head in his direction, signaling Ruslan to drag him to his feet.

He barely had the strength or awareness to fight back as I clamped and ripped, and his death was much less satisfying than the previous one. When he crumpled into a lifeless heap at my feet, I saw just how deep the river of ruby had gotten. "I think I'll need some new shoes after this," I sighed as if my greatest concern was my fashion choices and these predatory males were nothing more than toys for me.

"I am, in fact, King of the Iron Realm, so I think I can make that happen." Ruslan smirked, snatching my wrist and yanking me to him. His tunic was soaked in blood, as was mine, and yet I couldn't help the wave of desire that rose within me. I tipped my head back, exposing my throat to Ruslan, and he growled, diving in for that place on my neck where I loved to be kissed.

The groan that escaped me resounded around the cave, drowning out the whimpering in the background. "Perhaps we should leave our clothes here on our way out."

His teeth skimmed the sensitive place just below my ear. "I think that is a good plan."

"Then we'd better get to work," I breathed, and he nipped my ear.

"If you don't mind, I'd like to take these last kills for myself. After all, what kind of male would I be if I didn't deliver the utmost pain to someone who dared lay a hand on my mate?"

"Not the kind I would want," I murmured, yanking his mouth to mine for a biting kiss before pushing him toward the waiting guards. "Now show me how much you love me, Ruslan."

Those smoky eyes turned animalistic and rapacious as he

was granted an opportunity to unleash the darkest parts of himself. The most fucked up parts of him were not so different than my own, and that was what I loved most about him, about us – that we understood one another in a way others could not.

Pain was the way he expressed himself when words failed him. Choice was the way I controlled my life. Fate was what bound us together, with an unbreakable thread that kept me in his orbit despite my immediate hatred of him. Love was born from our understanding of each other's darkness, what we needed to move through this world in a way that made us feel safe and in control.

Ruslan selected a cleaving knife from the roll of metal instruments, chopping off fingers and ears and toes, sometimes ripping away a gag before a particularly nasty blow, dragging out the deaths of those who hurt me while amping up the psychological torture. All the while, I watched him work, watched his brutality, and I did not flinch. He finished each of them off by ripping away their cocks and balls, just as I had, and cursing them as they died for touching his mate.

The silence was deafening when the last one fell.

But in that silence was a peace I didn't know I could find; the sessions I'd completed with Zuriel could not compare to the heady feeling coursing through my veins. My body hummed from head to toe, buzzing with an electric energy that begged to be freed.

Never again would those males harm me; I had retaken every ounce of power they stripped from me, and I felt *fucking amazing*.

Ruslan broke the silence when he dropped his tools, the metal hitting stone with a satisfying ring that sang of finality. In three strides, he wrapped me in his arms, blood smearing all around us as we raced to rip our clothes off.

"That was the hottest fucking thing I've ever seen you do,

sprite, and I need to be inside you. Now," he growled as he ripped my tunic away with one hard yank.

"Fuck me hard, Ruslan. I want to come all over your cock to thank you for what you did for me." The words came out breathy, wanton, and I didn't care how needy I sounded, I just wanted *him.*

"Fuck..." he groaned, burying his lips in my neck and grinding his hips into me. Backing us out of the pool of blood, Ruslan steered us until we were among the hundreds of candles he'd placed in the cave prior to my arrival. Using only my feet, I kicked one boot off, then the other, Ruslan mimicking my actions and then stripping us both of our pants. Half the white flames surrounding us changed to black as he laid back on the bare floor, pulling me on top of him, flush with his hardness. "Ride me," he commanded, and I gripped his dick with one hand and positioned myself over him, sinking down with a delightful hiss as he stretched out my inner walls.

I was so fucking full of his cock, and looking down on him, I felt like a fucking queen. His pupils were nearly black from lust, and his hands gripped my hips and dragged me down deeper, eliciting a moan. The tattoos on his chest blended with the blood still coating us, making his already sinister-looking torso that much wickeder. I ran my hands across the hard planes of his shoulders and arms as I began to ride him, finding a rhythm that dragged me all the way off before dropping down again, and he cursed low as I worked him harder and faster.

Within moments, I was close to coming, my thighs soaked from watching him work and our earlier encounter in the lift. Ruslan would do anything for me – torture, kill, burn. There was nothing I could ask of him that he wouldn't do or wouldn't give, and instead of binding me to him through force, he had given me the space I needed to work out my feelings, even though it sent his anxiety over the edge to do so.

And Kazimir could barely go five minutes without insisting I owed him in some way or insinuating that he owned me.

The cacophony of our heavy breathing and slapping skin filled the cave where I had been chained, and as my walls began to flutter, I ground myself deeper onto Ruslan's cock. "That's it, sprite, come for me."

The most intense orgasm of my life speared through me, shattering everything I thought I knew and replacing it with a high that rivaled the peak of Vasvain. "I love you, Ruslan. You are my mate. My one and only. I choose you."

The roar that Ruslan released shook the cave with its ferocity, sending stones skittering and the firelights flickering. His hips pistoned into mine, and his hot cum filled me as he snarled. "I love you, Izidora. You are my mate. The fire in our souls belongs together, in this life and in all the rest."

And with those spoken words, we were joined in every way. Pain seared the skin between my shoulder blades, causing my back to arch forward. A strangled cry ripped from me, and then I was coming again, the pleasure of Ruslan throbbing inside me mixing with the sharp sting on my back. I panted through the wave of release, sweat dripping from me and onto my mate as our bond settled into place.

It was unlike anything I'd ever imagined, anything I'd experienced before. I thought I loved Ruslan five minutes before, but compared to what I felt as the bond settled in place, it was infinitesimally small. This feeling was infinite, pure, true, unconditional, and I *radiated* for the depths of it. No words could accurately paint the picture of this blissful feeling, but I found none were necessary between Ruslan and me – not anymore. Not when his heart beat for me, and mine for him.

"You have given me the greatest gift of all. This feeling... it is indescribable. I imagined what it would be like countless times, but this,

this is more than I could have dreamed. You are my angel, my sprite, and now my life."

Tears pricked my eyes as I *felt* the truth of his words. "Will your mark be covered by your tattoos?"

"No. I left a special place free just for this moment," he smirked. The moment he pushed my hips off of him, I ached for his closeness, not wanting to be separated, not yet anyway. I was still relishing this incredible feeling of boundless certainty and contentment.

"I'm not going anywhere."

"How did you know?"

"There are no barriers between us anymore. We are one."

His eyes glittered as he turned around to show me his back. There, just between his shoulder blades, was the outline of a perfect circle. I touched it with the devotion such a powerful mark deserved, and the one on my back tingled in tune.

The smile over his shoulder was devastating. "Let me see yours."

We switched positions, and I bared my back to him. His fingers traced the outline, sending another shudder through my body. Then his lips brushed the very center of the circle, the touch sending heat straight to my core. "You are exquisite, my mate," he purred. "I can't wait to make you my wife." He pulled me onto his lap, holding me against his chest like I was the most precious of gemstones. "I love you."

"And I love you," I whispered back. We remained locked in that embrace until the air became too cold to bear, and a body-wide shiver from me finally caused Ruslan to stir.

"I need to fuck you again, but this time I want to be clean while doing it." He scooped me in his arms, leaving the bloodied tools and bodies behind, along with our clothes, and carried me toward the lift that had been hidden deep in the Agrenak Mountains the entire time I'd been chained in that cave.

I swung my feet in time with his steps, a wide smile plastered on my face as I walked my fingers across my mate's muscled torso. "I don't think we'll stay clean for long, not with the way I want you to take me."

Ruslan groaned, the sound slipping from low in his chest. "Fuck, sprite, when you say things like that..."

"What?" I teased, my fingers stopping just above his pounding heart. "I didn't even tell you how my pussy clenched when you killed them for me."

"Izidora," he growled, a warning in his tone, and his whole body went tense beneath me.

It made my blood sing in the best way. I wasn't quite ready to step out of the dark, not when it felt so damn *good* to slip into it with Ruslan.

"Take me home," I said, breathless, and our fresh mating bond hummed with excitement.

Ruslan wasted no time, beginning to chant under his breath, the words foreign yet familiar, and I knew he meant to take us to Roc Palace – the home he built for us, where no other female had set foot. The cart, our clothes, all was forgotten when getting as close as possible to one another was an all-consuming thought. Within moments, we were standing in the center of our suite's bathroom, the giant shower flowing with natural hot spring water from the mountains beckoning us to wash away the gore and grime.

"How did that not drain all of your magic?" I asked, blinking up at him.

A secretive smirk pulled up the corners of his mouth. "Because I am the most powerful Félvér in all of Északi."

"You were holding out on me," I protested with a wry grin.

"You are not the only one with hidden thorns, sprite," he teased, carrying me toward the waiting shower. Ruslan could scarcely stand to put me down, and the entire time he spun the handles to release the flow of natural thermal water, his intense gaze pinned me in place. The moment steam rolled in our direction, he snatched my waist and directed me under the spray, sending a cascade of giggles from my chest. The world fell away with each brush of skin on skin, with each swipe of tongue against tongue, until we were infinite in that moment.

Nothing and no one would separate us now that we were one.

Now that Ruslan was my mate.

24

RUSLAN

Béke Day Six

I awoke with my mate in my arms.

She had accepted the bond.

I still could not believe it, but there it was, a solidified thread that was so potent I could feel its each and every shift between us as we dozed in our bed at Roc Palace, hidden away from the world. The first hints of light peeked through the heavy black curtains, and an idea formed in my head – one that I could not wait to carry out. Even though we had only gone to bed an hour before, I had to wake Izidora.

"Sprite," I murmured in her ear, planting a gentle kiss on her still-damp hair.

She grumbled incoherently for a moment before releasing a long sigh.

"I have somewhere I want to take you."

A yawn nearly unhinged her jaw, and she blinked blearily at me through the fog of sleep. "Where?" Her voice was thick and hoarse from how I'd made her scream my name over and over the night before.

"You'll see. Get dressed, and we can take a nap when we get back," I promised, running a finger along her bare shoulder.

"Ugh," she moaned, reaching her arms overhead and stretching like a lazy cat before bringing her balled-up fists to her eyes and rubbing.

I stroked her long locks one last time before throwing the covers back, earning my usual string of curses as I exposed her to the cold. Rushing to the closet, I threw clothes her way, and she dutifully pulled them on beneath the righted covers before slipping from the pile of blankets.

Before she got far, I wrapped her in my arms and uttered the spell that would bend space to move us to the shop of my favorite jeweler. He sourced the purest stones from the mines buried deep in the mountains of the Iron Realm, and no one could match his skill in crafting the finest jewelry from them.

The shop was among dozens of others in the lavish part of Radence, where the richest of Iron Fae and Félvér lived and purchased their necessities. Each storefront gleamed as if it had been recently polished, and not a hint of ice coated the stone beneath our feet, already cleared for the patrons that would not arrive for hours.

"I never got you another ring after the one–" My teeth clenched around the words, as guilt and shame rendered me voiceless and unable to finish the sentence.

But my mate was more than aware, and I felt her concern and forgiveness down our bond. She spun in my arms, chestnut hair spilling down her back as she tipped her head up to look at me. Our gazes collided with the force of an avalanche, and I saw the truth of the words she whispered in my mind in her shining eyes.

"I am so glad you allowed me the space to make my decision. That was what ultimately led me back to you. You have never truly trapped me, not since the first day."

"You are too fiery to trap. I could never have broken your spirit. It would have killed me to do so." My words held as much truth as hers, for I didn't know the meaning of love before she burst into my life with the ferocity of a wildfire, sucking all the oxygen from my lungs in her inferno. After seeing her shine so bright as she fought with me, still wearing that glamorous gold dress, I knew, deep down, that there was nothing that would please me more than watching her help me burn the world down and rebuild it anew.

I guided her to the lacquered red door of the shop, then rapped sharply on it, waiting patiently for my jeweler to appear. The male, still dressed for sleep, opened it with a huff.

"Ah, King Ruslan, please come in," the male bowed, his irritation melting away as he held the door wide for us to enter.

"Thank you for waking so early, Ambros," I greeted him, gesturing for Izidora to walk in front of me. Her jewel-like eyes went wide as we entered the male's cave of glittering gems.

"Anything for my best customer," he chuckled. "Now, what can I get you today?"

"Another ring for my mate." A smile tugged at my lips as she wandered to a shelf filled with deep red rubies. The entire shop was a veritable mine, with rough-hewn stone walls, wooden shelves holding gems of all colors, shapes, and sizes nestled in finely crafted settings. Ambros's work was not gaudy and over the top, as many jewelers defaulted to with gems of these sizes; he preferred a more delicate touch that allowed the stones to shine through.

Ambros winked at me. "Are you certain she does not have Dragon blood?"

"I must be rubbing off on her." I couldn't contain the joy that sparked through me, and my usual ruthless, cold countenance was nowhere to be found as I leaned casually against the counter, crossing my arms and waiting.

Ambros joined my mate in perusing the shelves of wares until she held a small fortune's worth in her hands. Watching her eyes light up as he explained the properties of each stone was worth every piece of gold it would cost me. I was lost in my adoration of her, and it wasn't until she nudged my mind that I focused on the words she spoke.

"I can't decide which one I like best. Can I have them all?" Her laugh shone brighter than all the stones in this shop.

I feigned chest pains as I gaped at the pile in front of her, but then I grinned, "Anything for my sprite."

On tiptoes, she kissed my cheek, and Ambros set to work, Izidora watching in fascination as he manipulated stones and metal with magic, weaving and binding and bracing them together until seven rings lay on a purple velvet cloth in front of him.

I selected a rectangular ruby surrounded by a halo of pointed diamonds and slid it onto my mate's finger. "This is my favorite."

"Then I will always wear this one." She beamed up at me and I captured her mouth with mine, inhaling her rosy scent, laced with a hint of plum. Her lips were soft and pliant against mine, and we melted together like it was more natural than breathing.

There was no way I could love anyone else as I loved her.

Ambros cleared his throat, interrupting our moment. Glancing up from my mate's flushed cheeks, I fished out a bag of gold for my favorite jeweler, and then he handed me a velvet-lined case holding all of Izidora's new rings. "Come back soon with your mate, King Ruslan. She has good taste."

"Expensive taste, too." I winked at her, and she rolled her aquamarine eyes, though she didn't bother denying it.

"See you soon, Ambros," Izidora threw over her shoulder as I tugged her along behind me. His chuckles followed us into the frigid morning air, and once we'd cleared the door, I pulled her flush, my hands all over her body, needing more of her, needing her closer. The fresh mating bond called for me to fuck her into oblivion, to erase every other male from her mind.

She gripped me with the same fervor, fusing her body with mine in every way, and I wasted no time moving us back to our bedroom at Roc Palace. The bed had not even cooled from our earlier departure, and with one powerful throw, she was on her back on the soft mattress, a breathy laugh escaping her.

Propping herself up on her elbows, she bit that damn bottom lip and raked her gaze over me. I popped open the case of rings, the precious stones glinting in the low light. "Strip then hold your hands out," I commanded.

With heated eyes, she rose, reaching for the buttons of her jacket and undoing them one by one before tossing it aside. Only then did her fingers brush the bottom of her tunic, and with the speed of a fucking turtle, she lifted it over her head, revealing inch after inch of her beautiful skin. The lace covering her breasts did not hide the peaks of her nipples, and my attention snagged on them before she trailed her hands over her flat stomach and to the waist of her pants. She shimmied them over her hips then laid back on her elbows again, lifting and pointing her foot in a clear indication that she wanted me to remove them for her. With one hand I tore the first leg off, then the second, until my mate was only covered in scraps of lace that looked so fucking delicious on her.

But she wasn't prepared the way I wanted her, not yet at least.

"Hold out a hand," I instructed, plucking one of her new rings from the box. She obliged, and I slipped them on one by one until her hand was heavy with stones. "Now the other." I snatched her closer once she proffered it to me, dragging a gasp from her throat at the sudden movement. Her nipples brushed against my shirt as I slipped the remaining rings on her petite fingers, and then I closed her hand and kissed the back of it before letting it fall to the soft blankets.

"Don't move," I purred, backing away slowly, drinking in the sight of Izidora's heaving breasts straining against the lace and flaring my nostrils to inhale the sweet scent of her arousal. Disappearing into the closet, I searched my treasury for the pieces that would look fucking fantastic falling down her chest and wrapping around her waist. Laden with priceless chains, I returned to the bedroom, finding my mate exactly where I had left her.

"Good girl," I praised, and a flush crept up her chest and to her cheeks. "Turn around."

She did, slowly, showing me her shapely ass as she flipped to her hands and knees before sweeping her hair over one shoulder. I closed the distance between us, letting the cool metal caress the skin of her back before wrapping the necklace around her pretty throat. The moan she released made my cock throb against my pants, borderline painful. Once the clasp was secured, I pulled her long locks free and braided them loosely down her back. "You're going to drip for me in more ways than one, mate."

A delicate chain glittering with star-shaped diamonds slid off my forearm and into my hand, and I brushed it along her bare waist before wrapping it there.

"Oh," she gasped, her skin shivering at my touch. Every stroke of my fingers was like tracing a line of fire over her body, and it took every ounce of my self-control to draw out dressing her the way I wanted.

I leaned down, placing my lips against the shell of her ear and ghosting my hands over her arms, between the jewels cascading down her chest, and finally settling them just above the lace covering her core. "I love you, mate. Turn around so I can see you decorated in my treasure."

The space between us was painful as I stepped back, but when she sat on her knees and faced me, the pain was utterly worth it. "Fuck," I swore, dick throbbing in the best kind of way. "I might have to add *you* to my treasury too. Because there's nothing more precious, more rare, or more exquisite than you right now, Izidora."

The smile that she wore was sultry, and she cocked her head to the side. "Perhaps you should put me on display for the whole realm to see. For *all* the realms to see. Show them who I belong to."

Fuck.

I groaned, long and low, and approached my mate, images of me fucking her in front of the other monarchs making me harder than the diamonds wrapping around her throat. The tendrils of gems that dripped from the collar joined even larger ones that lay against her chest, some balanced on her breasts, others dipping between where they strained against the lace confining them. The string of them wrapping around and around her waist made her shine with the brightness of a thousand suns, and I nearly fell to my knees at the sight of her.

My inner Dragon purred with delight.

"I think you need a few more pieces," I rasped.

She raised a heavy hand to my chest and flattened it across my racing heart. "Not until I get to see you," she said, her voice both soft and heated. Her fingers bunched up my tunic until my abs were revealed to her, and she drank in the sight of them and the tip of my dick bursting from my waistband. Once the fabric reached my chest, I tore it over my head, revealing every inch of my chiseled, tattooed torso. Her nails raked across my skin, tracing every line until she found the ones that led right to my cock.

"Fuck, sprite," I swore as she ghosted her thumb over the beaded tip.

"Were you going to get something else?" she asked sweetly, as if she didn't know exactly what she was doing to me.

Dragging in a ragged breath, I regained some semblance of control and with one swift movement, I caught her braid and tugged her back, bringing her hands away from me. "I am. And when I return, I want you playing with that pretty pussy for me."

The fire in her eyes flared as I stepped away and forced myself to return to the closet for the crown that would complete the ensemble. Teardrop diamonds perched atop rows of round and square gems, forming spikes that were as formidable as they were beautiful.

Just like Izidora.

I brought it on the velvet cushion that housed it all these years for her. Before I returned to the bed, however, I stalked to the windows and threw back the heavy curtains, letting the morning sun spill into the room.

When the light fell across her, my mate fucking *glittered*. She braced herself on an elbow, the other hand dipping between her spread thighs and stroking. The reflection of the thousand gemstones scattered across every inch of her, and I circled to her side with the crown in my hand, not wanting to cast a shadow on the most brilliant sight I had ever seen.

"On your knees," I croaked, unable to tear my gaze from the sight of her stroking lightly over her own skin. With teeth digging into her bottom lip, she returned to her earlier position, and I gently placed the cushion on the bed beside her. "Dip your chin."

She did, but the entire time, she watched me from under thick lashes. My nostrils flared as I tried to breathe at the sight of her submitting to me as I lifted the crown to her head. "My sprite. My mate. My future *queen.*" The piece settled across her head like it was always meant to be there.

And when she lifted her chin and gazed up at me with those aquamarine eyes that held so much life even after all she had suffered, the entire fucking world fell away. My mouth crashed against hers, tongue insistently parting her lips and tasting her. She groaned, hands slamming into my chest as I pulled her closer.

"Fuck, sprite, I love you so much," I said in her mind, unable to release her mouth for a second with the force of my need.

"And I love you, always."

Her nipples brushed against my chest, and I reached between us to cup her breast, running my thumb over the peak and pulling a groan from her throat. I rolled it again and again, pinching as I dragged out what was certain to be the most incredible sex of my life. Her hands trailed down my sides, and when one wrapped around the outline of my cock, I growled a warning.

"I want to savor every second of this, sprite, and if you keep touching me there, I won't be able to control myself."

"Then lose all semblance of control. I want you inside me."

Not even a heartbeat passed in the time it took for me to release her and rip off my pants. In another, she was flat on her back on the bed, spun so that the sun still spilled across her gem-coated skin, and the lace covering her center was pulled aside. She was so slick already, wetness dripping from her and pooling on the sheets beneath her.

"I told you that you would drip in more ways than one," I groaned, grasping myself and sliding up and down her slit, stopping to tease her clit before dipping down again.

"So you did," she whimpered, arching toward me, and trying to get me to sink inside her.

"Use your words," I chastised, stilling my movements and loving the noise of protest she made.

"I already did," she huffed, continuing to grind against me.

"I know. I want to hear it again," I smirked, leaning forward and bracing my free hand beside her head. "I want to hear how much you want me, how much you *need* me, every day for the rest of our lives, mate. I want you to scream my name as you break beneath me, loud enough for all the realms to hear. Because you are mine, and I am yours, and *nothing* will ever change that."

"Oh Goddess," she breathed, reaching around to grasp my back. "I want you, Ruslan. I *need* you, Ruslan. Make me come."

She tugged down the moment I pushed in, and we groaned in tandem. Nothing was better than being joined to my mate this way, making our bodies one, closer than any other possible way. We were one soul, one mind, in two separate bodies, except in moments like these. Our breaths synced as I began to move, stretching her out easily with how slick she was. The feel of her warmth around me, tightening down with each inhalation, was better than any wine, any herb, any feeling in this fucking world.

"Ruslan," she whimpered, digging her nails into my back.

My other hand slammed to the bed on the other side of her head, hips driving into hers and making her body shake with the force of it. The gems covering her bounced with the movement, catching the sun and scattering light all around us.

"You look like a fucking goddess," I rasped, reverent eyes sweeping over her. "My fucking Angel."

Her lashes fluttered against her cheeks as I moved. "Eyes on me," I commanded, and they flew open, locking with mine as I seated myself to the hilt. They widened at the depth, sun spilling into them and making them sparkle too.

"If I'm your Angel, then you're my Dragon, guarding me like these precious stones caressing my body," she breathed, mouth popping open as I dragged my cock all the way out, then slowly sheathed myself again.

"Can't forget that I'm also part Demon," I ground out, willing my movements to slow, to tease.

"There's only one Demon I don't mind haunting me," she said, head falling back as I hit that part of her that made her legs shake.

"Fuck, sprite." Her pussy clenched around me, and I rocked back and forth in that spot, wetness coating my thighs as she dripped – flooded – me with her arousal.

"More," she begged, and when she asked with that desperate noise following it, I had to oblige. I leaned back, digging my fingers into her hips to keep her in place while I fucked her, captivated by the way her breasts bounced every time I sank in deep, the way the crown on her head prevented it from falling back completely, and the way she fucking shone.

My abs tightened, and I ground my teeth and tried to breathe through the need to come. But her core throbbed, tightening over me, and I was nearly gone from the sensation alone.

I hiked her legs up over my shoulders, taking her deeper, and she gasped, mouth popping open as I climbed onto the bed with her because my sprite needed a little pain with her pleasure, just like me. "It's too bad that the collar is taking up so much space around your throat. I know how much you like when I take away your air."

"Oh fuck," she whimpered, and I leaned forward anyway, wrapping my hand over her throat and stroking my thumb across her lower lip.

"I'll have to settle for other methods," I purred, tugging her lip before releasing it and finding her breasts. I slipped the lace away from them, forcing them higher and exposing her nipples. My hips worked again as I leaned down and sucked one into my mouth, eliciting a cry of pleasure from her.

"Yes," she groaned, her breaths short and staggered, and she laced her fingers in my hair, guiding me to her other side. I rolled it around with my tongue before nipping it, then closing my teeth over it and dragging them back. "Oh, Goddess!"

I did it again, shoving myself to the hilt at the same time, and she ground against me, brushing her clit over my groin for some friction. *"Touch yourself."* She did, slipping a hand between us and circling her fingers while I continued sucking and biting her nipples, bringing her pleasure higher and higher until I knew we were both so close to breaking. *"Come for me. Scream my name and I'll scream yours."*

"Oh fuck," she whimpered, hands and hips moving faster until her walls clenched down and she cried out, over and over and over. "Ruslan!"

I held on as long as I could until the force of her orgasm yanked mine along with it, and with a roar, I exploded. "Fuck, Izidora!" My cock twitched and throbbed inside her, and I dropped to my elbows on either side of her, letting her legs fall with them. Breathing hard, I tried to regain a sense of time and space that had disappeared while we moved together.

"My mate." Izidora's words filtered through my mind, and when I lifted my head, the love in her aquamarine eyes amplified the feeling down our bond.

"My mate," I echoed, loath to remove myself from her. But somehow, I managed, removing the crown and setting it aside before unclasping the necklace and waist chain from her limp and spent body. Once she was fully bare, I cradled her against me, tracing swirls over her skin until her heart slowed and her breathing evened out. I turned over, hating that I had to release her to reach our two books, and then handed one to her, slotting myself as close as I could so we touched from head to toe while we read. She was utterly spent from the last few days of competition, our foray to Vasvain, and accepting our bond, so she snug-

gled into me and released a long sigh as she cracked open the pages.

Izidora was *everything* to me, and I vowed to do everything in my power to protect her without smothering her flame. I would take care of her, treasure her, pleasure her, and love her until my dying breath, and perhaps even beyond that, should we be so lucky as to perish together.

Whatever lay ahead of us, I knew one thing with absolute certainty – I would never be alone again.

25

KAZIMIR

BÉKE DAY SIX

All eyes were on me when I waltzed into the breakfast room wearing a black crown glittering with diamonds, like the jeweler had pulled the night sky down and formed it into my new headpiece. All eyes except the four I truly wanted.

Where the fuck were Izidora and Ruslan?

My vision flashed black before I sucked in a breath, wrestling for control with the binding magic. I ran a palm over my face after I'd regained a semblance of it, then scanned the room for a third time, counting every noble attending Béke save for the two of them. I wanted to break something, but I was the king of the Night Realm, and I needed to act like the cold, calculated ruler I was expected to be. Squaring my shoulders and lifting my chin, I piled food onto my plate then strode to the table where the other monarchs sat.

Queen Viktoria and King Consort Geza's eyes narrowed for a fraction of a moment before they schooled their expressions, but King Airre was the first to comment on my new appearance.

"Nice crown. Does this mean the Night Realm has decided on a change in leadership?"

The chair across from him was unoccupied, so I slid into it. "It does. I am now King of the Night Realm. I am afraid that Izidora will not choose me, so we thought it best that we have stable leadership in the face of uncertainty."

Queen Immonen's clear blue eyes cut my way momentarily before she lifted her drink to her lips and intently stared at the tapestry over my shoulder.

"I should think you also would like to keep a Night Fae ruler on your throne," King Airre offered, though his tone was unreadable, lacking sympathy or support.

"That we do. As High Lord Kaztar reminded me, House Vaszoly ruled prior to House Valynor." I bit into a roll slathered in butter, chewing slowly while the rulers of the Day Realm considered me.

"Does this change any of your other plans?" Queen Viktoria leaned in, voice dropping low with her question.

"It does not. The Night Realm was still attacked, unprovoked, and that will need to be answered, even if Izidora does not choose to return to her rightful home with me."

"Izidora does have a choice between two mates, you know," Queen Immonen hissed, unable to contain her words. The female was tense, fingers curled around her silverware and turning white. "The fate of our world rests upon this choice. It is not one she should take lightly."

King Airre shot her a look, placing his hand over hers in a soothing way. "What my mate means to say is that whomever Princess Izidora chooses, she must have a good reason for it."

Queen Viktoria made a low noise in her throat, and my attention immediately snapped to her. "Is there something you wish to say, Queen Viktoria?"

She waved her hand dismissively in my direction. "Only that

you males are all self-important and do not often deign to consider what us females may go through."

Queen Immonen tipped her already raised glass at Queen Viktoria. "I'll drink to that." Her eyes cut my way again before she sipped.

This was not how I wanted this conversation to go.

I was losing control of the situation, fast. The hand that rested on my knee tightened over it, nearly bruising myself as I reined in my anger. "But of course, you are right," I said in my most polite, most humble voice. "We males like to fight and fuck and don't think often about feelings or the consequences."

"There is nothing quite like the feeling of victory, though," King Consort Geza chuckled. "Especially after you bested the best of all the realms yesterday, King Kazimir."

I lifted my glass to the king of the Day Realm. "Truer words have never been spoken. My mount will sport some of his new armor today for the horseback competition."

"I suppose High Lady Domi will be the ultimate winner today," Queen Immonen said quickly, clearly wanting to change the subject. "Her horses and horsemanship are impeccable."

"That would give the Night Realm a solid lead," I grinned. "Are you sure you want that?"

Queen Immonen frowned, and the rest of the monarchs sitting around the table shared a low laugh. "Peaceful competition, that is what Béke is for," she responded sharply. "If you'll excuse me, I need a small nap before today's activities."

The scrape of wood on stone preceded her departure, her silky dress floating behind her as she rushed from the dining space. "I'm afraid I am also requiring some extra sleep. I look forward to our peaceful competition later," her husband echoed before following his wife to their temporary home in the Iron Realm.

Queen Viktoria and King Consort Geza remained quiet a

few seats down from me, so I turned my attention to my food, clearing my plate absentmindedly while I wondered where Izidora was.

Tuning into that tug in my belly that had allowed me to sense where she was, I found it to be faint, though not absent as it had been while we trekked from the Night Realm, through the Crystal and Day Realms, and finally into the Iron Realm to reach Radence. Excusing myself, I decided to follow that line and see where it led me.

After all, I was a king, and clearly, Izidora wanted a male who could offer her power and prestige rather than the other way around. But to show her that this change had taken place, I needed to find her, and then she would see that I could give her everything Ruslan had and more.

Between the ropes of magic in my chest, I called to my moonlight, pulling and manipulating shadows as I stalked the halls of Ryza, trying to remain inconspicuous. No one paid me any attention as the tug pulled me toward the main gates in the courtyard, and after a furtive glance around, I called on the binding magic to mix with the moonlight and cloaked myself in an invisible shield.

Out in the open air, the pull was stronger, so I called my wings to me and shot into the air, relishing their new thickness and strength since the binding magic had been gifted to me by the Fates. I flew for ten minutes in the direction of the Night Realm, curious as to why Izidora would be in this direction. The only sights below me were a smattering of houses and farms, closed up for the harsh winter, save for the animals bracing against the cold with their furry coats.

That tug had yet to lead me astray when I wanted to follow her, so I trusted that it was leading me in the right direction and kept flying until I spotted two small outbuildings that had been erected nearly against the sheer face of a large mountain.

Hovering in place, I searched the surrounding area for any sign as to what the buildings might hold, but it wasn't until the sun broke the clouds that I spotted it – the hint of a reflection of glass and metal buried into the side of the mountain.

With a hard flap of my wings, I was off again, eyes glued to the spot where I had seen the flash of light. As I drew closer the building took shape, cleverly hidden so that someone who did not know what they were looking for would miss it. There were four stories in total, but the top floor had thick panes of glass wrapping its expanse, and I flew close to a panel on the end, the interior partially obscured by a thick black curtain. I pulled away for a moment, checking on my magic to ensure I remained hidden, then pressed against the glass, trying to see what lay beyond.

The room was dark compared to the light flaring outside as the sun rose over the jagged peaks surrounding us, but after I allowed my eyes to adjust, I finally saw her – naked and writhing under Ruslan. His whole torso was covered in ink, and his arms caged her in as she arched off the bed and into him, her scream reaching my ears as she fell apart. Red and black flashed in my eyes, and I forced myself to fly away to regain control, lest I reveal myself and my new powers when I needed to hide them.

My nails drew blood into my palms, and I smothered a growl in my throat.

This place was hidden for a reason, and I needed to discover what else was hidden here. Any information would provide me with an advantage, especially since the Iron Realm had always been so secretive. Dropping to the floor below, I discovered what looked like a library and formal receiving area, and below that, an expansive but deserted kitchen and staff quarters. Returning to the top floor, I forced myself to fly to the opposite side, where two fireplaces roared in massive hearths surrounded by plush, luxurious furniture. Above the palatial home, a thin railing corded off a large section of rock, the center holding a heavy iron door. If I had brought my iron-resistant gloves, I might have attempted to open it, but as it stood, I needed all the magic I could get.

The temptation to return to the window was too great, and against Endre's voice yelling in the back of my mind to return to Ryza, I flew toward it, needing to know what the two of them were doing – if they were still fucking.

Images of the two of us working in tandem to bring her to orgasm flashed through my mind, my cock hardening from both anger and lust. She fucking loved it, having two males filling her, and yet she chose to continue to only fuck him when I wasn't around? She should be crawling into bed with me, letting me worship her and show her how well we moved together. I wouldn't hold back with her next time, letting all my previously caged desires out to play. They would have scared her before, but now it was clear she enjoyed being captive, and I did aim to please.

Their movements had stilled when I peeked around the curtain, pressing my hands flush to the cold pane. Izidora and Ruslan were still wrapped together, but both held leather-bound books. Izidora glanced up from hers, asking Ruslan something and pointing. Placing his volume down, he turned Izidora's book so he could view it, stroking her arm while he read and responded to her. I clenched my teeth as she batted her thick, dark lashes at him, then returned her attention to the book.

So that bastard had taught her to read.

Izidora had accused *me* of intentionally manipulating her into wanting to take the throne, for not giving her contraception, and for keeping her in the dark. Me, the male who had saved her, released her from her chains, who had spent the majority of his life scouring every corner of the continent for her. Ruslan had done *nothing*. He was directly responsible for her abuse, and yet she believed he loved her because he taught her to read? Ruslan was the one who had manipulated her, not me.

Bile rose in my throat and I crinkled my nose as I left them alone. She was clearly delusional or had some sort of magic placed over her if she thought that he was the better choice out of the two of us.

I had to save her again, to ensure that she returned to the Night Realm where she would be safe. Where she would be *my* queen, and she would never leave my side. She'd have a child in her womb before the following summer if it killed me. No one would touch her, would hurt her, again because I'd never let her out of my sight. If I had overcome the effects of whatever the Iron Fae did to me when they stormed Este Castle, I would have prevented *this*, whatever Ruslan had done to her.

She was mine, and I would save her again, even if I had to resort to drastic measures to do so.

26

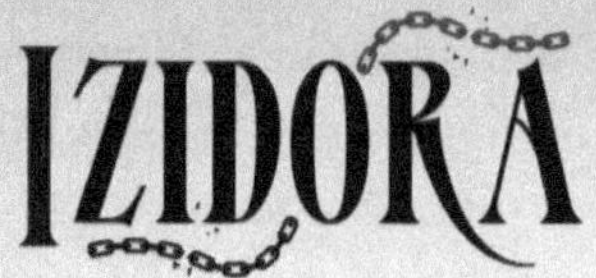

Unconditional love was rapturous, and Ruslan's devotion was endless. I didn't need my empath magic to feel the depths of his desire or the intensity of his infatuation. We spent the whole day in bed, and I could hardly walk by the time Drazen banged on the suite door, finally hunting us down to attend to our responsibilities.

"I could hear you fucking from the base of the mountain!" he shouted through the door.

I snickered, totally unashamed. Ruslan threw clothes at me, and I pulled them on as he jogged to open the exterior suite door for Drazen.

The half-Dragon walked into the living area with hands over his eyes. "Are you decent or will uncovering my eyes result in the removal of my hands?"

"You can open your eyes, Drazen," I teased, curling my legs beneath me as I propped my head on my hand, bracing against the couch.

He dropped his hands and looked between us before a wide grin broke out across his face. "Thank the Goddess you finally accepted the bond. But you are hosting Béke, Ruslan. You're needed to judge the horseback competition this afternoon. And you," he turned his attention on me, "have been nothing short of obsessed with horses since I met you. I expect high marks from you."

I rolled my eyes. Obviously, this was the competition I was most excited for, and I planned on flying around the courses on Mistik's back.

"Can you do it?" my mate complained as he scooped me up from behind. His arms formed a vice around my torso, pinning me in place as he nibbled on the crook of my neck. A squeal slipped out, and I tried to shove his hands away, only serving to make them tighten.

Drazen rolled his eyes. "No, it has to be the hosting monarchs. Don't even think about passing me the Iron Crown. I don't want it."

"Fine. We'll be ready shortly." Ruslan dragged me, squirming, back to our bedroom.

"I will be waiting right here, so don't get any ideas about crawling back into bed!" Drazen called after us.

Ruslan released me, and with a sigh I made my way to the closet, hunting for warm leathers. "He's no fun."

"I heard that!"

Damn Dragons.

"We'll come back tonight, mate." Ruslan planted a kiss on my cheek when I finished fastening a thick jacket all the way up to my neck. At least the snow had cleared around Radence, though the wind still chilled me to my bones.

Ruslan pulled on light-plated armor that moved as if it were leather, similar to the set he had gifted me a few days before, then threw me warm riding pants from where they'd been hidden in the back of the closet. "Thank the Goddess," I exclaimed, slipping off my current pants in exchange for the black ones that immediately warmed my legs. "This place needs to be straightened up," I said, glancing at the chaos. "It would help if I could keep my clothes on for more than five minutes. I'm constantly losing my favorite attire."

Ruslan chuckled, dark and low. "I'll just have to buy you everything in multiples, so there's always at least one item to be found."

I rolled my eyes, moving discarded, half-worn clothing around in search of another pair of boots, since my favorites had been irrevocably destroyed the previous night. "Where are my other boots?"

"Over there," he gestured toward the back with his foot. He fumbled with a strap just out of his reach, his muscles preventing him from getting the right angle to fasten it. After revealing the shoes and slipping them on, I grinned, returning to his side and securing his strap in place.

"Ready?" I asked, once he'd finished straightening himself.

"No, but I must judge," he laughed, leading me back to Drazen, who waited, arms crossed, for us.

Ruslan clapped Drazen on the shoulder, intentionally a bit harder than necessary, and then the three of us returned to the clearing where the strength competition had taken place the previous day, though the rings had been cleared or reformatted to accommodate the horseback riding events. Horses and people were already running about everywhere, preparing for the day's events.

No one noticed our arrival, allowing us a moment to gain our bearings. I spotted Liliana holding the reins to Mistik and Twilight, the horse Ruslan had gifted me, in the distance, chatting with Domi and Immonen. Ruslan's attention followed mine, and without warning he scooped me against his chest, bending me over and whispering in my ear. "Good luck, mate. My eyes will only be on you."

Then he released me, and I immediately craved him with a fierceness that stole my breath. Our mating bond was intense, more intense than anyone could accurately describe, and the pain of his absence speared through me as I took one step forward, then another. With one lingering glance over my shoulder, I skirted through the throng of people, blazing a path toward my friends. Liliana's face lit up when she saw me, her arms waving wildly despite it being obvious that I already knew where she was.

But the moment I closed the circle with the three females, their faces fell somber. Liliana's words burst out in a tumble of breath. "Kazimir has been named King of the Night Realm. I wanted you to hear it from me before you saw him because you deserved to know. None of us were around when the males made this decision. They just showed up in our apartments last night with Kazimir wearing a crown and the news that House Arzeni was now among the High Houses."

My jaw dropped. All his lies, all his manipulations, were so he could rest the Night Crown on his head instead of mine. This action only confirmed that I'd made the right choice in my mate. Kazimir was calculating in a way I'd never realized, and my blood boiled with renewed fury.

How did the others not see this in him?

Domi's nose crinkled as Liliana recounted the events, then nudged her with a sharp elbow. "Tell her what else."

"Oh! Right. Kazimir has *binding magic*." She whispered the last part with a hiss of distaste. "I managed to get it out of Endre last night, and Domi confirmed with Kaztar this morning."

"What's binding magic?" I asked, brows dipping together, confusion replacing shock as I wondered why the females seemed so disturbed by it.

Immonen cut in, her willowy frame tense with worry. "Binding magic has been known to corrupt the mind and soul of its wielders. There is a reason it is so rare. Most succumb to the madness that goes along with it. It is dark magic, Fates-gifted instead of Goddess-gifted like the rest of our magic. Essentially, Kazimir wields thick ropes of magic that render others immobile, like an actual rope, but it also blocks access to our Goddess-gifted power. If he were to bind you completely, you'd be utterly helpless."

My dream of the Goddess and my parents returned to me in full force. If the Goddess was warring with the Fates over the outcome for our world, it made sense that they'd gifted him with additional dark power to achieve the victory they sought.

A shiver wracked my spine as I felt a pair of eyes on me and a tug low in my belly. Domi's eyes widened a fraction before she schooled her features, and I spun on my heel to find Kazimir stalking toward me, a black crown resting on his brow.

Why did I still feel this tug with him when I'd accepted the bond with Ruslan?

I didn't have time to chase the thought as he stopped before me, towering over me in a way that was nothing less than sinister. My skin crawled as that oily aura exuded into the air around him, and with my new knowledge, my certainty was doubled, tripled, and I was grateful I had already made my decision because the way Immonen described it made me think that Kazimir could have bound me and forced it out of me if he wanted.

"You are glowing today, Izidora," Kazimir said, looking me up and down with his dark emerald eyes.

I stepped toward Mistik, needing something to do with my hands. "Meet us in the far arena," Liliana whispered before taking Twilight's reins and following Domi and Immonen away, giving Kazimir and me space to talk.

Wave after wave of emotion rose within me as he stood there, waiting for me to say something. The first that crashed through me was anger, for him taking the Night Throne away from me after he had worked so hard to convince me to want it in the first place – not that I still did. It was the principle of the matter, of his continued deceptions and games, knowing how ignorant and naive I had been in the months after they rescued me. The second was disgust as the oiliness swirled around him, bringing that manipulative side of him to the surface, laid bare for all to see. The third was fear, though that wave was smaller than it ever had been, thanks to my sessions with Zuriel and the slaughter of my abusive captors the previous night with Ruslan. The feeling of ripping their balls away still lingered, giving me a heady rush that I channeled into my magic.

I was fucking powerful, and Kazimir would not hurt me, not when I was prepared for a new type of attack from him. Armed with the knowledge Liliana had passed on, I tuned in to the flame-and-moonlight-wrapped crystal in my chest, stoking the white fire and filling the crystal with energy so that it lay in wait, ready to use on a moment's notice.

Viktor had taught me that the person who spoke first lost the power in the dynamic, so I continued to say nothing, checking Mistik over while Kazimir stared at me in a way that made me want to bathe and rinse the feel of his eyes from my body. The tension between us could have been sliced like a cake, and it was thicker than any dense dessert I'd ever eaten. Finally, I could take it no longer, and the pent-up fury burst from me like an explosion of fire.

"So you manipulate me into wanting the Night Crown and then take it from me?" My voice was pure venom, and I did not disguise the disgust in my tone.

Kazimir only shrugged and stepped closer. "We didn't want

the Night Realm to fall into the hands of a bastard from the Iron Realm."

My teeth clacked with how hard I bit back a retort about Ruslan, and it took several breaths dragged through my nose to be able to respond in a way that would not reveal that we had accepted our mating bond. Kazimir had been unpredictable in the worst type of way since he'd arrived in the Iron Realm, one moment the sweet male who had rescued me from the cave, and the next, a torrent of barely contained violence, unstable and unreasonable.

What would he do when he found out?

I knew then that I had to keep it a secret until Ruslan and I had convinced the other monarchs to ally with us over Kazimir. With this binding magic, Kazimir could lose his shit at any moment and have all of us bowing to his will.

I would never be powerless like that again.

"I appreciate the heads up," I gritted out, clenching and unclenching my fingers from Mistik's gray mane.

Kazimir stepped closer again, and Mistik tossed her head as if she sensed the emotions swirling beneath my skin. "I thought you wanted a king, Izidora. Here I am. I can give you everything Ruslan has, and more. After all, I'm the one who brought you back from the brink. I saved you. I can save you again, from him. Just say the words and I'll spirit you away, home to Este Castle, where you belong. We'll rule the Night Realm together like we were always meant to."

I could only blink at him. *Was he fucking kidding me?* All my growth was *on him*? But that statement wasn't the one that angered me most. "What I wanted was a male who was honest with me, who made me feel safe, who I could trust. You broke my trust, you manipulated me, you lied to me. Being a king does not make up for that."

Kazimir's eyes flashed dark, and my magic flared in my

hands, still hidden in Mistik's mane. "And yet you allow Ruslan to teach you to read? He is manipulating you, and you are allowing it. He is making you reliant on him, to teach you, to protect you, to take care of your emotions. How am I worse than a male who isn't secure enough to allow you to spread your wings and fly?"

The scoff that fell from my lips was as unbidden as Kazimir's presence in front of me. Everything he had just described was a direct reflection on him, and not on my chosen mate. Ruslan had fought through his own demons to allow me space to make my decision. Ruslan had empowered me, magically, physically, emotionally, and sexually, begging me to open up and become the highest version of myself. Trust was not an easy thing for me to give away, and yet my trust in Ruslan, especially when he returned with me to the cave where I had been chained, was the reason I accepted our bond that night.

But then, I realized, I'd never read in front of Kazimir. "How the fuck did you know he was teaching me to read?"

"How long was it after he kidnapped you that you started fucking him?" Kazimir redirected the course of our conversation, but I was not done. A violent storm swelled within me, threatening to unleash a torrent of hateful rain over his dark hair.

"Don't change the subject," I hissed. "How. Did. You. Know?"

All the times I'd felt eyes perusing my form, only to spin around desperately searching for the source of my unease and find nothing. *Was it always him?*

Kazimir took another step forward, raising his hands ever so slightly in supplication. "Just tell me what I need to fucking do, Izidora. You're mine, and I want you back. What the fuck do you want from me?"

"Nothing." I let the word fall between us, as cold and cruel as I could manage with the trembling that was weaving its way into my voice. My body flooded with adrenaline as I sensed the danger lurking mere feet away from me, mixing with the rage at his insolence, ratcheting up my heart rate as I prepared to fight.

"Sprite, what's wrong? I can feel your fear."

I ignored Ruslan's call down our bond, shutting him out because I had to survive, and that meant all my focus needed to be on the male in front of me. I even loosened the white-knuckle grip I held over my emotions the way Zuriel and Drazen had encouraged time and time again, waiting to use their intensity to my advantage.

"I spent my entire fucking life thinking about you. Searching for you. Every waking moment of every day revolves around you and has since the day you were born. I am the reason you are where you are right now. You should be grateful to me, and instead, you spurn me for a bastard, a mongrel bastard at that."

"He is more of a male than you will ever be," I snapped, rising to the goading Kazimir was so clearly giving me. My emotions were slipping through my fingers like sand, and I hurriedly tried to get a grip on them before information I did not want to share burst from my lips.

Kazimir closed the distance between us in three powerful strides, and in an instant, my sword was drawn from its hilt in the saddle and bathed in white flame. The arrogant male stopped an inch from my blazing blade, an amused twitch of his lips breaking up the ugly aura around him.

"You've gotten much faster, Izidora." He opened his mouth to say something else, but a horn cut through the air, and Ruslan's magically amplified voice called a start to the first event.

Without hesitation, I swung myself into the saddle, staring down from atop my mare's back at the male I'd loved first. "I am so much more than the female you tried to create," I said with a sharpness aimed to wound, and then I dug my heels into Mistik's sides and steered her toward the far ring, glancing over my shoulder to ensure Kazimir was not following.

While his legs did not move, his eyes did follow me until I rode around a makeshift building, cutting off his line of sight.

Liliana and Domi's heads were bent in hushed conversation when I reached them, and they quickly straightened at my approach. Something wild must have been in my expression because Liliana immediately reached out a reassuring hand as I jumped from Mistik's back.

My eyes burned as I looked toward the sky, fighting back tears of fear as my body returned to a less heightened state, adrenaline slowing its race through my veins.

"Are you okay?" Liliana whispered to me, pulling me in for a tight embrace.

"Yes," I choked out, my voice barely a whisper.

I hated that I felt so powerful and so weak at the same time.

She released me, holding me at arm's length, her seafoam green eyes both hard and soft. "I don't believe you, but I'm not going to push you to talk. Kazimir is a bitch, and Domi and I don't want to stay near him anymore. The three of us will stick together through the rest of this fucking feast, and then, I promise, I'll always stay with you."

"But what about Endre?" A tear spilled over, heating my cheek as it escaped to the ground.

"You are more important," she swore, and another choked sob escaped me.

"I missed you so fucking much."

"I know, me too."

The announcer's enhanced voice cut through our conversation, and I heard our three names being called to the first ring. Swiping at my wet eyes, I cleared my throat and straightened, facing Liliana and Domi with a determination to forget Kazimir and allow myself to be free atop Mistik's back.

"May the best rider win," Domi grinned, swinging into her mount's saddle.

Her banter brought a smile to my lips, and as I mounted Mistik again, I replied, "I see some tough competition out there, Domi. But I'm still confident in my abilities."

Liliana snorted, arriving at our level a moment later atop Twilight. "As long as it's one of us and not those dumb brutes, I don't care who wins."

"Together?" I asked, grinning at my friends.

"Together," they replied.

27

ZURIEL

BÉKE DAY SIX

The excitement in the thoughts of every person in attendance at the horse riding competition was like a torrent of rain against the mental barrier around my mind. If it weren't for centuries of practice keeping everyone out, it would have crumbled under the onslaught. Squeezing my eyes shut, I poured more magic from the light in my chest into the barrier, sighing in relief when the world quietened.

The other Telivér who chose to remain in the Iron Realm perched on borrowed beasts beside me, the group of us watching the scene unfold as riders mounted their horses and prepared to race through the obstacles.

Ruslan had just announced the start of the events, and as he descended from the stage, he searched for Izidora among the crowd. But my cousin was on the far side of the arena with her friends, all speaking with their heads bent close together. Their group was called first, and with her head held high, Izidora rode into the ring. I knew my cousin well enough to know that she was not as okay as she pretended to be, and with bated breath, I waited for her to begin the course. Ruslan watched her with the same intensity, and as I swung my surveillance to our right, Kazimir joined the other Night Fae and zeroed in on her as well.

The three of them were like anchor points for my attention, Izidora's heart-shaped face flush with excitement and exhilaration as she cleared obstacle after obstacle, Ruslan's pride as he beamed in her direction, and Kazimir's fury that tasted bitter in my mouth.

He did not know of Ruslan and Izidora's new mating bond, of that I was certain. If he had, he would have blown the whole realm apart already. I knew without having to slip into either of their minds that they'd accepted it; the way they looked at each other reminded me so much of Liessa and Ithuriel, and my chest panged at the memories of their tragic romance. My uncle told me he'd never been happier in his two and a half millennia of life, and I believed him when his glacial eyes sparkled with joy. The mating mark he bore between his wings was his greatest source of pride.

It was also his downfall. King Zalan was cruel, narcissistic, and controlling in a way that made even my skin crawl, and his presence at a prior Béke had already solidified my dislike. I didn't think it was possible to hate someone more than I hated King Azim, but when he forced Liessa and Ithuriel to fuck in front of him while he pinned her down, I knew there was no one I could hate more.

Then I watched him rip Ithuriel's wings from his back, leaving only bloody stumps in his wake. Ithuriel lost the ability to magic them away, leaving him in excruciating pain until he finally died shortly after Izidora was born. I knew then that he had joined Liessa in the beyond, and for that, I felt relief.

I waited for my cousin to emerge from wherever the wicked kings kept her, ready to help her win the war I had known was approaching for over two thousand years. It wasn't until I'd arrived in Északi that I understood the part I was to play in the Goddess's Prophecy, and it kept me here even when Rares and King Azim wanted to use me for their 'experiments.'

At least they'd given my partners and me the courtesy of privacy, unlike what King Zalan did to Liessa and Ithuriel.

The transformation in Ruslan since Izidora had returned with him to the Iron Realm gave me hope for the future of Északi. I had tried to remain as neutral as possible, knowing Izidora needed the space to work out her choice on her own, but secretly, I had rooted for Ruslan. I didn't know Kazimir, but after what I had witnessed since his arrival with the other Night Fae, I didn't care to know him either. My lips pressed together as I glanced sidelong at him once again; he was staring daggers at Ruslan. If I had reached out with my mind to read his, his thoughts would have been centered on regicide, without a doubt.

He was manipulative, obsessed, and volatile in a way Ruslan never was with Izidora. Not to mention the ego he carried like a badge of honor. How his companions did not see the darkness lurking within was beyond my comprehension. Why they allowed him to become their king and rule over them was even more so.

Mind reading was not a perfect science, but rather an art, and to remain undetected in someone's mind took incredible skill; it was a secret I had shared with no one but Ithuriel. The corner of my mouth twitched upward as I recalled Izidora's refusal to utilize her empath magic to render her opponent immobile. Stubbornly upholding our values must have run in the family.

These days, I almost refused to slip into someone's mind to read their thoughts, preferring to interact with those around me on equal ground. Besides, after over two thousand years of life, people were predictable, and their thoughts grew boring and repetitive. But Kazimir's mind was a complex web that I had barely begun to untangle, and I needed to know what he and his companions had planned during their travel to the Iron Realm. The Night, Crystal, and Day Fae had arrived as a group, and I suspected there was a united army behind them. Whether his army was fracturing with every one of Kazimir's slip-ups remained to be seen.

It wasn't a matter of *if* war was coming, but a matter of *when*.

And then it would be time for me to play my part.

My attention was drawn away from my inner thoughts when a cheer rose through the crowd of onlookers. Even one of the Demons released a whoop as Liliana, Izidora's best friend, sailed over an incredibly difficult jump that had tripped up every previous rider. Though her perfection cost her precious seconds, moments after she crossed the finish line her name appeared directly next to my cousin's on the magically enhanced scoreboard towering over the arena. Only their other companion, Domi, was ahead of the two, and the group cheered together as Liliana leaped from her black mount.

The Telivér were called to compete next, and I dug my heels into my horse's side, opting for the higher level course Izidora and her friends had ridden through, while many of the Shifters opted for the lower level course, and Konsteon, a Centaur Shifter, leaped over the obstacles in the middle ring. The time I'd lived was more than enough to perfect the sport, and as I sucked in a deep breath at the starting line, I rubbed my mount's shoulder, offering him some encouragement. He tossed his head, tensing beneath me as he prepared to launch into action.

The horn sounded, and we were off, wind whipping through my white locks of hair as we sailed over the first jump, landing lightly and angling toward the next. The stallion flew along the course as if he had Angel wings holding him aloft, and I lost myself in the flow of jump, gallop, turn, jump, until the largest one loomed ahead. Pulling up lightly on the reins, I slowed my mount, allowing him time to gather his haunches beneath him and launch us into the air, his hooves clearing the bar with a breath to spare. We raced to the finish line, slowing to a walk only after we'd cleared it. I patted his neck in praise as I studied our completion time and points. We clocked in a few seconds behind Izidora and her friends, and I guided my mount to the side, waiting for the rest of the Telivér to finish their turns.

My chest swelled with pride. The Telivér did not hide from the world as we had been forced to for so many years at the behest of King Azim and Rares. No one seemed to mind or treat us any differently, save for a few of the Night Fae, and for that, a spark of hope rose from within that this war would not be like the Great War between the Angels and Demons. One day, in the history books, they would call this the Age of Innovation, where the world changed for the better thanks to the brilliant minds of a few, most of whom held mixed blood and brimmed with power.

But all changes like this came with a steep cost; lives and blood were the usual payment, along with a measure of trauma and lingering strife.

Izidora waved me over once the last of the Telivér finished, and I tugged on the reins to direct the stallion in her direction.

"You were amazing, Zuriel!" she exclaimed once I dismounted and joined her huddle with High Ladies Liliana and Domi. Thanks to my gift, I also knew about the former's rise in station.

I shrugged off her compliment but allowed a small smile. "You three were as well. I see all your names topping the board." I dipped my head in the direction of the giant stone currently burning new names into its facade.

As Liliana and Domi craned their necks to glimpse the scores, I spoke into Izidora's mind. *"So you accepted the bond?"*

The blush that crept across her cheeks confirmed what I already knew. *"How did you know?"*

"A lucky guess from the way you two looked at each other when you arrived."

"Kazimir bothered me shortly after."

"I saw."

"Why do I still feel a connection to him if I accepted Ruslan?"

My brows lifted for a moment as shock hit me like a punch to the gut. That was not something I had an explanation for. A bond between three was nearly as rare as empath magic, and in my life, I'd only heard whispers of a few, and read even less in written texts from reliable sources. But I knew, because I was there, that the Goddess's Prophecy spoke of choosing between two mates. *"That I do not know. Perhaps you must speak the words to him to break the bond like you had to speak the words to Ruslan to accept it?"*

A subtle dip of her head acknowledged the suggestion before Liliana and Domi's attention returned to us. *"Do they know?"*

"Not yet. I want to keep it a secret for now, so Kazimir doesn't find out."

"A wise choice, cousin."

"High Lady Domi, my cousin tells me you breed horses," I said casually. Before she had a chance to respond, the announcer boomed over us all, calling for the next event – a race. "I'll take that as my cue to leave."

"See you later, Zuriel," Izidora called as I gripped my horse's reins to lead him toward the waiting Telivér.

"Remember, our training resumes tomorrow," I called over my shoulder.

After all, war was coming, and I could not allow my cousin to enter it unprepared.

28

RUSLAN

The crowd hummed with excitement as the officiants tallied the final scores of the horseback riding events. Those, combined with the scores of the previous days' events, would determine the overall winner of this Béke's competition.

The Iron Realm better fucking win.

The Fae, Félvér, and Telivér clumped together on the ground around the stage where I stood, patiently awaiting the slip of paper that would declare the winning realm. Izidora chatted animatedly with the Telivér, throwing her head back and laughing loudly at something one of the Demons said. Watching her slip into the carefree moment warmed my heart, especially knowing how much she had suffered since the arrival of the other Fae.

A male crossed the stage, handing me several slips of folded paper, and a hush settled over the competitors and onlookers as I unfolded the first. On it was the list of individual event winners, and when I saw Izidora's name next to two of the events, I couldn't smother the grin that broke across my face. One by one, I called out the names, the helpers behind me stepping forward with the respective prizes.

Izidora approached the stage, bouncing with excitement as I lifted a small leather bag from the male stepping forward, and handed it to her. *"You can put all your new rings in this while you ride."*

"You or Mistik?" Her eyes flashed to mine, filled with heat, and our bond thrummed.

"My dirty sprite."

She winked and sashayed her hips as she returned to the crowd. I watched her the entire way, forcing myself to remain in place when all I wanted was to snatch her in my arms and ferry her to Roc Palace.

High Lady Domi, unsurprisingly, was the overall winner of the day's event.

The final slip of paper contained the overall scores of the realms, ranked from lowest to highest.

Crystal Realm... Day Realm... Iron Realm...

I nearly crumpled the paper when I saw the fucking Night Realm had beaten the Iron Realm by *three points.*

Forcing myself to unclench my jaw, I looked up from the paper and locked eyes with the new king, whose smug, self-important expression told me he knew exactly what was written on this slip.

Fucking Kazimir.

The bastard even wore the Night Crown, flaunting his new status in my face even more so than in my mate's. But in the end, I got Izidora, and he lost.

So why was he not angry?

If it had been the other way around, I would have lost my shit, tearing everything and anyone around me to pieces to slake the utter anguish that would have consumed my soul. I was not a good male, but I fucking tried for Izidora. I would do anything for her, as evidenced by the way I tortured each and every male who'd kept her chained in that cave.

Shaking away my unanswered questions and dark thoughts, I cleared my throat and tried my best to sound enthusiastic. I was hosting, unfortunately. "The winner of the competition this year is the Night Realm."

Cheers erupted from the gathered Night Fae, and Kazimir sauntered toward the stage like he was the king of the Iron Realm too, escorted by raucous claps. Our gazes collided with the force of an avalanche, so many unsaid words flinging between us as he approached. The officiant stopped halfway between us, the large, elegant box he held hiding the ultimate prize.

With a dramatic flourish, he unveiled a goose egg-sized gem, the stone transforming from a deep green to a deep purple as a sliver of light pierced it. Each knuckle on my hand popped in quick, violent succession as Kazimir lifted the stone from its velvet setting and held it high for all to see. The gemstone was a new discovery, thanks to those tunnels carved into the mountains leading to the other realms, and this was our largest find to date. The Dragon in me wanted nothing more than to snatch it from his oily fingers and fly away to add it to my collection, but I resisted with every ounce of sanity left in me, because I needed the other monarchs to believe I was better than *him*.

With this goal in the forefront of my mind, I clapped my hands, allowing the forceful slaps to soothe that part of me that relied on pain to cope. As the crowd died down, I spoke again. "Please join us for a celebratory feast tonight at Ryza Citadel marking the halfway point in Béke. And remember, in two days, we begin celebrating our Goddess, who has granted Északi long-lasting peace in her generosity."

Not that that peace would last much longer.

The crowd began to disperse, and I immediately sought out my mate. She stood in a huddle with Liliana and Domi, their heads bent together as they whispered furiously. My heart twinged as I paused for a moment to watch her with her friends, something she'd never had before and something I knew she held onto dearly. Liliana was good to her, and I hoped that she would understand, for Izidora's sake, that she'd chosen me over Kazimir.

Though, with the furtive glances the three stole at the aforementioned male, I did not doubt that she would.

He had already rejoined the other Night Fae, the winter sun glinting off of his newly minted crown. My jaw clenched because *someone* in the Iron Realm had to have made it for him, and I would make it a personal mission to find out who. Ambros would never betray me like that, but he would know who did. And once I had them in my clutches, they'd feel the wrath that had been trained into me from childhood, and I'd slake a sliver of my fury by delivering the most delicious kind of pain to them until they begged me to end their life.

Fucking king of the Night Realm.

The heat that boiled inside me must have caught Izidora's attention, because not a moment later, her gorgeous aquamarine eyes snapped from her friends to me. Her brow pinched ever so slightly as she focused, and the raging boil transformed into a low simmer. I loosed a breath, feeling my shoulders relax as she soothed me. Even from a distance, she lent me strength and support. The corner of my mouth twitched up as I realized she and Zuriel had kept yet another secret from Rares and me about her abilities.

"Come to me, mate. I have not had enough of you yet."

Those gem-like eyes sparkled as I spoke in her mind. *"In a moment. I'm inviting Liliana and Domi to come with me tomorrow."*

"That is a brilliant idea, sprite. You are going to be so beautiful."

A blush crept across her cheeks under my fervent attention and pretty words, but she returned her focus to the conversation in front of her. I knew by the high-pitched squeal and bouncing from Liliana the moment Izidora told her friends what she had planned for the following day, and my heart melted at the sight of her excitement for my mate.

Being mated was better than I ever thought it could be. I felt safe in a way I never had, loved in a way I never thought was possible, and for the first time in my life, I relaxed into knowing that would never change.

INTERLUDE

All the lights in Vaenor had been extinguished, casting all the Fae in attendance in darkness. The crowd shifted from foot to foot as a strong breeze whipped off the dark ocean, crashing waves audible in the distance. Gradually, as if the Goddess were flicking stars down from the heavens above, lights flickered into existence, highlighting the faces of the lantern holders.

The lantern release was a highly anticipated tradition during Béke, especially when the feast was not hosted in the Night Realm. The king and most of the High Houses celebrated in the Day Realm, and the revelry was not as excessive as it had been two years prior when the Night Realm had played host. The night when all gathered to reflect on the past year and set intentions for the new always ended in an enormous party, and without parties on the preceding nights to lessen the appetite for another, the crowd vibrated with anticipation.

A chocolate-haired female stood amidst a crowd of young Night Fae at the rear of the group, most of the males surrounding her competing for her attention. She rolled her eyes at their antics, dismissing them one by one. The area around them brightened as the firesticks made their way to the back of the group, only spurring the males' efforts to win her attention. One went so far as to dangle the firestick just out of her reach in an attempt to draw her close enough to be able to kiss her beneath it.

But her brother had trained her well, and in several swift movements, she'd disarmed the suitor and snatched the light for herself. With great care, she brought it above her lantern's fragile paper encasing, dipping it to find the wick within. She was lonely, despite the constant attention of males around her, and this year, she knew, was the year the Goddess would grant her wish.

No other noble female in the Night Realm loved fighting as much as she did. Her long lashes and longer locks drew the attention and envy of all those around her, along with her striking seafoam green eyes. Most of the young females around her were friendly, but none let her close because they saw her as competition – and for good reason. Yet these young males surrounding her held none of her attention. She wanted someone older, stronger, and with enough will to match her own.

But most importantly, she wanted a friend – one who loved fighting, fashion, and fun just as much as she did.

It was that fervently held hope that lit the wick of her lantern, and it was the promise of the Goddess granting her the friend she'd always wanted that had her ignoring those around her. She prayed, holding the wish within her heart, like it was an essential part of her being, until the High Priestess began her melodic, solemn chant, signaling the gathered Fae to release their floating lights into the sky.

With one last look at the aqua-blue lantern, she opened her palms, allowing the fire to fill it and lift it into the sky, joining the thousands of others as the ocean breeze called them away from Este Castle.

Her eyes never left the lantern as it sailed away, and she remained steadfast in her spot until she could see it no longer. Only then did she join the throng of Fae searching for the nearest location to obtain a drink, many slipping indoors in an attempt to escape the night's wintry chill.

A breeze lifted the strands of her brown hair as she took one last look at the sky. She could have sworn the brightest star winked at her before returning to its usual lull of light. With a sigh, she followed the crowd into the castle, making the trek to the large ballroom where she'd find her family and a host of males offering her drinks and dances. She partied the night away without a care in the world, for she knew in her bones that in the next year, her wish would come true.

III

THE CELEBRATION

29

IZIDORA

The air was thick with the scent of amber. I whipped around, trying to gain my bearings amid the massive snow banks that surrounded me. Everything was white, save for tendrils of oily darkness slipping through the snow, sickening with its touch. Veins of black wound their way through the thick piles, melting them until I was knee-deep in water. And still, I could not find the source of the smell. My unbound chestnut hair lifted in a strong breeze that brought wispy shadows in on its wings. I flicked my fingers in an attempt to bring my magic to my palms, but nothing happened with the movement. My breath caught in my throat, panic clawing its way up as I felt utterly powerless.

Shit, shit, shit, I had to get out of here.

Without a moment's hesitation, I pushed off the rocky ground beneath me, but my legs were encumbered by the soupy water surrounding them. My heart galloped faster and faster as I struggled to run, and my crazed movements only seemed to thicken the water around me. A splash at my back sprayed water in every direction, and

I whipped around, a hand clutching my chest as Kazimir appeared from nowhere.

"You are mine," he growled, lunging for me, and I was helpless as his hand closed over my throat.

A gasp ripped through me as I bolted upright in bed, dragging Ruslan from sleep a moment later. Without hesitation, he cradled me against him, wrapping his arms around me protectively. "Shh, sprite, it was only a dream."

A choked sob caught in my chest as he continued to soothe me with gentle, circular strokes on my bare skin, the warmth of his large frame enveloping me and chasing away the chill of powerlessness. "It was *him*," I managed to choke out, and Ruslan only pulled me tighter.

"I'll always keep you safe, sprite. I am only a thought away," he promised.

Dragging in a serrated breath, I wiped my eyes and allowed his heat to relax me. "What time is it?"

He brushed his lips over my bare shoulder. "Time to eat breakfast."

"Good, because I could use a cinnamon roll to banish my nightmare," I said, eliciting a low rumble behind me. When I squirmed in his arms, he released me, and as I scooted out of bed, I was grateful that I had not drunk too much at the feast the previous night. "I'm going to shower before we go."

Ruslan was out of bed a moment later, throwing back the curtains hiding Radence from us, and the pinkish purple of dawn over the Agrenak Mountains was revealed. He tossed a little of his magic into the fire, bringing it to life, and I knew it was because he wanted to ensure I was warm enough. With happiness bubbling in my heart and banishing the lingering bits of fear, I strode into the bathroom and turned on the taps for the shower.

When I returned to our bedroom, Ruslan was reading, one

arm holding his book and the other thrown casually behind his head, his muscles flexing in the morning light. I paused for a moment to admire him, still in disbelief over how incredible he was to me. To others, he might be the ruthless king, but to me, he was soft and sweet, and the love I felt down our bond was deeper than any ocean and just as endless.

"Ready to go?" I asked, drawing his attention away.

With a smirk, he set his book aside and rose from the bed, revealing every naked inch of his body. "I will be in a moment." I gulped at his erection, my thighs dampening from the sight of it. "My eyes are up here, mate."

Jerking my gaze to his face, I blushed, then sashayed my hips as I walked toward the dresser filled with my clothes, dropping the towel away from my body as I did so. The growl that came unbidden was entirely too satisfying.

"If we didn't need to focus on winning the Day and Crystal Realms to our side, I'd fuck you against this until you went hoarse from screaming my name."

"Maybe later," I purred, pushing my ass out as I bent to pull undergarments from the bottom drawer. When I straightened and glanced over my shoulder, his expression was dark and playful, and he looked like he wanted to devour me.

"I'll hold you to that."

———

WE WERE the first to arrive in the dining hall, and once I'd realized that, I bolted straight toward the steaming pile of sweets, taking all the best pastries for myself. A sigh brushed across the back of my neck, and I whipped my head around to find Ruslan holding two plates filled with meat and cheese. I smiled at him, batting my lashes innocently. "Is one of those for me?"

"Since you will only eat these if I get them for you, yes," he teased, nudging me along with his leg. We settled at our usual table just as the other monarchs began to arrive, their entourages trickling in behind them.

Queen Viktoria and Queen Immonen sat across from me, and we fell into easy conversation, while Ruslan spoke with their husbands. An idea dawned on me as we chatted, and I knew Ruslan would approve. "Would you two care to join me today as I select my wedding gown? High Ladies Liliana and Domi will be in attendance as well."

Queen Viktoria's expression was open and bright, almost motherly, and it warmed me from the inside out. "It would be my honor. I still remember my wedding as if it were yesterday."

"I've never been to one, so I have no idea what to expect," I admitted, ducking my head for a moment. Then with a sigh, I continued, "I could use all the help I can get. Thankfully, Ruslan has taken care of most of the planning for me."

His regard fell over me as I uttered his name, and he gave my leg a light squeeze beneath the table. *"You are brilliant in your own right."*

"I'd be delighted as well. While the Night and Day Fae may have the best cloth weavers, the Crystal Fae have the best fashion sense," Queen Immonen boasted, tossing her platinum hair over her shoulder.

The smile spreading across my face was interrupted by a string tugging in my low belly, leaving me with a sense of rising nausea. My attention snapped to the Night Fae who sauntered into the room.

Kazimir strolled in with a swagger that made me want to roll my eyes, and as he piled his plate with food and walked toward us, my stomach threatened to return its contents to my plate. He wore the Night Crown with an air of haughtiness, with his nose lifted even higher in the air than normal and a shit-eating grin he flashed at everyone who glanced in his direction. The chair scraped obnoxiously against the ground as he pulled it back and joined us at the table. All our conversations ceased, and I did not need to be an empath to know that everyone at the table was wildly uncomfortable.

Tapping into that spear of crystal wrapped in flames and moonlight in my chest, I pushed soothing emotions into everyone around me, knowing that the shift in mood would be in everyone's best interests. With six people surrounding me, it was a bit difficult, but when Queen Viktoria's shoulders relaxed, I knew I had managed to pull it off. I couldn't wait to tell Zuriel.

"Thank you, sprite."

"You're welcome."

My magic had affected Kazimir too, and the oiliness that had surrounded his aura was notably absent. Warmth returned to his countenance, and he opened up conversation again. "What has everyone planned for the free day?"

The queens pressed their lips together, and as we locked eyes, I knew they would not speak of my earlier invitation. Thankfully, King Consort Geza offered words first. "I for one would like a day to relax. I am sore from all our competitions."

King Airre chuckled, then turned to my mate. "I'd like to see some of your new mines, King Ruslan." He dropped his voice conspiratorially. "My wife is fond of pretty things, you see."

Queen Immonen's eyes sparkled like gemstones as she shout-whispered, "Your wife is *very* fond of pretty things."

"Consider it done, King Airre. I will take you myself to one of our newest mines, where any rock you find is yours." Ruslan flashed him a winning grin, though it was all the ruthless king on display and not a friendly comrade. "Anyone else is welcome to join us on the expedition."

Kazimir contributed little else as our conversations drifted onto other topics like agriculture, trade, and new technologies, but he studied each word intently as if he were memorizing them and packing them away to review later. Ruslan explained how the lifts the others would see on their way to the mines had been created, then mentioned a few other inventions of the Iron Realm in the last few decades.

My mind was only half in the conversation, every hair on the back of my neck standing with Kazimir only two seats away from me. The dream still had me on edge, and I wanted to leave the dining hall as soon as possible. The moment Liliana finished eating, I caught her eye across the room, and she seemed to understand what I needed. Grabbing Domi by the arm, she pulled her toward me until the two of them stood at the end of the table. "We'll meet you in the courtyard in ten minutes?" she asked with a quick perusal along the table.

"Yes," I confirmed, and the queens across from me dabbed their mouths with napkins and rose from their seats. I felt two sets of eyes on my back as I did the same, though I only smiled at the ones closest to me as I hurried to leave.

Ruslan held my hand, our fingers touching until the last possible moment. *"I love you."*

"I love you," I replied, then followed the females into the hallway, where we parted ways so I could order a carriage from the stablehands while they dressed for our outing.

Fifteen minutes later, we rolled away from Ryza and toward the dress shop – supposedly the most exclusive in the whole Iron Realm. The five of us were a tight fit in the carriage, but no one seemed to mind as we laughed and gossiped on the way. The shop was near Steel, Liliana mentioned as we rolled past the Félvér club, and then she was 'forced' to recount tales of her experience for Queen Viktoria, who was fanning herself by the time we finally rolled to a stop in front of the wide-windowed boutique.

"Greetings, Your Highnesses," the female clad in soft black

clothing said, holding the door wide for us to enter as we emerged from the carriage. The space reminded me of the dance studio where Ruslan and Kazimir had pleasured me until I could no longer walk, with mirrors adorning every wall, some covered by racks of fabric or ready-made gowns. Unconsciously, I glided over to them, running my hands along the material and admiring the luxurious feel of everything in the shop.

To think, a little under half a year had passed since I'd left my chains behind.

I was so lost in thought that I did not hear Liliana's approach. "This reminds me of our first day together."

I jumped, clutching my chest as my heart leaped and sank, and I released a whoosh of air. "Sorry, you startled me." Regaining control of my breath, I paused, focusing on everything around us in an attempt to ground myself. "It reminds me of that, too. I'm so glad you're here." To show her my sincerity, I reached for her hand and gave it a squeeze.

"You're my best friend. I wouldn't miss it for the world," she replied, squeezing my hand in turn. "Now, let's see what they have to say."

We rejoined the queens and Domi on the far side of the space, where two Félvér and one Iron Fae female waited for us. "Natasha! Aliana! I didn't realize you two worked here," Liliana said when she noticed the two Félvér.

"Liliana, what a pleasant surprise," the dark-haired one replied with a wide grin. "We haven't seen you the past few nights at Steel."

Liliana glanced at me conspiratorially. "I'm trying to convince Izidora to come with me next time, Natasha."

Aliana's eyes trailed me up and down, and from the red tinge to them, I had to guess she had Demon blood. "Yes, Your Highness, you should come and bring your king with you. We'd have so much fun together."

Heat blossomed throughout my body as Liliana's tales, still fresh from our ride, rose to the front of my mind. "As much as I would love to join you, I don't think Ruslan would allow anyone else to touch me right now."

Liliana's dark brows pinched before they leaped up her forehead. "No fucking way! How did you not tell me?"

The two queens looked at each other in puzzlement before Domi's face broke into a wide, knowing smile. "You accepted then?"

"Yes," I breathed, grinning ear to ear as that thread that tied me to Ruslan hummed contentedly. "I was going to surprise you today since you'll see the mark when I try on dresses."

Before the words finished spilling from my lips, Liliana tackled me into a hug, throwing me off balance and stealing a laugh from my chest. "I'm so happy for you."

Tears sprang to my eyes as our contact allowed me to feel the full depth of her emotion. "I am happy, happier than I've ever been. Happier than I ever thought possible."

But there was still so much lingering trauma I needed to heal.

Could both be true at the same time? Could I truly be so incredibly happy and still suffer from what had happened to me?

Liliana held me at arm's length as I sniffed and blinked rapidly to dispel the tears that threatened to fall. "You deserve it too," she told me.

As Domi wormed her way in, the three workers excused themselves, offering us a moment of privacy. Queen Viktoria embraced me next, followed by Queen Immonen, the other mated female in our group.

"Izidora, being mated is the most incredible gift anyone could be given. I wish Airre and I hadn't fought our bond for so long. I am so glad you made your choice..." The queen of the

Crystal Realm blinked rapidly, platinum lashes fluttering violently before her eyes rolled to the back of her head.

"Immonen?" I whispered, heart pounding in my chest as something unearthly settled over me. The sound that the queen made next was something between a gasp and a choke, and as she collapsed, Liliana and I reached for her, our reflexes kicking in just in time to lower her gently to the ground.

"What's wrong with her?" I asked, attention flitting everywhere as I searched for the source of her distress.

"She's having a vision," Queen Viktoria stated, hands hovering protectively over her belly.

Immonen's body twitched again, arching off the ground, and Liliana cradled the queen's head in her lap so it didn't smack against the floor. "She's been having them often lately," she said quietly, glancing around us to ensure we were alone. The dressmakers' absence was a relief. I didn't think Queen Immonen would want anyone to see her in this state, let alone strangers.

With my empath magic, I reached for her, sending soothing emotions her way in an attempt to ease the tension lining her brow and the frown pulling down the corners of her mouth. But as I opened myself to her, I was hit with a wave of pure terror, so powerful that it turned my stomach over and inside out, and I immediately wanted to heave. I must have reacted in some way, because in the next moment, Liliana hissed, "Put your mental barrier up!"

Nodding, I did just that, and the emotions of the queens, Domi, and Liliana melted away, leaving me firmly in my own mental space. As I returned to myself, so too did Immonen. With a shudder, and then a few long, slow blinks, her eyes refocused, and she gulped down air.

"Shh, just lie still for a moment," Liliana soothed.

But Queen Immonen had a wild, crazed look in her eye, and I didn't need my empath magic to read the fear rolling off of her.

Her attention landed on me, and she grasped at my shirt, yanking me close to her with the desperation of a female possessed. "He can't know, he can't know, you can't tell Kazimir that you accepted the bond."

I stiffened, her proximity and the force with which she gripped me sending ice skittering down my spine.

"Please, Izidora! You can't tell him!" Immonen's voice reached a fevered pitch, and both Domi and Liliana placed reassuring hands on her in an attempt to get her to release me.

"Why not?" I asked warily, air lodging in my lungs as I waited for Immonen's response. I knew from the level of distress she displayed that whatever she'd seen in the vision could not be good.

She swallowed, twin sets of tears spilling over and tracking down her cheeks. "Once he knows... everything goes dark."

"What do you mean, everything goes dark?" Frustration speared through me, and I gritted my teeth against the rising tide of rage. "I thought choosing a mate was supposed to fix all of this!" My words came out harsher than I intended, but none of the females paid it any attention.

Some of the fervency lifted from Immonen, and she allowed Domi and Liliana to uncurl her fingers and sit her upright. With a sniff, she wiped her eyes and smoothed her hair before responding. "I don't know... the visions aren't always clear. I get flashes and impressions more than anything lately. And they shift so much... one day, I'll be certain of an outcome, and the next, the Goddess shows me something completely different." She paused, closing her eyes briefly as if she were trying to create the vision again. "But this, this *will* come to pass once Kazimir knows."

Goddess damn everything.

"Fucking Fates," Liliana swore, glancing at the heavens, then at the ground. "We can't exactly go around telling everyone about this vision either, because that would mean we know about Izidora and Ruslan's mating bond. Which we don't." She shot a pointed look at the gathered members of our group.

"Agreed," Queen Viktoria hummed, glancing over her shoulder in the direction the others had disappeared. "We must also swear the females to secrecy. The knowledge should not leave this room."

Another secret in the Iron Realm.

"You won't even tell your husbands?" I asked the two queens. Domi, I was already certain, would not tell Kaztar.

"I am the only queen in a continent of proud, arrogant kings. We females must stick together," Queen Viktoria stated firmly.

"As much as I love him, my husband is one of them," Queen Immonen sighed. "I will try my best to keep this from him, but as you know, Izidora, the mating bond gives us access to each other's minds. He's already in there asking if I'm alright after my vision."

I grasped her hands in mine. "Thank you, Immonen. Tell him we've got you."

"You can't tell Ruslan either, Izidora. He'd immediately kill Kazimir for the perceived threat against you. Your mating bond is super fresh, and he's already kind of volatile as it is." Liliana shrugged as if her statement was obvious. Which, I guessed, in a way it was. Ruslan didn't show his vulnerable side to anyone but me.

"More unstable than Kazimir?" I quipped, quirking a brow.

She huffed a laugh. "No, but Ruslan would burn the world down for you. Kazimir would... burn the world down for you, but in a different way."

I had to suppress a smile. Liliana had no idea what Ruslan would do for me – had done for me. A wicked thrill swept through me as the memory of us slaughtering my former captors together and then fucking while covered in their blood drifted to the forefront of my mind. I snorted and then helped Immonen stand. She swayed slightly before finally steadying herself. She smoothed her skirt, then said to me, "I don't know what will happen in the coming days, weeks, or even months, but if my visions are any indication, it is nothing good."

The Goddess had said as much when she appeared in my dreams alongside my parents. Choosing was supposed to be the fucking solution to everything, and to hear from Immonen that if Kazimir uncovered mine and Ruslan's solidified bond everything would still go dark did nothing but return my apprehension with roaring ferocity.

I chewed my lip as the two queens leaned on each other for support and made their way to a low sofa across the room. Domi squeezed my shoulder, then joined them, leaving Liliana and me alone.

"That definitely put a somber air on the day," I finally said, attempting to laugh to dispel the unease settling in my belly. But my core was cold and chilling more with every passing moment at the thought of what it meant for everything to go dark.

"Let's forget about it all and enjoy the day. Right now, it's just us about to design you the sexiest damn dress we can so that Ruslan falls to his knees when he sees you in the temple." Liliana succeeded in making me smile at the imagery of my strong, powerful male softening like melting butter for me.

"Why are you the best?" I joked, linking my arm in hers and closing the rest of the distance to the pedestal where Natasha, Aliana, and the Iron Fae female spoke with the queens and Domi in hushed tones.

When we reached them, all three lifted their gazes to me. "We swear not to speak a word of what we see today to anyone,"

Natasha said. "We swore an unbreakable vow to Queen Viktoria." The three lifted their wrists, and a faint line of gold lined each of them.

"Unbreakable vow?" I asked, my body shaking slightly.

What else did I not know about the magic of this world? Had Kazimir locked me in an unbreakable vow without my knowledge, and was that why I still felt him?

"Only crowned monarchs can make them, as part of the Goddess's balance," Queen Viktoria informed me. "This particular one will remain in place until you tell Kazimir that you accepted your mating bond with Ruslan. If any of them speak on the subject, they will die immediately."

"Thank you," I said, my shoulders loosening with the knowledge that Kazimir would not discover that Ruslan and I had accepted the mating bond until I was ready for him to know, and that there was no unbreakable vow I had been trapped in without my consent.

Liliana released me, and I stepped onto the pedestal, banishing the lingering worry and focusing on the spectacular array around me.

The dressmakers began scrutinizing me, circling and assessing and drawing imaginary lines with their fingers. Aliana spoke first after a thorough pass. "What style and color would you like?"

In a panicked glance in the mirror, I sought out Liliana, hoping for some assistance, but Immonen cut in with her suggestion first. "My dear, with your Angel heritage, you must wear white."

"White with lots of gems!" Liliana exclaimed. "This is the Iron Realm, and you're marrying the king of it."

I laughed, "I like both of those suggestions. Can you make something that is form-fitting? I want to really wow Ruslan."

"We can," Natasha confirmed. "If I may make a suggestion?"

"Please." I indicated she should continue.

"With your figure, you'd look incredible in something like this." She pulled a dress from a nearby rack, the bodice tight and nearly transparent with bones holding its shape. The skirt was cinched tight from the waist to mid-thigh, where it flowed in waves of light fabric in every direction, the train so long it was wrapped over another hanger.

My eyes widened as I beheld the elegant dress, and I nodded immediately. "Can we add some sleeves to it? It's quite cold at the moment." That earned a chuckle from the group, none of us accustomed to the bitter winter weather in the Iron Realm.

"Slip behind the curtain with me, and I'll help you into it. From there, we can make alterations," Aliana said, and I followed her a few steps away, shedding my pants and tunic while she unlaced the back of the gown. With great care, I managed to slip into the middle of it without stepping on the fine fabric, and the Félvér wriggled it over my body until the top of the bodice brushed against my breasts. I held it in place while she tightened the silk on the back, giving my cleavage a nice lift. She glanced up from her work and caught my eye in the mirror. "King Ruslan will not be able to resist you in this. The Iron Realm is sexy, and you, Your Highness, look sexy in this dress."

I had to agree with her. The dress was flattering in all the right ways and showed enough skin to be alluring while leaving some to the imagination. Aliana carefully bundled the train in her arms, helping me pivot so we could exit the room.

Stepping back into the parlor, we found my companions perching on the edges of their seats. Liliana squealed and bounced, while Immonen clasped her hands in front of her mouth, over a watery, close-lipped smile.

"You look stunning," Queen Viktoria enthused, her eyes alight as they roamed the dress.

Once I was settled atop the pedestal, the dressmakers worked together to fan out the train, careful not to step on it.

"Lift your hair so I can see your mate mark!" Liliana exclaimed.

Grinning, I twisted my long locks, then lifted them off my back, revealing the perfect circle between my shoulder blades. In the mirror, I watched my best friend swoon. But then the reality of Immonen's vision settled over me and I released my hair, hands shaking as I smoothed it. "No, my back needs to be covered. This mark has to be covered."

Liliana jumped to her feet and leaped over the train to my side, grabbing my hand and grounding me as panic sunk its claws into my chest. "Shh, take a breath, we will fix it."

My vision swam, but I nodded and sucked in a ragged breath.

"I have a perfect solution," the Iron Fae female said, crossing to the opposite end of the store and returning with an intricate, jeweled piece that had a thick collar and cascaded row after row of diamonds. "This will fit over your dress and make you sparkle."

"It's beautiful," I breathed, sweeping my hair over my shoulder so she could secure it and hide the mark once more.

A bubble of laughter burst around us, and I found myself brimming with joy as I stared at my friends, and then at myself in the full-length mirror. The dress was exquisite, hugging my curves in all the right places, the soft, billowy fabric making me look ethereal, and I knew the moment I added my wings to the ensemble, I'd bring all the realms to their knees. The thought heated my low belly in the most delicious way.

I couldn't wait for Ruslan to see me in this.

Liliana wrapped her arms around my waist and squeezed as we looked at ourselves in the mirror, and more than anything I was relieved to have her with me. She was the best friend anyone could ask for, and during the turmoil of Béke, she'd been a steadfast and grounding presence that I so desperately needed.

But my moment of joy was yanked away when a tug at my back had me snapping my head up and staring in the mirror, out the window, and into the street beyond.

KAZIMIR

Béke Day Seven

They were fucking wedding dress shopping. From my hidden spot across the street, I watched two of the females from Steel and another I did not know work on a white gown around Izidora, the queens, Domi, and Liliana excitedly chatting and sipping on wine while they participated in the farce. I ran a hand over my face, trying to calm my pounding heart as the black beast in my chest roared at me to break up their session and snatch Izidora and force her to be mine. That darkness was already simmering beneath the surface as I used it to cloak myself, remaining hidden from the ignorant females, and it took every ounce of restraint to keep it caged.

The last night I'd spent at Steel flashed in my mind, reminding me of how good Natasha had felt riding my cock while she sucked the tongue of another female whose name I could not recall. I ground my teeth as I realized their proximity to Izidora could lead to her discovering that I'd fucked almost all the females at that club in my time in the Iron Realm. But she had been fucking Ruslan, so she couldn't complain about it.

One day, this would all be behind us, and her belly would swell with my seed, our indiscretions forgotten. She was *mine*, and I was going to win her back.

I snapped out of my reverie when the Iron Fae female crossed the store toward shelves of glittering gems, selecting an intricate metal piece and ferrying it back to Izidora, who stood with her back to me. I could almost hear the oohs and aahs coming from the queens, Liliana, and Domi as it glittered in the light. Izidora turned slightly at their sounds, half-facing me and nodding profusely. She swept her hair off her back, and for a moment I thought I saw a flash of black marking her back.

What the fuck?

My blood boiled and I stalked forward, pulling on more of my magic to keep me hidden until I was nearly pressed against the glass storefront. But the bejeweled collar was already secured around her neck, and from it hung row after row of chains covered in diamonds, obscuring her bare back and wrapping around the bodice of the dress. I caught sight of the front in the mirror, the piece spilling over her stomach and breasts, causing her to look like she was quite literally dripping in gemstones.

I obsessively scrutinized her back for any hint of a mark, trying to see if she had accepted the mating bond with Ruslan. I needed to be closer or for them to remove the intricate jewelry from her body. Liliana wrapped her arms around Izidora's waist, and she returned the embrace, the two staring at themselves in the mirror.

"Fucking Fates," I cursed, and the black beast in my chest decided it had had enough of allowing me to lead. It began gnawing on my emotions and tunneling my vision, blackening the rim until all I saw was *her.*

Izidora's eyes snapped up, hardening as she whipped her head away from the mirror and over her shoulder, directly through the window to where I stood, cloaked in invisibility.

But she knew I was there.

She opened her mouth to say something, and I bolted down a side street, stone shops and houses with curling smoke flashing by me as I raced back to Fek. My trusty stallion pawed the snow as I approached and dropped my magic away in an attempt to regain control of myself. The beast inside me screeched in protest, trying to rise up again, but I shoved it down, heart racing, and leaped onto Fek's back. In moments, I'd yanked the reins and steered him in the opposite direction of the shops, cutting through side streets in a haphazard pattern as I tried to lose anyone who might attempt to follow me.

It wasn't until I returned to Ryza and handed over my mount to one of the stablehands that I realized my footprints would be visible to anyone who wanted to follow them.

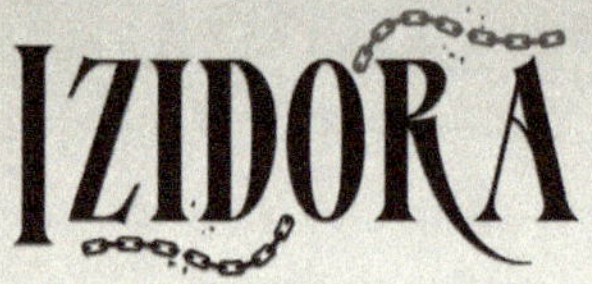 IZIDORA

Béke Day Seven

The spiral staircase descending into the tunnels beneath Ryza Citadel wound my thoughts up with each subsequent step. I couldn't shake the feeling of being watched, and after the combination of Queen Immonen's ominous vision and the feeling of eyes burning into my back at the dress shop, I was in a near-panic. I needed Zuriel to lead another session for me, because if I didn't get some relief from this clawing, clamping vice around my chest, I would die.

I burst into the subterranean antechamber, blowing past the Demons and Mages who lounged there and raced straight down the tunnel to Zuriel's door, banging with my fists until my cousin appeared in the doorway.

His white brows dipped in confusion before his gaze swept over me. "Izidora, what's wrong?"

"I need," I gasped out, feeling like I could burst from my skin from anxiety and fear, "I need another session."

Without hesitation, Zuriel swept me into his room and quickly closed the door behind us. The small couch that lined one wall was my destination, and I settled onto it, curling my knees to my chest and wrapping my arms around my legs as I gently rocked back and forth, trying not to scream in frustration. To his credit, Zuriel remained completely calm, easing the chair away from his desk and settling into it in front of me.

"Is this the rawness you spoke of?" I asked, hoping that I wasn't losing my mind.

"Yes," he said, sympathy lining his tone.

I nodded, closing my eyes for a moment and trying to suck in a breath.

Zuriel's deep, melodic voice filled the air as he asked, "What triggered this?"

"We were at the boutique, and when I was trying on gowns, I *felt* someone looking at me. I whipped around, trying to see who it was, but there was no one. It was so sinister, and I wasn't paying attention to my mental barriers. The utter filth..." I shook my head, shuddering at the memory of feeling naked, possessed, and scraped by the attention. My stomach clenched, and bile rose in my throat. Zuriel already knew about the mark, so I confessed what else had happened there. "And Queen Immonen had a vision. She said that when Kazimir discovers the mate mark, everything will go dark. What does that even mean? I thought once I made the choice, it would all be over. It would be easy. Everything would be okay. But it's not!"

I was spiraling, down and down and down into a whirlpool of turbulent emotions, and if I didn't escape the pull soon, I might drown in despair.

I was not okay.

The thought shortened my breaths, blanking my mind of any and all sense or reason, and then there was nothing but blinding emotional pain, so acute, so overwhelming, I wanted nothing more than to crawl beneath the covers and never emerge again.

"Release your legs so you can tap your shoulders. And breathe," Zuriel encouraged, his attention never wavering for me.

I eased my legs to the floor, crossing my arms over my chest and closing my eyes as I began the rhythmic tap back and forth. The sensation flared again, and I cried out, shuddering as flashes of memory surfaced from the dark corners of my mind where I had banished them.

"Please, no." The words slipped out before I could stop them, just like one of the worst of my memories. I tried to shove it down, shove it away because it was too painful. I couldn't do it. I couldn't relive it. I'd nearly died inside the first time, the last dimming spark of light inside me nearly snuffed out from it.

"You're safe, Izidora. No one can hurt you anymore," Zuriel soothed. "Feel it. Rewrite it. You get to change the ending now. You get to finish the story the way you want it to be. Give yourself that power."

Zuriel's words broke through the thick fog of fear, and when I sucked in a ragged breath, I noticed the dampness of my cheeks.

"O-o-okay," I whimpered, forcing myself back into that dark corner. I had to confront it to free myself of it.

He nodded, encouraging me, face twisted in loving sympathy.

The taps increased in speed as I mentally walked into the cave and watched the scene unfold, narrating for Zuriel.

"Get on your knees," the male snarled at a younger version of me.

I bared my teeth at him, planting my feet firmly into the stone ground. "Never for you."

A second male slipped forward, his torch barely lighting his face in the darkness of the cave. "How about for me, love?"

I spat in his direction without a second thought. The third's laugh slithered out of the void. "You're so close to being of age, pretty thing. Maybe we ought to get a taste of you after all."

I fisted my hands around the chains binding me, hoping I could fling them at one of the males quickly closing the distance between us and incapacitate him. One stalked from my front, while the others closed in on either side, and I felt trapped, helpless, and utterly alone. The other guards wouldn't help me, no matter how much I screamed.

They would not break me, I told myself.

I whipped one long chain to my right, using my dominant hand to its only advantage, and I managed to whack the male in the knee. But he only laughed and stepped on the chain, pinning it in place as he closed the remaining distance between us. I cried out as my own knee banged against the ground, forced down by his rough movement.

His grimy hand grabbed my tangled hair and yanked my head back so I was forced to look at him. "I think I'll take that smart mouth first."

With my free hand, I punched him in the groin, causing him to double over, wheezing and coughing. But my victory was short-lived when his companions were upon me, one taking his place holding my hair while the other delivered a forceful slap across my face. Copper coated the inside of my mouth, and I wasted no time spitting it straight at them.

"One day, you will die. And it will be by my hand," I swore.

The three of them laughed, and by the sinister tone of it, I began to think that this might truly be the end for me — the time when I lost it all, including my life.

The one I'd punched circled behind me, and every muscle in my body tensed, waiting for his disgusting touch on my flesh. With a loud rip, my tunic was torn away, leaving my top half naked and my breasts bared to the two males still pinning me in place.

"Can you believe we'll be the bitch's first?" the one holding my hair said, his other hand stroking my face. His touch made me want to vomit.

"Bet that pussy is tight," the one behind me groaned, and I gritted my teeth, watching, calculating, praying that I could find a way out of the moment.

When the one who held my hair made another pass across my face, I whipped my head to the side, ignoring the sharp sting in my scalp, and sank my teeth into his finger. He roared in anguish, dropping both hands away from me, and I surged to my feet, throwing all my weight backward in hopes of knocking the one behind me off balance and into the hard rock wall. But I missed, tripped over my chains, and cracked my own head, stars bursting in my vision.

I was on my back, chains tangled around me, and completely vulnerable, with three pissed off males looming over me. Tears sprang to my eyes, burning them as I fought to keep my head above water. It pounded furiously, a headache blooming behind my eyes, and as I tried to lift my head off the ground to sit up and defend myself, a wave of dizziness forced me flat again.

"Please," I croaked, unable to do, to say more.

"She's begging for it now," the slapper teased, elbowing his companions in their sides. He crouched over me, hands finding my pants, and he tore those away from my body too. "She's all mine. Beg for my cock again, baby."

"Fuck... you," I managed to say, clinging to my defiance like it was a liferaft.

"That you will, sweetheart," he laughed, unfastening his pants and freeing his cock.

The tears spilled over of their own accord, the pain in my head and my soul nearly too much to bear. My shoulders screamed in pain as the chains pulled them in opposite directions, his companions using them to drag me to my knees.

They'd made enough passing comments and lingered a little too long after feeding me or forcing me to exercise for me to be ignorant of what came next. For years, I'd felt their gazes on me, held my breath as they entered my space, tried to be demure or to be feisty, doing anything to survive. But when they were on duty, I couldn't sleep, couldn't breathe, couldn't think, out of fear they'd follow through on those disgusting promises.

And this was the day they decided to do just that.

With two fingers, he pried my jaw open, the other two snickering as I tried to twist my head one way, then the other, to get free. But my arms and my shoulders were locked in place, and the grip on my face tightened to the point of bruising. His cock was hard and pointing at me, and I tried to snap my teeth shut to prevent it from going into my mouth.

"If you don't do this willingly, we'll have to get the whips," he taunted.

My heart dropped to my stomach, and I stopped struggling. The tears dripped and dripped and dripped, racing toward freedom in a way I could not.

He slipped into my mouth, and I immediately gagged, stomach heaving up the contents of my meager meal that morning.

"Oh fuck," I moaned, feeling that same nauseated sensation rising within me.

"We can stop this at any time," Zuriel murmured, handing me a bag should I need to surrender the contents of my stomach.

"I need to do this," I managed to say, swallowing down the worst of it. "Then I can be free."

Zuriel only nodded, and I filled my lungs with as much air as I could before dropping back into the horrific memory.

He made a noise of disgust, pulling away from me as I retched. The other two laughed and teased him, but their words were a blur as the throbbing in my head increased tenfold. When I finally came up for air again, the three stared down at me with a mixture of disdain and sadistic intent. My chest heaved from the effort and my fear, and I closed my eyes, whispering to anyone, anything that could possibly save me, to do so in that moment.

"Get her up, turn her around," the slapper said to his companions.

"No!" I screeched, fighting them as they lifted me to my feet and pinned me to the wall. The rough stone cut into my face, and I gritted my teeth against the additional pain.

The one on my right whistled, long and low, and although I couldn't see his face, I felt his lewd eyes roaming my naked form. "She sure looks good from behind, doesn't she?"

I pressed my thighs together, shaking from head to toe as I was totally exposed and completely vulnerable. All I wanted to do was curl in on myself, to protect myself, but it was impossible.

I was so focused there that I didn't hear the leather hissing as it unfurled, and the moment the familiar whistle cut the air, I cried out instinctively. A heartbeat later, the whip dug into my back, and the heat that bloomed there told me the skin had split.

"Anywhere but here," I whispered to myself, holding my breath and forcing my mind to fly far away. A story my caretaker had told me when I was a little girl came to mind first, and I clung to it like the lifeline it was as I endured lash after lash.

"I repeated it over and over again as they tore my legs apart and scraped my front against the stone as they raped me. I wasn't even in my own body. I had to be somewhere else. To survive," I sobbed, my face, my nose, my tunic, my arms soaked. But I never stopped tapping, allowing the motion to free me from the confines of these long-hidden memories. "Why couldn't I do more? Why did I let them do that to me?"

"You did everything you could have done, Izidora," Zuriel soothed, affirming me when I needed it most. "What would you do now?"

The answer came to me immediately because I'd already been allowed the opportunity to reclaim my power from them. Flashes of Ruslan driving his sharp blade into the eyes of my former guards crossed my vision, and my ears were filled with the sweet sound of their screams as I ripped their cocks and balls away and watched them bleed out.

Letting that fuel me, I dropped back into the scene, using what had happened a few days before change what had happened to me when the three guards whipped and raped me to the point that I wanted to end my own life. "Ruslan and I storm into the cave ready to kill them all. By the time we reach my younger self, we've slaughtered everyone in our path. I fling my white magic over them, forcing them against the wall for Ruslan to slaughter while I collect little Izidora. I use my healing magic to close up her back, and then wrap her in my cloak. The one with the white rabbit fur that's so warm."

"And what do you say to her?"

"I tell her that her prayers were answered. That I *heard* her. That I came for her. That I'd always come for her. That she never had to tolerate the attention or the touch of a male she didn't want any longer. That she would learn to be powerful and make *them* cower at her feet, begging for mercy she wasn't obligated to give. That she would have her vengeance, and I'd stop at nothing to ensure she received every drop of blood she wanted for what happened to her."

The fire that had dulled to embers roared to life inside me again, filling me with energy and power and confidence and everything I needed to rise above what happened to me then, to rise above what happened to me now, until I was brimming with an inferno that needed no further fuel.

My eyes flew open and my breath fled in a rush, as I was filled with that familiar sensation of the heaviness being stripped away. It was as if a layer of skin had been shed, leaving me lighter and freer to move within myself.

My hands flew from my shoulders to clasp over my mouth as a sob threatened to escape. Yet this sob wasn't one of pain; it was one of joy.

"Holy shit, Zuriel," I choked out, and another wave of hot tears tracked down my cheeks. Tremors no longer wracked my body and fear no longer froze me from the inside out. Somehow, the slaughter of my abusers and the tapping had made me whole and settled in a way that was antithetical to the restlessness I'd arrived with.

My cousin tipped the legs of the chair back as he reached for a glass of water on the desk and handed it to me. I sipped from it, drying my eyes and nose on the cloth he offered as well.

"How do you feel?" he asked gently.

"That was the biggest release yet," I rasped, my voice hoarse from crying. Words could not adequately express the difference within me, for I felt both empty and whole, mended on the inside in a way that was only visible when I knit skin together on an open wound.

"That must have been a deep memory," he mused, studying me for a moment. "Now say your affirmations."

"I am safe. I am an insidious bloom. I am strong. I am powerful. I am brave. I am bold. Nothing will hurt me again," I repeated, focusing on feeling each and every statement and fusing them into the fabric of my being.

The Angel lifted the glass from my hand, then instructed me to cross my arms and say them again.

"I am safe."

Tap, tap, tap.

"I am an insidious bloom."

My shoulders began dropping away from my ears.

"I am strong."

My spine straightened, holding me steady.

"I am powerful."

My chest swelled with pride.

"Nothing will hurt me again."

The tapping never ceased, and with each subsequent pass

through the affirmations, I *felt* them grow within me, as if I were truly planting an insidious bloom in my soul, the blossom crowding out the horrors and the thorns threatening any thoughts of helplessness to stick around and see what happened.

Once I was full to bursting, I stopped the movements, a wide smile breaking across my face as I realized that I was *free* of the memory. I pulled it to the front of my mind again, but the panic, the terror, the inability to even face it was gone. It was as if I were watching it happen to someone else, or reading about it in a book. It was no longer mine in the sense that it lived inside me, but rather, it was a piece of my past that no longer held any sway over my present.

"Are you sure this isn't magic?" I asked Zuriel.

"I am certain, cousin. You are the one who has done all of the work to make these feelings happen," he promised.

"Guess I am pretty powerful, huh?" I said, arms dropping to my lap and resting there.

"That you are." Zuriel braced his hands on his thighs and pushed off the chair. "I'm assuming with the way you burst in here that you haven't spoken with your mate, and with the intensity of the release you had, he's probably losing his mind. Let's go find him and assure him you're alright."

I nodded, feeling slightly guilty that I had ignored his calls down our bond as I'd raced back to the citadel. He had gone into the mines to flaunt the Iron Realm's achievements, and I couldn't let my issues prevent us from succeeding in uniting the realms.

"Are you still in the mines?" I asked down our bond.

"We arrived in the citadel a few minutes ago. Where are you? I felt your terror, Izidora, are you okay?"

"I'm fine now. I was working with Zuriel. We're in the tunnels."

"Understood. My office?"

"We're on our way."

Returning to Zuriel's bedroom, I found him leaning against the desk, arms crossed and waiting for me. "Ruslan says to meet in his office."

"Then that is where we shall head."

———

THE SENTRIES outside the door snapped to attention as Zuriel and I entered the long hall that led to Ruslan. Most of the doors along the way were closed, no doubt because the advisors and nobles were off galavanting or celebrating. Only Ruslan seemed to continue to work while Béke wore on, though I suspected it was because he couldn't let go of control, not when those we did not trust wandered the realm. And with his newfound status, there was much he needed to acquaint himself with.

Was it really only a week before that we had killed King Azim?

The heavy wood door swung open, revealing Ruslan seated across from Drazen. Their conversation died when Ruslan's gaze collided with mine. We remained locked, even as he rounded the desk and swept me into his arms, squeezing me so tight I could barely breathe.

"Fuck, sprite, I'm so glad you're safe. It took everything in my power not to race home to you."

"I know, but you needed to show off for the other kings."

"You know you are far more important than they are. Nothing in this world is more important than you."

The sincerity of his words wrapped around my heart, warming it as his professions of love always did. *"I love you."*

"Love you more."

Ruslan finally released me, but he tugged me along behind him and settled me in his chair before rounding and bracing his forearms on the back of it. We faced Drazen and Zuriel, the latter having settled himself in a high-backed chair beside the former.

"Someone was watching me while I was trying on dresses," I blurted out, needing to get all the information out of me before someone else had a chance to direct the conversation elsewhere.

Behind me, Ruslan tensed, and I sensed his rising anger.

"But when I turned around, I couldn't see anyone. I just had this awful feeling like I was being watched. No one else saw anything either. The dressmakers even went outside to check. That's when I ran to Zuriel." I cleared my throat, prepared to confess more knowledge. Craning my head, I tried to show my mate the depth of my worry. "Kazimir cornered me yesterday at the horseback riding event and told me that you were manipulating me by teaching me to read. Except, I've never read in front of him, and you've certainly never helped me in front of him."

A muscle ticked in Ruslan's jaw, and he tilted his head to one side, then the other, cracking his neck along the way. "If he's been watching you, I will fucking kill him."

Good thing I hadn't told him what Immonen said after her vision.

Drazen slapped his palm on the wood in front of him, jolting both me and Ruslan. Some of that bloodthirstiness drained from him, and he sucked in a long breath before blowing it out. "You can't kill him now, Ruslan. Not while he's a guest here. It would go against our other goals."

"I don't give a fuck. Like I told Izidora before, *she* matters more to me than uniting the realms, freeing the Félvér, or welcoming others to our shores," Ruslan snapped.

Definitely a good thing.

"We can't even be certain he is the one following her. What if it's one of the other Night Fae? They can all fly," Drazen pointed out.

"But none of them can turn invisible or fully cloak themselves in shadow or light," Zuriel argued. "Both feats used to be possible, but in the last few centuries, that power has weakened."

"And that's why the Félvér are superior," Drazen muttered under his breath. None in the room disagreed, not when three of us had mixed blood and Zuriel was an Angel. He blew out a long breath, dragging his hand over his long hair and fidgeting with the pile of it atop his head. "I'll check out the dress shop and see if I can find anything there. A place someone could have been hiding across the street, perhaps."

"Thanks, Drazen," Ruslan said, his body still tense against my back. The half-Dragon pushed off from the arms of his chair and made to leave. Zuriel, with one last glance at me, followed, offering to help Drazen in his search.

As the two departed, I spun to my knees and faced my mate. "How were the mines?"

"King Airre was very impressed with what we were mining, and King Consort Geza was very impressed with how we were mining. I didn't reveal the extent of the tunnels in and under the mountains though. That's a secret best kept among those in the Iron Realm." His gray eyes still pinched with worry at the corners. "Are you sure you're okay? Why don't I take you to Roc to soak in the hot springs?"

That sounded incredible.

"Please do," I grinned, threading my fingers through the hair at the base of his neck and scratching lightly. He released a low groan, head tipping back to rest against the back of his chair. Without rising, he chanted the words to the spell that would move us, and within moments, we stood in the steam in the grotto beneath our home, my legs wrapped firmly around Ruslan's waist.

I slid to the ground, the safety offered by the springs and the session with Zuriel putting me at more ease than I had been in days. There were no windows, only one way in or out, and

Ruslan was with me. Kazimir couldn't reach me here. No one could reach me here. Ruslan seemed to sense that I wasn't in the mood for sex, and when I stripped out of my clothes, he watched with the adoration I'd come to expect from him when he wanted to show me just how much he loved me.

Leading me into the rolling water, he guided me along until we were in the deepest parts, and then he cradled me, whispering sweet affirmations in my ear and stroking soothing swirls along my back. With each passing breath my body unwound, and the water seeped into my bones, chasing away the last of the chill that lingered there. Floating in the healing water, I felt lighter, freer, than I ever had before, and with Ruslan attending to my every need, I let go, allowing the grip around my emotions to fall away and trusting that one of us would catch me should I need it.

RUSLAN

"You're certain you can summon them?" I asked the Iron Realm's High Priestess as she perched on the edge of a chair across from me. The midmorning sun glinted off the polished wood in my office, and I leaned forward to remove the glare from my line of vision.

"Yes, as long as we have enough herbs and a distraction for our guests," she confirmed.

"Consider it done. Take all the herb you need from the stores at Steel." I scratched a note to the manager and handed it to her. "The note also asks for his help in setting up... intimate spaces around the site. That and free-flowing herbs should be enough distraction for you."

She accepted the slip of paper in her dainty hands, then dipped into a curtsey. "Thank you, My King. I shall not disappoint." Then she glided along to the door, passing Drazen on her way out.

The half-Dragon plopped down in her unoccupied seat. "You busy?"

"Not at all," I said, leaning back in my chair and kicking my feet up on the desk. "What do you need, Drazen?"

"It was Kazimir that Izidora felt watching her yesterday. Confirmed the prints this morning after Kriath followed him out toward the mountains again."

"Fuck!" I swore, dropping my feet and banging my fists onto the desk. "I'm going to fucking kill him. He cannot keep terrorizing her like this." My chest heaved and I searched for something, anything, to slake this rage burning through me, because the need to protect my mate was driving me insane. Finding a liquor bottle, I threw it against the windows, the glass shattering with a satisfying crack, and the smoky scent of the liquid filled the air.

Drazen sat, arms crossed, his usual air of nonchalance on full display as I raged, waiting for me to calm down. "Your bond is fresh. Tell me again, why doesn't Kazimir know?"

"She said she still feels this pull to him," I grumbled, finally collapsing into the chair behind me. "Zuriel suggested she might need to speak the words aloud to break it off like she had to do to accept our bond."

"But to do that, she'd have to get close to him."

I nodded.

"And she does not want to do that."

I nodded again, tilting my head to the side and popping my neck to relieve some tension. Blowing out a breath, I replied, "Nor do I want her that close to him. Who knows what he would do when he found out? He's already stalking her."

"Well, she can't avoid confronting him forever," Drazen pointed out.

"I know. I'm trying to let her figure it out on her own, but fuck! I want her to be safe." I buried my head in my hands, trying to fight back the overwhelming urge to hunt her down and lock her in Roc Palace until Béke concluded.

"He won't fuck with her if you're around, Ruslan. Between the two of us and Zuriel, someone will be with her at all times from now on," Drazen promised, his tone softening.

"Speaking of Zuriel, are he and Izidora training?" I asked. She had been exhausted last night after the excitement of choosing her dress for our wedding, the subsequent terror of feeling Kazimir's attention on her, and then another session with Zuriel. I never asked what occurred in these sessions, but by the way she spoke of them, they were helping tremendously with her trauma. Despite her heightened emotional volatility and jumpiness, I thought they were working, too. Izidora told me that after each session, she felt like another layer had been stripped from her, and the transformation was incredible to behold from the outside looking in. The weight lifted from her left her shoulders looser, movements lighter, her breath flowing easier, and she bloomed more beautifully than I had ever imagined.

"As we speak. He told me he thinks there will be a war, and soon," Drazen informed me.

I lifted my head from my hands, only to discover the worry in Drazen's blue eyes and the stress lining his forehead. "And what do you think?" Because there was no doubt in my mind that Kazimir would wage war once Izidora broke off their bond.

"I agree with him."

"Are you still sending patrols toward the borders?"

He nodded. "I've asked the scouts to report back immediately if they spot large movements in the distance."

"Good." I blew out another breath, then pushed to my feet. "There's not much we can do but wait is there?"

"Nope," he replied with a wry grin twisting his lips. "And I know that's your least favorite thing to do."

———

THE MAKESHIFT ARENA had once again been transformed. All the event materials from the strength and horseback competitions had been removed and dark tents spanned the area instead, beckoning in revelers with the smell of sugary treats and warm drinks. A blistering chill had settled over the afternoon, and as the sun dipped beyond the reach of the mountains, the wind picked up, blowing Izidora's loose chestnut locks about.

In the center of the space, dried branches had been twisted and twined together to form an enormous tree, bags of herb hanging from the bare branches protruding at every level. The High Priestess stood before it, her acolytes twirling around it in a ritualistic dance that called to the deepest parts of us that were connected to nature all around us. The hairs on my arms stood on end as their chanting grew louder, drawing all in attendance closer to the dancing circle. The priestesses called flames to their hands, weaving them through the air as they illuminated the creeping night. Their magic bloomed, blending with their sisters' around them, until a ring of fire danced around the offering, lofted by the fast-moving priestesses.

"Fire is cleansing," the High Priestess shouted over the others' chanting. "Fire is burning. Fire is destroying. Fire is life." Her black robes billowed about her thin frame as if the wind that had been chilling us all had decided to blow all its attention on her. "Our Goddess, we offer you our souls this night. Purify our hearts for the coming year, and may you allow us to remain peaceful in your infinite wisdom."

The dancing priestesses halted in their tracks, fingers splaying forward as they shot their flames into the dried brush, lighting the tree from bottom to top. The offering caught immediately, smoky crackling filling the air and blasting heat around the open field. The sweet scent of the herbs followed moments later, and I inhaled deeply, filling my lungs with the drug. Down the bond, I sensed Izidora's confusion.

"Breathe deeply, sprite. The herbs will make you feel tingly and lightheaded, and if it gets to be too much for you, just let me know and I'll take you home."

"Is it like wine?"

"Not exactly. You'll know when it hits you. I promise I'll be by your side the whole time."

She chewed her bottom lip, and I knew she worried about Kazimir seeking her out in the darkness. *"Drazen has our guards keeping an eye on everything too. You're safe."*

Her aquamarine eyes speared into mine, captivating me with their ethereal beauty. Clasping a hand around her upper arm, I tugged her toward me, sweeping her hair off her shoulders and capturing her lower back. She arched into me as I kissed her roughly, claiming her as mine in front of the Goddess and all onlookers.

Someone cleared their throat beside us, and I growled a warning before breaking our kiss to see who dared interrupt me. Liliana waited there, along with Anton and Slavian, who both looked like they had trouble planned for the night.

"We've got another bag of herbs," Anton said as he produced a pouch from behind his back, "and you should smoke them with us, Ruslan. Like old times." A wolfish grin spread across his face as he waited for my response.

"Why not? We are celebrating the Goddess after all. Follow me." Izidora and Liliana linked arms and whispered conspiratorially as I directed us through the clearing toward a tent erected for my personal use at the far side. As we passed closer to the burning offering, the sticky sweet smoke thickened, and I checked on Izidora to ensure she was handling the herbs. It was her first time using them, and my mouth twitched up in anticipation of her reaction. We'd been fucking like crazy since accepting the bond, and the herbs would only enhance our sexual appetites tonight.

Dipping into the lavish tent, I fanned the flames burning in the braziers, casting more light into the space and heating it for my mate who tended to catch a chill.

"Thank you," she whispered down our bond, and I squeezed her hand in response.

I pulled her onto my lap as we settled on a half-moon-shaped couch, and the two young High Lords of the Iron Realm wasted no time preparing the herbs for consumption.

"We're going to have so much fun tonight, Izidora," Liliana said as she lounged beside us. "You've never been to Béke before, but tonight is one of the best ones. In the Night Realm, they use a lot less herb, and there's never any to go around freely after the burning begins. You'll feel more connected to nature than ever before."

"So what's the purpose of the burning?" she asked.

My curious little sprite.

"The burning represents a new beginning, like wiping the slate clean for next year," Liliana explained. "The herbs are supposed to help bring the realms together, forming new bonds and forgetting old grievances. And tomorrow night at the masquerade, we all get to pretend that we're meeting for the first time. The days after that are filled with arts of all kinds, including a ceremony where we release floating lanterns into the sky holding our most fervent desires for the coming year. The end is the most beautiful part of Béke."

"What did you wish for last year?" Izidora asked, snuggling into my embrace. I draped my arm around her, resting it against the back of the couch as I settled in.

Liliana blushed, and I had to press my lips together to suppress a smile. I'd never seen the fierce female be anything but unabashedly confident. "A friend."

Izidora's emotion flooded our bond, and she burst forward, leaving me forgotten so she could embrace her friend. I scented salty tears from both of them and decided to allow them some space, even though everything in me wanted to have her all to myself. But with the sanctity of our bond, I'd never have to worry about her permanently leaving me for anyone else.

Anton and Slavian had finished packing the herbs and Slavian lit the end with the tip of his finger, drawing a deep breath to fill his lungs with smoke. He passed the apparatus to me, coughing, and I repeated his action using my black fire. The rush from the herbs was almost immediate, and as I blew out rings, my connection to everything around me heightened, my senses simultaneously sharpening and dulling at the edges as if I were slipping into a dream.

My mate had sidled up to me again, an eagerness in her eyes that I was happy to oblige. Holding the herbs out to her, I instructed, "Go nice and slow so you don't cough."

Putting her lips to the end, I lit my finger, only allowing a tiny flicker to touch the herbs. She sucked in a breath, and I snatched the apparatus away from her a moment later, already seeing the inevitable choking. Izidora's eyes watered as she coughed out a lungful of smoke, eliciting a laugh from Liliana and rubs on her back from me.

"Damn," Izidora swore through wheezes. "You weren't kidding about going slow."

"It's the only time I want you to go slow, sprite," I purred, the herbs heating my blood in the most delicious way. The way Izidora's long lashes fluttered against her blushing cheeks made me want to capture her mouth and claim it mine.

Anton and Slavian snickered, taking the herbs off my hands. "We need to get more people in here so it will be a real party," Slavian commented as he lit the apparatus. He blew his smoke in Anton's face as he exhaled. "Go find the females."

Waving his hand in front of his face to clear the smoke, Anton shot back, "Why don't you?"

"Ugh," Liliana interrupted them. "I'll do it. You two will only seek out females when what we really need is more dick."

Izidora muffled a laugh beside me, and I turned my attention to her as Liliana brushed past the tent flap and into the night. Her pupils had darkened, and they only grew as she returned my gaze. "How are you feeling?" I murmured.

"Really, really good," she breathed, seeming at ease, and a peaceful smile spread across her lips. All I wanted was for her to be happy, and not taking matters into my own hands was killing me. Izidora wanted to deal with Kazimir herself, and even though she had accepted the bond, my promise to redeem myself still stood.

I brushed my knuckles across her cheek and she sighed, leaning into my touch. Slavian tapped me on the shoulder and I accepted the herbs from him, taking another long drag, welcoming in the sensation of the world around us, and releasing my worries with the dissipating smoke. Outside the tent, the sound of revelers, clinking glasses, music, laughter, and merriment filled the air as Fae, Félvér, and Telivér celebrated together.

Liliana brought some of that joy with her when she returned with a few of the Night Fae and Félvér in tow. She knew better than to bring Kazimir, at least. Endre, along with Kaztar and Domi, ducked in behind her, the former making quick work of placing himself next to her, across from Anton and Slavian. The noble Félvér were a tight-knit group, though I'd always been on the outside of it. The rest of them scattered along the couch, and two familiar females forced their way between myself and Slavian.

"Natasha, Aliana, long time no see," Liliana joked, and Izidora offered them a small wave.

The two smirked knowingly at me. "Your bride-to-be will

look stunning on your wedding day, King Ruslan. We made sure of it," Natasha said.

Izidora giggled beside me, her giddiness flowing down the bond. "So sexy, too. You'll rip it to shreds the moment we're alone." Her floral arousal hit my nostrils, and I inhaled it more deeply than the herbs, wanting to get high on her already.

My nose trailed along her neck, and I whispered in her ear, "What if I ripped it off in front of all our guests?"

A sharp intake of breath told me the herbs were opening her up to the idea. "Then everyone would see me."

"And they'd see me claim you, my mark sitting squarely between your shoulder blades as if my ring and my crown weren't enough."

She whimpered as my hand rested high on her thigh, slipping beneath the slit in the dark dress she wore. With my other hand, I unclasped the square diamond at her throat, allowing the cloak I'd given her to fall away and expose the deep V in the front of her dress. My tongue trailed along her collarbone, eliciting a soft groan. I pulled Izidora from the couch into my lap, holding her firmly there as my cock grew thick beneath her.

The air around us grew hazy as Anton and Slavian passed around more herbs, attracting more Félvér in with the heady scent. Some brought bottles of liquor and the acolytes with them until the tent was heating from the bodies alone.

My skin buzzed, and my whole focus went to drawing pebbles across my mate's skin. Snaking my arm around her waist and fisting her unbound hair with the other, I forced her to collapse against me, giving me the perfect view of her breasts. Tingles erupted across my palms at every point of contact, and that thread that tied us together hummed contentedly.

Both of us pulled smoke into our lungs the next time the apparatus was passed around, and we began floating higher, the world beyond the canvas tent melting away. Each person surrounding us was a kaleidoscope of color, some shining, others glittering, and most gleaming with pure ecstasy.

The open space at the front of the tent became a sea of bodies grinding against each other as the music filling the arena turned primal. The drums beat a rhythm that was both a deep, steady thrum and a rapid-fire of sound, and the chanting that accompanied it was disjointed to my dulled senses.

The young priestesses ground against Anton and Slavian, some of the other Félvér joining in their dance. Beside us, Liliana and Endre became wrapped around each other without a care for anyone near them. Izidora's long hair whispered between us, and every time my fingers brushed across her bare skin, it felt as if I had left a trail of fire in my wake. She leaned into my touch, circling her hips slowly, unconsciously as she watched the scene unfold.

"Do you want to play?" I murmured in her ear, my voice echoing in the space only we could occupy together.

"Yes," she breathed, a rosy flush creeping across her chest.

My cock twitched beneath her ass at her throaty tone. "No one else will touch you, mate, but there are other ways to participate." I ran my nose from the crook of her neck up to her ear, nibbling on it from behind as I moved a hand to the slit in her dress, bunching the fabric in my palm. "Watch them."

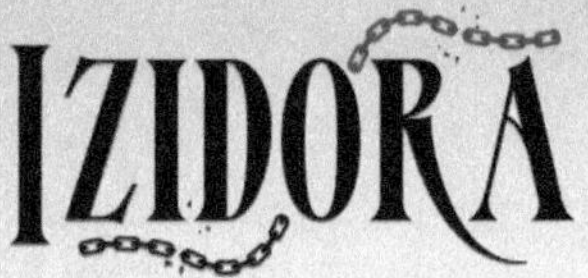 IZIDORA

Béke Day Eight

The herbs I smoked made me feel as if I were both floating and on fire, and my skin felt tingly and hot and stretched far too thin. My thighs were already damp, and the way Ruslan held me to him only made me want more. The hard shaft beneath me was a testament to his own desire. As the material covering my legs drifted higher, exposing my flesh to the heated, smoky air in the tent, I allowed them to drift apart, providing Ruslan access to the area that begged to be touched. My nipples were stiff and straining against the fabric covering them, and all I could think about was my need to be filled.

Desire like never before coursed through my veins, and the unbridled passion flowing through the room only heightened my arousal. Before me, the priestesses' billowy dresses began slipping down their shoulders as the males toyed with them, sweat slicking the rest of the fabric to their bodies as they danced. Two of the Félvér females from the dress shop were among them, moving between Anton, Slavian, and the priestesses.

Ruslan's fingers finally brushed the sensitive inside of my thighs, and I nearly jerked out of his firm hold at the touch.

"I've got you, sprite," he murmured in my ear. "Just let go and enjoy the show."

I nodded, unable to speak as he drew lazy circles too far from my heated center. Natasha pulled Anton in for a kiss, their tongues battling as he gripped her ass and bent her backwards. But she broke away from him, grasping one of the priestesses by the wrist and spinning her flush. Their hands roamed each other's bodies while Anton looked on hungrily from behind. When their plump lips locked, Anton sidled up behind Natasha and ground against her, his hands roaming from her body to the priestess's.

Ruslan's rumbling growl vibrated against my back as he discovered that I wore nothing beneath my dress. "It's a good thing you're wearing black because you're positively dripping. Does watching them turn you on?"

"Yes," I moaned as his finger slid against me. He teased my slit, and my breaths grew short, choppy, and I wiggled my hips, trying to get him to touch me deeper. *Fuck, I needed him deeper.* I already teetered on the edge, and it wouldn't take me long to come. "Please, I need more."

His answering chuckle was dark and sinister. "Maybe I'll have to fuck you right here while you watch them. You already made it easy for me. Was that your intention?"

My pussy clenched around his words. "Maybe."

His teeth nipped at my shoulder. "On the outside, you may be an Angel, but on the inside, you're a Demon, always wanting more of my cock, like a pretty little succubus."

A finger plunged into me, and the achingly slow exit had me panting, gasping, begging for more. "Ruslan, please..."

"Please, what?"

"Fuck me."

The hot breath fanned across my ear at the same time his deft fingers stroked that spongy spot on my inner walls. "Not yet. Keep watching."

The groan that left my lips was pained as I tore my attention from his fingers to the scene before me. Liliana's dress was hiked up around her waist and she and Endre moved together on the luxurious furniture, one of the Félvér I didn't know alternating between kissing her and fucking one of the priestesses he'd bent over the back of the couch. Endre and the priestess did the same, the four of them joined in a dance that sent fire straight to my core.

Unconsciously, I ground into Ruslan's hand, needing friction on my clit to come. His movements were slow, so fucking slow, as he worked me to the point of desperation. The wetness that seeped between us wasn't entirely from me, and his cock dug almost painfully into my ass. Grinding against it elicited a hiss from between his teeth, and I nearly purred with satisfaction. "Did you do this often before me?" I asked, unable to help my curiosity.

"Sometimes. But you here, right now, has me harder than a fucking diamond. Knowing how much watching all this turns you on has me wild with desire, and you have no idea how much I want to fuck you on this couch. To show them all that you are mine and you belong to no one else. I want the whole fucking world to see our mate marks and envy every moment I get to spend inside your perfect body."

"Even more than you wanted to fuck me after we slaughtered my abusers?"

The growl that rumbled against my back sent a delicious shiver down my spine.

"I don't think anything will top that, sprite. But this might be a

close second. It's a shame that we killed them all already. It was intoxicating to watch you surrender to the darkness."

His pace quickened as truth spilled from his lips, and more heat gushed between my thighs moments before I floated to the stars as my orgasm tore through me. "Fuck," I gasped, my hand reaching back and cupping Ruslan's neck as I held on for dear life, riding his hand like it was my own personal salvation and the only way to see the Goddess was through him. The tingles that spread from my toes to the ends of my hair were unlike anything I'd ever experienced, and it was as if my every nerve was alight with pleasure.

"That's it, fuck my hand, sprite. Fuck it until you come down from the heaven I sent you to. Because when you're back, I'm taking you to hell."

"Oh, Goddess," I breathed, my movements finally subsiding.

"We may be here tonight to worship Her, but I am your God, and tonight, you will also be worshiping me."

If I could orgasm from words alone, those would have done me in.

"On your knees," he commanded, and I wasted no time in obliging.

My mouth was a mosaic of sensations with my senses heightened by the herbs. The velvety skin of his cock gliding across my rough tongue was incredible, and as I took him deeper into my throat, the fullness of my mouth was exquisite. I moaned around him, gripping the base of his shaft with one hand and bracing the other beside me for balance. With all the slowness he'd given me, I worked him up and down, using my saliva to lubricate his skin.

"Fuck, Izidora," he groaned, his head tilting back in rapture as if he were thanking the Goddess for my mouth. His noises only encouraged me, and I sank down until I gagged on him before coming up for air. His hand threaded in my hair, guiding me into position again before he began thrusting upward and into my mouth. I felt eyes on me, but in my current position, I couldn't turn to see who was watching. That made my thighs slicken, and I dropped my hand away from his shaft, slipping it up the slit in my dress to touch myself.

"You look so fucking good worshipping your king," he growled above me, his cock throbbing and forcing my mouth wider. Tears pricked my eyes as he continued to thrust, my moans egging him on. Touching my sensitive nerves while high on herbs was like sparks bursting off a fire, each sensation taken to a level that I never knew existed.

His movements became erratic, and lust coursed down our bond, ricocheting as our highs amplified our connection. I worked quick circles over my clit, drawing closer to the edge, hoping we'd dive over together. With one last thrust, he buried his cock in my throat, hot ropes of liquid coating it at the same time my own arousal gushed down my thighs. The cry I wanted to make was stifled by his cock, but he knew that I had come all the same. I swallowed him down, and a moment later, Ruslan yanked me onto his lap, his tongue diving between my lips as he tasted himself on me.

Rough hands grabbed and lifted my heavy breasts through the fabric of my dress, and I arched into the touch, wanting the pinpricks spreading across my skin to consume my body like a wildfire. When we came up for air, I glanced over my shoulder to see Liliana had turned around, grinding against Endre with her fingers threaded in his hair, watching us. She winked at me, then turned her head to the side to kiss a priestess who had joined them.

Ruslan grabbed my chin and redirected my attention to him. "When I fuck you, I want you to scream my name. I want the fucking Goddess to see the perfect creation She made just for me, coming apart all over my cock."

"I'll scream loud enough for Her to hear me," I panted, breathless.

He growled, lifting me in one fluid motion from his lap and over the back of the couch. "My good fucking girl." Moments later, he was behind me, bunching my dress up on my back and entering me from behind. "Grab the couch."

I wasted no time digging my fingers into the plush fabric, bracing myself for the fucking my body craved. His thick length sliding into me was pure ecstasy, filling and stretching every inch of me until he could go no further. I hadn't realized I'd dropped my head until he yanked my hair back, forcing my eyes forward. "Watch," he commanded again.

So I did.

The dancers had nearly stripped out of all their clothes, most of the dresses pulled down, exposing breasts to the heady air, and all the males' chests were bare and coated in a slick sheen of sweat. Slavian had two females attending to him and each other, alternating between sucking his dick and kissing. His hands bunched both their long hair away from their faces, and his eyes were nearly black with lust. Anton was beside him with two males and a priestess, their limbs intertwined in a way I couldn't follow, not when Ruslan began moving inside me. Every slide through my slickness was like fireworks, and the force of his thrusts pushed me forward into the couch. I locked out my elbows in an attempt to remain in place, but they barely held under his onslaught.

"Ruslan," I moaned, my head arching back of its own accord as he hit the deepest part of me.

"Who are you praying to tonight?" he growled from behind me, stilling his movement as our hip bones touched. He circled his hips as he waited for my answer, and I nearly swore at the fullness.

"You," I panted, pushing back into him. "I need more."

His fingers dipped to my core, sliding around the stickiness coating my thighs. "Where?"

"My ass," I begged.

A gasp tore through me as he used my wetness to push a finger into my hole, delivering more erotic sensation to the already sensitive and heated area. "Yes," I hissed, widening my stance so he could slide deeper. At first, the intrusion was unwelcome, but the herbs had relaxed me, and watching the others had me more aroused than I'd ever been. Within minutes, Ruslan had two fingers in there, and the pressure was exquisite with his cock stretching my pussy.

A yank on my hair had me refocusing on the events unfolding in front of me. "Do you like watching the males or the females more?" Ruslan rasped, fucking me with fingers and dick, creating a rhythm so intoxicating I never wanted him to stop.

"I don't know," I panted, my attention torn between the females grinding their hips together or burying their heads between one another's thighs and the males entering each other from behind, with the last one pounding a female into the couch mere feet away.

"We'll have to do this again and again until we see which one you like better," he purred, spreading his fingers wider. Wetness dripped down my thighs as three of the priestesses lined up, the first on her back, the second on her hands and knees, lips locked on the first's, and the third licking the slit of the second while Slavian entered her from behind, much like Ruslan was doing to me.

"Fuck," I moaned, my walls tightening around him. "That's so hot."

"Which one?" Ruslan asked.

"The females and Slavian," I panted, my eyes locked on the two at the front of the line, their breasts brushing each other as they kissed, while the top one's hand slipped between the legs of the bottom one.

"Mmm, I can agree with that," he replied, slowing his pace to match those of the group. "I love watching you embrace your sexuality, sprite. Now be a good girl and take more of me, show me exactly how filthy you want to be."

He slipped a third finger into my ass, and I whimpered from his praise and the pleasure he delivered. Every nerve was strung tight, and my body was on fire. I was so close to the edge, but Ruslan was holding me back from falling off of it. "Please, Ruslan, I need to come."

"Then scream my name to the stars."

He tugged my hair forcefully, delivering a bit of pain with pleasure and causing me to arch my back so he could deepen the angle. The thrusts he delivered were brutal, our skin slapping together and mixing with the wet and sloppy sounds around us. A bead of sweat trickled down my back, sticking to the fabric of my dress, and my arms gave out as he forced me into the back of the couch. His hand dropped away from my hair, reaching around to clasp the front of my throat instead, cutting off the tiniest bit of air. On the herbs, the sensation was heightened, and stars danced in my vision, coating the others in a shimmering light. I was closing in fast on my release, and after a few heartbeats, I let go.

"Ruslan!" I screamed out to those stars, my chest shaking with the force of it. The orgasm was so intense, my entire body shuddered, and my walls sucked his cock in, latching onto it as his movements grew ragged.

"That's it. Come for me," he groaned. "Let them know I am your God."

"Fuck, yes, you are my God," I gasped out, riding wave after wave of intense release. He released my throat, both hands coming to grip my ass as he swore under his breath, finishing deep inside me, mixing his arousal with my own.

He clutched me to him, straightening my back against his chest. "You are so fucking sexy when you scream my name. And so fucking mine."

I felt like I floated among the stars, body alight in the best of ways as he pulled out of me. I was too overwhelmed with sensation to speak, and my arms trembled with how hard they worked to hold me up.

"Are you ready to go, or do you want to stay for a while longer?" Ruslan asked, his breath hot against my sweaty neck.

"I think I'm ready to go," I managed to say, the tent swaying as I took a step. He caught me by the arm before I pitched to the side, pulling me close.

"I need to speak with the High Priestess before we go, but then I'll take you home, mate," he promised, tucking me under his arm as we traversed the sea of bodies.

Liliana noticed our exit, throwing me a soft wave before turning her attention back to Endre. Domi and Kaztar were nowhere to be found, and I wondered if I had imagined them joining us or not.

The cool night air was a slap to the face as we exited the tent, and when I tiled my head toward the sky, the stars danced and sparkled in a way I'd never seen before, as if our ritual had pulled the heavens closer to us.

Judging by the position of the moon, hours had passed since the tangled web of branches was lit, rather than the mere minutes it had felt like while we worshiped the Goddess in an entirely different way. The flames of the offering were nothing more than embers, and the High Priestess stood beside them in a thin shift, the chill in the air not seeming to bother her. She glanced up from her reverie as we approached, noting the disarray of our dress with piercing eyes. "Did you manage it?" Ruslan asked her, still holding me.

She nodded slowly. "Yes, everything we planned fell into place perfectly."

"Good," he replied. "Enjoy the rest of your night, Priestess."

She swept into a curtsey, only rising when we strode away through the camp toward the waiting horses. My eyes begged for me to close them, even while we walked, and I sighed as waves of fatigue washed over me. "I don't think I'll be able to ride back."

"You can ride in front of me, and I'll tie Mistik to my saddle. I've always got you, sprite. Always." True to his word, he clutched me to his chest, not letting me slump as we returned to Ryza. My eyes could scarcely stay open by the time he laid me in our bed, and I let him undress me, turning into my pillow the moment my clothes were gone, and surrendering to the void that beckoned me.

34

KAZIMIR

I was so damn tired of the cold. Buried in my warmest jacket atop Fek, we trekked again into the Agrenak Mountains, on the hunt for another stag to feed the attendees of the masquerade ball that evening. In the Night Realm, we would have hunted elk with dogs, not trudged through banks of snow in search of hoof prints.

At least on this ride, my hangover wasn't so terrible. After spending the better part of Béke smoking herbs and drinking every night, my body had acclimated to the abuse that kept the binding magic at bay – while I was rolling. The memory of our last hunt had me grinding my teeth, still seething that Ruslan had made me look incompetent and weak when the black fire spewed from his mouth to stop the avalanche from killing us.

I was the savior, the one who acted with a level head under pressure, but one action on his part completely overshadowed my own. The other monarchs had been cozying up to him ever since, when it was *my* mate we'd ridden all the way to the Iron Realm to rescue. It was as if the other monarchs had completely forgotten why we were here. Our army was probably preparing to pack up and march on the Iron Realm as we rode into these Goddess-forsaken mountains.

Would they change their minds by the time the army reached us, and disband their soldiers with orders to return home?

The Night Realm did not have enough warriors to wage battle alone – not with the few we'd managed to gather on short notice before departing for Béke. Fek tossed his head, and only then did I realize how hard I gripped his reins. With a muttered apology to my mount, I unclenched my hands and refocused on the group in front of me. Ruslan and Drazen led the pack along a different route than before, stopping occasionally and leaping from their mounts to study the snow before directing us one way or another.

The binding magic purred in my chest, whispering ideas into my ear of how to take Ruslan out, to remove that option for Izidora so she would be forced to choose me. It was ironic that the opposite of those thoughts had plagued me on our last hunt.

Better to be the one to kill than to be killed.

I could use my magic to pull a rock loose high above, sending it cascading down in the front, and with how long our line of riders was, he'd be trapped unless he took to the skies or spewed black flame again. I'd have to ensure the volume was more than before and not allow him any time to prepare. Though close to the front, Endre and the two High Lords of the Day Realm rode alongside some of the mixed-bloods Izidora seemed so fond of. I couldn't kill my best friend, not after everything he'd done for me and almost killing him with my magic before.

Grinding my teeth, I occupied my mind with the myriad of ways I could feasibly kill Ruslan without it being so obvious. As we wound up into the mountain, we came across a ridgeline with a steep dropoff on one side. Could I incapacitate Ruslan's horse and send them both plummeting into the ravine? From far away, no one would see the tendril of binding magic around his ankle that would prevent him from accessing his magic. Yet much to my dismay, he kept his mount flush with the rough wall that formed the other side of the path, too far for a slip of his mount's footing to send them careening over the edge.

Weren't there large beasts that lived in the mountains, attacking passersby at random? Perhaps I could form my magic into the shape of one, sending it leaping from the snow and startling his horse, the jumpy beast sending them falling. My imagination ran away from me, and as I assessed every possible scenario, time to act ran out.

We drove through a thick patch of snow nestled between two faces of the mountains and left the ravine behind. Up ahead, Endre shouted, gesticulating wildly at something in the distance. Ruslan and Drazen leaped from their mounts, followed by Endre and the others. With a grumble under my breath, I slid from Fek's back and crept along behind the Crystal Fae. We bunched together among the snow behind a series of large boulders, silence reigning over us.

As if called by my will alone, one of those enormous beasts lingered on the mountainside a hundred yards away. Even from a distance, he looked like he was one wrong move away from attacking. Thick, white fur covered his body, and his eyes were a blood red that pierced into our hunting party as he scented our arrival. His blocky head lifted from where he snuffed the ground, and one of his massive paws swiped at the snow in front of him, clearing the drift impeding his path. As he lumbered forward, two more beasts were revealed behind him, and both Drazen and Ruslan began swearing.

"Everyone, back to your mounts. We need to leave," Drazen instructed in a rush.

These beasts had gifted me an opportunity on a snowy platter.

The two new arrivals lifted their noses and sniffed, the closest one releasing a roar that shook the mountains on either side of us, and charged.

"Go!" Endre and Viktor shouted at me simultaneously, and the latter grasped my arm and hauled me along beside him as we sprinted to our horses at the back of the line. Around us, rocks perched on high overhangs began tumbling down, and the heavy pounding of three sets of paws against the ground sent more snow sliding down the mountains.

The beasts were faster than any of us, covering distance with ease and closing in on the back of our hunting party. I jammed my foot into a stirrup and hauled myself onto Fek, yanking the rein back on one side to turn him in the opposite direction. Pure, unfiltered fear lined the faces of those in the back, and fuck, as much as I wanted Ruslan dead, I couldn't lose Endre, not when I'd already lost my father, Kriztof, and the twins. Digging my heels into Fek's sides, I urged him forward, catching up with Viktor and Vadim who were already racing away, opening a path for the others. The two checked over their shoulders repeatedly to gauge our advance, not focusing on the harrowing path before them. Three vicious roars ripped through the air, so violent that the rock wall beside me shook from its force.

"Watch out!" I shouted as a precariously perched rock tipped forward, feet from where Viktor and Vadim were about to pass. Their horses were smart, and both swerved at the last moment to avoid being slammed by the projectile. It cracked upon impact with the ground, and I held my breath as my stallion and I careened toward it. We needed to jump to clear it, but the ground beneath his hooves was icy and slick.

Fucking Fates, I hadn't come this far to die from a fall.

Fek sailed over it, and I wasted no time couching low on his neck to offer him the stability he needed to land without slipping. But the moment his hooves touched the ice, they slid, and he neighed a warning as we shot toward the side with the ravine. Without hesitation, I unleashed the binding magic, using it like an anchor to keep us from falling over the edge. The ropes around Fek's belly and my hands stopped us a breath before, and I glanced to the side, noting the sharp rocks that would have impaled us and the rushing river that would have swept us away. We panted for a moment before King Airre pulled up his horse and melted the ice beneath us, providing us safe passage back to the center of the trail.

Another roar shook the canyon, and I wasted no time redirecting my mount forward. Thanks to King Airre, the way was cleared for the rest of our hunting party, and hoofbeats pounded into the ground as we raced back the way we'd come. Only once we reached a wide opening in the path did we finally slow, counting our numbers to ensure we had all made it safely. Aside from a gash in Drazen's horse's rear, everyone was unharmed.

Releasing a shaky breath, I dismounted, sweat pouring down my temples, until my heart slowed to an even pace once more. I sought out Endre, pulling him in for a much-needed embrace. "I'm so glad you're alright," I said, shaken as the reality of almost losing my life and the life of my best friend sank in.

"I've never seen a Fehérmedve before," he replied, a slight tremble wracking his countenance. Viktor, Vadim, and Kaztar joined us a moment later, all breathing sighs of relief.

"Seeing one Fehérmedve is rare, but three at once? It couldn't possibly be a coincidence," Viktor hissed with a glance at Ruslan, Drazen, and the mixed-bloods. "They're obviously preparing an attack. Did Liliana tell Izidora about our plan?" He leveled a lethal gaze on Endre.

"Why are you looking at me instead of Vadim?" he snapped,

the tension obvious in his frame as he uncharacteristically bit back at our friend.

"You're the one that's fucking her," Viktor replied coolly.

"That's enough," Vadim snapped. "We're all on edge right now, so drop it. Don't speculate, Viktor, and don't accuse my sister of betraying us. She's loyal."

"Since when are you defending the Iron Realm, Vadim?" I snarled. "Is it because you've finally found kindred spirits in Anton and Slavian?"

He shoved against my chest when I took a menacing step toward him. "I'm fucking loyal to you, asshole!"

"Knock it off!" Endre shouted, and his tone brokered no room for argument. If our normally quiet and sensitive friend sounded like he was ready to throttle us, then we stopped and listened.

Running a hand over my face, I sucked in a steadying breath, blowing it out along with my apology to Vadim. Kaztar watched on as we reconciled, and minutes later, we all acted as if nothing had happened. Endre healed Drazen's mount, and the other Fae shot us questioning side eyes until we were all remounted and trekking down a different path in search of food for the masquerade.

It wasn't long before we came across a giant stag, and Ruslan wasted no time in killing it, using his Dragon wings to soar over the snow and collect it the same way he had before.

"About time. We can finally return to the warmth of Ryza," King Consort Geza joked as the stag was strapped to the litter.

I grunted an acknowledgement. "It's a good thing the Iron Realm only hosts every four years."

"So true, my friend. So true," he replied, urging his mount forward and joining with his High Lords as we wound our way down from the mountains and into the valley that held Radence. No one wanted to remain among the peaks for any longer than necessary, and we all took solace in that we'd finally captured and killed our dinner.

Ruslan looked like a fool, having taken us into his precious realm's wilderness twice and twice almost dying. Perhaps this was the incident that would sway the monarchs of the Crystal and Day Realms back in my favor.

My opportunity to end Ruslan's life had passed, but one day, he would bleed beneath my sword, and I took comfort in knowing that day drew near.

35

IZIDORA

Béke Day Nine

On my way to the sparring ring at Ryza Citadel, I ran into Zuriel. My body itched after days of inactivity, begging for movement despite the slight headache behind my eyes. The males were off hunting for the dinner that would be served during the masquerade, and the tug around my middle was driving me crazy. Exercise was the perfect distraction and solution to my restlessness.

"Zuriel! Care to join me?" I called out to him. He glanced at my leathers and plaited hair, amusement twitching his lips upward.

"I don't believe we've ever sparred with swords. Show me what you can do, cousin." We walked together into the open air, a slight bite in the wind sending shivers through me.

Better get moving to warm up.

Liliana bounced into the courtyard a moment later, calling for me when she spotted us.

The Angel dipped his head in greeting. "Lovely to see you again, High Lady Liliana."

My friend eyed him appreciatively, and I rolled my eyes. She and Vadim were more alike than she cared to admit, and after watching her the previous night, I had no doubt that she would rival his own prowess by the time she finally decided to fully commit to Endre.

"We'll have to settle for Zuriel as a sparring partner today. The males are all out on a hunt," I joked.

"I promise to take it easy on both of you. I've only had two millennia to train," he said casually as if everyone lived for thousands and thousands of years.

I resumed walking, shaking my head as I tried to fathom the stretch of time. So much had happened to me in my relatively short lifespan. I couldn't imagine what else would happen if I lived to Zuriel's age. Fae only lived for a few hundred years at best, and the Félvér, I'd been told, varied based on their heritage.

We trekked to the barracks in the courtyard at Ryza, finding the rings nearly empty and with plenty of space for us to use. A few young males trained at the end closest to us with older ones who shouted instructions and corrections when they faltered or made mistakes.

Across my back, I carried my new short swords, though I'd left the full set of armor behind, not needing full-body protection for some light sparring. I smiled to myself, Ruslan's thoughtfulness in both choosing the gift and the design of it melting my heart for the second time.

I waited for Liliana and Zuriel to select weapons from the rack of training equipment. Liliana opted for a long knife and axe, and I pressed my lips together to suppress a smile. She and Endre were made for each other, if she could only accept his love for her and he could step up to be what she wanted him to be. He had the potential, if he would only open himself to believing it.

Zuriel only picked up a dagger, a hint of mischief in his icy eyes, and vaulted over the fence to the training ring before walking to the far end so we had plenty of space.

"Let's go, Izidora." My cousin called me out first, and grinning, I stepped forward to face him.

As I unsheathed my blades, the veins of silver in the dark gray metal caught the light, highlighting the long-stemmed roses etched into the blades. Positioning myself, I held one high in front of me while I let the other rest at my side, not entirely passive, but not entirely aggressive either. Zuriel stood motionless in front of me, not even blinking as he waited. A light breeze flitted through the ring, pulling strands of chestnut from my plait, and yet he still did not move.

My left foot raised as I prepared to take a step forward, and in a blur of motion too fast for me to comprehend, he knocked the blade from my left hand. It clattered off to the side, and, off balance, I stumbled forward and nearly into Zuriel's waiting dagger. At the last moment I twisted, backstepping with my right foot to avoid the blade, but I was even more open than before.

He lunged, and I parried, my single blade meeting his sliver of a dagger a breath from my shoulder. Using only his thin blade and skill, he backed me all the way to the fence. It was as if every move I made, he knew I would make it before I did.

"Are you sure you've never spied on me while I sparred with Drazen and the other Félvér, Zuriel?" I laughed as I blocked his blade from slicing my neck.

His ice-blue eyes twinkled with excitement. "You mortals are so predictable."

"We are no–" I started to protest, but while I was distracted with my opinion, he snatched a hidden dagger from my thigh and held it to my side. "I yield," I huffed, and with a knowing grin, he returned my weapon.

"I can do better than that," Liliana bragged, hopping from her perch on the railing and striding toward us.

"I'd like to see you try." I took her place beyond the fence, leaning on it with my elbows as I watched my cousin and best friend spar.

Liliana lasted no longer than I had, quickly backed up no matter how she rolled, dodged, and parried with the knife and then the axe. Once she yielded, all of us now breathless, I asked, "So why do I train with Drazen and not you?"

"Because Drazen is a more reasonable opponent than I am. You'll never catch me," Zuriel said, amusement dancing in his tone.

Liliana and I shared a look, and without hesitation we sprung into action, blades singing as they swung through the air. And yet, two-on-one my cousin still managed to best us both without losing his composure. We collapsed in a heap of sweat on the ground after three consecutive losses against the Angel.

"You have over thousands of years of fighting experience. It's totally not fair," Liliana complained, tucking locks of sweaty hair behind her ears.

"I am not the one who said 'I can do better than that' if my recollection serves me." Zuriel mimicked Liliana's bubbly voice with surprising accuracy, and we burst into laughter.

"Two thousand years of memories is enough to start getting some confused, Angel," Liliana bantered, batting her long lashes in his direction.

I huffed a laugh, then sat upright with a groan. My body was sore and worn out, and the restlessness that had plagued me for days melted away with the amount of energy I had expended. Training like this needed to be a daily priority, otherwise my thoughts would continue to spin out of control. The sessions with Zuriel helped tone down the level of my reaction, but they had not completely banished the fear of Kazimir following me. Strength and skill were important to maintain, especially because only the Goddess knew the next time he would appear unannounced, hidden so that I could only feel him.

The thought sent a chill skittering down my spine.

Ruslan wanted me to tell Kazimir we'd accepted our bond and break my tie to him as Zuriel had suggested initially. I still hadn't told Ruslan about Immonen's vision; the dread that had settled in my stomach at the thought of whatever darkness came with it was too much to share with him. We still had to break apart the alliance of the Night, Crystal, and Day Realms and secure the safety of our people. Keeping those thoughts and fears away from him was difficult when I heard his every thought and felt his every emotion down our bond. My extensive practice at mental shields for my empath magic was the only way I was maintaining the box around that information.

Liliana interrupted my thoughts with a giggle, watching Zuriel gather the borrowed weapons and stride off to put them away. "He's cute."

"You're so bad." I rolled my eyes, but my words were all tease.

Clopping hooves drifted over the barracks and into the training ring, signaling the return of the hunting party, and I hopped to my feet as I sensed Ruslan growing closer. "He's back!"

"Now who is bad?" Liliana elbowed me in the ribs, causing me to flinch and giggle.

"Hey, at least he's my mate," I pointed out, then vaulted over the fence, followed a moment later by Liliana.

Zuriel fell in step beside us as we left the barracks. "How long has it been since you've seen him?"

"He left early this morning." I bit my lip as we rounded the corner and my mate materialized. I couldn't help myself as I ran to the stables and jumped into his arms the moment he dismounted.

Ruslan spun me around in circles until I pounded on his

chest. "Put me down unless you want me to throw up." The movement ceased, and when my feet hit the ground, I stumbled into him, the world spinning a little too much to remain upright. I giggled anyway, giddy that my mate had finally returned to our citadel.

"I missed you too, my sprite." He planted a kiss on my forehead. "I have to get this stag inside for dinner, but I promise I will find you shortly."

Antlers wider than I could stretch my arms greeted me when I turned around to see what the horses pulled. The stag was nearly bigger than the steeds combined. An involuntary gasp slipped out. "That could feed all of Radence."

"That's the plan. We will feast well at the masquerade tonight." Servants had secured ropes around the beast, and as Ruslan stepped away, he hefted one over his shoulder, joining Drazen and the others to drag the litter inside.

"I'm going to give Mistik and Twilight treats and then I'll be in our apartment," I called out as I watched them go, most of the party already having retreated to the warmth of Ryza. Liliana and Zuriel must have gone inside when I ditched them to run to Ruslan because they were nowhere to be found. Sighing, I decided I would be quick to the stables and back so as not to be alone for long. It was also bitterly cold, and the warmth of our apartment called to me, along with a much-needed bath.

As soon as I had made my decision, the hairs on the back of my neck rose.

Someone was behind me.

My entire body stiffened, just as his powerful, low voice hit my ears.

"Izidora."

I spun to face Kazimir. He was dressed in thick clothing from the hunt, but it did nothing to hide the warrior's body beneath.

My skin crawled at his closeness, and I took a step back, needing to put distance between us, for my own safety.

But he stepped forward. "We nearly died today in the mountains."

If he thought the words would make me feel sympathy for him, it did not work, and honestly, my life would have been a lot simpler if he had died. Fuck, the war we all knew was coming, yet continued to dance around, would never come to pass if he did.

I opened the well of empath magic inside me, reaching out with invisible threads to brush against his emotions. It was my safeguard against his new, volatile binding magic, and I hoped that I would be quicker to act on my magic than he was, if it came to it.

"Are you not going to say that you're glad I'm alive?" He was persistent in his attempts to sway me, though I would still fault him for it.

"I'm glad you're alive, Kazimir," I gritted out, hating that I was yet again placating a male who sought to control and manipulate me. Focusing on my magic rather than our conversation, I prepared myself for whatever madness he might unleash on me.

Anything to survive.

The invisible tendrils of my empath magic brushed against his emotions, and I tried to delve deeper, winding my way through the tangled mess that protected his heart and mind.

"You could have lost both of your mates today. Why aren't you more upset?" He ran a palm over his face, then rested it on the back of his neck while he regarded me.

I was only half listening, determined to discover his intentions before he could act on them. "Because I don't know that you're telling the truth," I quipped, more than ready to end the conversation. But I was so close to passing the barrier...

Rage flared from him at my questioning of his integrity, dragging me to the center of his heart.

There.

Flashes of feeling overwhelmed me almost instantly as my magic latched on to his emotions, flipping through them like they were pages in a book. Never before had I ventured so deep into someone's psyche, and I nearly vomited at what I found.

Desire-filled fantasies of me before my rescue. Desperation to keep me while we were at Zirok. Jealousy over my close inter-actions with the Nighthounds. Adoration as I spoke to the people of the Night Realm. Love as he drank me in while I wore the golden dress. Fear as Iron Realm soldiers ripped me away from him. Grief upon finding his father dying minutes later. Fury as he raced through the woods searching for me. Laying with my clothes at night. Protectiveness over images of my belly swollen with child. Obsession to bind me to him by any means necessary.

I yanked back with horror, but in my haste, I brushed against his binding magic, causing it to flare to life and give chase as I lost control of the tendril. It was thick, ropey, and vile, with a hellish desire of its own, grasping at my magic as I frantically pulled away, barely managing to slip through its corrupting fingers.

Kazimir's chuckle was filled with depravity, sending a shiver of fear down my spine. "Did you find what you were looking for, Izidora?" He lunged, capturing my throat in his hand before I could react. Gasping for breath, I rose to my tiptoes, trying to relieve the pressure on my neck. With my right leg, I kicked out, landing a heavy blow to the inside of his knee. He grunted, his grip loosening just enough for me to suck in a breath. I locked my hands together and brought them with all the force I could muster on the crook of his elbow. He released me completely, and I stumbled backward and away from him.

"Don't touch me," I snarled, calling white magic to my hands, ready to defend myself.

I was not powerless in the face of the monster Kazimir had become.

"You are mine. I will touch you whenever I want. Don't you feel the pull between us? You want it as badly as I do." Kazimir merely jerked his clothes straight and faced me again, unruffled by my strikes.

"Maybe I did once, but no longer. Something is wrong with you, Kazimir."

His once-kind emerald eyes darkened, and his lips curled into a sneer. Two thick black ropes like snakes landed at my feet with a dismissive wave of his hand. They uncoiled and moved of their own accord, slithering toward me. I blasted each of them away with white magic before they could get close, then called my wings and floated backward and away from the sinister magic.

Better to have a third movement option.

Kazimir sniffed the air around us. "I smell your arousal, Izidora. It clings to your thighs."

Bile rose in my throat. "You are insane."

Faster than I thought possible, he had me pinned to the ground. With all my strength, I pushed against him, screaming for help. Panic clawed its way up my throat, and my mind blanked on what to do to defend myself as he caught my hands together and shoved them above my head. The other gloved hand found my mouth, silencing me. "I went crazy when he took you. I had to, to get you back. You just need to understand the depths I would go to, the darkness I would fall into, for you. Then you'll choose me."

Kazimir had said as much before, but I had already made my choice. The *right* choice. But if I called on Ruslan for help with Kazimir pinning me like this, he'd kill him. He wanted so badly to win the other monarchs to his side, and I feared if he killed the new king of the Night Realm, they would turn against us. I didn't want everything to go dark because of me.

"Zuriel! Help! I'm in the stables."

"I'm on my way."

The hand that covered my mouth shifted slightly, and I did not hesitate to bite down, hard. "You bitch," he seethed, a stinging slap whipping my head to the side.

But the pain sharpened my focus and fueled my rage, which I redirected to my magic, spearing it into his mind. The last thing I ever wanted to do was torture anyone with my empath magic again, but he'd crossed a line, and I wanted vengeance.

His back arched and he fell away, writhing in pain as I focused all my energy on sending the whipping sensations I knew all too well across his back. I'd suffered hundreds of lashes, yet they still stung my back as I forced Kazimir to feel them too. My eyes burned with unshed tears as I struggled with my breath, bearing the pain so I could deliver more to Kazimir.

Zuriel dropped from the sky beside me as Kazimir screamed in agony. My cousin looked at the red mark across my face, then at the writhing male in front of me. "I'll take it from here."

Releasing my hold on him, I stalked away as Zuriel caged Kazimir in a net of light. "If you ever touch her again, I will not hesitate to kill you. You are a despicable excuse for a male."

Zuriel backed away with me, holding his magic until we were out of sight of the male I had loved first. Adrenaline still flooded my veins, and I hurried through the halls of Ryza, my heart pounding in my chest as I struggled to gulp down enough air. I took the spiraling stairs that led to our suite two at a time, and once we were safely behind closed doors, I let go. Tears flowed freely down my face, and I heaved breath in and out until Zuriel shook me gently to get my attention.

"Follow my breath," he instructed. I focused wholly on my

cousin as he took me through a familiar set of breathwork until I calmed down.

I was safe. There was no cave. I was not trapped. I was not powerless.

Not a moment later, Ruslan burst through the door with a wild look in his eye. He rushed to my side, and through our bond I felt wave after wave of concern. "Izidora, what happened?"

I dried the last of my tears and then snorted with not nearly enough disdain. "Kazimir attacked me. I think I handled it pretty well."

Zuriel dipped his head in agreement. "I never thought I would see her willingly do it, but she tortured him with her empath magic."

Ruslan pulled me into his chest, cradling my head against his furiously pounding heart. Rage rolled off of him like a storm rolling into the valley, and I had to work to block out his emotions and focus on my own. His arms trembled around me as if he fought with everything he had not to haunt the halls of Ryza and rip out Kazimir's throat. "You are fierce, my mate, and I am proud of you for standing up for yourself."

"I sense a but," I stated.

"*But* I am not okay with him hurting you. If something should happen to you, I would never forgive myself, and I wouldn't be long for this world without you in it. Waiting for you to tell him that we accepted our bond is killing me."

Guilt slammed into my gut, the secret I had been keeping from him weighing heavily on me. But I couldn't tell him what Immonen saw, not when we didn't know what the dark meant. Instead, I skirted around the truth, and my voice was small as I whispered, "I have this awful feeling that the moment I tell him, something horrible will happen. I don't have an explanation for it, but I feel it in my bones to be true. Maybe it's my empath magic or something else, but I think we need to wait until Béke is almost over."

He blew out a frustrated breath, his arms twitching as he continued to hold me. Sensing he needed more reassurance, I pulled back, then cupped his face, running my thumb across the beard that covered his strong jaw. "I know this is hard for you. You've empowered me to be able to hold my own. As you said before, you want to be able to concentrate on the battle in front of you rather than worrying about me. This is practice, for both of us."

My words took the edge off his fury, but the violence in his eyes had not faded. "We will continue training, every day. And you will continue training with Zuriel as well, but do not exhaust your magic as you have been. It's more important that you have some to spare than to grow your well. Understood?"

His tone brokered no room for argument, not that I wanted to challenge his points. "Understood," I replied, stroking his face and massaging his arms until he relaxed around me.

Zuriel cleared his throat, drawing our attention. "The Telivér will all be in attendance at the masquerade. We will watch over you, and I'll have Xorrek and Gozzak trail Kazimir the entire time." He paused as if he was considering a confession, and my stomach dropped as I feared he would reveal what I'd told him in a moment of despair the previous day, but had obviously not told Ruslan. To my relief, his next statement was an affirmation of my own belief without revealing how either of us knew. "Kazimir's mind is fracturing, and I fear Izidora is correct in her assessment that breaking the lingering string between them will set him off. We should plan it strategically."

"Thank you, Zuriel. See you later," Ruslan said, the thanks and dismissal both clear in his tone. The Angel slipped out the door with one last parting look, leaving me alone with the male whose only desire was to see no harm befall me.

"Come, let's shower and read before the masquerade. It will take your mind off things." Ruslan held out his tattooed hand and I accepted it, allowing him to lead me to the marble bathroom. I let him wash the sweat and dirt from my body as the heated water poured over us both. With each swipe of soap, Ruslan instilled safety in my muscles, in my bones, until finally, I was clean in both mind and body.

But rage simmered just beneath the surface of my skin, and I knew it was my own. Kazimir dared to lay a hand on me in violence, and I'd already proven time and time again what happened when a male touched me in a way that I did not want. Determination settled over my shoulders like a cloak of armor, and I vowed in that moment to give my fucking all to breaking his alliance with the Day and Crystal Realms.

The Iron Realm was my home, and its king was my safe space and my mate. Our bond was more powerful than any magic on this planet. United, we could do anything, and I steeled my spine as I reminded myself of that fact, reminded myself just how fucking strong I was. I only hoped that my strength and our determination were enough to see us through the challenges that lay ahead – both on and off the battlefield.

36

LILIANA

Béke Day Nine

When the guards outside Izidora and Ruslan's apartment allowed me entrance, I immediately burst in, calling out for my best friend. I needed to see if she was okay after what I'd witnessed in the Night Realm's temporary accommodation.

I'd just emerged from a shower when my brother, Endre, Viktor, and Kaztar returned to our suite after another hunt. Before I'd finished dressing, Kazimir burst into the room, cursing Zuriel for stealing Izidora away from him. I crouched at the slit in the door to the room Endre and I were sharing, listening to Kazimir recount *his version* of what happened when they arrived back and he found Izidora waiting for him.

It took every ounce of my willpower not to slam the door open and tell him how fucking wrong he was. Kazimir's perspective was slipping by the day, and I no longer trusted him. Domi shared my views, and after Immonen's vision, the two of us had promised each other never to be in the suite alone with him. If only Kaztar, Endre, and Vadim had listened to us when we told them about the changes we saw in Kazimir.

Of course, my brother had every excuse in the book for him. Vadim had searched for Izidora longest, seconded only by Kazimir, and I was sick of hearing him say, 'of course he's going crazy, we spent all that time looking for her, only for her to be his mate and get stolen away.' The next time those words fell out of his mouth was the time I was going to punch him in the face.

Even Endre, the sensitive, sympathetic male, could only find loyalty for Kazimir. His empathy only went in one direction, and that was to his best friend. Each day that passed, we fought more and this chasm opened between us that I wasn't sure how to cross.

Which was why I jogged through the halls of Ryza dressed in the most casual of clothes, my attire for the masquerade ball tucked safely under my arm, to my best friend.

"Liliana?" Izidora's voice was small and strained, floating toward me from the bedroom. I burst through the door a moment later, finding her and Ruslan curled up in matching robes, each with a book in hand. Izidora set hers aside as I approached.

"I came as soon as I could. Tell me what happened." Without regard for Ruslan, I jumped on the bed and snuggled in beside her. He smothered a laugh and returned to his book, though the twitching muscles in his jaw told me he was probably trying to drown himself in the words so he didn't rip Kazimir to shreds with his Dragon talons.

Izidora's aquamarine eyes hardened as she sucked in a breath, and I reached my hand to hers, grasping it in mine and stroking the back of it. "After our training, I went to find Ruslan, and after that I decided to visit Mistik and Twilight before returning inside. Only, Kazimir lingered after the other males had gone, and he cornered me. I tried to influence his emotions, but his magic tangled with mine, capturing it as I tried to retreat. And the things in his mind…" She shook, her hands fisting the sheets so hard her knuckles turned white. "He wants to impregnate me so I'll have no choice but to accept our bond."

I gagged on her words. "He is sick. I'm so sorry you had to experience all that."

"It gets worse." Her eyes flashed, and I realized I'd never seen her so angry.

I groaned, flopping back against the pillows. "Tell me."

"He threw his binding magic at me, then when I defended myself, he pinned me to the ground. I bit him, and he slapped me. So I used my empath magic to make him believe he was being tortured. Thankfully Zuriel was nearby and heard the commotion, helping me get away from him."

My mouth popped open in shock. "Okay, first, you are a fucking queen with your magic. He deserved everything you gave him and more. I can't believe he hit you. What the fuck! If the others knew, maybe they'd change their minds about him."

Hitting females was one of the most frowned-upon actions in the Night Realm, and most of the males I knew, especially the ones who went through Knight training, would never stand for actions like that.

Ruslan released a pained growl, then flipped his book over on the bed. "Liliana, I know that I am putting you in an awkward situation by asking you this, but what is the Night Realm planning? Did you bring an army with you, waiting in the Day Realm to attack?"

I bolted upright. "You know I can't tell you that. My brother… Endre…"

"What if we tell you what we want for the continent? The fact you rushed here for Izidora…" Ruslan blew out a long breath. "I believe I can trust you, Liliana. And I don't give this information, or my trust, away easily. I'd do anything to protect my mate – your best friend. Wouldn't you?"

Izidora reclined against the headboard, watching us volley back and forth.

I considered his proposal, and these topics we'd danced around since our arrival. I was caught between two realms, with my family in one and my best friend in another. While I normally loved being the center of attention, I hated that I was in the middle of it like a fucking flag on a tug-of-war rope. Though I wasn't the only one. Izidora was that flag between Ruslan and Kazimir, but Ruslan had already won – though Kazimir didn't exactly know that yet.

"I promise I won't repeat what you're about to tell me to anyone," I said. "But I can only offer you the barest details in return. Mostly because I don't know the big ones."

Ruslan cocked his head while he regarded me, mulling over his decision. "Alright. Once I hear what you have to say, we can work out other arrangements for what to do with it."

"Deal," I replied, holding out my arm. We clasped ours together, sealing our agreement before Izidora.

She uncrossed her arms and leveled a serious look in my direction. "You know Ruslan and I have mixed blood, along with thousands of others in the Iron Realm."

I nodded slowly, waiting for her to continue.

"The other realms have a blood purity mentality that makes people like us not so welcome. And with the purebloods from other continents also wanting to live here, we aren't sure how the other realms will react to that. You have been so accepting of me – of us, that I think, I hope, you would support our plan to unite the realms under one banner and welcome all peoples to our shores."

Before I had a chance to say anything, Ruslan added, "I think we've proven that power does not come from blood purity. All I want is for the Félvér and Telivér to be able to roam the continent without fear of being treated as pariahs or locked out of spaces for having mixed or different blood."

"Like the separate spaces for nobles and non-nobles in the Night Realm," I said, hoping I understood their goal.

"Exactly," Izidora replied. "We've been working all of Béke to show the monarchs of the Crystal and Day Realms that we're trustworthy and honorable so they side with us when this is all over. We don't want bloodshed to make the right thing happen."

I nodded, sympathizing with their points. "Honestly, I think you've won Queen Viktoria over. Queen Immonen too. Whether King Airre will follow her advice is a different story, but honestly, other than a handful of people I can think of back in the Night Realm, I don't think you'll have as much opposition to the free movement of people through Északi. I can't speak for the other realms though. It's time for a change."

Izidora's shoulders dropped in time with a whoosh of air from her lungs, and she pulled me into a tight hug. "I'm so glad you understand and agree."

"Thank you, Liliana," Ruslan murmured, his gray eyes softening as I embraced his mate.

"I love you – both of you," I said. It was true; I did care deeply for both of them, having felt an immediate connection to each from the moment we first met. Last Béke I'd asked the Goddess for a friend, and I was not passing on the gift she'd offered. "I'm grateful that you let me be the third wheel in your relationship, Ruslan."

He rolled his eyes and slicked back his dark hair. "I would say you are a welcome addition, but..."

I threw a pillow at his face, and with lightning-fast reflexes, he caught it and tucked it into his lap, shooting me a smirk. Izidora snickered beside me, hiding her mouth with her hand.

"I believe it is your turn to impart information?" Ruslan said, lifting a brow.

"Only because I can't throw another pillow at you right now," I huffed. "Fine, here it goes. There is an army in the Day Realm, probably arriving on the border with the Iron Realm on the day of your wedding. They planned to march after the feast was over and take you by surprise. Not that you'd be surprised anyway, even before I told you that. I think it's pretty obvious what's going to happen – to everyone." I sighed, brushing my damp hair over my shoulder and straightening my spine. "I can't tell you numbers or anything like that, but I can tell you that I don't think it would take much for the Day and Crystal Realms to send their warriors home instead of attacking. Like I said, I think you've won over Queen Viktoria, and without the Day Realm's soldiers, King Airre wouldn't risk his own. Especially because he has seen your power, Ruslan."

Izidora blew out a breath and tangled her fingers in her hair, combing out knots while she waited for Ruslan to speak. The male sat unnervingly still, and the hairs on the back of my neck rose as my body sensed a predator rising to the surface within him. "Thank you for telling me, Liliana. I promise no harm will come to Vadim or Endre while they are in the Iron Realm because of the information you gave me."

"And Domi," I added.

"And Domi," he confirmed. "You have a sharp mind. What would you do to push the other monarchs to break their alliance with Kazimir?"

The fact that Ruslan respected my insight made me feel valued in a way I'd never felt in the Night Realm. Females there were often seen as lesser than the males, and I'd always wanted to be recognized for my wit and intelligence that matched Viktor's, if not surpassed it. "Tell them what he did to Izidora earlier. Mention the stalking too, to drive home the point."

Ruslan nodded. "Anything else?"

"Kazimir's binding magic isn't well known since it was gifted to him when we were in the Crystal Realm. Maybe revealing that will sway them?" I offered.

"Noted," Ruslan said before stretching his neck to the side and releasing a series of cracks into the air around us. "Why don't the two of you spend the rest of the afternoon getting ready? I'll give you some space. I need to talk to Drazen anyway."

Izidora perked up, eyes sparkling with mischief as she shot me a conspiratorial look. "I think that's a great plan," I responded for us.

Ruslan yanked Izidora into his lap, tangling his fingers in her hair and kissing her deeply. "I'll miss you, sprite."

The way they looked at each other simultaneously melted and broke my heart. I wanted that so badly for myself, and yet Endre would always side with Kazimir, and I would side with Izidora.

Why couldn't he see the truth?

"I'll miss you," she whispered back, a soft smile spreading across her face. I couldn't tear my eyes away from the purity of the moment. He released her, crawling out of bed and striding to the dresser where he searched for clothes. Reaching for a pillow, I slammed it into my face moments before I heard the robe hit the floor, and Izidora roared with laughter.

"Shut up, you wouldn't want me to see him naked, Izidora." My voice was muffled by the pillow.

"Definitely not. You're already lusting after Zuriel. Can't have you salivating over anyone else in my family," she laughed. "It's safe for you to come out now."

I dropped the pillow from my face, revealing a dressed Ruslan standing at the end of the bed, watching us like the prey we were compared to him. "Zuriel is the only male in the Iron

Realm who isn't interested in you, Liliana." The corner of his mouth twitched up as he teased.

My mouth popped open in mock protest. "Do I hear a challenge?"

He huffed and made to leave. "I've known Zuriel for forty-three years. He doesn't talk about his past much, but he's never looked twice at a female in all the time he's been in the Iron Realm. Or male for that matter. Anton and Slavian, on the other hand." He shrugged, and with that last jab, he disappeared into the living space beyond.

Izidora snickered before knocking my shoulder with hers. "Anton and Slavian would crawl on their hands and knees to you if you asked."

I rolled my eyes. "I know. Why can't I find a male who will actually make me submit? I want to be challenged, not the other way around."

"So that's why you're growing bored of Endre? Because you already have him?" she asked, weaving her way around me and rolling out of the bed and onto the floor.

I followed her into the bathroom, the large windows filled with the dying sunlight. "Not that. We've been fighting a lot. Mostly about you and Kazimir. He is siding with his best friend like I am siding with you. We're trying, it's just," I searched for the right words, "hard? Awkward? He knows there are things that I'm not telling him, just like I know there are things he isn't telling me. It's hard to have a relationship with so many walls between us."

Izidora had twisted locks of hair in her fingers and was using her magic to dry and shape them. "I get that. I couldn't have a relationship with Kazimir until I started tearing down the walls I built to protect myself while I was chained in the cave. Maybe when this is all over?"

I lifted a shoulder in a half-shrug. "Maybe. Or maybe he's not the one for me and Zuriel is."

She smacked my shoulder playfully. "He's my cousin!"

"Yeah, but then we'd really be family," I laughed, turning my attention to my own damp hair. "So tell me, how'd you like the herbs?"

Izidora blushed a deep shade of crimson. "I want to do it again. Maybe in a few months when this crazy mating bond has had time to cool off." She chewed her lip as her eyes went glassy and a faraway expression crossed her face.

"Two dicks at the same time? Sign me up," I giggled, belly heating at the thought of fucking Endre and Slavian at the same time.

"Isn't it great to be utterly worshiped like that?" Izidora grinned into the mirror, examining a spot on her cheek.

"Fuck yeah." I paused for a moment, concentrating on the pieces at the back of my head. "Maybe that's my problem. I need two guys to handle me instead of just one."

We fell apart laughing, tears blurring my vision as I clutched my stomach.

"I think you might be right, Lil," she teased.

"What are you wearing tonight?" I asked her, and she shrugged.

"Ruslan got it for me. It's in that bag." She gestured over her shoulder to a black bag hanging on a hook on the wall. "I haven't looked at it yet."

"Let's see what the king has picked out for you this time," I grinned, unfastening it and reaching for the fabric.

The dress was all intricate black lace, with an off-shoulder design that immediately had my stomach clenching. The skirt was silky and flowing, and as I flipped it over, I saw what I feared. The back was low enough that Izidora's mate mark would be visible. The mask tumbled from the bag, and I barely caught it before it reached the ground. The lace matched the dress, while the feathers on either side of it were soft and shiny like the skirt.

"Oh, it's so pretty," Izidora said, lifting it from my hands and turning it over in hers. "What's the dress like?"

She stepped around me to examine it, and her breath immediately caught in her chest. "I can't wear this." Her voice sounded so pained that it nearly gutted me.

"I have an idea," I said, racing into the closet in the bathroom. Row after row of dresses hung there, most only worn once and only during the last few days. Finding the dress she had worn the previous night, I pulled it from the rack. "How attached are you to this?"

"Not particularly," she said, cocking her head to the side. "Why?"

"Good," was my response as I grasped the skirt in my hands and pulled.

Ripping fabric filled the air, and Izidora's eyebrows shot up her forehead. "What are you–"

"Hey, trust me I know what I'm doing. I wouldn't ruin a fine dress for no reason," I laughed, interrupting her.

"Fine, I'll let the master work," she joked, and I grinned as the last of the fabric fell away.

"Alright, let me show you," I said, redirecting us toward the mirror. Shaking out the fabric, I ripped it again, leaving one long strand instead of a loop. Positioning her arms, I draped the fabric over them, then pulled on the ends to bring it forward. "See? You can wear this and it will cover the mark on your back while not diminishing the impact of your dress."

"You are a genius, have I ever told you that?" Izidora chuckled with a small smile, her eyes filled with relief.

"I know," I grinned, stepping away. "Ruslan will return soon and we should be ready when he does. Can't have him any more annoyed with me than he already is or I'll never get to snuggle in bed with you two again."

That earned a laugh from Izidora, and we returned to the mirror, gossiping and readying ourselves for the masquerade that I hoped would be less tumultuous than every other event over the last nine days.

37

KAZIMIR

The grand ballroom at Ryza Citadel had been transformed into a gaudy, garish show for the Goddess, complete with the head of the stag bedecked with holly and red berries. Red was the only color that stood out among all the dark tones, and even then, it was the color of blood. Every one of the hundred or so tables was sprinkled with tiny gemstones, and the plates set out for the meal were hand-carved metal.

I hated every bit of it.

Especially because the intention of the masquerade ball was to be anonymous, and every Fae tried their best to be, some even going to great lengths to change their hair and eye color for the evening. As for me, I wanted everyone to see the new king of the Night Realm and show me the respect I deserved.

But there was only one person whose adoration I wanted, and at the moment, she was impossible to find. The ballroom was packed with people, thousands having turned out for one of the most anticipated nights of Béke, and more arrived by the minute. A tug to my left caught my attention, but my view was blocked by heavy silk curtains draping from the ceiling. Cursing, I pushed through the crowd, my jaw tightening as my crown did not automatically part them. I'd at least donned a full-face mask that left my eyes and mouth free, pretending like I cared about the spirit of the event.

The garnet carpet led me to an alcove piled with soft pillows and furs and a large group of partygoers standing in a circle before them. Clustered around them were smaller sets of groups, like the planets orbiting the sun, and I stalked my way past, searching for a petite frame and aquamarine eyes I'd know anywhere.

The string that always led me to Izidora informed me she was nearby, but these damn outfits were making it impossible to tell people apart. If I didn't know what my friends were wearing, I'd never have spotted Endre among the group, presumably with Liliana at his side.

And where Liliana was...

A flash of blue caught my attention, and I ripped my attention to the back of the group, where a pair of icy blues stared daggers into me. I allowed my lips to twitch up at the corners as I locked eyes with the Angel who had sought to keep me from my mate earlier that day. He hadn't bothered to significantly alter his appearance either, his white hair on full display as it swept past his shoulders.

I sipped from my drink and moved out of his line of sight, circling the outer ring like a predator hunting its prey. With Liliana and Zuriel around, Izidora would not be far. Though, I hadn't caught sight of Ruslan yet either. He was arrogant enough that I figured he'd come dressed as himself, maskless and parading himself about for attention.

Before I could slip further into the crowd, a hand caught my shoulder and spun me to face them. "There you are, King

Kazimir," High Lord Soma of the Day Realm said, High Lord Domon accompanying him. "You didn't try very hard to hide yourself."

Slipping into my king role, I offered them both an easy grin. "And neither did you."

Both males wore golden robes in the style of the Day Realm, with matching golden half-masks on their faces, accentuating their dark skin.

"Where are Queen Viktoria and King Consort Geza?" I inquired.

"Psh," Domon waved a hand dismissively. "They are trying to blend in. I'll leave it up to you to find them. Quite a challenge, I think."

I seized the opportunity to scan the crowd in the center of the ballroom, not seeking out the Day Realm's monarchs, but rather looking for Izidora and Ruslan. To my increasing aggravation, I found neither. "They must have put a lot of magic into their appearance," I teased, "for I cannot find a sign of either of them."

The High Lords chuckled beside me. "Will you join us for dinner? There are no place cards tonight."

I sipped from my drink, letting the alcohol burn my throat before responding. "It would be my honor. We shall have to find a table with pretty females to keep us company too."

"Here, there is no shortage," High Lord Soma commented, making an appreciative perusal of the group to our right.

"Lead the way." I swept my hand before me as a gong reverberated throughout the room, silencing conversations and sending bodies rushing to find a place at a table. As the Day Fae turned their backs to me in search of a spot, the grin slipped from my face, annoyance gnawing at my fingertips as I dug them into my palm. I hated that I was forced to sit in their company rather than spend my time seeking out the one person I wanted.

That tug came from my left again, and I whipped my head to the side. But I saw nothing through the throng of people. One by one, they claimed high-backed wooden seats along the massive tables slicing through the ballroom. Each was draped in iron-gray tablecloths adorned with that damn dragon symbol Ruslan seemed to favor. The thought of him with *my* mate and being unable to find either of them had me yanking back a chair with extra roughness as I settled at a table, surrounded by Fae in elaborate costumes.

Liliana breezed past me on her way to a table on the opposite side of the ballroom. I nearly rose from my seat to follow her, since she would know where Izidora was, but a purring voice to my right froze me in place. "King Kazimir, don't you look handsome tonight." Taya's burgundy hair tumbled down her back, matching the color of the wine in her goblet. Like me, she had not put much effort into concealing her identity, and I wondered if she placed herself purposefully in my path.

My cock twitched against my dress pants at the memory of her lips around me on our first night in the Iron Realm. If her hair were only a little more brown, and her eyes blue instead of gold, she could have passed for Izidora. It was a much better fantasy than the one I'd attempted to play out over the years.

Lifting her hand, I brought it to my lips and planted a kiss on the backs of her fingers, letting my mouth linger for a moment after. "Taya, you look stunning."

She batted her long black lashes at me before lifting her drink and sipping from it. "How fortunate I am to sit next to a king during the masquerade."

"Fortunate indeed," I replied. "Have you met High Lords Soma and Domon of the Day Realm?" With a dip of my head, I indicated the Day Fae seated across from us.

"I have not had the pleasure," she purred. Both of the males introduced themselves to her, while she introduced the females surrounding us; some had mixed blood like her, given the variety of their features, while others were decidedly Iron Fae.

How long had the Iron Realm been up to this shit?

Sure, the females were pretty, exotic even, but the mixing of blood was something no reasonable Fae would want to do, even among the Fae races. It irritated me to no end that I was the only one of the Night Fae who took the slightest issue with what had been happening here. It was one thing when only Izidora was part Angel, but to see more and more crawling out from their hiding places set my teeth on edge. If we were going to win a war against the Iron Realm, these mongrels would pose a challenge none of us were prepared for.

Taya pulled my attention back to her when she ran her slim fingers along my arm. "I loved watching you win all those strength competitions," she flirted. "Makes me think about all the ways you could throw me around."

She definitely put herself in my path.

A sultry smile spread across my face as I perused her form. Her face was mostly covered by a glittering gold mask that matched her eyes, and the dress she wore gave her ample cleavage an extra boost. Her tanned skin was on display through various cutouts in the green dress, though it wasn't like I hadn't seen what was underneath the scraps of fabric already. "I might have an idea or two."

Her eyes darkened with the lust in my tone. She bent her head toward me, the feathers on her mask tickling my cheek as she whispered in my ear. The words spilling from her lips went straight to my cock, along with her hand as she brushed it up my thigh.

But my attention was ripped away when chestnut hair floated through the air out of the corner of my eye. Ignoring the female creeping closer to me, I chased down those tendrils until I saw her.

Izidora and Ruslan appeared together in the middle of the space, making an entrance only after everyone had scrambled to find a seat. The two were dressed head to toe in black, subtly flaunting their mixed blood status with the masks they wore. Ruslan's was in the shape of a dragon's head, with his eyes altered red to match his sigil, while Izidora wore a black lace mask with feathers arcing toward the sky, a black mirror to her own wings. She looked like a fallen Angel standing beside the heavily tattooed male.

I tracked them through the ballroom, those long locks spilling down her back and over a shawl that covered the skin there. She turned her head to say something to Ruslan, and my eyes locked on the shift of her hair and that fabric, looking for the circle I thought I had seen while she stood on the pedestal in the dress shop.

A frustrated growl slipped past my lips as I failed to certify my belief, too far away to get a good look at Izidora's back. "Forget her," Taya whispered in my ear, her nails digging into my thigh. "She can't give you what you're looking for anyway."

"And you can?" I challenged, raising an eyebrow.

She sucked her bottom lip between her teeth before wetting it with her tongue. "Definitely."

38

IZIDORA

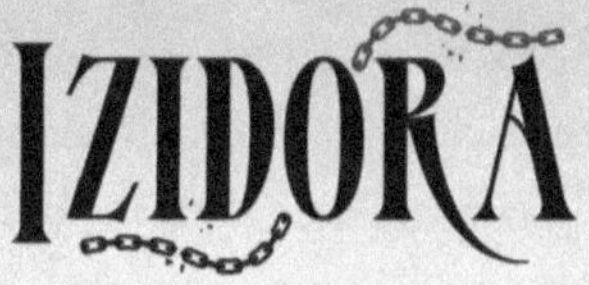

Béke Day Nine

Ruslan and I stood outside the grand ballroom doors, waiting to make our grand entrance. Even as we had walked down the hall toward it, the sound of revelry drowned out any conversation I might have tried to have with my mate. Raucous laughter, clinking glasses, and an undercurrent of music all pricked my ears.

I chewed my lip, twisting the rings on my fingers and adjusting the shawl around my shoulders as a mixture of anxiety and anger swirled in my belly. We'd stayed away during the pre-dinner mingling to avoid the stalking tendencies of Kazimir and because Ruslan needed more time to calm down. I spent a chunk of my magic working Ruslan down from a rage before we left because he wanted to murder Kazimir on sight. But our goals were bigger than Kazimir laying an unwanted hand on me, and we could not fail at bringing the other monarchs to our side. Besides, once Queen Viktoria heard of what happened, I had no doubt she would officially break away from Kazimir.

But logic and rage didn't remove the fear lingering in my

body, even after a few more sessions with Zuriel and reclaiming my stolen power, and I couldn't convince myself I was safe so long as Kazimir was around to raise the hairs on my arms or send chills down my spine.

Thank the Goddess Béke ended in five days.

My heart pounded as the doors opened for us, and the moment we crossed the threshold, nausea churned in my gut. Kazimir's eyes immediately found me from one of the lavish tables near the center of the room, and I felt them ghosting across my skin and leaving a slick trail in their wake.

I peered up at the male I was to marry on the last day of the feast, my chest warming as that thread tying us together hummed contentedly with our proximity. I slipped my hand into his as he sauntered to a table in the center of the room, where Liliana and Zuriel already waited. Drazen and a few of the Demons were at nearby tables, and I breathed a sigh of relief with the ring of protection surrounding me. I'd proven earlier that I could manage Kazimir with my magic, but knowing I wasn't alone in my fight brought me more comfort than I could adequately express.

Ruslan sipped from a goblet of wine on the table before clearing his throat and tapping the metal with the flat blade of a knife to garner the attention of the room. A hush fell over the crowd, amplifying the sound of scraping chairs as people turned to give the king of the Iron Realm their attention.

"Welcome to the masquerade ball, honoring new beginnings for all of us. Tonight, there are no foes – only friends. It is my honor to have in attendance a number of people from far-flung continents who plan to make Északi their home in the future. It is my wish that you find them among the masked crowd and get to know them just as you would any other Fae in attendance. With that being said, please enjoy the meal and dancing once the food is cleared." Ruslan lifted his glass into the air, and the thousands in attendance did the same before sipping.

A smattering of claps sounded through the space, softened by the hanging silks and plush furnishings. Ruslan pulled out my chair, and I batted my lashes at him before settling myself into it. He pushed me closer to the table before taking his seat beside me. I reached out to cup his face, my fingers brushing against the soft stubble lining his jaw. "We're making progress."

He turned his head into my palm, kissing it. "That we are."

After seeing how segregated nobility was from the common Fae in the Night Realm, I knew I wanted to live in a place where all were equal. While the idea of ruling was still far from the front of my mind, I still wanted to change the world so that no one had to suffer for who or what they were. No one would be chained, physically or metaphorically, by their past, titles, or blood status so long as I was around to do something about it.

The dark red wine in front of me tasted like pepper and blackberries, and I drank down an entire glass, Ruslan refilling it without hesitation, before casually sipping from it again. The relaxing effects began to take hold, dulling the edge of my anxiety as the ballroom buzzed with activity. We fell into conversation with those around us as the first course was served, and I was grateful to mingle with new people, getting to know them and their stories. That was what the ball was about anyway – opening ourselves up to new connections.

My wineglass was refilled again during the second course – a bright orange soup that was hearty and warm. Both were drained to the dregs, and my head felt lighter without all the worries weighing me down. Liliana and I laughed too hard at a deadpanned joke from Zuriel, and by the time I finally caught my breath again, I was giddy and blissfully drunk.

"How long until the main course?" I asked Ruslan.

"A few minutes," he replied, sipping from his whisky and

circling a finger over the back of my hand, painting goosebumps on my flesh. *"Why? Can't wait until tonight to have me?"*

A blush crept across my cheeks, heating them more than they already were. *"Now that you mention it."*

His response was a wink.

I glanced at our dinner companions and placed my napkin on the table. "Please excuse me for a moment, I've had a bit too much wine."

"I'll go with you," Liliana offered, her chair scraping back in time with mine.

We linked arms as we crossed the ballroom, both swaying slightly from the three glasses we'd consumed. "I appreciate you tagging along. I might need help with this dress," I laughed, looking down at the skin-tight attire that encumbered my strides.

"Ruslan sure wants everyone to know what they can't have," she giggled, tossing her chocolate hair over her shoulder as we entered the bathroom down the hall.

After struggling with the layers of skirts, I tossed the shawl onto the hook on the door to free my arms for navigating them up my legs, finally managing to hoist them high enough to relieve myself. While I waited for Liliana to take her turn, I looked myself over in the mirror, smoothing out any wrinkles and ensuring my mask was firmly in place. My thoughts drifted, and I absentmindedly braided and unbraided my long hair, soothing my fraying nerves. "Do you think we'll convince the other realms to unite?" I asked Liliana as she preened in the mirror.

"I think once you tell them what Kazimir did today, the odds are good," she replied with a casual shrug of her shoulder. "He's obviously not going to stop until he gets you, though. I don't know how King Airre and Queen Immonen will feel, since they are mated. Rejecting one mate and accepting another? It's complicated."

I blew out a breath. "Tell me about it. Sometimes I wonder, why me?"

"I still stand by what I said before. Prophecies are vague as fuck and it's us who adds interpretation to them." She finished glossing her lips, rubbing them together and turning toward me. "Ready to go?"

"Yep," I said, popping the P and dropping my fingers from my braid.

Liliana pushed through the door to the hallway first, and the breeze of air that dusted my face carried a hint of amber. I stiffened immediately, calling my magic to the surface of my skin, feeling the heady rush of power from holding it there protectively around me. The sounds of revelry drifted toward us, and I scanned the vicinity for any sign of Kazimir.

But there was none.

A shiver licked its way down my spine, and I grasped Liliana's arm.

"Are you okay?" she whispered, sensing my unease.

"Let's just get back to the table," I murmured, quickening my pace until we were in the safety of the numbers of the ballroom.

I dropped into my seat moments before servers came around with slices of the massive stag the males had killed on their hunt, and I accepted them numbly, speaking and eating without really being present.

Every moment of unease over the course of Béke, when I felt as if I were being watched, sensing that string that tugged me to Kazimir but never discovering him, played over and over again in my mind, circling along with a single question.

What else did his new power do?

39

KAZIMIR

BÉKE DAY NINE

I fucking knew it. Izidora had braided her hair over her shoulder by the time she exited the bathroom, and when she and Liliana swept by me in a rush to return, I saw it.

That Goddess-damned black circle between her shoulder blades.

But why did I still feel this pull to her?

Could it be that the choice in the prophecy wasn't about choosing a mate at all?

The words I'd seared into my brain repeated themselves as I searched for answers.

"The ones that are part of all will be born under a full moon
Her white light will fill the land
But her mates darkness will rise
Kings will fall
Rivers will run with blood
There is a choice
Follow the light

Descend into the dark
The harrowing pass decides it all"

The words offered no more clarity during that review than any other time I'd repeated them. No matter which way I turned the puzzle, I couldn't crack the code. But if there was still this connection between us, I still had a chance.

Taya waited for me to return to the table with her nail resting on her lower lip, her eyes flaming with lust. She was no Izidora; she was not my mate at all. But that didn't mean I couldn't use her to satiate the desire and fury pounding through my veins. Besides, she only wanted my crown. From my years navigating the Night Realm's vicious political scene, spotting a social climber was as easy as breathing.

So, all through dinner, I indulged her advances, flirting shamelessly and brushing my fingers against her bare skin. The Day Realm's High Lords were forgotten; Izidora was not. I wouldn't mind if she glanced my way and saw the attention I poured into Taya. Perhaps she might grow jealous enough to pull me aside so we could talk, and then I could tell her my theory that she didn't have to choose at all. I fucking *hated* Ruslan, but if I had to tolerate him to share my mate...

I'd still kill him in the end, one night while he slept. Make it look like an accident, and the only solace Izidora would find would be in my arms. She'd be mine – only mine – somehow, and I'd do fucking anything to make it happen. The binding magic prowling in my chest snarled its appreciation for our plan, and I had to press my lips together and sip from my drink to hide that I hadn't been paying attention to what Taya was saying.

Music floated from somewhere in the massive space, saving me from having to make up an answer to a question I didn't hear. "Care to dance?" I asked Taya, proffering my hand.

She batted her lashes through the slits in her mask. "I would love to."

Around us, people were rising from their seats, throwing back the last of their drinks, and leading partners to a quickly expanding dance floor. Servants scurried to clear tables, dodging revelers and other workers alike. I spotted Liliana and Endre across the sea of bodies and led Taya in their direction, only for my lips to curl into a sneer when Izidora and Ruslan appeared beside them moments later.

This was my opportunity to make her jealous.

I remembered the sensual way we'd danced at the studio on the outskirts of Radence, how our bodies had molded and moved once she finally let go of her anger at me. My cock hardened, and I quickly pulled Taya flush with my front as we ground to the beat of the music, hoping she'd think it was all for her. The tune changed from a primal beat to a flowing, musical piece, and I immediately shifted into the role of a king courting a female, showing off my dancing prowess for those around us.

Taya was a good dancer, expertly flowing through the steps, the fabric of her dress creating a flurry of movement that attracted the attention of many. Her golden eyes never left mine as we danced, and as the song reached its climax, I gripped her waist and lifted her into the air, spinning her before setting her down on the other side of me. My gaze dropped to the swell of her breasts, but on the way back up, it was torn away. Beyond her was Izidora, hair unbound and spilling down her back like a chestnut waterfall, looking up at Ruslan like he was the only air she needed to breathe.

I needed her attention.

The song changed to a haunting melody, and Taya closed the distance between us, entwining our legs as I propelled her backward in a sensual dance the Iron Realm was known for. She tilted, and my hand dropped to her lower back to support her.

Her hips ground against mine before she peeled herself upright and brushed her hand against my chest. I spun her again, closing in on Izidora and Ruslan just in time for Taya to repeat the motion. The scraps of fabric she called a dress barely covered her skin, and every male around us watched on as we danced, whether they had a partner or not.

After the third dip, I yanked her upright and into my chest with a low growl, dipping my head to brush my lips along her ear. "You are so sexy. I can't wait to get you alone."

I lifted my eyes to find Izidora watching us, her lips thinned into a flat line and her brows pinched ever so slightly. Her gaze flicked from Taya to me and back before Ruslan twirled her, breaking our connection. Taya had flushed a pretty shade of peach at my words and proceeded to show me just how much she wanted us to be alone.

Around and around we went, always within sight of Izidora and Ruslan. Dipping and yanking and twirling until we panted for breath with the intensity of our movements. When the music died away, applause erupted around us, drawing my attention away from the female in my arms and to the gathered audience, only a handful of couples left in the center of the dance floor.

Izidora and Ruslan. Drazen and Natasha. The Angel and a female I did not know. Viktor and Aliana. Domi and Kaztar. King Airre and Queen Immonen. And finally, Endre and Liliana.

The tension among the dancing couples was tight enough to suffocate, and I quickly bowed to our audience, raising Taya's hand to my lips and kissing it reverently to the sound of more applause. When the music resumed, I leaned in and whispered in her ear. "Let's get out of here. I need to be inside you."

Her breath hitched, and as I pulled away, her eyes flamed with lust. "My place or yours?"

"Mine. I'm just down the hall."

I made a show of tugging her along behind me, our fingers

twined in a way that signaled we weren't just going to fetch a new drink. As we passed Izidora and Ruslan dancing at the fringes, I winked at her, then pushed into the crowd and out of sight, Taya in tow. That faint string between us vibrated nervously, and I smirked, my victory as sweet as I knew it would be.

40

RUSLAN

Béke Day Ten

"You need to tell the Félvér females to stay away from Kazimir," I instructed Rares as I stood in his office beneath the halls of Ryza. "Izidora was up most of the night last night worrying for Taya because she disappeared with Kazimir during the ball. He is not stable."

The old Mage huffed, not deigning to look up from his writing to respond. "Affairs between kings is not my area of expertise. He is your equal. You take care of it."

In the span of a breath, I had a hand planted on either side of the paper he scribbled on, my bared teeth inches from his face. "Do you forget who I am, Rares?"

He narrowed his eyes as he finally lifted his gaze from his work, his lips pulling apart to reveal his creepy, toothy grin. "No, My King. But since you refuse to let me continue my experiments, I fail to see how the Félvér are my problem any longer."

"Do you consider yourself to be their creator?" I hissed. "You've always liked playing Goddess, Rares. You can't turn your back on them now because you're pissed at me."

The Mage's face reddened as I called him on his bullshit. Izidora and I were the crown jewels, his greatest accomplishments, and he couldn't stand that we had more power and backbone than him. But that's what happened when he wanted to play Goddess without regard for the consequences.

"Fine," he spat, as if the word was a bitter potion. "On one condition."

I lifted a lazy brow. "I'll bite. What do you want?"

"At least let me study the new babes born to Félvér parents. I need to keep track of the winged ones especially, since they tend to have more physical ailments."

Rares was fucked in the head, but I couldn't deny his logic. I'd rather have healthy babes born in the Iron Realm, and if it were unavoidable, know how to help them. "Done. But none of the fucked up shit you used to do to us. Only assessment and observation. No potions. No magic unless I give explicit permission." I pushed back off the worn wood, tired of intimidating the man who had spent so long torturing me. "See to it that the word gets around to the Félvér not to get close to Kazimir."

Rares grumbled his response, but I at least heard him say he would take care of it. I left him hunched over his desk, allowing the heavy wood door to slam shut on my way out.

The tunnels beneath Ryza were eerily empty of people and noise, as most of the residents had sought other accommodations since being given free rein over the Iron Realm and encouraged to mingle with our guests. What I had done was good, right even, especially with how well our plans unfolded.

I'd gifted Zuriel a suite near ours a few days ago, especially since Kazimir had not stopped his menacing ways. He still leered at Izidora every chance he got, and clearly followed her to places he should not. Izidora was strong, as I had trained her to be, and she could take care of herself, but I wasn't leaving anything to chance – not with him still around. With everything

Zuriel had done for me – and Izidora – lately, he more than deserved a change in status.

Same with Drazen. I'd given him a similar set on the floor below so my general and all-around assistant was close by.

The long halls leading to my office allowed my mind to wander over the good deeds I'd done lately and onto the next steps in my plan to unite the realms and free the Félvér. More papers awaited my review before I could break for the day and find my mate. We would then head to the courtyard where the sprawling artisanal fair was already underway.

What would she wish for?

My greatest wish had finally come true, and our bond hummed as I reached down it, offering a soft caress against her mind. She returned one, a small, simple gesture to some, but just knowing she was there at any time to offer a whisper of comfort soothed the ache of loneliness in my chest, if only for a moment.

There was nothing I could wish for really, other than saving the Félvér from bloodshed in a war; I doubted the Goddess would, or could, answer that wish – not if it was as we suspected, and the Goddess battled with the Fates over the outcome of Északi.

The rest of the day passed in a blur as financiers, business owners, and lawyers rotated through my office like clockwork, all needing something from their king. By the time mid-afternoon rolled around, my head pounded from stress, and I needed a drink. Taking a break from my desk, I poured two fingers of whisky into a glass and stood by the window, watching over my kingdom as I sipped from it. My back was to the door, but I sensed the moment my mate slipped into the room, trying to be quiet so she could sneak up on me. If it weren't for the bond signaling her arrival, the scent of roses and plums would give her away every time.

I pretended not to notice her until she was moments away from grabbing me. In one swift motion, I downed my drink, tossed the glass, and hooked her to me, forcing her back against the glass window in front of me. "Did you really think you could surprise me?" I purred, caging her with my body.

Her floral arousal mixed with a hint of fear filled my nostrils, and I inhaled deeply, savoring that I could still make her heart pound.

"No," she whispered, looking up at me through long, dark lashes and chewing on her lip.

I caught it between my thumb and forefinger and ripped it from her teeth. "Sucking on that pink pout is my job," I reminded her.

Her fingers darted out from behind her back and walked their way up my chest until she cupped the side of my face, scratching at my beard with her nails. "It's also your job to help me buy a lantern."

I cocked my head as I gazed down at her. "Is that so?"

She nodded. "You are the one with all the money, after all."

"I see that I have spoiled you," I grinned, tracing my fingers along her collarbone. "I'm not mad about it."

She shrugged, some of her hair falling over her shoulder as she did so. "Me either. Now let's go." Her smile was breathtaking as she slipped from beneath me and tugged on my hand until I followed her to the door.

I stopped her in her tracks, needing to show her I was still in charge. With a tug, she was in my arms, and I bent her backward to prevent her from going anywhere as I hovered my lips over hers. "Say please."

"Please," she breathed, and I rewarded her with a brush of my lips over hers.

"Good girl," I said, releasing her from my embrace and intertwining our fingers. "Where is your cloak? It's cold today."

"Liliana has it," she replied.

"And where is–" I stopped mid-sentence when I opened the door and discovered Liliana flirting with the guards stationed there.

With a flick of her hair over her shoulder, she ended their conversation and left one of the young males standing with his mouth slightly agape as he watched her jog to catch up with us. She handed Izidora her cloak, and my mate fastened the large diamond at her throat before tugging the fabric around her to keep her warm. I smoothed the back of it, ensuring every bit of warmth it provided was given to her.

"Thanks," Izidora beamed up at me, so much love in her eyes that it almost physically hurt.

"I'll always take care of you," I reminded her.

"Can you two be less in love for a bit? I'm struggling over here," Liliana grumbled, and I tore my gaze from Izidora, lifting a brow at her.

"Trouble with Endre, or did Zuriel turn you down?" I guessed with a teasing lilt to my tone.

"I don't want to talk about it," she huffed, and I dropped it, since she and Izidora had likely hashed it out already.

The halls of Ryza buzzed with activity, excited voices echoing off the stone walls as people streamed out the main door and into the courtyard that bustled with activity. All morning, artisans had arrived, setting up booths from the barracks to the stables and everywhere in between. Color danced in all directions in front of the citadel, and it was nearly wall-to-wall with people.

"Where do you two want to go first? Over there," I indicated the direction of the stables, "is where you'll find stones, salves, and fresh goods. While over there," I indicated the direction of the barracks, "you'll find metalwork, woodwork, and other crafts. In the middle is where the lanterns and other Goddess-related artifacts are."

Izidora's stomach rumbled, and I had to suppress a smile. "Snack first," I said decisively.

"Are there sweets?" she asked.

"Of course there are. We'll make ourselves sick on them."

The crowd parted for the king of the Iron Realm, opening up an easy path for Izidora and Liliana to follow behind me. We found Drazen at a stall shoveling the treats in his mouth. The vendor offered brown sugar-coated balls with honey to dip, and by the looks of the empty cups beside him, Drazen had already had more than a few.

"Drazen! I didn't know you had a sweet tooth," Izidora laughed as he sheepishly looked up from his half-full cup.

"I don't. These are my favorite treats, and I can only get them during Béke," he mumbled through a mouthful of food.

The shopkeep tsked at him. "I've told you for the last several years that if you come to my shop I'll make them for you anytime."

"I think he needs the mental block of only eating them during Béke, otherwise he wouldn't stay in shape," Liliana teased, running a finger along the muscles of his free arm.

Drazen swallowed the last of his food and nodded. "Exactly."

The shopkeeper handed over four more cupfuls, and I paid her before the four of us continued our stroll around the stalls. Izidora and Liliana, unsurprisingly, stopped at several jewelry stands, oohing and aahing over the finely crafted rings and necklaces. Izidora wanted a set of tiny bands meant to fit around each knuckle, and I gladly handed over coins for them. The smile that crossed her face as she slipped them on was enough to make me weak at the knees.

"You're going soft." Drazen elbowed me in the side as we followed the females around.

I snorted. "Only for her. I still expect perfection from you and the guards. One fuck up, and you're done."

"Uh huh," Drazen responded, stealing a pastry from my cup.

I rolled my eyes and did not rise to his test. The throng of people around us was so thick that it was difficult to move, and the smells drifting on the breeze were an overwhelming mix of herbal concoctions, sharp metal, and sugary treats. I crinkled my nose at the combination, wishing for once that I didn't smell everything. Drazen did the same, though our female companions didn't seem to notice when they stopped in front of a stall selling soaps, candles, and salves. We waited several paces back to avoid the worst of the combination, and mutterings of 'My King' filled the space around us as my subjects offered me the proper respect. I nodded in acknowledgment to most of them, though I refrained from speaking. Even though the Félvér numbers grew every year, power was still respected most of all in the Iron Realm, as with every other realm on the continent.

And I was the most powerful Fae, and Félvér, in the whole of it.

Finally, Izidora and Liliana returned to us, the two casually passing off their new items for us to hold before linking arms and beelining to a stall at the end of the stables. Mistik's gray head popped out of the open door, and she neighed merrily when she noticed her rider.

Drazen smothered a snicker as I followed, my arms laden with goods, smelling as unkingly as possible with the floral scents rolling off me. "What was it you wanted the other realms to see? Wealth, strength, and power?"

"Fuck off, Drazen," I grumbled with a hint of amusement.

Once Izidora finished giving her mare attention, I suggested we select lanterns for the following day's events before all the good ones were gone. Drazen led the way through the crowd until row after row of paper lanterns stretched toward the open doors of Ryza Citadel. They were a kaleidoscope of color, ranging from light hues that were cheery and bright to deep hues reminiscent of the night sky.

"What color is your favorite?" Izidora asked me, her eyes wide with the vast selection before her.

"I always get black," I stated, lifting one so dark it swallowed up all the light around it.

"Last year I got a light blue," Liliana said, standing on her tiptoes to gain a better view of the lanterns at the opposite end. "This year I think I might buy a green one."

"What about you, Drazen?" Izidora asked.

"I'm leaning toward this red one," he replied, selecting a scarlet color that reminded me of the blood I had spilled killing Izidora's former guards.

"Wander until you find a color that speaks to you," I encouraged my mate, gesturing for her to continue walking. With a wry grin, I dumped my armload of goods into Drazen's unsuspecting hands and followed her away while Liliana perused the lanterns nearby.

Slipping my freed hand into hers, I allowed her to lead me through the people, some bent over the spread of lanterns, examining the color and quality and asking questions about the craft. Every time Izidora stopped to admire one, I took the opportunity to scan our surroundings for any sign of Kazimir. Some of the other Night Fae were huddled together off in the distance, but thankfully, there was no sign of the new king.

King Airre and Queen Immonen were picking through a set of pastel-colored lanterns a dozen feet away, and I greeted them as we approached. "Your Majesties, are you finding everything you're looking for?"

"Oh, yes, these hues are lovely," Queen Immomen enthused, then turned to kiss Izidora on either cheek in greeting. "What color are you thinking, dear?"

Izidora lifted a single shoulder, then dropped it, her focus on the array of paper lanterns. "I haven't seen anything that I'm drawn to yet."

"I think I know just the one for you. It was a few stalls back," she exclaimed, tugging Izidora by the hand through the crowd. I kept a watchful eye on them as they lifted one after the other, examining them and chatting merrily as they did so.

I took the opportunity to speak to the king of the Crystal Realm without our mates around to distract us. "So, King Airre, I've been meaning to speak with you alone regarding King Kazimir, but I'm afraid my other duties have kept me quite busy."

"Oh? What about him?" King Airre responded, his attention divided between the lanterns and me, in an attempt to dissuade anyone around us from listening to our conversation by making it appear unimportant.

"Yesterday, after we returned from the hunt, he attacked Izidora." I allowed the words to fall with a seriousness that befitted them, my voice hardening over each word.

King Airre sucked in a sharp breath, subtly shaking his head after. "Did he lay hands on her?"

"Yes, he struck her across the face, then forced her to the ground and choked her." My fists clenched, nails digging into my palms as my fury flared anew.

The king's head snapped up. "Is she alright?"

"She was badly shaken but managed to defend herself until Zuriel, the Angel, came to her aid," I replied.

"I have let many things slide during my reign, but one I have never condoned is violence against females," the king of the Crystal Realm spat out, as disgusted with Kazimir's actions as I hoped he'd be.

"He is the newly crowned king of the Night Realm, but I find it inexcusable as well." Izidora and I had not been public about accepting the mating bond because of her worry that Kazimir would snap and do something crazy when he found out. But I knew the final card I needed to play to convince King Airre to break his alliance. Dropping my voice and leaning in so others would not overhear, I said, "Izidora and I have accepted our mating bond. You can understand how difficult it is for me to allow him to wander the halls of our home unchecked."

King Airre blanched, his lips drawing into a thin line before they broke into a grin and he clapped me on the shoulder. "Congratulations, King Ruslan. I am pleased for you both. I wish you all the happiness the Goddess has to offer. Being mated was the best thing that ever happened to me." His attention turned to his wife, still poring over the lanterns with my mate a few stalls away.

"As with me," I agreed, returning the gesture. "I hope we can continue to build relations between the Iron and Crystal Realms since we share such special bonds."

He regarded me for a moment before answering. "I would like that very much. Would it be possible to arrange a... private dinner for the monarchs of Day, Crystal, and Iron tonight?"

The wicked grin I wanted to display remained hidden beneath my carefully practiced mask as I answered. "That can be arranged. Why don't we dine on one of the balconies overlooking Radence? There is one with a lovely view I'm sure you would appreciate."

"As long as you have some fires going. It's too cold here," King Airre chuckled, feigning a shiver to emphasize his point.

"Noted. I'll send someone to fetch you this evening," I promised.

Izidora and Queen Immonen returned moments later, both carrying lanterns. The queen's was a light lilac shade that matched the color of her dress, and her husband immediately voiced his approval of her choice, kissing her until she shoved at his chest, claiming he would crush her selection.

Izidora returned to my side with a lantern so white that it nearly filled the whole courtyard with light. "It's perfect," I grinned down at her, tucking a lock of chestnut behind her ear.

"I think so too," she smiled back, melting my heart with how happy she was.

"You've always been my light in the dark, and now your lantern will guide mine to the Goddess like the beacon of hope that it is." I pulled her flush against me and pressed my mouth to hers, not caring who viewed their king showing his devotion to their future queen. In only a few days, we'd be married, mated, and crowned together, and I couldn't fucking wait.

A throat cleared behind me, forcing me to break away from Izidora. Drazen and Liliana waited there, both holding the lanterns they'd selected, plus the black one I'd picked out for myself. "Ready to go to the other side?" Liliana asked, her seafoam green eyes dancing with amusement.

"First, we need to make a trip upstairs. I have a feeling we'll be buying more," Izidora laughed, lifting some of her items from Drazen's precarious pile. I snatched my lantern before it tumbled to the ground, then grabbed Izidora's before saying goodbye to the king and queen of the Crystal Realm. The crowd had thinned, making it easier to navigate the distance between us and the open doors of the citadel. A small smile tugged at the corner of my lips as I carried our things inside.

I had spoiled Izidora, but she deserved it, and I wouldn't have it any other way.

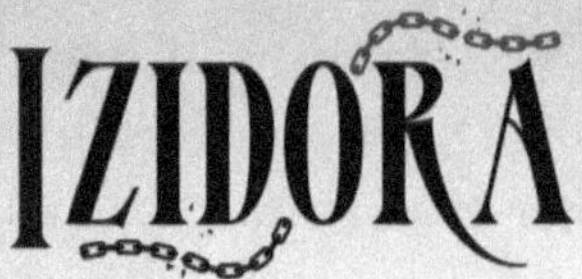IZIDORA

BÉKE DAY TEN

The large terrace overlooking Radence was finely decorated for entertaining our noble guests. Fire tables like the ones Ruslan had used when he asked me to marry him ringed the round table, blasting heat on the dark, chilly night. Soft candlelight flickered on the table and above us, adding elegance and romance to the atmosphere.

When Ruslan told me that King Airre had asked for a private dinner for the monarchs, without Kazimir, my heart leaped to my throat. The time spent winning them over, slowly but surely, had paid off. We would be able to unite the realms, bring peace, and allow all peoples to live in harmony with one another. Zuriel and the other Telivér, as well as the Félvér, had mixed and mingled with them as well, and their presence melted my wariness away like the snow on a sunny day.

The six of us settled around the round table, blood-red rose petals decorating the center so nothing blocked our views of one another. Servants appeared and disappeared with fine wine and delicious food, and no one's glass was ever empty. The monarch of the Crystal Realm needed to be thoroughly flattered before we broached the subject of Kazimir, and Ruslan ensured that success with the fine meal he arranged.

I was seated between the two monarchs of the Day Realm, while Ruslan sat across from me, between the two monarchs of the Crystal Realm. The placement felt balanced and non-threatening, seeming to place us all on equal ground.

Queen Viktoria's colorful attire stood out among the six of us, the bright, warm yellow of her dress almost replacing the sun as the stars winked to life above us. King Consort Geza wore a matching yellow ensemble, the color nearly as deep as his voice. He was by far the biggest male I'd ever seen, and yet he exuded a warmth that put me at ease. "King Consort Geza, what part of the Day Realm are you from?"

"Believe it or not, I am from a tiny fishing village close to the border with the Iron Realm. Growing up, I could sit on the tip of my father's boat and gaze upon the peaks of the Agrenak Mountains," he replied, then lifted a piece of flaky fish to his mouth and chewed slowly.

"It sounds lovely. I'd love to explore more of the continent. I spent too long in one place." I sipped my wine, savoring the crisp taste as it washed over my tongue.

"I agree. It is far too cold here in the Iron Realm. You are welcome to warm your bones in the Day Realm anytime," he chuckled.

"I will hold you to that," I grinned back.

"And you must visit us in the Crystal Realm," Queen Immonen exclaimed, lifting her glass of wine to me.

I mirrored her. "Absolutely. You said this white wine is from one of your vineyards?"

"It is. King Ruslan has good taste," she enthused, glancing at my mate.

"In more than one respect," he replied, shooting me a look that held enough heat to make me blush.

Dessert was a fluffy vanilla cake with fruit-filled frosting, and I nearly moaned at the way it melted in my mouth. Sweets would never cease to amaze me.

Queen Viktoria chuckled beside me. "I have the excuse of growing a babe in my belly to eat an extra slice of this."

"I'll have to train twice as hard tomorrow for the next two slices I'm eating," I replied, shoveling another forkful in my mouth without regard for proper decorum.

"Do you train every day?" she asked, dabbing her mouth with a napkin.

"I do. It is what makes me feel strong, powerful, like I can defend myself after so long of not being able to." The queen flattened her lips, concern passing over her brow. She had seen the scars on my back the day we shopped for dresses, so she knew just how powerless I had been. "It was thanks to my training that I was able to force Kazimir off me when he attacked me yesterday."

A hush fell over the group like my words had sucked all the oxygen from the space around us.

"King Ruslan mentioned that. Can you tell us exactly what happened?" King Airre requested, his words careful and slow.

Before describing our encounter, I sipped from my wine to steady myself. "The males had returned from the hunt while I was training with the Angel, Zuriel, and High Lady Liliana. I ran to greet Ruslan, and afterward, he helped carry the stag inside. I watched them go, only to be stopped when Kazimir approached. He told me you almost died in the mountains again, trying to make me feel sympathy for him. When I didn't give him that and tried to leave, he used his magic to stop me, slapped me, called me a bitch, shoved me down, and tried to choke me. Thankfully, I was able to get him off, and

Zuriel was nearby to assist me in returning to the citadel safely."

Queen Viktoria shook with anger, throwing her napkin onto the table as she scoffed. "Unbelievable. And he calls you his mate. No male would *ever* treat their mate that way."

"I can confirm that," King Airre offered, the grip around his fork so tight I thought he might bend it.

"There is more." Ruslan released a heavy sigh, lifting his glass and swirling the wine in it. "Kazimir has binding magic."

"Binding magic?" The queen of the Day Realm spit the words out like a bitter potion.

I nodded. "When he attacked me, the magic he threw at me was like two black ropes, crawling toward me. They were sinister, slithering almost, and if it weren't for my training, I wouldn't have been able to blast them away as quickly as I did."

King Consort Geza made a disapproving noise in the back of his throat. "In the Day Realm, binding magic is the worst of omens. It only breeds evil in the heart of its bearer. How long has he been in possession of it?"

"According to my sources, since the Night Fae stopped in the Crystal Realm," Ruslan answered for me, and I was grateful that he did not reveal Liliana as our source of information.

King Airre paled, nearly matching the shade of his blonde hair. "How... how did we not know?" He and his wife held a long look, and I gathered that they spoke mind to mind.

Their connection broke, and he returned his attention to me. "We knew they kept secrets from us because when we arrived in the Day Realm, they revealed your heritage, Princess Izidora. Kazimir had plenty of time to convey the information between arriving at Blire Palace and entering Aress Keep, but he chose not to disclose until he was under pressure to do so."

"It appears the Night Realm holds many secrets. Who knows what else they aren't telling us?" King Consort Geza mused, reaching for his wife's hand across the table. I leaned back to provide them space to embrace.

"We must not ally ourselves with the Night Realm any longer," his wife declared, and for the first time all evening, my chest loosened.

Their alliance was breaking apart, and there would be no war.

"The Crystal Realm will no longer ally with the Night Realm," King Airre seconded, Queen Immonen also offering an affirmative nod.

"It is a relief that you understand the severity of our situation. Kazimir is dangerous, and as you can see, Izidora wants nothing to do with him. We are ready to be mated, married, and crowned in a few days. I hope you will remain in the Iron Realm following our wedding and coronation to celebrate with us."

Ruslan certainly knew how to turn up his charm when he wanted to. Even after all this time, he continued to surprise me with different sides of himself.

I realized it hadn't been that long – not really. Still, the way I felt about Ruslan transcended time, lifetimes even, and I simultaneously felt that I'd known him forever and would never know him long enough.

"Only if you continue to provide us with these delectable treats. I'm afraid my babe loves them a little too much," Queen Viktoria chuckled, smoothing a hand across her belly.

"What the little princess wants, she gets," King Consort Geza cooed, thumb brushing across the back of his wife's hand.

The conversation returned to lighter topics, and Ruslan grinned impishly across the table, the heat in his eyes promising a thrilling celebration after we'd finished our royal dinner.

"Only a few more days until you're mine in every possible way, sprite."

"I can't wait."

42

KAZIMIR

BÉKE DAY ELEVEN

I knocked on the door to the Crystal Fae's temporary residence after breakfast, having slept so late I nearly missed it. I'd been up all night again with Taya, whose sexual appetite was nearly insatiable. It was a good thing I had my own pent-up sexual frustrations to work out, and she was a good substitute for the female I truly wanted.

King Airre had asked me to come alone, so I snuck away from Endre, Viktor, Vadim, and Kaztar, who were all off gallivanting about the Iron Realm doing shit I didn't care for as Ruslan continued to flash his obnoxious wealth for all the realms to see.

King Airre himself opened the door, much to my surprise, and he ushered me inside before peering up and down the hall, no doubt to ensure no one would be eavesdropping at the door. I strode into the room, brimming with self-confidence until the sight of Queen Viktoria and King Consort Geza stopped me in my tracks. Recovering myself, I said, "Ah, Queen Viktoria, King Consort Geza, I wasn't expecting to see you here."

"Please, have a seat," King Airre said from behind me, and I squared my shoulders before dropping onto a leather couch across from the monarchs of the Day Realm and adjacent to the chair Queen Immonen perched in. King Airre settled himself in a chair opposite his wife, and suddenly, the visit seemed more like an interrogation than a friendly chat.

"Is King Ruslan joining us?" I asked, trying to keep my tone neutral. Glancing around the room, I noted the absence of the Crystal Realm's High Lords.

"No, it will be only us talking," Queen Viktoria said, her eyes holding a hardness to them I'd never seen before.

The binding magic slumbering in my chest woke as I sensed a looming threat. Running a hand over my face, I tried to appear calm and collected as I reclined back against the couch. "What would you like to discuss?"

King Airre leaned forward, bracing his elbows on his knees as he leveled his gaze on me. "Kazimir," he started, trailing off before clearing his throat and straightening. "You have not been completely honest with us."

His informal use of my name irked me, but I waited for him to continue. When he didn't, I asked, "How so?"

"Did you receive any new magic recently?" King Consort Geza's tone was flat and directed at me like a well-thrown spear.

"How recently?" I asked, lifting a brow.

But Queen Viktoria was having none of my games. "Cut the shit, King Kazimir. You may be a ruler now, but when you came to us, you were a High Lord. We put the lives of our people on the line for a cause *you* convinced us to join, and yet you didn't reveal all your information."

Who fucking told them about the binding magic?

Gritting my teeth and shouting down that black beast rumbling in my chest, I retorted, "Because what I gained was extremely valuable and would help us in the war. If Ruslan had found out before we launched our attack, it would have put us at a disadvantage."

"So you do admit that you gained new magic?" King Airre pressed.

"Yes," I spat out like it was venom, my vision darkening as that magic thrashed in my chest, begging to be released.

"And what is it?" he asked again, his tone condescending.

How dare they corner me and scold me like a petulant child.

With a wave of my hand, I released a snake-like rope onto the table separating us, expanding it so it engulfed the table, wrapping around itself. Making a fist with my hand, I commanded it to squeeze, and moments later, the metal groaned until it collapsed inward with a screech.

"Binding magic," Queen Immonen hissed, looking from the table to me with utter disgust.

Banishing it with a dismissive wave, I turned my attention to her, King Airre stiffening on the fringes of my vision. "Yes, binding magic. I can throw these ropes around Ruslan and the other mongrels, suffocating their magic until we can slaughter them all. We will win because of this."

The queen of the Crystal Realm's eyes turned white, her head dropping back as her empty gaze fell toward the sky. King Airre burst by me moments later, supporting his wife as the sight claimed her. The monarchs of the Day Realm gripped the edges of their seats, waiting for Queen Immonen to return to us. I half rose, planning to leave, but a sharp look from Queen Viktoria stilled me.

Several minutes passed before Queen Immonen gasped, clutched her chest, and whipped her head forward. "What did you see, my love?" King Airre asked, stroking her platinum hair as he kneeled beside her.

She shook her head. "I need time to make sense of what I saw. There was... so much."

His brows pinched, but he nodded. "Later, then."

Scooting along the edge of the couch, I took King Airre's former seat, allowing the mated pair to sit together on the couch, and finally I felt like I had some power over the situation unfolding before me.

But Queen Viktoria sliced right through it. "The Fates are seeking to manipulate you, King Kazimir, and I want no part of their games for my daughter." Her hands covered her swelling belly as if the simple movement could protect her unborn child from the evil lurking within me.

"So, what, you want to break our alliance?" I growled, gripping the arms of my chair so hard the wood beneath my fingers protested.

"The Day Realm will not fight with the Night Realm should you decide to attack the Iron Realm," she declared, and her husband made a noise of affirmation.

The wood snapped as I dragged my attention to King Airre. "And what of the Crystal Realm?"

He glanced from his wife to me, then back before finally blowing out a breath. "We will not fight against the Iron Realm either."

"Are you fucking kidding me?" I seethed, my anger rising like a tidal wave and smashing into me before I could even begin to control myself. "Who told you about this? Who betrayed me?"

King Airre pressed his lips together, and I ripped my focus to Queen Viktoria. "Your malevolent magic is not the only information that helped us arrive at this decision," she said sternly.

"Oh? What else is there?" I ground out through clenched teeth. My leg bounced as I tried to banish the overwhelming urge to rip every piece of furniture in this room to shreds.

"We heard that you attacked Princess Izidora," she replied, her eyes narrowed on me and disapproval emanating from her pores.

The muscles in my jaw worked overtime as I forced myself to breathe through the darkness threatening to suck me under. "From whom?"

"You did it in the middle of the day, in a courtyard filled with people. Did you really think no one would notice?" King Airre snapped, his patience worn thin. He pinched the bridge of his nose, giving his head a slight shake. "Willfully harming a female is one of the most frowned upon actions in the entire continent. We cannot stand by you now that we have definitive proof of what you've done."

Yet, none of the Night Fae knew what had happened, and I had ensured no one was around by the time I cornered Izidora. Which only meant one thing...

This was entirely Ruslan and Izidora's doing.

Somehow, the two of them had uncovered the exact nature of my magic, and that, combined with Izidora attacking me with her empath magic, had swayed the other monarchs to betray our cause.

Snakes, every last one of them.

I had fucking hated King Zalan for this very reason – all the political bullshit, backroom deals, and self-interested maneuvering he'd done with the other realms, especially within his own. There was no redeeming the other realms, and I didn't need shit from them to win this war. I would do it all on my own and prove to them they shouldn't have broken our alliance.

Backstabbing bastards.

"Did she tell you she tortured me?" I growled, the memory of the whips stinging my back still just as fresh as the day it had happened.

"Who tortured you?" Queen Viktoria questioned, the disbelief in her tone only serving to piss me off more.

"Izidora. She's an empath, you know. Her magic is just as deadly as mine," I pointed out.

"Her magic is only deadly if she uses it for the wrong reasons, and from what I know of her, she would never willingly harm someone unless her life was in peril," Queen Immonen rebuked, finally recovering from her vision. The glare she offered me was lethal, like she wanted me to freeze to death on the spot, and I was certain if no one was around, she might have done just that.

Shooting to my feet, I towered over the seated monarchs, fists clenching and unclenching rapidly. "So that's it then? You're choosing *them* over me?"

"We never said that," King Consort Geza placated, raising his hands in the air as if he were trying to calm a wild beast. "Only that we would not fight with the Night Realm against the Iron Realm."

"Fine. Then I guess we are finished here." Without waiting for a response, I stomped through the room, throwing the door open with a bang, and stalked down the hall until I found myself in the stables, with a wide-eyed stablehand rushing to fetch Fek.

All I saw was red as anger and malice battled for control within me, and without even acknowledging the stablehand, I snatched Fek's reins and spurred him on. We flew down the path leading into Radence, and I didn't stop until we reached Taya's house. Flinging the reins over the hook outside, I banged on the door until the female appeared.

"Kazimir–" she started, but I shoved the door open and captured her in my arms, kissing her roughly as I backed her to the bed.

I sucked her lower lip into my mouth, biting hard enough to bruise, and she whimpered, her nails digging into my back and raking down, bidding me to give her more. Without warning, I broke our kiss and shoved her backward, splaying her out for me. All she wore was a silver dressing robe, and I ripped it open, bracing my hands on either side of her as I sucked a nipple into my mouth. She cried out, arching into me, and I used my teeth to rake across her nipple before moving on to the other one.

Her hands grasped at my tunic, and I broke away momentarily to rip off my jacket and tear my tunic over my head. Pushing her flat against the bed with one hand, I used the other to cup her center. "So fucking wet already, Taya. I need to be inside you. I need to fuck you hard. Can you handle that?"

She whimpered as I stroked her folds. "Yes. Fuck me as hard as you want."

Slapping her core, I said, "Good girl. Grab the headboard."

Without hesitation, she slipped out of the arms of her robe and turned to her knees, both hands gripping the metal posts propping up the back of the bed. She remained there as I unlaced my pants and heeled out of my boots. The mattress dipped as I put my weight on it, and I wasted no time lining my hardness with her swollen center. The dried cum stains from our fucking the night before remained on the inside of her thigh.

"You didn't wash me off."

"Never," she moaned as I swiped the head of my cock up and down her slit.

With my free hand, I slapped her ass, hard, leaving behind a red handprint that would surely bruise. Something between a yelp and a moan left her lips. "Again," she begged.

I repeated the motion on her other cheek, leaving matching handprints for her to remember me each time she sat.

"Keep going," she begged, and I spanked her five times in quick succession, each strike harder than the last. The wetness that poured out of her core dripped onto my cock, mixing with the moisture beaded there.

"Beg me to fuck you," I commanded, and her pussy clenched in response.

"Please, please fuck me, My King," she whined.

"Why?" I asked, giving her center a few lazy strokes with my fingers.

"Because you're my king, my hero, my savior, and I want you to make me come."

I couldn't deny that.

Without warning, I speared into her from behind, seating myself fully without giving her time to adjust. She cried out, knuckles whitening as she gripped the poles for support. The pounding I gave her was relentless, violent, and shook the whole bed. If it weren't for her grip, we probably would have broken the wall.

I punctuated my thrusts with slaps to her ass, letting the force of my strikes satiate the sting of betrayal from my alliance falling apart and Izidora being the cause of it. My nails dug into Taya's hips as I gripped her harder, yanking her down on my cock as I thrust it into her, imagining I was doling out the punishment to Izidora instead.

She'd been so fucking bad, and I'd allowed it to go on for far too long.

Taya panted as I brought her closer and closer to climax, her cries becoming broken and desperate as she called my name over and over. "Kazimir, please, I–"

"You may call me my king, my savior, or my hero – nothing else," I growled, spanking her for her insolence.

"Yes, My King," she mewled, arching her back as I ground my hips into her.

"You take my cock so good," I praised, and she lowered herself further, still gripping the poles, so I could deepen the angle. The position bared her puckered hole to me, so I spit onto it, then gathered some of the wetness from her thighs and circled the mixture there. "I'm going to fill your ass with my fingers."

"Please, My King. Give me everything you've got. Make me come."

I worked a finger in, and she pushed back shamelessly into me, her ass sucking my digit down before pushing it back out again. Through her inner walls, my cock and finger rubbed against each other, adding to the already incredible sensation of her tight holes. By the time I worked a second finger in, she was vibrating with barely restrained tension, moments away from coming.

"Don't you dare come until I tell you," I growled, seating myself fully inside her.

"Yes, my hero. I will wait for your command to come," she panted, hands trembling around the bars.

With my one free hand, I slapped her ass again, the red beginning to deepen to purple. "Tighten your grip."

She did, and the combination of my fingers in her ass and the tightness of her pussy caused me to see stars. "Yes," I hissed, driving my hips harder and deeper. My balls tightened with my impending release, and I thickened inside her. Her walls began fluttering in response, and I chased her to the edge before allowing her to let go.

"Come for me," I growled, releasing ropes of my seed inside her as I plunged my fingers in and out of her ass. Her center milked me dry as she came, crying out and arching her back so deeply I swore my cock was in her stomach.

Dropping her hands from the bars, she panted, unable to move. I pulled out of her, then went to wash myself quickly in the adjacent bathroom, returning to her bedroom once I heard her shift off of the bed. She was wrapping the robe around herself, and I closed the distance between us, capturing her for a bruising kiss before allowing her to fasten it.

As my heart rate returned to normal, so did the rage that had neared a boil within me. I quickly redressed, then wandered into the living space, where she stood in a small kitchen pouring herself a glass of wine. "Want any?" she asked casually, like I hadn't been screwing her senseless minutes before.

"No thanks. I need to get back."

"Will I see you tonight at the lantern release?" she questioned, a hint of hope in her voice.

"Sure, we can release ours together," I offered. It wasn't what I truly wanted to do, but I could play along in hopes of flaunting it in Izidora's face.

A smile spread slowly across her face. "See you then."

I nodded, then returned to the bitter cold and my waiting mount. Maybe stringing Taya along with the promise of more was wrong, but she was always willing to let me sink into her pussy and forget everything else, and that was exactly what I needed.

But I also needed to address the real problem if I wanted a solution to it, and that meant getting Izidora alone. Plotting how to do exactly that filled my thoughts as I returned to the citadel.

43

ZURIEL

BÉKE DAY ELEVEN

All around Radence, lanterns and fires winked out of existence in a slow wave, starting at the edges of the city until only the citadel's fires still burned. Then they too were extinguished, bathing Radence in complete darkness. The galaxy of stars above joined the crescent moon in casting a hint of light over us, but no more. A sky this clear during the winter was rare, without a cloud promising snowfall in sight. It was as if the Goddess wanted this night to be remembered by all present.

Of all my years in the Iron Realm, I'd never participated in the lantern release. Truly, I'd never wanted to, even though some of the other Telivér did during the years when the Iron Realm did not host Béke. But this year I relished buying one of the paper lanterns, accompanied by the Demons. Something sparked in my chest as I stumbled upon a light teal one, and I smiled to myself as I picked it up and paid for it, clutching it against my chest like it was the most precious gift I'd ever received.

Silence reigned among us as we waited for the ceremony to begin.

The most important members of the Iron Realm and all the guests were situated on a balcony overlooking the entire city, and at the very edge of it, a raised dais allowed the High Priestess unparalleled access to the worshippers. The black dress she wore whipped in the wind as she called for us to open our hearts to the gifts the Goddess would bestow, her voice magically amplified to carry around the valley. She continued her speech, becoming more impassioned with each subsequent sentence.

I tuned her out as small flaming sticks were passed among those of us who did not have fire magic. The Iron Fae and Félvér reached inside their lanterns, igniting them with a spark from the tips of their fingers. Beside me, Izidora called on her white flame, holding it to the wick of her lantern and filling the already stunningly white paper with even more brightness. Beside her, Ruslan did the same, the black flames darkening the black paper.

The two lanterns competed for space, one fighting off the darkness and the other sucking the light away.

Before me, pinpricks of dim, colorful light rippled into existence as the Fae and Félvér lining the streets of Radence joined us in igniting their lanterns. It was as if the stars overhead had fallen to the ground and scattered themselves across the land, stretching well into the distance. Where did the sky end and the ground begin?

"... hold in your heart your deepest desire, and reveal it for the Goddess to see," the High Priestess boomed over the crowd. I closed my eyes, but instead of opening my heart, I opened my mind.

"I wish to find a way forward for Endre and me," Liliana wished.

"I wish that Liliana would choose me above everyone else," Endre wished.

"My wish is to be known as a great general after the war," Viktor wished.

"I wish that my true love would make herself known so I can finally settle down," Vadim wished.

"My wish is for some new pussy to show up at Steel," Slavian wished.

"Please, Goddess, don't let my friends die in the coming war," Drazen wished.

"I wish that Ruslan would allow me to continue my experiments," Rares wished.

"I wish that Atros would admit how he feels," Anton wished.

"I wish that Kaztar would see Kazimir's true side," Domi wished.

"Goddess, please keep Domi safe in our home during the war. I couldn't live with myself if anything happened to her," Kaztar wished.

"I wish that we could have peace," Izidora wished.

"I have nothing to wish for, Goddess. You have granted me all I have asked for in my mate," Ruslan said.

Closing my mind off from those around me, I opened my heart to my one and only wish.

"I wish for war."

The High Priestess began chanting, a haunting melody that raised the hairs on my arms. The song speared into me, as if she'd sent a tendril of magic into each of us and pulled our heart's desires straight from our chests. One by one, hands dropped away from lanterns, allowing them to float away. Reds, blues, greens, purples, and pinks in every shade and hue filled the sky, creating a rainbow of color among the stars.

But one black and one white lantern stood out amongst the colors. They raced toward the heavens, overtaking the ones released before them until they towered over us all. The crowd's attention followed the two as they danced with one another through the sky, soaring higher and higher, seemingly propelled by magic. They peaked, pausing in midair and floating as if they were gazing down upon the world beneath them.

And then, everything fell into place.

The white lantern lit by white flame exploded with brightness, evoking cries of reverence and horror and forcing people to shield their eyes from the blinding light.

But I did not avert my gaze as Izidora's lantern highlighted every detail in the Iron Realm and beyond, filling the land with white light.

Thoughts around me rang out with curses, but the ones closest to me were filled with realization as the finality of the prophecy settled across each and every noble Fae in attendance. There was no denying that Izidora was the prophesied one, and Ruslan along with her.

It truly was a tragedy that Izidora had wished for peace, because in the coming year, there would, without a doubt, be war.

Her eyes were as wide as the full moon as her focus bounced between the lanterns, Ruslan, and me, and neither of us bothered to hide the truth from her or each other. Ruslan and I locked eyes above her, and a slight dip in his chin told me he understood as well as I did what the blinding moment meant.

The Goddess's Prophecy was coming to pass, and it was time for everyone to choose a side.

***

INTERLUDE

The magical history teacher droned on, and three young Night Fae propped their heads up with their hands in an attempt to stay awake. But one by one, they dropped to the table in front of them, their eyes drifting closed while their thoughts drifted to anything but the history of magic. Outside, the sun shone, spilling through the stained glass and onto the teacher's desk, almost begging him to end the lecture so the younglings could stretch their wings and fly.

With a heavy sigh, he snapped his book shut, startling the three from their slumber. The messy-haired one woke first, rubbing the heels of his palms into his peridot eyes to clear them. Beside him, the emerald-eyed one yawned and performed a lazy overhead stretch, while the one on the end with the neatly-styled hair took his time rising, blinking wearily as the room refocused.

"This is my last day teaching you three before our summer break, and while I know you'd rather be out there learning to fight with swords, the lessons I am teaching you are important," the teacher scolded. "One day, the lessons you learn in here could save your life. History tends to repeat itself, and more often than not, those who rise to power lose it in the same way as they gained it."

"Yes, sir," they grumbled in unison, straightening in their seats and blinking to clear the last fog of sleep.

"Good, now, during the Age of Prophecy, many with the sight had near-constant visions, some even dying from lack of sleep due to them. The most prophetic seers had round-the-clock observers waiting to scrawl down anything they said. As for the rest... well, there was so much chaos that many of those slips of paper were discarded as nonsense, never expected to come true. Scholars have tracked events that unfolded exactly as prophesied in the centuries since, and only a few viable candidates remain out of the hundreds of slips still in existence. Many have been tossed out as events unfolded differently or the world changed enough that their predictions were irrelevant. Of those unfulfilled prophecies, magical historians believe only three will ever come to pass: the Goddess's Prophecy, the Five Brothers, and the Torn Veil."

The youngling with the peridot eyes interrupted the teacher. "Why only those three?"

"Because of certain lines in them. For example, from the Goddess's Prophecy, there is a line speaking of a white light filling the land. No Fae in Északi possesses magic of a white color, which means something in the future will have to happen to bring white magic to the continent. The Five Brothers speaks of seeking refuge in a distant land, and the Torn Veil speaks of our world dying. As you can see, none of those has come to pass yet, and it would take an enormous upheaval to make them happen. History tends to repeat itself, as I have said many times, therefore, they are likely to come to pass during times of immense change on our continent. Everything has been relatively peaceful in Északi for hundreds of years, and in the continents beyond for longer than that. The last great war was between the Angels and Demons in Keleti. Even the skirmishes we had in Északi do not compare to that. No, there needs to be an event on that scale for these prophecies to come to pass."

The teacher paused, all but one of his students' eyes glazed over again. Placing the heavy leather-bound tome on his desk, he turned to the chalkboard behind him and began scribbling instructions on it. "Your summer reading will be these three prophecies, as well as an essay on the work of a seer from the Age of Prophecy. I will see you three at the end of the summer. Enjoy yourselves."

The one with peridot eyes scratched down the assignment while the other two packed up their belongings and sprinted toward the door. "Have a nice summer, Professor!" they called over their shoulders, disappearing down the hall. The one they left behind heard their whooping cry as they burst into the sunshine. He took his time packing his belongings, gave their teacher a heartfelt thank you, and then followed his friends into the warm air.

"C'mon, Endre, it's time to have fun!" the one with sage green eyes said, punching him in the arm.

"Your idea of fun and mine are a bit different, Viktor," he replied.

The third one threw his arms over the shoulders of the other two, yanking them close to him. "We're going to spend the whole summer at Este Castle. My father promised he'd be there the whole time instead of out looking for the lost princess."

"Children! Come this way," Endre's mother called out to them.

"Mother, we're not children anymore. We're fourteen now," Endre chided her as they traipsed through the garden toward the waiting female.

"You three have grown up so fast," she said, eyes shining as she examined them. "Kazimir, your father wrote, and he said to tell you he's sorry that he won't be at Este Castle to greet us, but that he will join us as soon as he's able. Now come, I've made you some cookies to celebrate your break from lessons."

The youngling's arms dropped away from his friends' shoulders, and he slumped inward on himself as he followed his friend's mother inside their home – the place he had called home too often since his father was called away to search for the lost princess.

Endre bumped his shoulder, drawing his attention away from the floor. "I know you were looking forward to seeing him, Kazimir."

"Yeah. Since mother died, all he can think about is the princess. I wish he would come home more. No offense meant, I like staying here with you, but sometimes I wish he'd be the one asking me how our lessons went at the end of the day," Kazimir replied.

"Hopefully, he isn't caught up too long with whatever is keeping him away."

The emerald-eyed one offered a half shrug. "Hopefully."

IV

THE CLOSING

44

RUSLAN

Béke Day Twelve

"So what's the lineup for tonight?" I asked Drazen, who held several sheets of paper in his hand, shuffling through them as he tried to find his place.

"A ballet, fire jugglers, another dance, dog trainers, someone telling jokes, a poetry read–"

"No poetry," I cut Drazen off before he could finish. "Give them something for their time regardless, but there will be no poetry tonight."

His ocean-blue eyes lifted from his papers, along with a raised brow. "May I ask why?"

"Because of what happened to Izidora," I said, cracking my knuckles as the memory of her flashback in my tent during our trip between the Night and Iron Realms surfaced in my mind. "The last time she heard poetry, she lost touch with reality. She told me that her female keepers used to force her to recite it and punish her if she messed up."

Drazen paled, though his eyes flamed with anger. "That's so fucked up."

I nodded, lifting my glass to my lips and relishing the burn of alcohol in my throat. "That isn't even the worst of it. I forced her to tell me everything before I killed her guards. I wanted to feel every ounce of rage imaginable as I tortured them."

Drazen blew out a breath. "I don't blame you."

"So, no poetry," I emphasized.

"No poetry," Drazen repeated. "Anything else I should screen out of here?"

"Anything with whips." The scars across Izidora's back were enough to make me consider banning them in the Iron Realm. It was unfortunate that they gave us such an advantage over other Fae.

Drazen scribbled something in the margin of his paper. "Alright, I think that's it for me. Need anything before I go?"

"No, that will be all. Thanks, Drazen," I said, downing the last of my drink and hissing out the burn.

Drazen only made it halfway out the door before he leaned back to say something. "King Airre and Queen Viktoria are here, and they'd like to speak with you. Should I let them in?"

"Of course," I replied, hurriedly straightening the mess on my desk as the other monarchs entered. "Can I get either of you a drink? I do have water in here, Queen Viktoria."

She waved me off, the golden bangles around her wrist jingling. "We'll only be here a moment."

"Please have a seat." I gestured to the two lavish chairs across from me.

They did, the queen resting a hand on her belly. "We spoke with King Kazimir."

I raised a brow. "And?"

"We have broken our alliance with the Night Realm," King Airre declared. "We'd appreciate it if High Lords Aake and Soma could have an escort out of the Iron Realm."

"Consider it done," I replied, then shouted for one of the guards at the door.

"Yes, My King?" Kriath said, poking his head into my office. "Please fetch Drazen for me."

"Right away," he replied, closing the door softly behind him. Drazen appeared moments later, having evidently not gotten far.

"How can I help?" he asked, looking between the three monarchs in the room.

"Can you arrange an escort for two High Lords returning to the Day Realm through Ferzo Pass?"

Drazen turned his attention to me, a silent question in his gaze. I dipped my chin to signal my approval. "Absolutely. When would they like to leave?"

"As soon as possible," Queen Viktoria said. "We need to slip them out of the Iron Realm to stop the advance of the Crystal and Day Realms' forces."

That the king and queen were so forthcoming with me after all this time was a relief. The monarchs of Északi liked to be reserved in their thoughts and opinions, lest they reveal an advantage to a potential adversary. "Please make the arrangements before you take care of the evening's entertainment," I instructed Drazen, and he nodded.

"I'll send a messenger to your rooms when the males are ready to depart." He addressed the monarchs. "The stablehands will saddle their horses in the meantime."

"Thank you, Drazen," King Airre said warmly, Queen Viktoria echoing the statement.

Once Drazen hurried to arrange for the High Lords's departure, I asked, "Do you think King Kazimir would try to prevent them from reaching the army?"

Queen Viktoria slumped in her chair. "I do not know what to make of King Kazimir anymore. But I will not risk my people by putting blind faith in someone who has *binding magic*."

"I understand the sentiment completely, Queen Viktoria," I replied. "What else can I do for you?"

"Nothing, King Ruslan. You've been incredibly helpful," King Airre said, rising from his seat. He offered his hand to me, and I clasped his arm in farewell.

"I hope to see you both tonight for the performances," I said, standing respectfully as they departed.

"We will be there." Queen Viktoria offered me a warm smile before disappearing through the door King Airre held open for her.

When it clicked shut, a wide grin rippled across my face, and I threw my head back in a manic laugh.

We fucking did it.

Kazimir was destroyed and discredited before Béke was even finished. The other realms readily broke their alliance, and I looked like the hero instead of the villain. Everything was playing out exactly as was needed to advance our agenda, and I couldn't wait to tell Izidora the good news.

"Sprite, I have something to tell you."

"You sound relieved. What is it?"

"The Day and Crystal Realms have broken their alliance with the Night Realm."

Her excitement coursed down our bond, mirroring my own.

"Zuriel is happy for us too. Do you think there will still be a war?"

Her question halted my exhilaration because my gut reaction was yes, and I knew she wanted to avoid bloodshed. If Kazimir hadn't been so aggressive with her since his arrival in the Iron Realm, I might have said no. But he was unstable and unsupported, and that was a deadly combination.

"Unfortunately, yes. I don't see Kazimir letting this go. You need to tell him that you accepted our bond and want to break off his."

I could almost see Izidora's annoyed expression – scrunched nose, a little huff of breath, eye roll – from my office.

"I will."

"When?"

"Tomorrow, I promise. Then we can have our wedding in peace."

Our bond hummed contentedly as we both basked in the knowledge that we'd be married in only a few days.

"I can't wait to tear that dress off you and call you my wife and my queen."

"Zuriel is rolling his eyes like he knows you're saying dirty things to me."

"When am I not saying dirty things to you?"

"Good point. We're almost finished with our lesson for the day, and then I'll see you in our apartment?"

"You will."

She disappeared from my mind, but the echo of her never really left me – not anymore.

———

A STAGE HAD BEEN ERECTED in the ballroom, spanning an entire wall, with heavy gray velvet curtains lining either side and firelights controlled by a host of Iron Fae casting color on various parts of the stage. In front of it, rows and rows of chairs were arranged in a semi-circle, but at the back, a heavy table on a riser hosted more luxurious seating for the nobles of the realms in attendance. Outside the ballroom, the halls bustled with vendors selling treats to enjoy during the show, and I purchased a bagful of sweets for Izidora before carving a path for us into the ballroom. King Airre and Queen Immonen were already seated, and Izidora rushed to her side, Liliana and Domi joining them moments later, their heads bent in giggled conversation.

What they always had to chat about, I had no idea. I selected two seats for us, ensuring there was at least one on either side so

Liliana had a place to sit as well, and poured three glasses of wine from the bottle waiting for us.

The ballroom buzzed with conversation as people navigated the rows and rows of chairs facing the stage, and I dipped my head to Zuriel and the other Telivér as they walked in. They ambled toward the back of the room, slipping into a nearly empty row close to us, for which I was grateful. Moments later, the Night Fae joined us, Kazimir's dark attention falling over Izidora immediately. As if she felt it, she glanced away from her conversation, eyes narrowing before she pointedly returned to it.

That's my fucking sprite.

She and Liliana bid goodbye to the other females, then joined me. Izidora chose to sit on my right, where there was less space between the Crystal Fae and us, preventing a large group from squeezing between. Liliana settled on her other side, and I passed the metal goblets in their direction, wine nearly sloshing over the rims.

"You know what I like most about you, Ruslan?" Liliana said.

"No idea," I deadpanned.

"You know how to pour a drink," she laughed, tipping back the glass and chugging. She sighed when the wine had vanished, then held out the goblet. "Can I have more?"

Rolling my eyes, I grasped the bottle and made a show of watching it fill to the brim before stopping. "Is that enough for you?"

"Yep," she said, popping the P. Izidora laughed at her friend's antics, and I squeezed her leg beneath the table.

"Do you need me to top you off too, sprite?"

Shamelessly, she pushed her glass to me. "Sure do."

I had to lean down the table for another bottle to fill her glass, and she eyed me hungrily while I did so. "Like the view?"

"It's definitely the nicest in the ballroom," she said, chewing her lip.

I caught her face in my hand, using my thumb to peel her lip away from her teeth. "Don't make me fuck you while the whole realm watches."

Her eyes heated, and she took the wine from me, pouring it into my glass instead of her own. "Better get drunk first."

"Is that a challenge?" I purred, snatching the alcohol back and filling her drink to the brim.

"Maybe," she whispered, her fingers trailing along my exposed forearm, tracing a tattoo there.

Our flirty encounter was interrupted by the scraping of chairs behind me, and I whipped around as the Night Fae took their seats to my left. Kazimir sat beside me in an open challenge, and I almost lost my shit and tackled him right there.

He was not allowed to be this close to my mate.

A growl rumbled in my chest, and Izidora's grip tightened on my arm in warning.

"Ignore him. He wants the attention, to make you look bad in front of the other realms. He probably knows we turned them against him."

She was right, but that didn't soothe my inner Dragon, who wanted to fight and protect his mate. I greeted every other Night Fae except for him before turning my back. I wasn't an empath, but the anger radiating off of him at the blatant disrespect was palpable, like pinpricks of hate spearing into my skin. Izidora's brows pinched like she felt it too, so I reminded her to block the emotions of everyone around us.

She nodded, eyes closing momentarily as she worked to block out all the demands on her attention pounding into her like a thousand silent raindrops. Our bond was thick, strong, and unbreakable, and while it acted like a steady stream of emotion and thought to one another, I couldn't begin to comprehend the enormous toll all of that took on her. I only hoped I didn't contribute even more stress to her with my own inner turbulence.

When she reopened her eyes, revealing those beautiful aquamarines I wanted to drown in, she looked lighter, her shoulders falling lower and a sigh escaping those perfect pink lips. Lifting my glass, I offered her a toast. "To a lovely evening with my future wife."

Her smile was devastating as she raised hers in turn. "I cannot wait."

Anton and Slavian dropped down on Liliana's other side, both holding glass bowls of popcorn. Slavian looked pointedly past me at Kazimir, raised his eyebrows, then shoveled a handful of food into his mouth, not caring that he missed and some fell to the floor around him.

"You alright over there, buddy?" he asked, slurring his words, and I rolled my eyes again.

"I am your king, Slavian, not your buddy," I scowled, leveling the same stare at an equally drunk Anton.

"Ruslan, you gotta come out to Steel again soon and bring Izidora. She had so much fun the other night at the ceremony," Anton whined, lifting his drink and sipping from it.

Liliana tossed her hair over her shoulder and perused the two noble Félvér beside her. Then, she dug her hand into Slavian's bowl and stole his food, casually popping piece after piece into her mouth. The two fixated on the movement like hounds drooling over their dinner. "I'll come any night," she said suggestively, saving me from having to respond to my High Lords.

Slavian's eyes flared with hunger, and three different scents of arousal hit my sensitive nose. I lifted my wine to my lips and sipped, trying to cover the smell. Izidora watched the exchange with barely veiled amusement, and for a moment the male behind me was forgotten.

Before their flirting could go any further, the lights dimmed around us, signaling the start of the performances. I scooted my chair closer to Izidora's so I could touch her – not in a sexual way, but rather because I wanted to feel her against me and know she was safe.

The same announcer from the competition greeted us, outlining the evening's entertainment and bolstering the excitement of the crowd. "For our first act, we have a ballet! Please welcome the dancers to the stage."

The crowd applauded as he departed, lights dimming momentarily before music filled the space and dancers leaped onto the stage. An array of colorful lights followed their movements, some acting as a landing pad for the astonishing leaps the dancers took through the air. They floated across the stage as if they were Crystal Fae dancing on water, movements so airy and elegant it was hard to imagine gravity having an effect on them. Beside me, Izidora leaned forward ever so slightly, enraptured by their movements. As the tension in the music heightened, the dancers twirled faster and faster, weaving flawlessly in and out of one another until the music stopped altogether, freezing them in place. A beat of silence passed, all dancers still as stone, the crowd holding its breath in anticipation of what would happen next. The lightest of notes cut through the stillness like the clanging of metal, and the dancers began flowing like a stream, running off in every direction as the music faded out.

Cheers followed them offstage as the audience went wild for their act, and after a few whistles they returned to give a series of bows and accept the flowers offered to them. Once the excitement had died down, the announcer returned, introducing the next performance. "Those of you on the front row might want to lean back if you don't want your eyebrows singed," he warned. "Please welcome the Firebreathers!"

A troupe of Iron Fae and Félvér took to the stage, splitting into groups of three across. On one end, a series of flaming hoops were lit, and the performers took turns leaping through them, displaying their bravery. In the front, a group juggled flaming balls and batons with expert care, and I covered my smirk with my hand as the crowd gasped as time and time again the three held the flaming balls in their hands without getting burned. Little did they know, the three performers in the front were all half Dragon Shifter, so the fire did not burn them. On the other side, three performers were setting up for their finale, building what looked like a mountain out of crates and boxes and covering them with gray sheets. The other sets began working their way around, giving them the space they needed to continue their uphill build, until finally they rose high above the crowd. One raced to the top, flaming batons in hand, and paused, surveying the area beneath him. Then with a mighty roar, he tilted his head back, brought the baton close to his face, and exhaled, breathing fire into the air and spewing it over the heads of the crowd. Once the flames died down, the crowd erupted in applause, and the performers bowed to the audience and tore down their set in rapid succession.

We watched another dance after the Firebreathers, then listened to a male tell jokes for far too long. By the time the hounds and their masters walked onstage, Izidora and Liliana were drunk, giggling, and falling all over each other beside me. I squeeze my mate's leg under the table to get her attention. "You're going to like this one, sprite."

"What are they going to do?" she asked with a slight hiccup.

"Watch and you'll see."

She leaned her head on my shoulder, and I sighed contentedly, reaching across to stroke her hair and turning my head to plant a kiss on her forehead.

The trainers shouted commands at their dogs, and they

pranced across the stage, never looking away from their masters as they remained glued to their sides. They sat obediently when they halted, spun on command, then returned to their place. One pair broke away, centering themselves on the stage. The trainer produced a length of rope, showing it to the dog, then used a ladder to place it on a newly-erected stone wall at the end of the stage. The dog remained stationary while his master placed the rope, his eyes never leaving his prize. On command, the dog sprinted toward the wall, launching himself into the air as he scaled it, and snatched the bit of rope before backflipping off of the wall and landing lightly on the ground.

Izidora gasped beside me, her head lifting off my shoulder as her hands covered her mouth in shock. "That was amazing!"

"I thought you might like it," I smiled down at her.

Our attention returned to the stage, where the second dog jumped through the flaming hoops of the Firebreathers, fearless in his flight as he chased his master. After the fifth hoop, he turned sharply and raced to the second trainer, whose arm was thickly padded and extended to the hound. With an incredible display of force, he lunged for it and latched on to the padding, not letting go as the second trainer lifted him into the air. Only when his master shouted the command to release did he back away and begin barking at the second trainer.

"That is so fuckin' cool," Liliana slurred, clapping her hands.

"Agreed," Izidora said, wholly captivated by the show.

After a few more displays of obedience, the two pairs ended their act to an absolutely enthralled audience, the unique performance winning everyone over.

The ballroom brightened after they exited the stage, and the announcer returned, relaying the intermission information. I blinked rapidly at the change in light, and as my eyes adjusted I glanced to my left. A smug Kazimir still sat there, looking pointedly at me and then at my mate. Ignoring him, I returned my attention to Izidora. "Do you want to move around during the intermission or stay here?"

She yawned, covering her open mouth with the back of her hand. "I think I'll move around. Otherwise, I might fall asleep. I had too much wine."

"But I need more," Liliana declared, shaking the empty bottles on the table in front of her.

"I can get you both more," Kazimir offered behind me, and Liliana glowered over my shoulder, a threat of death flashing in her eyes.

"On second thought, I think I agree with Izidora. I've had too much wine." The ice in her tone rivaled the glaciers in the Agrenak Mountains, and the wine must have emboldened her because words sharper than icicles speared out of her mouth. "Why are you sitting there, Kazimir? No one wants you here. You should just leave."

Izidora's eyes widened, and I snapped my head around just in time to see Kazimir shoot to his feet, eyes turning black. "I am your king, Liliana, and you will address me as such."

"How about no?" she challenged, and I held my breath, calling on my magic to defend the females sitting beside me.

"I will not tolerate your disrespect," Kazimir snapped, banging his fists on the table and causing the silverware to jump.

Seconds later, Vadim and Endre had their hands on Kazimir's arms and shoulders. "Liliana has had too much to drink, Kazimir. She won't remember what she said in the morning. Let's go get some food from the halls before the theater performance starts." Vadim tried to soothe his mad king, but the asshole shrugged him off.

Scraping back his chair, Kazimir leveled a disdain-filled look on Liliana. "Drunkenness is no excuse. Do better."

Vadim and Endre shot apologetic grimaces in our direction

as they followed Kazimir out of the ballroom, and I released the breath I had been holding before cracking my knuckles one by one.

"Fuck him. You definitely made the right choice, Izidora," Liliana grumbled, tossing her long hair over her shoulder.

"I think so too," she confirmed, looking up at me with so much love I couldn't imagine her making any other choice.

"I love you, mate."

"I love you too."

I ushered the females into the hall, keeping them close to me and using my heightened Dragon senses to watch for Kazimir. We ended up wandering around, mingling with people here and there, but the three of us were on edge from our earlier encounter. As the crowd began returning to their seats, I made a split-second decision. "Why don't we skip the theater performance?"

"What would we do instead?" Izidora asked.

"We can go to Roc and enjoy the hot springs on the ground floor. No other female has set foot there, and I don't want to bring Liliana with us unless you say it's okay."

Izidora's aquamarine eyes softened, and she reached up to cup my cheek.

"You take such good care of me, Ruslan. No one has ever taken my thoughts and feelings into consideration like you have. You make me feel like the most special female in the world."

"Are you two talking through your bond again?" Liliana huffed, crossing her arms and rolling her eyes.

Izidora snickered and turned to her friend. "Yes. Do you want to come with us to our *real* home?"

Liliana lifted an eyebrow. "Real home?"

I dropped my voice so no one could overhear our conversation. "Roc Palace. I built it for Izidora and myself to enjoy, away from the citadel."

She swiped at her hair, then shrugged, as if she were trying to hide her jealousy. With how intoxicated she was, she couldn't cover her pinched expression and the way her attention drifted down the table toward Endre. "Sure, let's go."

"Follow me," I instructed, searching our surroundings for the stalker.

Slipping down a side hall, I navigated us to an empty room where we wouldn't be disturbed. There was an entry on both sides, so if someone had followed us, when they barged in they would think we had exited through the other door. Taking a deep breath, I tapped into the well of black fire in my chest, then grasped both the females' hands. The low chant of the spell to move us spilled from my lips, and Liliana jerked her hand as the magic settled over us. I tightened my grip, needing to concentrate on the words as I worked.

And then, we flew faster than light through the distance between Ryza and Roc as I bent space to return us to our home. When we halted in the entryway, I released them, and Liliana braced her hands on her knees, panting and swearing as she regained her bearings.

"The first time is always the worst," Izidora soothed, rubbing circles on her friend's back.

"What... the hell... was that," Liliana managed to say.

"Mage magic," I smirked. "Quite handy isn't it?"

She lifted her seafoam green eyes from the polished stone floor. "It's something." Straightening, she swayed slightly, and Izidora caught her arm to steady her.

Inhaling deeply, my shoulders relaxed with the knowledge that Izidora would be safe for the evening, tucked away in Roc Palace. Down the bond, I felt her loosen, that frantic energy that had been consuming her disappearing like smoke in the wind.

"To the hot springs?" she asked.

"Let's go." I led the way down the stairs to the bottom floor, and as we pushed through the door, the humidity blasted us, clothes immediately sticking to our skin.

"Wow, this is incredible!" Liliana exclaimed as she surveyed the space.

The underground grotto was all-natural, the stones still rough, as hot water piped up from a hole dug into the side of the mountain. Using my earth magic, I had shaped a few seats into the pool after my first few uses, wanting a place to recline rather than having to stand or squat in the water. Low lights flickered to life as we moved further into the space, enchanted so they created the perfect ambiance for relaxing, depending on the bather's mood.

Both females began tying their hair on the tops of their heads, and I turned my back to them as I stripped from my finery and laid it across a stone bench. The water soothed my soul as I entered it, the warmth seeping into my muscles and the healing minerals working their way into my skin. Ducking under the water, I wet my hair, slicking it back as I emerged. I waited to turn around until I heard splashing, Izidora and Liliana submerged in the water up to their collarbones.

"There are seats over there." I gestured to my left, and they glided through the water until they reached them. I joined them there, and the opaque green water swirled around us as a small geyser exploded with fresh heat.

"Why haven't we used this more?" Izidora groaned, sinking back into a comfortable position.

"We are always too busy. I had to ensure you were properly trained and strong." I planted a kiss on her forehead and scooted onto the rocks next to her before lifting my arms from the water and bracing them on the rock ledge behind me. She snuggled closer, leaning her head against my chest as Liliana took the seat across from us.

"You are the first female to set foot here besides Izidora," I told her.

"Really? Why?" she cocked her head to the side, studying me.

"Because I wanted this place to be special for her – for us. I never wanted her to feel like she was an afterthought."

"Fuck me, why can't I find a male like you?" she groaned, and Izidora giggled beneath my arm.

"Do you mean a villain, a king, or something else?" I smirked.

"For what it's worth, you may have started as a villain, but I don't think you are anymore – not really," Izidora murmured, lifting her head from my chest to look at me.

"Then I am not doing my job in scaring you enough, sprite," I whispered, my hand reaching from behind her to grasp her throat.

"The scent of your fear mixed with your arousal was and always will be my favorite combination."

A rosy red crept up her chest to her cheeks, and I knew it wasn't from the steam swirling around us.

Liliana interrupted our moment with a scoff. "How about a male who thinks about me first? I'd settle for that. You saw how Endre chose Kazimir over me earlier."

"I'm sorry, Lil," Izidora said, floating through the water to embrace her friend. I let her go, knowing that the two of them needed each other.

Wanting to change the subject away from the one that plagued my every waking thought, I asked, "So what does Izidora's dress look like?"

Liliana's mood shifted immediately. "Nope, I am not telling you a thing. You have to wait to be surprised."

I protested, but she and Izidora held firm, insisting that it would be better if I waited. After that, conversation floated around our upcoming wedding, the decor the temple would have as we took our vows and our crowns before the Goddess, and our plans for after Béke.

We remained in the spring until we grew lightheaded and sweat poured from our temples. As we dried off and prepared to return to the citadel, a twinge of sadness speared my heart, for in a few days' time, Béke would be over, and I did not know for certain if Liliana would stay or if she would return with her brother and the Night Fae to the Night Realm.

For Izidora's sake, I wanted her to stay.

45

KAZIMIR

Béke Day Thirteen

"Liliana didn't return to the apartment last night," Endre told me as he sank onto my bed.

I adjusted the Night Crown in the mirror, glancing at my downcast friend as his messy black hair fell into his face. "Where do you think she went?"

He buried his face in his hands. "I don't know. Somewhere with Izidora. Maybe she stayed with her."

The tension between Endre and Liliana had been growing during our time here, and the purple circles under my best friend's eyes showed his stress. They were on full display as he lifted his gaze to meet mine in the mirror. "Why did you threaten her last night? She would have come back if you hadn't been a dick."

Buttoning up my jacket, I replied, "Liliana needs to know her place. If she chooses to remain a citizen of the Night Realm, then she must obey her king. If she chooses to pledge her allegiance to the Iron Realm, then she's not my problem. But she won't choose a side, therefore, she belongs to me."

A flicker of annoyance swept through me. The answer should have been obvious to him. Instead, his peridot eyes dimmed, and he pushed off from the bed with a heaviness that was, unfortunately, all too relatable. "Liliana will go where Izidora does. Do you really think you can convince Izidora to choose you at this point?"

Time was running out – the following day, Izidora and Ruslan would marry and be crowned as the monarchs of the Iron Realm. Which meant I had one last day to get her alone and tell her my theory of the prophecy, that this tug between us still existed because she could choose both. Not that I had told Endre or any of my other friends what I had seen during the masquerade. I needed their continued support in this, and so long as they believed Izidora hadn't yet chosen a mate, I could continue to establish my rule.

I also hadn't told them we were on our own with the war we planned to wage against the Iron Realm.

"I have a plan," I replied coolly.

Endre heaved a sigh. "I wish you would tell me. Or Viktor. Or anyone, really. You spend too much time in your own head, Kazimir."

"No one understands the pain I'm going through," I ground out, jerking my jacket one last time before facing my friend.

"And no one will unless you tell them," Endre retorted. "Did you forget that the rest of us lost our brothers too? We're all still grieving over here. But we're pushing that aside to help you, and you are being an asshole to everyone. Figure your shit out." He stomped from the room without a backward glance.

I remained motionless, rooted in place by my friend's harsh words. Endre rarely snapped, so his words were like a slap to the face. I returned to myself when I heard Vadim say, "The parade starts in half an hour. We need to get going."

"Yeah, I know. He's almost finished in there," I heard Endre mumble through the walls.

Gathering myself and slipping into my kingly facade, I entered the living area where the Night Fae, minus Liliana, waited for me. Domi's eyes were hard, and she quickly busied herself with her nails when I entered. "Shall we?"

Without waiting for a response, I swept through the room, out the doors, and into the hall where servants and guards all wound their way to the front doors and into the afternoon sun. The parade would take place on the main thoroughfare in Radence, and at the end of the course, the nobility had special seats and a private area to tie up our horses.

Fek stomped his foot when we arrived in the stables to collect our mounts, his glossy black mane shining in the sun. I rubbed his nose, offering him a lump of sugar before mounting and guiding him through the crowd trailing into the city. A light dusting of snow from the previous night's storm coated the roofs and sides of the road, and the bright sun glinting off of the snow speared into my eyes. Fek's hooves clopped against the slush-covered cobbled road, the snow there trampled by the hundreds of feet that had already crossed it as people fought for the best view of the upcoming parade.

The stone houses and buildings we passed were overflowing with people eating and drinking as they celebrated the last days of Béke. Ales overflowed and spilled along the ground, meat roasted over open fires, and people sang off-tune, grasping each other by the arm as they went round and round. Their carefree spirits almost made me feel normal, but the day's mission was never far from the front of my mind.

I had to find Izidora. I had to get her alone. And I had to tell her that she could still accept our bond.

Making her jealous hadn't worked, though I hadn't regretted

my time with Taya at all. She fucked like a goddess, and sinking into her tight pussy had been the relief I needed these past few days.

Turning down a side street toward the road that led to the private seating area, I scanned for any sign of Izidora, or of Liliana, Drazen, or Zuriel, because wherever they were, she was likely close by. The string that tugged me to her was faint, and I maintained a bit of focus there, waiting for it to tell me which direction to go. As we stepped closer to the stands, it began thrumming. I picked my head up, searching for a hint of chestnut hair among the crowd.

I spotted her just as we halted at the posts where a dozen horses were already hitched, and a handful of young males stepped forward to take our reins. Without looking away from Izidora, I handed mine off, not waiting for any of the other Night Fae to join me before I slipped into the crowd, headed in her direction.

Unfortunately, she was surrounded by her friends, which made discreetly pulling her aside impossible.

"There you are. Let's go get seats beside the fire," Vadim said, hand latching onto my arm. I tore my gaze from Izidora to find him, Viktor, and Endre waiting.

"Yeah, sure. It's cold as fuck," I replied, falling in stride with them as we made our way toward a row of seats on the lowest level. The fire in front of them offered a surprising amount of warmth for how small the flames were.

"Slavian told me these were created with a special type of magic that allows them to put out a lot of heat without taking up too much space. They're portable too, so they can be moved around when necessary. They only need to use their magic to relight the fire," Vadim said as if he was reading my mind.

"The Iron Realm certainly has been busy with its inventions

the last few decades," Viktor grumbled, no doubt trying to think of something useful to create for the Night Realm. He hated not being the smartest or most strategic in a room, and he fell behind as Ruslan and Drazen flaunted one new creation after another.

That tug in my belly caught my attention, and I glanced over my shoulder to discover Izidora and Ruslan arriving with their troop of followers. She didn't even look at me as she walked by, heading up the stairs to the highest level. She and Liliana took the seats in the middle, and a pained noise slipped from Endre's throat as Liliana ignored him too.

Vadim rubbed him on the shoulder reassuringly. "I can't believe I'm comforting you over my sister, but it will be okay, Endre. Give her time."

"Yeah, I know," he mumbled, facing forward once more.

King Airre and Queen Immonen arrived moments later, two of their three High Lords in tow, and behind them Queen Viktoria and King Consort Geza arrived with High Lord Domon.

Where were High Lords Aake and Soma?

I didn't recall seeing them the previous night at the talent show or theater performance either. A horn blasted in the distance, cheers rippling through the crowd of onlookers, leaving me unable to dwell on those thoughts.

The parade had started.

The air filled with bright, happy music, and everyone craned their necks to the left, straining for the first glimpse. Every few minutes, an explosion sent streaming ribbons into the air, the colorful strings catching on the breeze and drifting away, some falling over the crowds while others mixed in with the snow.

It wasn't long before the first part of the parade finally rolled around the corner, and the spectators whooped in excitement. A group of Iron Fae used their earth magic to guide the giant contraption down the street, allowing it to stop some distance away. It was too far for those in the stands to watch comfortably, but the performance didn't last long before moving on. This time, they rolled to a stop in front of us, and the Iron Fae disappeared to allow the entertainment to go unblocked.

The performers appeared from nowhere, bursting out of the wooden ship on wheels and acting out a scene where the male and female Fae battled against one another for control of the wheel. When the females finally won, they stood at the bow and saluted, remaining in position as the ones below pulled the ship forward again.

It disappeared around the corner only to be replaced by another platform, artfully decorated with an intricate metal cage with a bejeweled sphere on top that glittered in the sun. People climbed out from between the bars, singing a tune before disappearing back inside and moving on to the next section.

Three more passed before an idea struck me. Glancing around, I noted that everyone was enraptured with the latest entertainment, no one paying the slightest bit of attention to what was happening around them. Carefully, I slid from my seat, calling shadows to me to blur my form as I slipped away from the seats and ducked beneath them.

Thank the Goddess I had taken the end seat.

Next, calling on the silvery part of my magic, I snaked it up through the stands and around the back to where Izidora sat with her friends. Her focus was on the performance, and holding my breath, I brushed my magic against the clasp around the heavy, bejeweled necklace that she wore. With great care, I broke the clasp, directing the necklace to fall to the side and down between the slats in the stands. It hit the ground with a thud beside me.

I called on my binding magic, combining it with the moonlight, and rendered myself invisible. Hurriedly, I stepped back and leaned against one of the thick wooden poles holding the grandstand together, heart pounding.

"Shit!" Izidora cursed above me.

"What's wrong?" Ruslan asked.

"My necklace fell to the ground, scoot over so I can go find it. It's one of my favorites."

"I'll get it for you, sprite, you should enjoy the parade."

"No, it's fine, I need a drink anyway."

"Are you certain?"

"Bring me something," Liliana chimed in.

Izidora laughed, and my stomach clenched at the bright, airy sound. "Will do."

Her footsteps were light beneath her petite frame, but when I heard her boots crunch into the snow, my heart leaped to my throat. I could scarcely breathe as she approached, then bent to search the snow for her necklace. It only took her a few moments to uncover it, and she dusted it gently with the sleeve of her jacket before straightening.

A faraway look rested on her face, as if she were deep in thought about something. The expression held as she walked straight past me toward the private dining area just around the corner. I waited, holding my breath until she rounded it before following. My footsteps were muffled by my magic, and as I crept closer, her laughter hit my ears again. When I reached the corner, I peeked around it and saw Izidora hefting two mugs of hot wine, throwing a giggle and a thank you over her shoulder at the lone attendant.

This was my chance.

Izidora strolled back in my direction, headed for the stands where all the nobles attending Béke were preoccupied. She threw a glance over her shoulder, then looked straight ahead again, her teeth sunk into her bottom lip. Her bright, aquamarine eyes scanned the area in front of her as if she were searching for something.

Me.

The moment she rounded the corner, I snatched her to me, slapping a hand over her mouth and wrapping the other around her waist so she couldn't escape.

"Hello, Izidora. We need to talk."

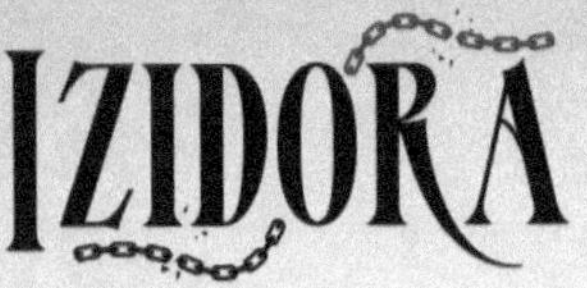

46

IZIDORA

Béke Day Thirteen

A hand clamped over my mouth, and I smelled him – amber. My flailing limbs struggled against the male who trapped me to his chest, my heart pounding wildly out of control as adrenaline flooded my veins. I dropped the mugs of hot wine, and they fell into the snow without a sound. Cursing, I continued to fight Kazimir, but he dragged me backward and away from the stands where my mate waited for me.

"Shh, stop fighting," Kazimir purred in my ear, and my eyes jerked to the young male manning the drink stand. But he seemed oblivious to the fact that Kazimir had me in a choke-hold. The male I had loved first dragged me against my will toward where I'd left Mistik.

Fuck.

Kazimir's intentions became crystal clear at that moment, and I snapped out with my teeth, hoping to graze his skin in any way I could. The moment I did, a corrupted black rope circled my head, gagging me as it bit into my mouth. "All I want to do is talk, but you need to listen to what I have to say instead of screaming for help or screaming over me."

The muscles in my neck strained as I fought against the bitter binding, but despite my obvious attempts to get his attention, the young attendant still did not notice my peril as Kazimir dragged me toward the horses.

Kazimir's laugh sent an icy chill skittering down my spine. "He can't see you. He can't hear you. No one will find you until I am ready for them to."

I screamed as much as I could behind the gag in a last-ditch effort to call for help, my throat vibrating with the force of my cry. Kazimir did not even acknowledge the level of distress he brought me, and that might have been the most terrifying part of this encounter.

Was this monster always lurking inside him? Had I not accepted him during those first few months outside the cave, would this have happened sooner?

In one swift motion, Kazimir threw my legs over Fek's back, then vaulted onto his stallion behind me, snatching the reins and kicking him into a gallop. Houses flashed by us as we raced down the street, which was devoid of life as the whole of Radence was preoccupied with the parade.

But I was an insidious bloom, and I needed no one to save me byt myself. I had reclaimed my power, and I had trained for this, and I would not be afraid.

Kazimir crushed me against him, and I struggled to free myself from his grip. Searching for the powerful white flames inside me, I called to them, stoking them higher in preparation to blow us off the street.

But nothing happened.

That's when Immonen's words drifted back to me. *Binding magic blocks access to our Goddess-gifted power.*

My eyes widened as panic clawed her way up my throat,

stealing my breath as we raced to Goddess knew where. I tried again, grasping for my precious magic, but it slipped through my fingers. Cursing Kazimir, I dug my nails into his arm, shoving down with all my might, trying to break his grip.

The laugh he left in my ear was so sinister that my entire body went cold. Another malicious rope bound my hands together, and it was then that I felt truly helpless and utterly powerless for the first time since I'd left my cave.

I couldn't save myself.

Tears pricked my eyes, and I fought with every spark of hope left within me to crush the overwhelming feelings threatening to render me immobile. I was a fighter, a survivor, and I would not give up on myself – not ever. This insidious bloom had one final thorn, willing and able to prick, and I knew, without a doubt, it was my only chance of survival.

"Ruslan!"

"Sprite? What's wrong? Where are you?"

"I don't know. Kazimir took me, we're riding through Radence. I don't know these streets, they aren't familiar."

The roar that burst from Ruslan shook even the homes around us, and Kazimir snapped the reins, urging Fek faster.

"Please hurry."

"I will find you, sprite. No one will ever hurt you again."

"He bound me, I can't access my magic. I'm scared."

"Me too. But we have survived so much already, and we will again."

I tried to look up toward the sky, searching for my Demon Dragon, but Kazimir's hand threaded through my hair and shoved my head down, causing me to cry out against my gag. "No one can see us." Another rope wrapped around my eyes, blinding me from our path forward, and tears overflowed as I surrendered to the mercy of another male again.

But I was not giving up; no, I was doing what survivors did

best – biding my time until I was certain I could strike. And then, I would offer Kazimir the same mercy I had offered the males who abused me in the cave.

Death.

Fek's pace slowed, and Kazimir pressed his chest into me, forcing me to lean forward as we began an uphill ascent.

"I think he is taking me into the mountains."

"I know, I'm almost there. Stay strong, Izidora."

Insidious bloom, insidious bloom, insidious bloom...

"That's right, mate. You have so many hidden thorns. Prick him with them all."

I hadn't realized I'd spoken my mantra down the bond, but I was grateful for Ruslan's reassurance.

The ground leveled out beneath us, and Kazimir pulled Fek to a stop, the stallion's sides heaving from the effort of racing away from Radence. The poor beast deserved better than the madness that was his rider. Kazimir jerked me off of him, throwing me to the ground with my limbs still bound and mouth still gagged. My head cracked on a rock, and I cried out around the rope in my mouth. He used the tight binds to jerk me upright, then removed the rope around my head so I was forced to look him in the eye. Blood trickled down the side of my face, wet, hot, and metallic.

But he did not care. Why did I ever think he cared?

"Izidora, listen. The prophecy states 'there is a choice' but it doesn't say what that choice is. I'll share you with Ruslan. I already know you accepted a bond with him. There is still this string between us, don't you feel it? That means you can choose me too. You can have two mates." Kazimir's tone grew more desperate as the sentences spilled out of him, his emerald eyes begging me to hear his words and accept him too.

But he had hurt me. Stalked me. Made me fear for my life. Left me so on edge that I couldn't walk alone for fear of him doing exactly this to me. My eyes narrowed on him, and I willed my white fire to burn him on the spot. But, of course, his malicious magic prevented me from using the *one fucking thing* that leveled the playing field.

Fuck him. Goddess damn him. He would die for this, by my hand or by Ruslan's, and that time was fast approaching.

I bit down on the gag and launched myself at him, aiming my shoulder for his gut to knock him off balance. With lightning-fast reflexes, he caught my shoulder inches from his torso, then gripped my upper arms and stood me on my feet. The gag disappeared as if it had never been there, and Kazimir snatched my hair in one hand and my waist in the other as he trapped me against him and forced his mouth over mine. My body revolted, and I bit down with all my strength on his tongue. Metallic liquid coated the inside of my mouth, and when he jerked away with a roar, I spit it in his face.

"You will kiss me!" He slapped me, hard enough that my head whipped to the side and stars coated my vision, then crushed my jaw between his fingers and forced me to look at his disgusting face again.

Instead of faltering, I laughed – a crazed, wretched sound that perfectly mirrored my internal experience. All the rage I had locked inside myself bubbled up, bringing out the hardened, ferocious, pissed-the-fuck-off side of me that I loved best. I let my voice drip with disdain, not bothering to suppress or hide my true emotions. "I've had worse done to me, Kazimir. You aren't the first, though you will be the last."

I was so fucking tired of males thinking they could use me how they wanted.

"You will give in to me," Kazimir hissed, spitting blood. "You will choose me. You will mate me. You will forget him and come home with me. We will be king and queen of the Night Realm."

I sensed Ruslan's approach, our bond like a beacon despite the magic binding me and cloaking both me and Kazimir.

"It's too late for that," I purred, batting my lashes and baring my teeth. "I do not want to be mated to you, Kazimir. I am breaking off our bond and choosing *only* Ruslan as my mate."

And with those words, an invisible string snapped between us.

Kazimir turned feral, a snarl unlike any beast I'd heard tearing from his throat. My bindings fell away, but an explosion of moonlight and oily darkness blasted all the snow around us, throwing me backward and cracking my spine against a large boulder. Pain shot through every nerve in my body, and my throat was scraped raw from the scream.

It was drowned out by my mate's roar as he dropped from the sky, his massive membranous wings casting us in shadow as he breathed black fire. Not a speck of white was left in Kazimir's eyes as he rolled out of the way of the flame and faced Ruslan head-on.

"I should have let you die in the avalanche," Ruslan snarled.

"You should have." Kazimir took a step to the left, circling an enraged Ruslan, both males hunting for an opening. He threw his sinister black rope at my mate, whose talons slashed through them as if they were nothing more than air.

"You're going to have to do better than that," Ruslan taunted.

They traded magic blows back and forth while I tried to heal my spine. The pain roaring through me was more intense than any whip lashing I had experienced, and every small movement felt like it took ten times the normal effort.

Immonen's vision and subsequent warning flashed through my mind, intensified by the swimming in my head.

"Zuriel! Can you hear me?"

"I'm here, where are you? Ruslan went crazy and left the parade

before we could get an answer out of him. Everyone dispersed thinking something horrible had happened."

"Kazimir kidnapped me. We're somewhere in the mountains now. I don't know where. Please hurry, I can barely feel my legs."

"I'm coming."

"Why don't you sheathe those talons and fight me like a Fae? That's what you wanted, right?" Kazimir challenged.

"I don't need talons to destroy you, Kazimir." Ruslan shifted out of his Dragon form, cracked his neck, and drew his sword. Flames licked the blade as he held it high, ready to pounce.

Kazimir sidestepped to his saddlebags, yanking out his own blade. The males circled each other, each waiting for the other to make the first move. When Kazimir leaped into a flurry of strikes, I tuned in to my magic, the crystal flickering and filling with power as I opened myself to every intense emotion for the male I'd loved first. I needed every drop of my power to end this, so I gritted my teeth and allowed the barriers around my worst memories to fall away, drawing on every painful emotion that cascaded through me. Tears overflowed of their own accord, mixing with the blood trickling down my face.

Then, I surrendered to them.

With a cry that held years of anguish, I directed my magic at Kazimir, willing his feet to stick to the muddy ground and sink into it like quicksand. The clash of blades rang through the mountain pass as Ruslan stepped in, and as Kazimir lifted a foot to shift away, my magic yanked it down and stuck it to the ground.

Sweat poured from my temples and down my aching spine from the effort of holding Kazimir still, and I gasped for air as agony speared through every fiber of my being. My focus slipped, overwhelmed by the intensity of *everything,* and a sob wracked my chest as Kazimir managed to unstick his foot a moment later.

Ruslan had already started to attack again, and the males fought with a ferocity I'd never experienced before. Desperation flooded me as I willed and willed him to stop moving, my magic flaring over and over inside that crystal as I called on it.

Had I used too much when trying to heal myself?

My entire body trembled, and I knew instinctively that I was closing in on burnout.

Ruslan's heavy blows backed Kazimir toward the mountainside, and when he was within mere feet of the rock, spears shot out from the wall, one catching him in the leg, the other scraping his shoulder. Blood gushed from the wound in his thigh, but he was a male possessed, and being impaled did not stop his crazed movements. His next three blows were like lightning, the last catching Ruslan's right shoulder and cutting deep.

"No!" I screamed, leaping to my feet despite the roaring agony in my body, hand raised and blasting white energy at Kazimir. The impact propelled him backward, flattening him against the ground and sending his sword clattering away as he tumbled over and over himself.

Ruslan gritted his teeth, switched his sword to his left hand, and hunted Kazimir down like the prey he was. Ruslan was the apex predator not only in the Iron Realm, but in all of Északi.

And he was my fucking mate.

My legs buckled, unable to support my weight any longer, and I fell to my hands and knees. My heart raced wildly out of control, and my lungs burned as if the white fire that lived in my chest had decided to consume them.

Why hadn't I trained for this? How could I be so stupid as to neglect one of my greatest assets?

Ruslan kicked the fallen sword further away as he passed it, but Kazimir had already recovered and was on his feet. He reached for a dagger sheathed in his boot, then pinched it between thumb and forefinger by the blade, as if he were going to throw it at Ruslan's broad chest.

The three of us were poised on the edge of that blade for a moment, and I held my breath, waiting to see which way we would fall. Time slowed to a crawl, and Ruslan paused, eyeing Kazimir's dagger warily. What was left of my magic I called to my hands, ready to throw a shield in front of Ruslan should Kazimir decide to throw.

Ruslan had expressed time and time again that he would die without me; what he didn't know was that if he perished, I would want to follow him into death too.

Why had I never told him that?

The thought robbed me of breath.

"If she won't have me, then she won't have anyone," Kazimir snarled, then hurled the blade. I threw a shield of white magic in front of Ruslan, pouring every last drop I had into it, desperate to save him.

But the blade sailed past Ruslan and buried itself in my chest.

47

DRAZEN

Zuriel screamed my name as he sprinted down the main thoroughfare in Radence, pushing parade goers out of his way like they were nothing more than insects. I'd never heard the Angel speak above a normal volume before, so I immediately spun to see what the fuck had gotten into him. He careened to a stop in front of me, the people around us falling silent to hear what the Angel had to say.

"Kazimir has taken Izidora into the mountains. Ruslan went after her, but she is badly injured. We need to hurry."

Oh, fuck.

I immediately hunted the vicinity for any of my soldiers, finding a handful in the distance. Their attention was already on us thanks to Zuriel barreling through the crowd.

"Artur! Disperse the crowd and make sure our guests are entertained in the ballroom." My second in command saluted me from across the street, then shouted orders at his legion.

"Are you armed?" I asked Zuriel.

He shook his head.

"You, give me your sword, and your chains." I pointed to one of the soldiers who stood watch a few feet from us. The male readily handed the sword to Zuriel and the chains to me.

Viktor, Vadim, and Endre pushed against the tide of people a moment later. "What's going on?" Viktor demanded, his brow furrowing as he took in the sight of me strapping iron chains to my waist and Zuriel doubled over and sucking down air.

I debated lying for only a moment but decided the three might want to stop the fight rather than join it. "Kazimir kidnapped Izidora and took her into the mountains. Ruslan went after them. We need to stop this before they all kill each other."

The Night Fae male gave a firm nod. "We're going with you. No one will die today."

"Good, because we need to move. Now."

Craning my neck over the crowd, I discovered a fairly empty side street, then shouted for everyone to move out of my way as I led our group down it. Once we'd cleared the throng of people, we broke into a run, racing until we found an open square. Without breaking stride, my lapis lazuli wings sprung from my back, and I shot into the sky, searching for prints in the snow around the stands where Izidora was last seen. Zuriel unfurled his white feathered wings and leaped into the air, flapping them lightly as he hovered and scanned the area with me. The Night Fae were not far behind.

"Zuriel, do you know where they are?" I shouted over the wind.

"Izidora didn't know. My guess is they went toward the Day Realm border."

Kazimir wouldn't know many other routes out of the Iron Realm, so that made sense. I banked right, studying the snowdrifts below for any sign of disturbance.

"Over there!" Endre shouted, pointing a little to the right.

The hoofprints appeared a moment later, and we banked as a group, our shadows highlighting the tracks in the snow. We flew along them at breakneck speed, wings flapping furiously to propel us toward the jagged peaks that held what was sure to be a bloody battle.

The prints tracked up a steep incline and disappeared along with the snow, having been blown away with the wide arc carved into the ground. Following the mountainside, we searched the mud for any sign of Izidora, Ruslan, or Kazimir, the wind battling with us from above. An anguished roar shook the peaks, and we leveled off just in time to see a knife sink into Izidora's chest.

Ruslan fell to his knees, clutching his own chest as the pain reverberated down their bond and overwhelmed him.

"Fuck!" I swore, snapping my wings shut and dropping to the ground beside my cousin. Zuriel landed beside Izidora, already chanting in Angelic as he pulled his cousin into his arms.

I threw up a barrier of rock around the four of us as Kazimir called black whips to his hands. There was no life in his eyes, both having been entirely replaced by mania.

"Kazimir, no!" Endre dropped behind his friend and yanked him back by the shoulder. He turned on his kin, and the four of them locked in a battle of fists and magic, three against one.

"Here!" Around the barrier, I tossed the iron chains at Viktor, and they clattered to a stop at his feet.

They could use all the help they could get.

Viktor yanked off his jacket, then scrambled to the ground to snatch them up, never turning his back on the crazed Night Fae behind him. Without missing a beat, he launched into action again, the three working together to corral Kazimir toward the flat rocks at his back.

They needed to put those fucking chains on him and subdue whatever madness had taken hold.

I returned my attention to Ruslan and Izidora once I was certain Kazimir was thoroughly distracted. Ruslan had crawled to Izidora's side, so I scooted backward, maintaining the wall in front of me, until the four of us were huddled together behind it.

"Sprite, please wake up, please you can't leave me, I need you," Ruslan babbled incoherently. Zuriel's brow furrowed and he chanted faster and faster, a hint of panic breaking through his words. Izidora was pale, too pale, her fur jacket soaked in blood, though the knife was still lodged in her chest. Ruslan's voice was strained with worry, and he collapsed on his side, never losing contact with his mate. While he might feel her pain, he would not die – not unless he took his own life after Izidora passed.

I would not let that happen.

The freshness of their mating bond made it nearly impossible for him to help us, everything shared between them still so amplified and raw.

"Shit, shit, shit," I cursed over and over, like it would change what was happening before our eyes. "She's dying, Zuriel."

"I'm doing everything I can," he snapped, hovering his hands over her and spilling a flow of magic into her so thick I was certain he would burn out at any moment.

A commotion across the barrier captured my attention, and I lowered it just a hair to see what the Night Fae had done.

"You almost killed her, Kazimir!" Endre screamed at him, his face red and peridot eyes shining. Kazimir was on his knees, face bloody but eyes clear and hands bound behind him in iron chains. "Is that what you wanted, truly?"

He shook his head, and despite the wall between us, I smelled his shame. Whatever magic he possessed controlled him to a point where he acted beyond his own interests.

That in no way excused his actions.

With no one else to lead, I rose and stepped around the

barrier, fisted hands holding blue flame in a clear threat. "Get him out of here. Now. Leave the Iron Realm. If you return, it will be taken as an act of war."

Endre, Viktor, and Vadim shared a panicked look.

"Is she going to be okay?" Kazimir asked, looking distraught, as if his actions hadn't fucking caused all of this.

"You don't deserve to know," I snarled, allowing the blue fire to flare with my anger.

His face crumpled, and his kin hauled him to his feet. Vadim and Viktor hooked their hands under his arms and leaped into the sky, carrying him, as his magic was locked away by the iron. Endre paused for a beat as if he wanted to say something, but he just shook his head and flared his wings to follow the other Night Fae.

I waited until they were out of sight before lowering the barrier, and what I found beyond it stopped me in my tracks.

48

LILIANA

"We have to go!" Vadim burst through the door, bloodied and bruised. Domi, Kaztar, and I had returned to our temporary residence in the Iron Realm after my brother and his friends raced from the parade, creating chaos in their wake.

Viktor and Endre dragged a bound and broken Kazimir in behind them, his face even bloodier than my brother's. Kaztar jumped to his feet, mouth parting slightly as he took in the sight of them. "What the fuck happened?"

"There's no time to explain. If we don't get out of the Iron Realm, now, we're all dead," Viktor snapped.

Kaztar needed no extra incentive to pack his and Domi's bags. He was insanely protective of his wife, and Domi and I shared a worried look as the males scrambled to get their shit together. My brother stood guard over Kazimir while Endre and Viktor raced between rooms, grabbing and shoving everything they found into bags without a care for ownership or tidiness.

Kazimir only hung his head and remained kneeling on the floor, unable to look at me or anyone else. That damned crown was nowhere to be found, and iron chains bound his wrists.

My stomach dropped as my brain started working.

What did he do? And where was Izidora?

"Why aren't you moving, Liliana? We have to go!" Vadim shouted at me.

"I'm not leaving." I crossed my arms over my chest. "Where is Izidora?"

A choked sound emanated from Kazimir's chest, and my fury landed squarely on him. "What did you do?" I hissed, stalking forward, fists trembling by my side. When he didn't respond, I shoved at his chest. "What did you do, asshole? If you hurt my best friend, I'll kill you myself."

"Hey!" Vadim shouted at me, and with murder in my heart, I tore my gaze from Kazimir to my brother.

"What?" I snapped.

"Now is not the time. We need to go," he shot back.

Domi stalked to my side, crossing her arms as we stared down my brother. "Not until we know what happened to her."

"She's dead or dying, who knows? We can't stay and find out," Viktor snarled, shoving what looked like one of my dresses into a bag with extra force.

"Are you fucking kidding me?" I screeched, turning on the king of the Night Realm. "What the fuck is wrong with you! What did she *ever* do to you to make you want to kill her? You stalked her, you hurt her, you intimidated her every–"

"Enough!" Viktor shouted, forcing me to sidestep as he barreled toward us, arms laden with our bags.

Endre reached for Kazimir, and he and Vadim hauled the broken male to his feet before heading for the door. Domi and I shared a long, knowing look, and I gave her a nearly imperceptible nod before she took Kaztar's outstretched hand and allowed him to lead her toward the open door.

"Liliana! Please come on." My brother begged me to join him, his face pained and concerned as I stood my ground. "Mother and father will kill me if I leave you behind."

"You're not leaving me. I am choosing to stay." My voice trembled with my barely contained rage, masking the grief that threatened to suck me under and never let me go.

Izidora had to be okay.

The Goddess wouldn't grant my wish only to steal it away, would she?

Endre looked stricken, his beautiful peridot eyes shining with worry. "You're staying?" He dropped Kazimir's arm and took three steps toward me. "Liliana, you will die, we will die, if we stay."

"Izidora is my best friend. I am not leaving her." But my voice was strained as the male I was falling in love with looked at me like I was the air he needed to breathe and I alone was responsible for suffocating him.

"Please, come with me," Endre begged, half stumbling as he fell to his knees before me.

Every fight over Kazimir and Izidora, every harsh word we'd said to one another, every sensual touch we'd shared, all hung in the air between us. My heart broke as I opened my mouth to speak, then shut it again before I drew a serrated breath and said the words I had known were inevitable.

Yet they shattered me anyway.

"I can't," I whispered, brushing his messy locks away from his face.

Endre sucked in a breath, then with a slowness we didn't have time for, rose and embraced me as if it was the last time we would ever touch. His mouth captured mine in a searing kiss, tongue twining against mine. Two strong hands grasped my lower back, and Endre bent me over as he deepened our good-bye. His messy black hair brushed against my forehead as he broke us apart. "I love you, Liliana, so I will wait for you until you are ready to find me again. I will always wait for you."

My vision blurred as he spun away from me, leaving me breathless and without a moment to respond to his words.

Vadim looked between Kazimir, Endre, me, and the rest of the Night Fae fleeing the citadel. "Fuck!" he roared. "Take care of yourself. I've taught you well. Love you, Lil."

And with that, the two males I loved most of all vanished down a chaotic hall, racing for their lives out of the Iron Realm.

49

ZURIEL

Béke Day Thirteen

Thank the Goddess, Rares appeared from thin air to help us. His oath to the Iron Crown compelled him to protect its wearer, and although it was not his own, Ruslan was in excruciating pain.

"Help me," I begged the man responsible for my entrapment in the Iron Realm, letting my dislike of him wash away as I tried to save my cousin's life. I'd poured more magic into her than I had thought myself capable of, keeping her heart beating while the Night Fae had battled just beyond a wall Drazen erected to protect us.

They'd led Kazimir away in chains, and if I hadn't been so busy trying to save Izidora, I would have taken a shot at the pathetic male before he disappeared.

The old Mage dropped to his knees beside me, immediately chanting in a rhythmic way, waving his hands in a circle around the knife still lodged in her chest. "The knife needs to come out, but she will bleed out the moment it is dislodged. I can use my magic to stem the flow of blood if you can *carefully* remove it."

"I can do that," I promised, focusing all my attention on the tip of the knife somewhere deep inside her.

Rares's chanting quickened, and I waited for the jerk of his head to wrap my magic around the blade and begin the most precarious lift of my life. One wrong move would end in tragedy, and I would not let my cousin die here – not when she was destined for so much more.

Drazen paced back and forth behind a collapsed Ruslan. "Stay still," I snapped at him. "We need to concentrate."

He didn't argue, settling himself down with his back to us, keeping watch should anyone attempt to return to finish what Kazimir had started.

Slowly, painstakingly, the knife began to retract, the silver of the blade invisible beneath a layer of ruby.

"That's it, keep going," Rares gritted out, resuming his spell while his gnarled hands clenched and twisted over Izidora's heart.

The blade tapered, and sweat dripped down my back as I focused on keeping it perfectly steady and upright, not wanting it to knick another blood vessel on its way out. Ruslan groaned, pushing himself upright and blinking slowly, his gray eyes cloudy with pain.

Almost there.

The tip was nearly visible, and I held my breath until the knife floated above her chest. I snatched it from the air, tossing it away so it could not harm her any longer.

"Is she going to be okay?" Ruslan rasped, and Drazen shot up from his seat, eyes raking over the four of us on the ground.

"Yes, but she is in a very fragile state right now. I need tools in my office to finish healing her," Rares muttered, still focused on stemming the blood flowing from Izidora's chest.

"Touch me," Ruslan panted as he crawled closer, putting both hands on Izidora's legs.

Drazen rushed to his side, dropping into a crouch beside him. "You are weak, Ruslan. You can't move us in this state."

"I am the most powerful Félvér to ever exist. Watch me," he growled, though the bite he intended for his words wasn't there.

Rares and I placed hands on his outstretched arms, and with a grumble, Drazen joined us. Moments later, Ruslan moved us through space until we ended up on the floor in Rares's office. The old Mage immediately barked orders to help him. Drazen rushed to fetch hot water and clean bandages, while I found the potions and instruments he required.

Ruslan was pale, his lips nearly drained of all color, but he managed to lift Izidora onto the table so we could work on her. The gentleness with which he placed her was something I never thought I would see from him, and my heart twinged for the pain he was in.

Bracing his hands on the table, he stopped the sway of his body, his attention wholly focused on his unconscious mate. "Izidora, please, please come back to me. Find your way back. I know you can do it. I'm here, *please*." His words slipped out so broken that I thought they might break me too. His knees hit the ground beside the table, but his hands never left his mate's arm as he rested there, feeling Izidora's pain as well as his own. Ruslan refused to let anyone stop what they were doing for her to heal the gash on his shoulder.

Rares worked over Izidora for hours, sending Drazen and me to fetch or create things for him. Eventually, he ordered Ruslan to sit and Drazen to fetch him food and water.

"Drink this," Rares instructed, tossing a small vial at Ruslan.

"What is it?" he asked.

"It will make you feel better."

After everything Rares had done to Ruslan, I never expected him to willingly drink anything Rares offered without a detailed explanation, but he pulled the stopper and tipped it into his mouth without further complaint. His eyelids drooped, and I rushed around the table, catching him under his arms as he collapsed.

"Just put him in a chair," Rares muttered, not bothering to glance up from Izidora.

I dragged him to a plush one in the corner, propping his head against the wall with a pillow. "You fixed her heart already, what is left?" I asked Rares.

"Her spine. She must have fallen into something, and it looks like she tried to heal herself. I'm undoing what she did so I can fix it properly. Otherwise, she'll never walk again."

Fuck.

"Fuck," Drazen swore, echoing my thoughts, standing in the doorway with food and water in hand. "You have to fix her, Rares."

"What does it look like I'm doing? After all the nonsense Ruslan has pulled in the past few weeks, I honestly shouldn't. But here I am, and you both should be grateful," he snapped.

Setting the tray aside, Drazen raised both hands in supplication. "Trust me, we are. You tell us what you need, and we'll make it happen."

Rares jerked his head in acknowledgment, and we lapsed into a tense silence, waiting for the outcome of Kazimir's actions to be realized.

RUSLAN

Béke Day Fourteen

The breaking dawn woke me and I bolted upright, glancing around until I recognized that I was in my bed at Ryza Citadel.

How did I get here?

The events of the previous day cascaded into my mind like an avalanche – the parade, Izidora's kidnapping, Kazimir throwing a knife at me only for it to sink into Izidora's chest, using what was left of my strength to move us back to Ryza.

Panic gripped me, and I became frantic as I ripped my attention to the bed beside me, needing Izidora to be there, to be alright, to be safe. Her chestnut hair fanned around her, and she rested on her back, arms crossed over her stomach.

"Sprite?" I whispered, leaning my face down to her torso and listening for her heartbeat. It was there, but sluggish, as if it struggled with each slow beat. The rise and fall of her chest was even softer, and my whole body trembled as I examined her. Shaking her shoulder, I said, "Wake up, Izidora. You're safe. You're with me."

She didn't move. Didn't respond. Didn't even flutter her dark lashes against her cheeks.

No, no, no, no, no, no, no...

A sob stuck in my throat, trying to escape as I shook her again.

Why wasn't she waking?

I *needed* her.

"Oh good, you're awake." Zuriel's melodic voice startled me, and I nearly jumped out of bed at his sudden appearance.

"Fuck, Zuriel, you scared the shit out of me. What's wrong with her? Why won't she wake up?" My voice broke on the last two words, and I examined my mate again, seeking a sign that she was stirring.

The Angel sighed, looking at the floor and nudging the rug with his toe. "Kazimir broke her spine somehow. Rares spent all night repairing it after he fixed her heart." He tucked his white hair behind his ear, then looked up to meet my gaze. "She would have died if it weren't for him."

I opened my mouth to respond, but the door banged open behind Zuriel, and a breathless Liliana burst into the room. "Is she awake?"

Zuriel shook his head, and I had to bite my cheek to stem the prickling in my eyes. I turned away from them, trying my best to hold it together, but I fucking failed.

A sob wracked my chest as I stared down at my beautiful mate, alive yet so close to death. The tears overflowed one by one, dropping onto the clean tunic she wore. My heart shattered into a thousand jagged shards, slicing me from the inside out. The pain was so acute, so overwhelming that I couldn't breathe, couldn't think.

A roar of agony tore from my lips, and I threw myself over her unmoving body, cradling her with the tender care only her mate could give her. Her rosy scent filled my nostrils, but it wasn't enough. I needed to hear her laugh, for her to offer me an unguarded smile, for those bright aquamarine eyes to sparkle as I called her my sprite.

My breath was ragged as I tried to fight through the inferno of emotions raging through me, consuming every piece of light she had given me. I wanted to burn the whole fucking world down to avenge her, but the idea of leaving her side to do so stabbed me in the gut and twisted.

I reached down our bond, begging her to feel me, to hear me, to come back to me.

"You are so brave, my mate. So bold. So fearless. So powerful. You tried to save my life, when, in fact, you already had, the moment you gave yourself over to me. Without you, I am nothing. My heart beats only for you. I breathe, only for you. And I promise, I will finish what we started. The other realms will join us, and when you wake up, we will kill him – together. It's always us against the world."

———

Can't get enough of Izidora, Ruslan, and Kazimir? Pre-order the final installment of Izidora's story here: https://a.co/d/16GShaJ!

If you enjoyed Dark, please consider rating or reviewing on Amazon, Goodreads, BookBub, or any other platform you prefer to use! Your support means everything, and taking a few moments of your time to let others know how much you liked the book is appreciated.

Subscribe to my newsletter for a spicy bonus scene featuring four of the Nighthounds and one very lucky lady! And if you need some therapy after that ending, join the discussion in Lacey's Insidious Blooms Facebook Group or <u>Discord - Lacey's Insidious Blooms</u>.

Where to connect with Lacey:
Instagram - @laceylehotzkyauthor
TikTok - @laceylehotzkyauthor
Discord - Lacey's Insidious Blooms
Lacey's Insidious Blooms Facebook Group
Goodreads - Lacey Lehotzky
Amazon - Lacey Lehotzky
Pinterest - Lacey Lehotzky

Merch & Signed Copies:
www.laceylehotzky.com

AUTHOR'S NOTE

Much like Izidora, many of us don't realize that we're still in survival mode, just moving from one moment to the next, never processing the depth of our pain. As I sit here writing this, I recognize that this is the game I am playing with myself as I juggle all of life's current challenges.

Sitting with those emotions, *feeling* them, and letting them go, is hard. Sometimes, it feels as though if we work through the pain, then we will lose a part of our identity. Sometimes, the pain was awful enough the first time that the thought of returning to it is too much to bear. Sometimes, we just don't have the proper support to heal in the way we need. Sometimes, we're lying to ourselves about just how okay we think we are.

While Zuriel isn't a therapist, I tried to do my best to relay through Izidora's experience what EMDR therapy was like for me. EMDR saved my life. If I hadn't been for the therapy, I would never have known the profound difference between thinking I was safe and *feeling* I was safe. If you've ever done this work, I am so proud of you. If it's something you've considered, I can't recommend it enough.

Thank you for being on this journey with me, and if you are struggling, know you are not alone.

United States

USA Suicide and Crisis Lifeline: dial 988

Crisis Text Line: Text REASON to 741741

United Kingdom

SHOUT: text SHOUT to 85258

Samaritans: call 116 123 (free from any phone), email jo@samaritans.org, or visit some branches in person

National Suicide Prevention Helpline UK: call 0800 689 5652

Australia

Lifeline: call 13 11 14 , text, or chat online 24/7

ACKNOWLEDGMENTS

Wow! Three books published in a year (ish). I couldn't have done this without you, my amazing readers. Thank you for loving Izidora's story as much as I do. Thank you for your kind messages on social media, hilarious memes about ACOLAD, and sharing in this experience with me.

To my team – my alphas, betas, ARC readers, Street Team members, and PAs, you rock. Thank you for spreading the word about Chained, Light, and Dark. Thank you for all your invaluable feedback. Thank you for sharing this series with enthusiasm. Thank you for talking me off the ledge. Thank you for your undying support, both personally and professionally.

To Beholden Book Covers - Thank you for another amazing cover and fancy chapter headers!

Courtney - Thank you for everything. From our heartfelt to hilarious conversations, I know every time you pop up in my messages I'm in for a treat. Thank you for being my friend, reader, and confidante.

Lisa - Thank you for being a super fan and coming to my aid whenever I need it. Thank you for helping me spread the word about ACOLAD, always being down to try something new, and being a great friend.

Kat - Thank you for being just as obsessed with me as I am with you! Your assistance, flexibility, patience, has been incredible since we started working together. Thank you for being part of my team and growing with me, and I can't wait to see what we'll do next.

Kaitlin - How lucky am I to call you both an editor and a friend?! The past year has been crazy for both of us, but I know it's because we're both leveling up in our lives. I am so proud to call you my friend, and so proud of all the work you've put in (much like Izidora).

Kristina - You're welcome for Chapter 18.

Nicole - Thank you for always being down to listen to me vent, spill the latest tea, or generally give great perspective on life. I am so grateful your video popped up on my feed and I reached out to you! Thank you for letting me be your first dark romantasy series and sharing your love of this story.

To my author friends - KL, Sam, KC, Amarah, Logan, I literally couldn't do this without you. You guys keep me sane, help me grow, and are an invaluable part of this journey. I'm so glad we're in this together.

To my friends - Matt, Sam & Alex, Christen & Justin, Kristin, and everyone at Gracie Raleigh, thank you for your continued support as I grow as an author.

To my family - Thank you for all your support, mentally, emotionally, with this process. Thank you for indulging me as all I can talk about these days is books. I promise one day I'll have something else to talk about again!

Andrew - My mate. Us against the world, always. Thank you for every moment you've given me and this series. Thank you for holding me while I sobbed, cheering me as I met goal after goal, and for every moment between, whether I needed to talk something out or just needed an encouraging hug. I love you from the depths of my soul.

ABOUT THE AUTHOR

Lacey is a writer, photographer, and author of the Amazon bestselling dark fantasy romance series, A Choice of Light and Dark. She is most often found with her nose in a book when she isn't training to be a fighter like her main characters. Lacey has her best ideas while traveling, where she finds inspiration for people and places in her books. She especially loves exploring the dark side, writing characters with deep flaws and even deeper trauma, and strapping her readers in for an emotional roller coaster that will leave them begging for more.